"ONE OF THE BEST CRIME FICTION WRITERS IN AMERICA TODAY."
—NELSON DeMILLE

Praise for the Novels of Linda Fairstein

Night Watch

"Fairstein is in vintage form here, weaving the rape and murder stories together with great detail and clarity . . . a real winner from the legal thriller master."
— *Booklist* (starred review)

"[A] thrilling procedural, a tasty soufflé of escargots, Beaujolais, cocaine, and murder that will entice the author's many fans." — *Library Journal* (starred review)

"Both devotees and new readers alike will delight at the return of Alex Cooper. . . . The book is completely engrossing and hard to put down." — *Vineyard Gazette*

"Fairstein . . . delivers another compelling story. . . . Fans of *Law & Order: Special Victims Unit* will enjoy the behind-the-scenes perspective." —The Associated Press

Silent Mercy

"Gripping. . . . Each outing with Alex brings a new view of this character and the city in which she lives."
— *South Florida Sun-Sentinel*

"Linda Fairstein has delivered another compelling crime novel set on the all-too-real streets of New York . . . a worthwhile read that fans of the *Law & Order* TV series will savor. After finishing *Silent Mercy*, readers will eagerly seek out her other novels."
— *San Francisco Chronicle*

continued . . .

"Fairstein excels at describing New York's complicated religious history as well as the vagaries of the city's legal and religious politics." —*Publishers Weekly*

"[Fairstein] puts the pedal down on page one and keeps it there until the dénouement in Nantucket Sound. Ms. Fairstein separates her work from others because she brings the grittiness of her career to the pages. . . . Unlike most crime novelists, she worked in gritty for a long time and it shows. Second, she uses the digging skills of her craft to inform the story with authentic historical context, weaving it into the plot. The author has researched the hell out of *Silent Mercy*." —*Martha's Vineyard Times*

"Fairstein keeps the suspense level high." —*The Kansas City Star*

"A tough-to-put-down ending that will leave fans ready for more." —*Booklist*

"Shows the power and importance of faith, but also how it can be corrupted. Fairstein excels at describing New York's forgotten religious history. . . . She also expertly weaves in the legal machinations and the politics that plague the court system, while offering a new view of this character and the city in which she lives." —*The Miami Herald*

"The detection . . . is first-rate." —*Kirkus Reviews*

"An exciting, action-packed tale with quite a wallop." —*Midwest Book Review*

More Praise for
Linda Fairstein's Thrillers

"Fairstein . . . makes the legal issues more exciting than any high-speed chase." —*The New York Times*

ALSO BY LINDA FAIRSTEIN

LINDA FAIRSTEIN

NIGHT WATCH

A SIGNET SELECT BOOK

SIGNET SELECT
Published by the Penguin Group
Penguin Group (USA) Inc., 375 Hudson Street,
New York, New York 10014, USA

USA | Canada | UK | Ireland | Australia | New Zealand | India | South Africa | China

Penguin Books Ltd., Registered Offices: 80 Strand, London WC2R 0RL, England
For more information about the Penguin Group visit penguin.com.

Published by Signet Select, an imprint of New American Library, a division of
Penguin Group (USA) Inc. Previously published in a Dutton edition.

First Signet Select Printing, April 2013
10 9 8 7 6 5 4 3 2 1

SIGNET SELECT and logo are trademarks of Penguin Group (USA) Inc.

ISBN 978-0-451-41614-8

Printed in the United States of America

PUBLISHER'S NOTE
This is a work of fiction. Names, characters, places, and incidents either are the
product of the author's imagination or are used fictitiously, and any resemblance
to actual persons, living or dead, business establishments, events, or locales is
entirely coincidental.
   The publisher does not have any control over and does not assume any
responsibility for author or third-party Web sites or their content.

ALWAYS LEARNING   PEARSON

For Justin Feldman
Forever, my love

Evil is unspectacular and always human,
And shares our bed and eats at our own table.

W. H. Auden

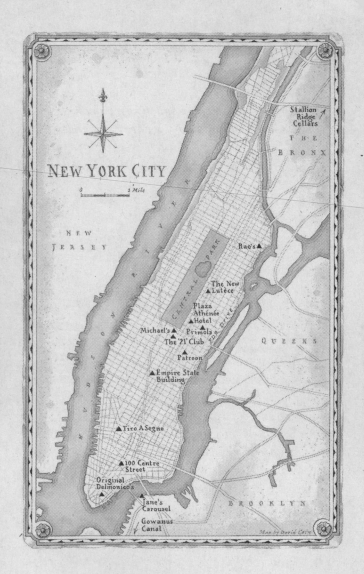

NEW YORK CITY

0   ½ Mile

NEW
JERSEY

THE
BRONX

Stallion
Ridge
Cellars

Rao's ▲

The New
▲ Lutèce

Plaza
Athénée
▲ Hotel

Michael's ▲

Primola ▲

The '21' Club

Patroon

▲ Empire State
Building

QUEENS

Tiro A Segno ▲

▲ 100 Centre
Street

Original ▲
Delmonico's

Jane's
Carousel

Gowanus
Canal

BROOKLYN

Map by David Cain

One

Bones. Human bones the length of a man's thigh. I stopped short at the sight of more than a dozen of them stacked like a cord of firewood just steps in front of me.

I paused to catch my breath before heaving my shoulder against the thick wooden door for the third time. The sturdy threshold, reinforced with rust-covered strips of wrought iron, had withheld assaults by barbarian invaders throughout centuries, so I didn't have much hope that it would yield to my slender frame.

The cobblestone alleyway that led back up a steep incline to the center of town was dark, except for a sliver of light that sliced through it like a laser from the two o'clock angle of the waning crescent moon.

"It's some kind of sick joke, Gaspard." I raised my voice as I addressed the perpetually drooling basset hound that was probably sleeping soundly just inside. There was no one else around to hear me, and I was trying to stay calm though staring at this cache of skeletal remains.

"There were no bones here when I left the house for dinner."

I was dead-ended outside the entrance to the grounds of the ancient mill—a medieval *moulin*—that Luc Rouget had converted into his home on a hillside in Mougins, a perched village in France that overlooked the glittering Côte d'Azur and the city of Cannes.

I glanced down again, trying to calculate how many dead men it had taken to create this ghastly tableau. The bones looked yellowed with age, but maybe that was a trick of the night sky. I picked up my head to return to the business of wrestling with the old iron door handle, which I had never before known Luc to lock.

I could hear voices in the distance, coming from below the house, where the dense Valmasque Forest surrounded the village. Deep voices of several men carried up over the stillness of the hillside, punctuated by the shrill laughter of a woman.

It was an early-spring night, cool and dry, but I had already worked up a sweat as I struggled against the mammoth door. I turned to make my way back up the slope to find Luc and our friends, but my left heel caught in the uneven spacing between stones. I nervously braced myself against the wall to disengage it, and as I kicked loose, my foot grazed the top of the mound behind me.

Several of the bones smacked against the ground, rolling or sliding out of sight in the darkness past the entryway. I leaned down to try to catch a couple but missed entirely. Too much good wine over too many hours had affected my judgment—like my decision to return home alone—and my balance.

The voices seemed to be getting closer to me, as though the interlopers had breached the wall at the bottom of Luc's property and were approaching his house. They were no longer loud and laughing, but whispering among themselves.

The pile of bones that had looked so sinister to me moments earlier was scattered across the cobblestones. My own doing, of course, but now it seemed as haphazard and benign an accumulation of debris as though Gaspard had dragged them home from the woods after an evening of foraging unsuccessfully for live prey.

More than a decade as a prosecutor in the Manhattan District Attorney's Office had provided enough fuel to stoke my imagination, even in the midst of a vacation, when presented with the slightest opportunity. But I shivered reflexively as I looked down. There could be no innocent explanation for the sudden deposit of a collection of human bones.

I unstrapped my sandals and stepped out of them. I was jumpy and slightly intoxicated. It was only a short walk from the cul-de-sac in which I found myself trapped to the center of town, the public square where Luc's restaurant anchored this quaint village known for its culinary landmarks.

I hugged the wall of the old mill as I retraced the route up the slope, the cool stones beneath my feet radiating chills as though I had dipped them in cold water.

Suddenly, at the top of the alley, I saw the figure of a large man, filling the opening toward which I was headed. He lifted his arm and shined a flashlight in my direction, blinding me momentarily. I twisted my head away, and when I looked up again, shielding my eyes, he was gone.

Why hadn't I asked him for help? The liquor had slowed my reflexes and clouded my thought process. I should have called out to him, but I feared he might have been lurking near Luc's home because he had something to do with the skeletal remains that had been planted there just a short time ago.

Better to be in the public square than cornered where I was, so I forced myself to move more quickly. Twenty or thirty paces and I emerged directly onto the narrow main street of the old village.

At least it was lighted by the dim glow of antique streetlamps, even though there wasn't a person in sight. Off to the left was a row of small shops, galleries, and restaurants that led to the car park and the road out of town. I turned to my right, where the bakery and apartments above it were all shuttered tight for the night.

The main street snaked in a circular path, winding and climbing through the tiny village to its highest point, where la Porte Sarrazine, the great fortification built in the twelfth century to protect the *Mouginois* monks of Saint Honorat from attacks, still stood watch over the countryside below.

I had separated from our group there on the ramparts above the village, and now I was too anxious and agitated to work my way back up to find them. I hadn't taken a purse or cell phone with me. I hadn't anticipated the need for either.

But the restaurant Luc owned was in the center of the village, within my sight. It was not that long after the normal closing time, and I hoped one of the staff would still be cleaning up and could get a message to Luc to come home immediately.

I walked in the dead center of the street, oblivious to the pebbles that poked me underfoot. I kept reminding myself that I was in one of the safest places imaginable, a village that looked like a movie set for a caper with Grace Kelly and Cary Grant.

I had come to know Mougins as a small piece of paradise, tucked into the foothills of the Alps in the southeastern corner of France, to which people from all over the world traveled, simply in order to dine elegantly and well. No third world gratings covered the windows of the pricey shops, rarely did anyone lock doors of villas decorated with works by old masters and modern artists, and the tiny residential population bragged that this town had no reason to keep statistics about violent crime. There simply wasn't any.

I ran toward the patio of the restaurant and ducked beneath the trellis that bordered the outdoor tables fronting the town square. Something on the ground in my way stopped me cold, and I bent over to see what was there.

Skulls. Obviously human. Three large human skulls stacked to form a pyramid at the entrance to the only three-star restaurant in the village of Mougins.

Two

"I don't know if you've ever met my friend Alexandra Cooper," Luc said to the young policeman who appeared at the house shortly after eight o'clock in the morning. "Alex, this is Claude Chenier."

"*Enchanté, madame,*" the officer said, nodding at me though refusing to crack a smile. His expression was as stiff as the pleats in the pants of his light gray uniform. "No, we've never been introduced, but I've seen you around the village. Good to meet you."

"My pleasure." We were on the terrace outside the house on a sparkling late April morning. "We're just having our first coffee, Claude. Would you like some?"

"Yes, thank you, if you don't mind."

I stood up to go back into the kitchen to pour another cup. Beyond the grounds of Luc's property, over the deep green of the dense growth of trees in the Valmasque, I could see the water of the Bay of Cannes that had given its colorful name to this stretch of the Mediterranean coast.

"I hope we didn't create too much extra work for you last evening." Luc was speaking English for my sake. He was bilingual, born in France and educated in England, before returning to take over the empire started by his father, the legendary restaurateur Andre Rouget. Although my affair with him had done less for my language skills than for my spirit, my comprehension was far better than my ability to converse about anything serious.

"*Pas du tout.* No trouble at all, Monsieur Rouget."

I stirred the sugar until it dissolved and then I carried the cup outside, setting it down on the table. "I have to apologize for creating such a commotion in the middle of the night, Claude. Won't you sit down?"

He shook his head. "I'm not sure what you mean, *madame*. Commotion?"

"*Agitation*, Claude. But I think Alex is mistaken. Nothing you need to be concerned with."

"Aren't we talking about the bones I found last night? The human skulls?"

"No, darling," Luc said, reaching across the table for my hand. "I'm sure Claude doesn't even know about them yet. Give me a minute with him, will you?"

"I thought you went directly to the gendarmerie after you brought me home?"

I had raced up the hill to find Luc as the last of the revelers at our party were finishing their champagne. Together we walked back to his restaurant—Le Relais a Mougins—and went inside, careful not to disturb the skulls, to retrieve the key to his property that he kept in the office above the dining room. Luc assured me that he hadn't locked the door and that I was probably just skittish alone in the dark alleyway, fooled by the work of village pranksters.

When we got to the house, he was as startled as I that he couldn't even insert the key. The lock had been jammed, and as he patiently whittled away at it with his pocketknife, a piece of bone—the size of a small finger—splintered and spilled out of the opening.

Luc settled me inside and inspected the grounds to be sure that no intruders had made it over the garden wall. I finally fell asleep an hour later, certain that Luc was going to the police station to report the incident and to ask the officer on duty to photograph and collect the bones.

"At three in the morning? Is that what you really thought?" Luc asked, winking at me as he got up from the table. "Like this is *CSI: Mougins*?"

Claude Chenier was still stone-faced. I was sitting with my back against the stucco bench of the sunny terrace, looking up at him. He was about my height—five-ten—and almost as slim as Luc.

"What bones are you speaking of, *madame*?"

"My wallet's just inside the door, Claude." Luc pointed to the kitchen counter not fifteen feet away and headed to it.

"I didn't actually come just now for the money."

"Nonsense. Your guys did a great job for us. No party crashers, no media, no out-of-control guests," Luc said, taking a handful of bills from his alligator wallet. "Don't look so startled, Alex. It's not a bribe. Claude was off duty last evening and he supplied the private security team for our party."

Claude did a quick count of the money. "*Merci*, Monsieur Rouget. It's very generous of you. My men will appreciate it."

Luc put an arm around the young man's shoulder, as though to steer him past the swimming pool to the heavy old door that had offered me so much resistance earlier this morning. "They earned it. We had a wonderful time."

I could tell Luc was embarrassed that he'd misled me into thinking he had made a police report already. Of course there was no need to awaken everyone in the village for what he'd almost convinced me by daybreak was a practical joke. And though the joke had been a distasteful one, I tried to switch off the "on-duty" part of my brain that was always thinking like a prosecutor.

"You must come by some evening with your girlfriend for dinner, Claude, eh? To Le Relais, for the new spring menu."

I smiled as the officer nodded in agreement. I knew that my favorite NYPD detectives, Mike Chapman and Mercer Wallace, would envy a police department in which there were no rules against taking meals at pricey restaurants "on the arm."

Mike, who worked Homicide, and Mercer, in the Special Victims Unit—one of the few African American detectives to make first grade—had become my most trusted friends in the twelve years I had served as a prosecutor.

"Very well, then. We'll set a date." Luc's chiseled features weren't classically handsome, but his smile was warm and slightly crooked, in a sexy way, and always drew a grin in return from me.

Claude held his ground despite the fact that Luc was trying to usher him out. We hadn't gotten much sleep and were planning a lazy day alone together. Claude pocketed the wad of cash and turned back to question me.

"May I ask again, *madame*, what bones are you talking about?"

Luc rolled his eyes and shrugged his shoulders, but I

answered anyway. "Let me show you, Claude," I said, putting down my coffee cup as I stood to walk out to the alley.

"Alex, they're not there any longer."

"What do you mean? If you didn't alert the police, then what did you do?"

"I removed them," Luc said. The sun reflected off the metal of his wire-rimmed glasses, so that I couldn't see his expression, see whether or not he was joking.

"You what?"

"I picked them up and carried them back to the restaurant for safekeeping."

"With your bare hands?" I sounded as exasperated as I was exhausted. "Did you even think it might be worthwhile having the police examine them for fingerprints?"

Claude was tugging on his narrow black uniform tie as he listened to us bicker, never taking his eyes off my face.

"*C'est fou.* Don't be ridiculous, Alex."

"How about the skulls? You moved those, too?"

Claude looked at Luc. "*Crânes?*"

"*Oui. Trois crânes.* Very old ones, Claude. I have them in my office." Luc turned his back to me. "You must understand something about Alex, Claude. *Elle est procureur de la ville de* New York."

"*C'est vrai, madame?*"

"Yes, it's true. I'm a prosecutor."

"Alex is in charge of sex crimes in Manhattan. *Tous les crimes sexuels,*" Luc said, trying to impress the stolid young cop, which didn't seem likely to happen. Then he patted Claude's shoulder. "It explains why she always sees something sinister when there really isn't cause for concern."

I playfully put my hands against Luc's back and pushed

him toward the edge of the pool. "If I riffed about the secret sauce for your escargots half as dismissively as you just nailed my career, you'd probably carve me up and serve me for dinner."

"With that very sauce, *mon amour*. Not only would it be tasty but also all the evidence would be devoured."

"How Hitchcockian," I said, turning my back.

"Are you ready for a swim to cool off that temper a bit?" He spun me around and lifted me from the ground, dangling me over the water, while he addressed Claude Chenier. "And you, my friend, the bones she's talking about are older than this village, but I'll cart them over to headquarters as soon as you like. Or do you want to come with me now?"

Luc put me down as Claude answered him.

"I was trying to get you alone, Monsieur Rouget, to explain to you the reason I came here this morning. But since Madame Cooper is a professional, I'll tell both of you."

"A reason you're here, beside the money?"

"*Oui*, monsieur, I was sent by my captain," the young officer said, hesitating before he looked Luc in the eye. "There was a body found just a few hours ago."

"Whose body?" Luc was all business now, his blue-gray eyes as icy as steel, his hands planted firmly on his hips.

"A young woman. We don't know who she is. I was sent here to ask for your help with an identification."

"Why *my* help?" Luc's pale face had reddened.

"Because we think she was on her way to your celebration last night. The captain believes she might have been one of your guests."

"Of course we'll do whatever you need," I said, thinking of the hairpin turns on the narrow roads that led from the *autoroute* to this hilltop. "On her way to our dinner party, Claude? Was it an accident, then? A car crash?"

"Perhaps an accident, *madame*, but it didn't involve a car. They were taking her body out of the pond when I was dispatched to come here. It's either an accident, Ms. Cooper, or the young lady was murdered."

Three

Half an hour later we were standing at the edge of Font-merle Pond, twelve acres of water that bordered the enormous forest, almost completely obscured by the green pods of lotus flowers that would bloom later in the summer.

Claude Chenier had passed us off to his boss, Captain Belgarde, who greeted Luc with a handshake as he tossed his cigarette into the murky water.

"Alex, this is Jean-Jacques Belgarde. Jacques, I'd like you to meet Alex Cooper."

Luc was going through the motions, but his attention was focused on a yellow blanket spread on the ground on the far side of the pond. "He's married to an American and lived in Baltimore for fifteen years, so his English is better than yours. What's happened here, Jacques? Who is she?"

Two men were navigating a pontoon back to our position. The morning stillness was ruptured by shrieking birdcalls—dozens of different sounds and cadences—

probably occasioned by our unexpected presence in this natural sanctuary.

"Not my forte, Luc. I haven't seen a body since I left military service."

"And the slow-motion ferry?"

"Nothing works in the pond but a flat-bottom boat. These pods put down roots that tangle oars or anything else that tries to move through. The boat'll reach us in a few minutes."

"That old guy steering the platform looks familiar."

Belgarde called out to Claude and asked who was poling the pontoon, carrying the other officer back to this side.

"Sorry, I don't know his name. He's how you say? The *veilleur de nuit*. He's the one who found the lady."

"The night watchman," Luc said. "Of course I know him. Emil. He used to be the caretaker for Pablo Picasso's home, just across from the pond. When I was a teenager, I used to make runs on my motorcycle with food my father sent to Picasso when he didn't feel like coming to town for dinner."

The great artist had spent the last twelve years of his life in Mougins and was one of Andre Rouget's regular customers.

"Pretty swell takeout," Jacques said. "There you go. Three years in town and I've never met this Emil, didn't even know his name. I've heard about him though—that he's a real loner. Works the midnight shift for the park service just so he doesn't have to deal with people."

"How would anyone see a body in this pond, especially before daylight?" I asked. Some of the leaves were three feet in diameter, overlapping one another and appearing so thick that it looked as if I could walk across on them to the other side.

"That brings us back to you, Luc," the captain said. "The deceased is dressed entirely in white. It's the clothes that stood out so obviously against the dark water and leaves, even in the dead of night. Sweater, lace camisole, long cotton skirt—and it's not even summer yet. My officers tell me you hosted a party last evening. A dinner in white."

"Guilty, Jacques, but all my guests were accounted for," Luc said, shading his eyes with his hand. "Why didn't they load the body on the boat and bring her to the dock?"

We were watching the pontoon's slow progress through the lotus leaves.

"I've been instructed not to move the woman. We'll go across to her."

"Fine. Perhaps Alex should wait here."

"I'm more useful with the dead than you are, Luc. Does this mean, Captain, that there's a *médecin légiste* on the way?"

"A medical examiner? I wouldn't know where to find the closest one. I've never had the need. But there's a local coroner. We're trying to get our hands on him now."

"Surely you're not going to leave this woman outside for hours, exposed to the elements?" It wasn't just the insects and eels above and below the water, but foxes and wild boar that gave the forest its unique character.

"We'll move her as soon as we're ready." Belgarde spoke sharply to me. "Tell me about the event, Luc. Your idea, this *Diner en Blanc*?"

"No, not mine. It's been going on in Paris for a quarter of a century, and more recently in New York, Montreal. Who knows where else? I thought I'd bring the concept to Mougins. A touch of civility before tourist season overwhelms us."

"You and I have shirts on our backs because of the tourists," Jacques said, cupping his hand over a match as he lighted his next Gitanes. Judging by the pile of butts, he had smoked enough cigarettes in the last couple of hours to blacken the lungs of the purple herons observing us from the middle of the pond. "You feed them, and I'm the uniformed lost and found for their cameras and car keys and iPads. What are these dinners, *mon ami*?"

The pontoon snagged on a stand of lotus fronds, and the old man used his pole with great deliberation to free the slow-moving vessel. I watched while Luc talked.

"One of my father's friends returned to Paris in the eighties, after a long time away. He wanted to see a lot of acquaintances, so he made his contacts and people agreed to meet all together, for dinner, even though they didn't know one another. By the time François assembled his list, there were too many of his friends to fit in a restaurant or home, so he suggested they meet at the Bois de Boulogne.

"Everyone was to bring not only their own food but also tables and chairs, wine and glasses, silver and table linens. And all were to dress entirely in white, so the two hundred or so guests could spot one another inside the park."

Jacques inhaled and raised his eyebrows. "That's legal, in an historic landmark?"

"*Je ne sais pas.* François made the rules. The hell with the law. He just wanted everyone to enjoy themselves."

"It worked?"

"So well that it's grown to incredibly larger numbers each time. Four thousand people in the plaza at the Cathedral of Notre Dame two years ago. Last August, when I was invited for the first time, six thousand showed up in the courtyard of the Louvre."

"That's astonishing. And not mobbed by outsiders?"

Luc smiled. "Only friends, and friends of friends. Each time there is a different organizer, deciding who is in and who is out."

Jacques blew smoke rings in Luc's face. "Clearly, I was out when you drew up your list."

"*Alors*, my pal, you don't Tweet, do you?" Luc waved the smoke away with his iPhone.

"I'm too old for that bullshit," Jacques said. I guessed him to be a decade older than Luc, who was forty-eight. "That's how you invite?"

"Till the very last minute, the Parisian organizers never revealed the location of the dinner. Part of the fun, I guess. Then on the actual day of, they blast out the landmark—whatever it is—and people descend on their Metro stations with all their gear."

"So for you, Luc, the place was la Porte Sarrazine?"

"Exactly. The peak of Mougins, with that spectacular vista over the valley. I broke the rules and provided all the food and drink from the restaurant. Guests just had to bring a blanket to sit on. The classic French *pique-nique*, full of romance and mystery, no? Ladies in white dresses and men in linen shirts. Pâté de foie gras, poached salmon à la Relais, cheeses, and chocolate truffles. The very best wines and a night of great *amitié*, great friendship."

"I hope you saved me something," Jacques said, rubbing his belly, which protruded over the belt of his uniform. "White's not my best look."

Luc was reliving the magical evening he had created, while I was fixed on the body across the shore.

"And you, Alexandra, did you enjoy?"

"Very much so. Until this news. Until now."

"How many guests?"

"Sixty in all," Luc said.

Jacques snorted. "I didn't know you had that many friends in town."

"I don't, *Monsieur le Capitaine*, but some of my friends have friends," Luc said, laughing at Jacques's candid remark. "The only three-star joint in a resort filled with restaurants, a mecca for gourmands? Yes, there has been some pretty fierce competition for me these last few years."

"Not to mention that you got your stars the easy way."

"How so?"

"You inherited them from your father."

Jacques's comments were getting to Luc. "When my father hung up his toque for good and retired, everyone thought the glory days of Le Relais were over. He had created the most acclaimed restaurant in the region, only to lose two of his stars in the last five years while he tried to hold on to the place."

"Too much time chasing tail, eh? Those were still the rumors when I got to town."

"Give it up, Jacques. That's rude. I'll invite you to next year's dinner, okay?"

"You inherit that, too?"

"What?" Luc was fuming. I could see the muscles in his face tense up.

"That philandering thing. Is that why your wife split?"

"If you're not going to be respectful to Luc," I said, "then would you at least try not to make a fool of yourself in my presence, Captain?"

"*Je m'excuse, madame,*" Jacques said, bowing his head in mock respect. "I didn't know this was a serious affair."

"It's none of your business what kind of relationship it is, Jacques," Luc said, moving closer to me.

It seemed that the captain had pinned his hopes on a connection between the corpse and my lover, simply because she was clothed in white.

"Even if it's the reason that you're leaving for New York?"

Luc wagged his finger back and forth. "Not leaving, Jacques. I'm opening a place there for the winter season, when things are slow here."

Claude Chenier stepped forward and circled us to get onto the rickety wooden dock that was about to receive the flat-bottomed boat.

"Perhaps it's time to tell the captain that someone left piles of bones and skulls on your doorsteps during the night," I added, to bring the point to Jacques's attention. "Maybe there is a link to what happened here."

"What do you mean? Tell me, my friend."

Luc ignored both of us and followed Claude onto the dock. "Let's get this done first, then I'll show you what Alex is talking about."

The other officer got off the pontoon to make room for the three of us. Luc boarded and identified himself to Emil. They embraced, speaking rapidly in French, and briefly reminisced about the past, while Jacques and I followed and grabbed onto the railing that sided the boat before it took off again.

"You have a list of all your guests, Luc?"

"Of course. It's in my office. I'll have it for you as soon as you get me back to town."

By the time we were halfway across, the mosquitoes

had found every exposed piece of my flesh. I swatted them away from my mouth and nose.

"Are you familiar with this part of the forest?" Jacques asked Luc.

"We all played here as kids. I know it pretty well."

"Have you been lately?"

Luc clearly didn't like the tone of the question.

"Just the other day, in fact. Before Alex arrived. You could create an entire meal from this pond." His sarcasm wasn't lost on Jacques.

"I've never been fond of frogs' legs."

Luc squatted and reached into the water, wrenching loose from its roots in the mud a green frond that housed the small bud of a lotus flower. "A real culinary delicacy, Jacques. Every bit of this plant is edible." Luc peeled open the flower and showed us the seeds before he swallowed a handful, almost daring the police captain to speak what was on his mind. "Tastes just like chestnuts. And the roots themselves cook up like sweet potatoes. We served them last weekend."

There was no dock on the shoreline of the pond where the body had been retrieved. Emile gently beached the boat, warning us to hold on as it slid in hard against the muddy embankment.

Jacques disembarked first, then Luc, who extended his hand to help me off. The captain walked toward the covered body, squatted at the far corner of the blanket, and drew it aside to reveal to us the back of the young woman.

The white clothes were still sopping wet and clung to her skin. Her head faced away from Luc and me, obscured by the clumped strands of long brown hair that crossed her cheek.

"You know the girl, Luc?" Jacques asked. "You bring her lotus picking with you the other day?"

I spoke before Luc could answer, though I resented the captain's question. "Don't show your ignorance, Jacques. She's been in the water only several hours."

His silence suggested he didn't know anything about postmortems.

"See her skin, Captain?" I walked to his side and kneeled in the muck, face-to-face with the deceased, whom I guessed to be younger than I by seven or eight years—maybe she was about thirty. "There are no wrinkles, no 'washerwoman' effect, as we call it at home. She hasn't been dead very long."

"And that stuff—that pink stuff coming out of her mouth," he asked, barely able to look at her face again, "what's that?"

"Do you know whether someone tried to revive her?" I asked.

Jacques pointed at Emil. "He says he attempted to resuscitate the girl, to press on her chest." Jacques simulated the motion of CPR in midair, keeping his distance from the body. *"C'est vrai, Emil?"*

The weathered old man nodded in the affirmative.

"It's foam, then," I said, looking at the mushroom-shaped froth that oozed from her mouth and nose. "It's the mixture of oxygen and water with mucus created in her airway when she was fighting to breathe. Come look, Luc. Do you know who she is?"

He moved slowly around the outstretched legs of the body, no more comfortable in this setting than the captain of the local police.

"You've taken photographs, Jacques?" I asked, waiting for Luc to get next to me.

"Just with the camera I keep in the car. And Claude's cell phone. An inspector is coming from Cannes sometime later today to manage the investigation."

I had no faith that the integrity of the forensics in this case would be preserved, or that Jacques was terribly concerned about that. I took the ends of a few of the tangled strands of hair and lifted them gently so that Luc could see the girl more clearly—despite the distorted features of her gaping mouth and foam-covered nostrils—so that he could tell Jacques he had been mistaken.

"That foam is a pretty good indicator that this poor creature was alive when she was submerged," I said to the captain. "You really need to get a professional team here quickly to move her before you compromise the chance for a coroner to find marks or bruises under her clothes."

I looked up at Jacques to be sure he understood the importance of what I was telling him, but he was more interested in the expression on Luc's face.

"Alex asked whether you know who she is," Jacques said. "Why don't you respond?"

Luc rested a hand on my shoulder and squeezed it hard as he kneeled beside me. I let go of the girl's hair when he answered. "Of course I know who she is, Jacques. Her name is Lisette. Lisette Honfleur. She used to work for me in the restaurant."

Four

"Busman's holiday, Alex? Isn't that what they call it in the States?" Jacques asked. "Working your way through your vacation?"

It was an hour later and we were sitting in Jacques's cramped office in the gendarmerie of Mougins. The bulletin board behind the captain was littered with celebrity headshots—movie stars, many of them in town for dinner during the Cannes Film Festival throughout the years, thanking the police for one courtesy or another.

"This is all in your capable hands now, Captain. I've got another week here to relax with Luc," I said, turning my head to offer my lover some reassurance, although it didn't seem that would help. "I'm sure you'll have things sorted out by then."

I'd been schooled in murder investigations by the best detectives in New York. The ignorance Belgarde displayed at the crime scene would have shocked Mike

Chapman, and I harbored little hope that these village cops would know what to do next.

One of the captain's men had been dispatched to the restaurant to carry back the bones. They sat on the floor in a large wooden wine crate between Luc and the desk, the three hollow-eyed skulls meeting my gaze with a blank stare.

"Tell me about Lisette, Luc."

"I thought we were waiting for the investigators to arrive."

"They've been delayed and I'm curious. Tell me about the girl."

"It must be at least five years since I've seen her, Jacques. Maybe more than that."

"Really?" the captain said, rocking back and forth on his ergonomically correct office chair. "Why so long between visits?"

"I fired her. That's probably the reason."

"She couldn't stand the heat in the kitchen?"

"Lisette wasn't involved with food. She helped with the books. My accountant placed her with me. He knows more about her than I do, for sure."

"How long did she work with you?"

"Five, maybe six months."

"And you let her go, why?"

"Because she liked to help herself to the cash, Jacques. A little too much, a little too often."

"*Ah, oui. Les doigts collants.*" The captain saw that I looked puzzled by his words. "Sticky fingers, Alexandra. A common problem in Luc's business."

Tax officials in France sat on restaurant owners like hawks, because so much of the business was in cash transactions. And the ready access to all those euros—and occasional dollars—must have been a temptation to the young woman working alone in an office above the chic dining room.

"My ex is the one who actually caught Lisette with her hand in the till."

Luc had been divorced amicably from Brigitte, his wife of fifteen years, who lived close by with their two kids. He was devoted to the children.

Jacques's chair was on casters, and he rolled himself toward the corner, where several dilapidated file cabinets stood. "So we have a record of the theft, you think?"

"I never reported it."

"No?"

"There was no point. I didn't think she had stolen that much money in such a short time. No need to jam her up. We just—we just let her go."

"No need to have the taxman in your house, finding out you cook your numbers, eh, Luc?" Jacques scooted back in place behind the desk. "I bet they get that pink foam off her face, she was a looker, this Lisette."

I studied Luc's somber face as he answered. "She was a handsome girl."

"Handsome enough to tempt you?"

"No, Jacques, she was—"

"I realize I'm offending you, Alexandra, but it would be stupid of me not to ask."

I nodded at the smirking captain while Luc finished what he wanted to say. "I was at the point in the breakup of my marriage, Jacques, that I wasn't beyond temptation. No secret there. That wasn't the issue. Plenty of guys in town were attracted to Lisette, but I wasn't one of them. There was a profound sadness about this girl— *une tristesse*—not just in her appearance and the way she carried herself, but in her whole spirit."

Jacques's head rolled as he leaned backward with his chair. "Ha! You were looking for something perkier, my friend, like a sex crimes prosecutor? Is that what you're telling me?"

There wasn't much of my usual good-natured humor in reserve since first seeing Lisette's body on the edge of the pond, and I had no interest in performing for the captain, who seemed to be growing ruder by the minute.

"Perhaps the next time you're in New York, you'll come visit me in the courtroom. I'm long on facts and fairness and the occasional outrage, Captain, but I've never been accused of being sad. Buy me some Dewar's at the end of the day, I might even convince you I'm having a good time," I said. "Now, Luc planned an absolutely delightful day for me. If you've got any more questions, you'll find us at the restaurant tonight. *Ça va?*"

Luc fished a business card out of his wallet. "This is my accountant. He knows a lot more about Lisette than I do."

Jacques was practically sputtering as he saw me reach for the door handle. "But you can't go yet."

"You can't possibly be holding him?" I asked, warming up to the incredulity that often preceded my outrage.

"I'm not holding anyone. I have no idea what happened to this girl. It's *your* brain I want to pick, Alexandra. I thought you'd help me with this—this situation."

"Such a strange way you have of asking for assistance, Jacques. The experts are on their way. What is it you need from me?"

"So drowning like this. Is that always murder? Must it be a homicide?"

I didn't take my hand off the door handle. I saw no reason for Luc and me to involve ourselves in this mystery. "Not necessarily. Most drownings are accidental. People fall out of boats or into deep water and can't swim. They panic and struggle to reach the surface, and sometimes doing that they exhaust their energy reserves. Or they swallow large quantities of water at the same time that air is escaping from their lungs. Alcoholics fall facedown in three inches of water, and because they're barely conscious they're unable to roll over."

"And the doctors know it's an accident because . . . ?"

"The totality of the circumstances, Jacques. Sometimes from witnesses, in other cases because the evidence points to only one conclusion. Do you know facts you haven't told us? Any idea how Lisette got to the pond? I didn't see a car there. And it's a long walk in from the road." I was talking at high speed. "Do people really swim in that water? It hardly seems the site for an accident."

"Well, no, I wouldn't think—"

"A few instances of drowning are suicidal. Think Virginia Woolf, Captain."

"Who?"

"You don't read enough, Jacques. An Englishwoman," I said. "She walked into a river after loading her pockets with heavy rocks, which took her to the bottom and made it impossible for her to survive. Manic depression."

"So she was sad, too, this Woolf person?"

"Not sad like Lisette," Luc said. "Mentally ill."

"And you know this girl wasn't a psych case? Is that what you're saying?"

"I haven't a clue, do you understand? I don't know anything about her except that she was quite comfortable stealing from me."

"Then there's murder," I said. "Someone may have held Lisette's head underwater until she drowned. An ugly death. If she was conscious when she went down, she would have been struggling, both to breathe and to get free of her attacker. Then the coughing and choking would have begun as she took on water, and convulsions next, before respiratory arrest and death. Minutes, probably. Achingly long minutes during which she knew she was likely to die."

"So who am I looking for?" Jacques Belgarde put his fingers to his lips for several seconds before he spoke again. "Someone who—"

"Someone? Maybe more than one. Who knows what it took to get her into the park in the middle of the night?" I asked. I didn't tell him I was reminded of the voices I'd heard when I was trying to get Luc's door open. "The autopsy will eventually tell you whether she was drinking or drugged. Perhaps there are bruises on her neck, under her clothing."

"This will spook the tourists for certain. The mayor will be on my ass to solve this one fast."

"Just like in New York," I said. "Political fallout is a common side effect of homicide, Captain."

"Talk to my sommelier, Jacques. Some of the younger guys on my staff may remember who her friends were and who dated her. Maybe they even kept in touch," Luc said. "Or they might be aware of who else she crossed, besides me."

There was a knock on the door and Claude Chenier entered, pushing us farther inside as he extended his hand with several pages of paper in it. "For you, Captain. From Paris."

"That was fast," Belgarde said to his young officer, lighting another cigarette.

"We can't be sure, sir. It's just a name check and a guess at the girl's age."

Chenier backed out as the captain glanced at the documents, then looked up at Luc and shook them in his direction. "The National Police. They seem to know your Lisette Honfleur, too. They share your low opinion of her character."

"I didn't say I had an opinion, Jacques. I don't know—"

"Is that her criminal record?" I asked.

"It is indeed," Jacques said, coming out from behind his desk and bending over to scoop up one of the skulls, spinning it around to examine it more closely. "Not that it tells us why someone targeted you with these human remains, Luc, but maybe we know where they came from."

"What does it say?"

"Two arrests, both fairly recent. Shoplifting from a boutique on the Left Bank, and last year, theft and vandalism from the catacombs."

"The Catacombs of Paris?" I looked at the discoloration of the stack of bones in the crate at Luc's feet. The idea that they might have been hundreds of years old, stolen from the underground ossuary created in miles of caverns and tunnels that once housed the stone quarries beneath the city's streets, made more sense than that they were a recent find. "Why would anyone want to steal bones of the dead?"

"Not to worry, Alexandra," Luc said, shaking his head. "It's only the French who would make a tourist attraction of our mass burial practices for the poor. Don't try to put a good reason to it."

"But someone is connecting them to you," I said.

"From the remains of—what?—six million humans on public display?"

"Minus these three or four gentlemen," Jacques said, poking the wine crate with the toe of his tall black boot. "A token from the 'empire of death,' as the ossuary was so aptly named. What is it, Luc? What message was Lisette sent to deliver?"

Luc squeezed my hand, urging me to exit Belgarde's office. "When you figure it out, Jacques, I'm sure you'll let me know."

"I'm glad, Alexandra, that you asked Luc to call these bones to my attention."

"He would have done it anyway," I said, thinking to myself that it was later rather than sooner as I'd asked him to.

But the captain couldn't let us go without a parting shot. "So at three this morning, Luc, when you didn't pay any attention to what Alexandra asked you to do, where did you go instead?"

Five

My head rested against Luc's back and my arms encircled his waist. I wore a helmet as I always did when riding behind him on his Ducati.

"Are you okay?" he asked, starting the engine. Like so many Europeans, Luc favored his motorcycle for trips to Cannes, allowing him to weave between cars stuck in heavy seasonal traffic and park almost anywhere in town.

"I'm fine." Luc knew me well enough to call my bluff. When we'd said good-bye to Jacques Belgarde, he had left me outside the police station to go to the restaurant to make sure everything was in order for the luncheon service. I returned to the house and tried to work Lisette Honfleur out of my thoughts by swimming laps in the pool. The temperature was brisk enough to refresh me after the turn of events during the night.

"You don't sound fine. Did Jacques get to you?"

"No, Luc. It's not about him. I'm ready to go, really. We can talk later."

It was noon on a spectacular day as we started out from the old village. I remember how tightly I clutched Luc the first few trips down from Mougins's crest several visits earlier, as he navigated the steep roads on his powerful bike. The twenty-minute ride to Cannes was all downhill, past farmhouses built centuries ago, bordered by tall cypress and olive trees that lined the route to the highway.

"It's the girl, then." He was speeding up now, leaning left into the first curve of the descent.

"Of course it's Lisette," I said, picking up my head though my words got lost in the wind. I wanted to know as much as Luc did—whether she had a family and who would deliver this devastating news to them; what her background had been that led her to the lifestyle of petty thievery when she'd been offered the possibility of a good job at a chic three-star restaurant; who had brought her to Mougins last night, dressed as though she planned to attend our party.

Now I trusted Luc on the Ducati Multistrada, no longer clinging to him as at first, but taking my cues from his body that I had also come to know so well over time. We shifted from side to side as though one rider guided the powerful machine. There was no opportunity for conversation as we raced onto the highway and sped south, reaching the crowded streets of Cannes, where Luc worked his way through midday traffic jams and commercial loading zones to come to a stop a block from our destination.

We both dismounted and packed our helmets into the saddlebags. Luc reached for my hand and pulled me toward him, and I accepted his warm embrace. He stroked the back of my head. "We'll talk at lunch."

I nodded as we headed around the corner to La Croisette, the grand boulevard that formed the iconic image of the French Riviera. Royal palms created a majestic centerpiece as far as one could see in either direction, reminding me that the town had originally been built as a mild-weather winter resort for the very rich more than a century ago. The great hotels—the Carlton, the Martinez, and the Majestic Barrière—looked like elegant fortresses, matrons of an era gone by, on one side of the road, while a brilliantly colorful band of beach umbrellas lined the strip of sand at the water's edge.

"Are we going to L'Ondine?" I asked.

"That's your favorite, isn't it?"

"Far and away." We had sampled many of the seaside restaurants, but this one was special to me. Luc's father had taken us there on my first visit. He had a maxim that had served him well in the business: the best restaurant is the one where you are best known.

"That's where I reserved."

We were arm in arm crossing the boulevard. Like all the resorts on the Cannes waterfront, the restaurant was down a flight of stairs from La Croisette. Plage L'Ondine had a glassed-in dining room, but we chose always to rent lounges and a large umbrella—eye-catching in a cheerful canary yellow with clean white trim—to sit outside on the beach and swim in the Mediterranean between courses.

The maître d' was an old friend of Luc's, who greeted him enthusiastically and kissed me on both cheeks. He led us to our usual spot, telling us that rumors about the success of last night's dinner had already circulated throughout the food community in Cannes. Apparently the bad news about Lisette hadn't traveled quite as quickly.

Luc was indeed well-known here. A waiter appeared

instantly with a bottle of champagne and a menu for me as we made ourselves comfortable on the chairs. The royal blue umbrellas to our left and the bright pink ones to our right marked neighboring establishments, filling for the afternoon with locals, tourists, and visitors from the sleek yachts that jammed the colorful port.

The waiter filled our glasses and disappeared before we clinked them together. "Cheers, Alex. Ask me whatever you want and let's get on with the day. Everything else here is perfect."

"Tell me all you know about Lisette."

"Darling, you're more exasperating than Jacques Belgarde." Luc pushed his sunglasses on top of his head and squared off to me. "I barely had anything to do with her. You know the long days and nights I spend in the restaurant, charming the guests. Well, trying to, anyway. She was upstairs in the office a few hours, two or three times a week. She always seemed down, like I told him. Her entire demeanor was off-putting to me, so I had no reason to engage her. I thought she was a druggie, too."

"You didn't say that."

"Because I don't know for sure. Why make it worse for her?"

"It can't get any worse for her than it is. And you didn't report that crime to the police." I wondered whether Luc really had anything to hide from the tax authorities.

"Sip your drink. You're here to relax and I don't want all those bubbles to go to waste."

"When we left the police station this morning and you went back to your office, did you talk to anyone else about Lisette?"

"I wanted to see how many reservations we had for lunch, to make sure all my VIP customers were well seated. I went back to take care of business before I took the afternoon off to attempt to seduce you," he said, signaling the waiter to come back.

"That doesn't answer my question."

"Yes, yes. Okay? Yes, I called Brigitte to tell her about the girl. Is that a problem for you?"

"Of course not."

"I called her because they had such a tremendous catfight when Brigitte accused Lisette of stealing from me. Everyone in town knew there was bad blood between them. I wanted to see if she'd heard from Lisette lately. I'd prefer Brigitte not be dragged into all this."

"And did she know anything?"

"Nothing, Madame Prosecutor. Now, is this inquisition going to go on all afternoon, or can we order something to eat?"

"I apologize, Luc."

"You don't doubt that Jacques is going to show up at Le Relais tonight, do you? I promise you he won't be able to resist. It will only cost me a good meal—a big one—with some serious wine, and you'll know all the dirt he's dug up by nine o'clock."

"I'm sure you're right."

"You're like everyone else who comes to Mougins after all. You see our precious hilltop from the highway and you think it's Camelot. You believe it's a magical medieval village where time stands still and only good things happen."

Since our relationship began, my frequent jaunts to the south of France had become a form of escape for me. I didn't delude myself about that. More than a decade of prosecuting the most heinous crimes in a city where violence flourished 24/7 made me especially susceptible to the nonurgent lifestyle that Luc so enjoyed.

When I was alone in New York, I tried to separate out how much of the pleasure and excitement of the relationship was my love for him and how much was the fairytale aura of life in this romantic enclave. Once I reached Mougins, it was a hopeless task to even contemplate making that decision.

"Now I know it's like every place else in the world. That's a good reality check for me," I said, pulling the crewneck sweater over my head and realigning the straps of my bathing suit. There was no purpose to a menu when I was out with Luc. "What's for lunch?"

The waiter stepped forward to take our order. "We'd each like to start with the salad of tartare de crabe et saumon. And then we'll have grilled langouste to follow, okay?"

The spiny Mediterranean lobster was entirely different from its American cousin. I had a home on Martha's Vineyard, where I'd first met Luc at the wedding of two of my best friends. I'd introduced him to all the culinary treasures of my little island in the Atlantic—clam chowder and fried clams from the Bite, lobster hauled in the same day and harpooned swordfish from Larsen's Fish Market, lobster rolls and root beer at the Galley, grilled striped bass at the Chilmark Tavern, and mussels steamed in garlic and oil at the Beach Plum Inn—and Luc reciprocated with all the most delicious foods in the South of France.

"I'll never be able to eat dinner," I said, sipping the cool champagne as he reached over to pat my stomach.

"It's my goal to fatten you up."

"You've got a good shot at it this time. I don't know how many laps I can do after a few glasses of champers."

I put my head back on the cushioned pillow of the lounger. This was only Sunday, and I didn't have to fly home for another week—enough time to put behind me the trial of the serial rapist I had just taken to a successful verdict, and before I needed to prep for the more difficult child abuse case I would prosecute in June.

"Laps? I'm thinking more like a late afternoon nap, Alex." We had both stretched out on our lounge chairs, facing each other. Luc was tracing the outline of my shoulder with his fingers. "You need to make up your mind about Saturday night, you know. It has to be exactly as you like."

April 30 was my birthday—thirty-eight this year—and we were going to celebrate it together in a week. "I told you, Luc, no party. Last night was enough of that."

"The restaurant, then?"

"No. You'll end up working the room with your fancy guests instead of sitting with me."

"Have you picked another place? Another chef?" He slapped his hand across his chest and feigned disappointment. "How many stars?"

I laughed. "Do you remember my first time here? The first dinner we had together? Because that was my very favorite."

"Of course I remember it. I brought out all the stars in the heavens for you. Well, I shall do that again, if the weather gods cooperate."

On my first trip, I had taken the direct flight to Nice, arriving in mid-morning. We drove to Luc's home in Mougins, spent a day reacquainting ourselves with each other, and at nine that evening, fully refreshed and lovingly restored, I came downstairs to find a lavish table set for two on the terrace. The pool had been surrounded with votive candles, Smokey Robinson serenaded me from within the house, and two waiters from the restaurant ferried back and forth with silver-domed servers holding one delicacy after another. The sky had never seemed so star-filled.

"That's what I'd like it to be—just the two of us."

"Then it's settled."

I kissed my fingertip and placed it against his lips. "And you'll be in New York just ten days after I go back, right?"

"Everything's in place, yes. The decorating is practically done and the equipment has arrived. Almost all the hires are complete."

"An opening date?"

"Not so fast. We'll have a month of tastings first. Dinners to which we invite friends, sort of try out the whole deal on them. The spring and summer months will be a sampling, a transition, while we're going full bore over here. Then I'll be ready for a real launch in the fall," Luc said. "I hope you've been collecting names for me. I'll need plenty of gourmand guinea pigs."

Luc was attempting a very bold move in a difficult financial market. With silent partners backing him, he had purchased a building on the east side of Manhattan and planned to re-create the elegant restaurant his father had started so many decades ago, the one that almost every critic on both sides of the Atlantic had for years and years declared the finest dining in the city: Lutèce.

I had a loyal group of friends in the district attorney's office who would be only too happy to submit themselves to the haute cuisine of the new Lutèce kitchen.

Luc was a restaurateur, an executive chef who owned and managed the restaurant here and would do the same in New York. He had his father's sense of style and creativity, but wasn't the guy in the kitchen, holding the food to the flame.

The waiter was back to refill our glasses and offer an amuse-bouche—something to excite our palate—in this case a medley of seafood, courtesy of the chef. Luc sat up and put his feet in the sand, readying himself for the delicious meal to follow.

"I thought the catacombs had been closed," I said. "I didn't realize you could still go down there and root around."

Luc groaned. "Get this all out of your system—bones and bodies and burial vaults—before the langouste is set in front of me, darling; I'd like to enjoy eating it, if you don't mind. Have you ever been inside the catacombs?"

"I made the mistake of accepting the invitation of a friend who's a medical examiner in Paris, five years or so ago. A tour was his idea of an excursion, I guess, but it's one of the creepiest places I've ever been."

We had entered through a narrow spiral staircase to the dark chamber way below the street surface that led to miles of tunnels beneath the city. The only sound breaking the silence was the gurgle of a hidden aqueduct coursing through an adjacent cavern wall. There was hall after hall of carefully arranged remains, floor to ceiling—centuries of dead Parisians who had been moved here in mass burials after widespread contamination of the city's cemeteries. Rusty gates barred visitors from reaching areas that were too unsafe—or perhaps too gruesome—to be part of the tour.

"They were closed temporarily after some vandalism

three or four years ago. Then reopened. That happens now and then."

"You've been there, too?"

"Many times, Alexandra. And no, I've never been tempted to carry off any bones."

He was licking his fingers to savor every last bit of the marinade.

"Did you ever go to the catacombs with Lisette?"

"No and no and no and no to all the ridiculous things that cross your mind."

I thought for a minute. "What if there's any significance to the numbers?"

"Which numbers?"

"Three skulls in front of Le Relais," I said. "And you're the only restaurant in town that's got three stars."

"And you've got a wonderfully fertile imagination that you should use to think about all the things we can do the next time you can sneak off for a visit here."

We had started to eat in earnest when the maître d' hurried to our chairs with a portable phone in hand.

"I'm so sorry to interrupt you, Luc, but it's the police. He says it's very important."

Luc stood up. "Damn Belgarde. He's determined to make himself look more stupid than Inspector Clouseau at this point."

"Not for you. It's for *madame*," he said, extending his arm with the phone. "It's American police."

Luc threw his hands in the air. "I can't believe this. You're on holiday, Alexandra. Doesn't anyone in your office get that? There are five hundred other prosecutors for Battaglia to lean on. Surely someone else is competent enough to do what you do?"

"Anyone and everyone on my team." I blushed as I

put down my glass on the small table between our chairs. I had promised Luc that I wouldn't even charge my cell phone during the week here, so that we'd have a real chance to experience life together, without a professional interruption.

"Hello, Coop?"

Not even the static on the small phone that had been carried too far from its base could muffle the distinctive voice of NYPD homicide detective Mike Chapman.

"Yeah, Mike."

"Did I catch you in the middle of a foie gras or anything? Is your profiterole melting?"

"Make it quick."

"Forgive me for skipping the 'bonjours' and all that, but I had Luc's secretary run you down."

"Obviously."

Luc folded his arms and walked away, but the maître d' wasn't ready to relinquish the phone to me at the height of the hour his reservations were calling in. He remained at my side.

"You've got to come home, Coop. Pronto. Next plane out of paradise."

"Not this time," I said, and though I was bursting with curiosity, I knew Luc would be furious if I even asked Mike why he had called.

"Mercer needs you. It's serious, kid."

"Something happen to Mercer?" The heightened concern in my voice got Luc's attention. He knew that Mercer Wallace had covered my back more times than I could count. There was very little I wouldn't do for him.

"Yeah."

"He's hurt?"

"Calm down, kid. He's just fine, physically. What happened to him is that he's saddled with the biggest case of his career and he wants you to help him. At the moment, it's your archenemy who's calling the shots."

"Pat McKinney?" The chief of the Trial Division spent much of the average workday trying to stab me in the back with a serrated knife. "What does McKinney want with a rape case?"

"Visibility, I guess."

I took Chapman's bait. "What makes it so big?"

"I caught the squeal. Collared the guy in the first-class cabin on a flight to Paris."

"The perp is French?"

Luc's eyes were riveted on me as I started to talk and show interest. Now I was the one who took a few steps back.

"Lives in France, but he's West African. Rich as Croesus. Son of an exiled African leader and he's rumored to be the next president of the Ivory Coast, give or take a revolution or two in between. Head of the World Economic Bureau—called the WEB. You know who that is?"

"I have no idea."

"I thought you specialized in Frenchmen."

"You're beginning to break up on me, Detective. You might find yourself disconnected if you get too snarky."

"Mohammed Gil-Darsin," Mike said. "Go on line and check him out. The French call him Baby Mo, even though he's in his fifties, or they just use his initials— MGD. Anyway, a maid at the Eurotel Hotel down in SoHo claims he raped her."

Everyone in the South of France knew Papa Mo, the overthrown dictator of the Republic of the Ivory Coast, who had gone into exile here—following the example of Haiti's Duvalier—with millions of dollars stolen from his country's cocoa-rich coffers. I didn't realize he had a son who was a figure in the international economic community.

"Did you say a maid is the accuser?"

"Yeah, a housekeeper at the hotel. Best suite in the joint, at three thousand clams a night. She was doing turndown service in the room and he came out of the shower starkers. She tried to back out and he threw her onto her knees."

"Nobody dead, Mike?" He was probably the best homicide detective in the city, assigned to Manhattan North, but he had never worked special victims cases.

"Nope. Alive and kicking back."

"So what are you doing with a rape case?

"Working Night Watch, Coop. All the craziest shit happens on Night Watch."

Six

Luc was toweling down after a swim in the bay by the time I got off the phone with Mike. His voice was as ice-chilled as the champagne. "I'll take you back to the house to pack up, Alex. You can fly up to Paris late afternoon and connect to home."

"Not this time. I'm not going."

"Detective Chapman losing his touch?" Luc asked, cocking his head.

"I'm on vacation. He just needed to be reminded of that."

"He has no boundaries with you, darling," Luc said, defrosting with the news that I wasn't racing back to take the case, leaning over to kiss me on the forehead. "Big news?"

"Sounds that way." I had handled more than my share of high-profile cases. Sex crimes could snag headlines like no other category of offense and usually for all the wrong reasons. The alleged perp is a celebrity, the victim is the daughter of a high-powered businessman, a junkie is attacked in a landmark location like Central Park, or the offender's occupation shocks New Yorkers' sensibilities—school principal, star athlete, elected official.

"Are you tempted?"

"I learned long ago there's no upside to being handed the big case in the glare of the media spotlight. There's already one supervisor who's jumped all over this. I hope for Battaglia's sake he gets it right."

I leaned back against the cushioned pillow and tilted my face up to find the sun. Paul Battaglia was the district attorney of New York County. At sixty-five years old and in office for more than two decades, he was regarded as one of the country's premier figures in law enforcement. He had appointed me to run his Sex Crimes Unit and relied on my superb team of colleagues to manage these cases that presented such unique issues to prosecutors as well as to the voting public. Hand-chosen for their combination of skills, the unit's members were brilliant and compassionate, tough litigators and fierce advocates for our severely traumatized victim population, but only after they made factual determinations that the crime had occurred and the right offender was identified.

"Isn't it odd that Battaglia didn't call you himself?"

"It's a good thing as far as I'm concerned. That's why I'm staying put."

"Why do you think he didn't?"

"I'm not good at second-guessing him. I've told you that." Battaglia's political instincts were first-rate. And while I had come to question his gamesmanship in some of my more recent investigations, he had in turn relied more heavily on the longtime chief of the Trial Division, Pat McKinney, whose most valued trait was the consistency to which he played yes-man to the prominent prosecutor.

"The bad guy is French?"

"What else did you hear?"

"Nothing, nothing else," Luc said.

"The tables are turned, aren't they? I suppose you want *me* to talk shop now," I said, wagging my empty glass in his face and grinning broadly. "I suppose this interests you more than your pyramid of skulls."

"Okay, I'm an open book." Luc spread his arms out in the air. "Ask me anything, then tell me all you know."

I thought he would see past my fake smile, but I tried anyway. "So when you told me you were going to the gendarmerie at three this morning, where did you really go?"

"Aha! So you're taking your lead from Jacques now? Asking the questions that he asked? That's beneath you, Alexandra. It's exactly like I said. I took the bones to my office, but decided there was no urgency to involving the police in the middle of the night."

"You were gone more than an hour."

"Now you're bluffing, Ms. Cooper. I may have to cut you off the booze," Luc said, taking my glass from my hand and turning it upside down. "You were sleeping so soundly when I came in, you couldn't have had any idea what time it was. If you're implying that I was off clipping lotus blossoms in the pond, I'll take you to the airport right this minute."

"Just practicing my cross-examination skills, darling. If you fill me up, I promise to be more polite." I righted my champagne flute and extended it to him. "You want to hear about your rapist?"

"Oxymoronic, darling. This is France. We don't have rapists."

Luc and I had argued about that issue more times than I could count. He was trying to return the insult.

"Your women just under-report because of the general attitude toward sexual violence in this country. And you have a justice system that doesn't know how to deal with these crimes."

"So what happened?"

"Mike says the guy was staying at the Eurotel."

"Not exactly the Plaza Athénée." Luc wasn't impressed with the perp's choice, a French-owned chain of moderately priced hotels, fine for the business traveler but without the luxurious appointments he liked.

"Well, he was in the presidential suite. Twenty-eighth floor, with views down to the Statue of Liberty."

"That should have cost him plenty."

"It did. He arrived Thursday night for meetings on Friday and was due to leave last evening. The front desk gave him the courtesy of a late checkout at six p.m., because he was on the final flight to Paris."

"Air France number nine from JFK. Eleven-twenty departure. I know it well."

"Scheduled for a quick dinner with his daughter, who's an assistant to the French ambassador to the UN, before the flight."

"Busy man," Luc said. "Where was his wife?"

"At home in Paris. Or should I say at one of their homes. So the maid bumps into the headwaiter from room service, backing out of the suite with the tray table. She was anxious to get the room turned over so the manager could sell the suite again, or upgrade some VIP on a Saturday night arrival. So at five forty-five, the waiter tells her he thinks the room is empty, 'cause he didn't hear any noise inside when he opened the door to get the tray. But it's huge, according to Mike. The living area alone is thirteen hundred square feet—and there's a bedroom and two baths."

"She went in?" Luc asked.

"Yes, the waiter told her she could get to work. So she announced herself and called out 'housekeeping' several times—just to be sure the guest was gone."

"But he wasn't."

"How could she have known? The waiter closed the door behind her, and as she started to straighten up the room and strip the bed, out from the bathroom comes our perp."

"He was—about to leave?" Luc asked.

"Apparently not. He was naked. Completely naked. Just out of the shower."

"She should have taken off," he said emphatically. "She should have left at once. She obviously caught him off guard."

"I hope you're just playing devil's advocate. *He* obviously surprised her. She'd been told the room was unoccupied, okay? She announced herself, loud and clear, while the door was still open. She apologized and tried to back out. She told him she was sorry."

"What stopped her from leaving?"

"The perp did. He grabbed her by the wrist and told her not to go, not to be sorry. She was scared, she told the cops. Frightened of him and just as frightened that she'd lose her job if she got into a screaming match with a high-rolling guest."

"Did he threaten her?"

"I don't know the exact words, but Mike said he did."

"Well, if Mike told you, then it must be so," Luc said flippantly, spearing a piece of crabmeat and devouring it.

"It doesn't really matter what was verbalized, the guy threw her onto the bed. He lifted the skirt of her uniform, ripped her panty hose, and penetrated."

Luc snapped his fingers. "Just like that?"

"Not just like that, okay? He had a head start by being naked, and aroused as well. He pinned her to the bed and was inside her briefly until she pushed him off, within a few seconds."

"And that's rape in your country?"

"I'm not done." Forcible penile penetration, however slight and for however short a period of time, established the elements of the crime of first-degree rape. "Then he pushed her onto her knees, on the floor, and demanded oral sex. When he ejaculated, she spit it out."

Luc had no smart answer for that fact.

"Semen on the carpet, on the wall of the room, and on her uniform. Sort of supports what she's saying, don't you think? And they'll have DNA results by the end of the day."

"So I guess he missed his plane," Luc mused, stabbing another piece of the salad.

"To the contrary. The entire episode with the maid took twenty minutes, start to finish."

"Not exactly a seduction, even for the most convincing Frenchman."

"The hotel surveillance photos have him rushing out a bit later, toothpaste smeared across his cheek. A quick dinner with his daughter and he actually made it to the airport in time to board. If it wasn't for the thick fog at JFK and an hour's flight delay, he'd have reached home and be having brunch with his wife just about now."

"I can't imagine what makes that such an important case in the States," Luc said, pushing the salad aside in anticipation of his langouste. "She's just a chambermaid, after all."

I hoped my sunglasses concealed the expression in my

eyes. "I see. So that makes her—what? Not worthy of belief? Not entitled to justice? Or makes the perp too powerful to have our system bother with her?"

"No, no, darling." Luc was searching for a way to back off his obvious prejudice. "I just mean it's not international news, really, is it? That's why Battaglia isn't looking for you. Maybe one day of tabloid headlines, then back to business. Not likely to make the light of day in the French press."

"I'll bet you tonight's caviar that you're wrong."

Luc was enjoying himself now. "And I was going to order up the finest beluga. Almas caviar, from Iran. It's white, and among the rarest in the world. Shall we say a small tin for twenty-five thousand?"

"I'll settle for something a little more subtle."

"And why do you think you can win? It's only seven in the morning in New York. I guess by dinnertime here we'll have a clue."

"Maybe if I tell you his name, you'll concede on the spot."

"So you buried the lede, did you? You know who he is?"

"I'm certainly betting that you do," I said, as the waiter approached with a tray and Luc nodded approval of the large grilled langoustes that were set in front of us.

"I hope you don't spoil my appetite, Alex. Who's the guy?"

"Mohammed Gil-Darsin."

Luc lost all interest in lunch and focused his attention on me. He let out a low whistle, clearly surprised by hearing the name. "MGD? The detectives must be pulling your leg, darling. It simply can't be."

"Why is that?"

"Well—well, he's—uh—he's brilliant, for one thing.

He's very popular in France, not to mention his political future at home. He's got a fabulous wife." Luc was stammering he was so agitated. "Mo's a player, all right—but—uh—that's different. I simply don't believe he'd rape anyone. He wouldn't have to, Alex. He's quite attractive. Brains, power, money—all of that. I mean, really, darling—a chambermaid?"

I sat back on my chair and exhaled. It was as though every conversation I'd had with Luc about my work since we'd met had gone in one ear and out the other. If this was his attitude, I knew how most people hearing the news would also react.

"Do you know him?" I asked.

"Papa Mo has lived in a villa in Grasse for thirty years." Grasse was the town adjacent to Mougins, whose thousands of acres of jasmine and hyacinth had long made it the perfume capital of the world. "He was my father's client long before he was mine."

"He was a dictator, Luc. And a thief."

"A scoundrel, maybe. I didn't care much for his politics, but he's a charming man."

"I asked if you know MGD."

Luc looked away from me, at a distant point out in the bay. "Of course I do, Alex, though not very well. He isn't a close friend or anything like that. He's a client, a customer. He was just in the restaurant for dinner a week ago."

Seven

I had no appetite for lunch. Luc, it was clear, was happier eating than talking to me.

The sun, the champagne, and the lack of sleep the night before combined to knock me out on the lounge chair. When I opened my eyes an hour later, Luc was napping also.

Nina Baum, my college roommate—and still my best friend—had tried to put the brakes on my love affair with Luc. She liked him and understood what I found so appealing about him—his intelligence and accomplishments, his great sense of style and adventure, his romantic courtship of me—Nina got all that.

But she worried about the superficial nature of our relationship. I had no time for Luc when I was experiencing the demands of a trial that required all my intellectual energy and emotion. And I had little understanding of a career that appeared to be so glamorous, in contrast to mine, with problems no greater than overcooking the entrée or recommending the wrong wine—a career designed to provide pleasure to a consumer for as many hours as a great meal lasted.

As Luc worked ferociously hard to open a new business in New York, I had come to appreciate the demands on a restaurant owner and many of the obstacles in the way of success. Had he absorbed nothing about the somewhat bizarre but fascinating professional world that gave me such great satisfaction?

He lifted his head and squinted at me. "Where are you, Alex? What are you thinking?"

"Nothing serious. I'm mesmerized by the view."

"That's as it should be," he said, reaching over to me and squeezing my hand. "Another hour? This is the only spot in the world where I think I can let go of everything and nap."

"Fine with me."

On the other hand, my great friend Joan Stafford was entirely in favor of the way I had plunged headlong into this relationship. The writer and her husband, Jim Hageville, a world-renowned journalist, had married at my home on the Vineyard. Luc was a longtime friend of Jim's—which added instant respectability to his credentials—and we met at my home on their wedding day. As much as Joan championed my legal career, now she was rooting for me to give up the often grueling work of the courtroom and move here to Mougins permanently to be with Luc.

When I'd boarded the flight to Nice the night before last, I was entirely in sync with Joan's plan. But at this very moment, I thought Nina was right. I was in love with a man I hardly knew. The aspects of the long-distance romance that made it so exciting and titillating were also the very things that made it impossible to get inside each other's daily life and routine.

I looked at my watch. It was two-thirty on a Sunday afternoon, and eight-thirty in the morning at home. I felt a tinge of regret about agreeing to stay off my BlackBerry during this trip. Mike and Mercer came from backgrounds as different from mine as one could imagine, but we had the same respect for the criminal justice system and the same value for the dignity of human life. Both of them had helped train me—every bit as much as the lawyers from whom I'd learned—in the art of investigating cases, in the search for the truth that characterized the way a great prosecutor's office worked. Mike's call—and Luc's response—had unsettled me.

I rolled on my side away from Luc and covered my shoulders with a yellow-and-white-striped beach towel. I wondered whether Lisette's body had been removed from the edge of the pond yet, and if there were any forensic experts in this area who would assist in the death investigation.

The anxiety gnawed at me until I pushed this morning's images out of my mind, and I fell asleep again. I didn't awaken until Luc kissed me on the top of my head.

"It's almost four o'clock. Another swim and we go?"

I stretched my arms up in the air to reach Luc's face. "It's warmer in the pool. At the speed you drive that thing, I'll form icicles on the way up to Mougins if I get wet here."

"Off we go, then. I've got all those hungry mouths to feed."

The sun was already dropping lower in the sky as I pulled on my sweater and slacks and gathered my belongings. "Do you have a lot of reservations for tonight?"

"Completely full. And you know how happy that makes me. There's a private party in the back of the main room,"

Luc said. He had created one of the most beautiful dining spaces in France, which complemented the exquisite food and premium service. "We'll turn each of the tables in front over twice. And you and I are dining in *le zinc*."

"Perfect." *Le zinc* was the bar attached to the restaurant. The elegance of the dining room with its crisp white linens, shining Christofle silver, crystal wineglasses, and the soft spring green of the painted trim was a sharp contrast to the turn-of-the-century feel in the much cozier adjacent room. It was intimate in the most casual way, a long wooden counter that Andre Rouget had rescued from a Parisian bistro and transported to the restaurant, across from a row of tables that sat beneath nineteenth-century posters warning of the dangers of *l'absinthe* or glamorizing the nightclubs and brothels of the day.

The maître d' appeared in our path as we headed for the staircase. There was rarely a bill for Luc when we dined at a friend's restaurant. Professional courtesy would come in the way of payback for the owner and management of L'Ondine when they wanted an evening in the country. Luc folded a tip into his extended hand and we thanked the maître d' for the delicious afternoon.

"We're not alone tonight, did I tell you that?" he said, as we climbed the steps back up to La Croisette.

"You mean, apart from Captain Belgarde?"

"That will put a damper on the evening," he said, catching up to me at the top and taking my hand as we crossed the broad boulevard. "Yes, one of the guys who's going to supply the wines for New York is visiting here. I had no choice but to invite him to join us."

"That should be lovely."

"We have so few nights together that I hate to fill them with business."

"For me it's great fun. I get to learn so much about what you do. Do you like him?"

"He seems like a decent guy. And he certainly knows his business."

We dodged the steady parade of cars and motorcycles and tiny Vespas that coursed through the thoroughfare with little concern about speed limits.

When we reached the motorcycle, Luc removed our headgear from the saddlebags and I stuffed my tote inside. I fastened my hair into a ponytail at the nape of my neck, strapped on the shiny blue helmet, and climbed onto the backseat. At this moment I didn't bear any resemblance to the serious prosecutor who made it a point to appear like a complete professional in the office and courtroom.

Luc looked at his iPhone before he pocketed it. "Brigitte e-mailed me when you were napping. Belgarde's already called to ask her about the dead girl," he said, shaking his head. "She's going to drive to her mother's tonight and stay till all this blows over in town."

"So I guess she's taking the kids?"

"Yes," he said, getting into place on the bike.

I was talking to his back. "And you want to see them before she goes?"

"I'd like to."

"I don't blame you, Luc. Just drop me at the house and I'll meet you at the restaurant whenever you like."

He reached back with one hand and stroked my thigh. "Thanks, darling."

"You worry about the silliest things. I'm pleased you want to see them. They don't need to have this murder case churning around them, just because you and Brigitte knew the victim."

I was well aware that figuring out how to maintain his intimacy with his children was a major stumbling block to Luc's plans for a second restaurant in New York.

The narrow side streets of Cannes were packed tight with parked cars and commercial vans. I nestled into my usual position against Luc's back and swayed with him as he maneuvered the territory he knew so well. The first few blocks were almost on flat ground, filled with shops selling all the luxury goods for which the French were known. But then the streets began to merge together, more modest businesses and residences side by side, as we climbed out of the busy city headed due north on the Boulevard Carnot.

I was daydreaming with my eyes closed once we left the dramatic scenery of the old harbor and grand buildings. The highway was a drab road, with strip malls built up on either side. Traffic was already intense, and Luc began to weave among the cars that started and stopped at each intersection and traffic light. He was an impatient driver, and I was used to the rhythm he set as he picked up speed to charge the great concrete hill.

The bike dipped sharply to the left and seemed to kick into a higher gear. My head snapped back, bringing me out of my reverie as I tightened my grip around Luc's waist.

"Easy!" I screamed out to him, but the word was lost between the noises of the engines and car horns all around us.

Luc was on a tear, passing three cars on the right as he gunned the powerful Ducati to surge forward. I grabbed at his lean frame to find some skin to pinch to express my discomfort, and when I did, he simply shook me off and continued at the same breakneck speed.

It must have been the day's events that were getting to Luc, and maybe Brigitte's sudden decision to leave town with the two kids, pressuring him when he least needed another concern. I twisted my head around to the left to check where we were and whether there was any reason—other than his nerves—for this erratic driving pattern.

I could see that he had skirted a bad collision a hundred yards back, a four-car pileup that would have everything backed up until it was cleared.

Luc was trying to say something to me now, but it was impossible to hear him. I leaned in against him and could figure only that he was trying to tell me to hang on. When I turned to the right and looked back, I could see why: two men on motorcycles, both in leather jackets with upturned collars, wearing polarized sunglasses beneath large black helmets, seemed to be in serious pursuit of us. They were also off to the right on the shoulder of the paved road, following in the very path Luc had carved out for himself.

There was nothing for me to do but flatten myself against Luc's back. His shirt was flapping against the skin on my cheek, whipped up by the wind and the velocity. At home, in the city, a ride like this would have been virtually impossible without a police car intervening in a matter of minutes. But speed wasn't an issue in this part of the world.

I wanted to be off the motorcycle, and I wanted to be anywhere but clinging to the back of a man I thought I loved but barely knew. I shook off that thought and tried to be rational. What if these two guys weren't chasing him? He was putting us both in danger, and I was getting dizzier from the combination of those ideas and the

swinging motion of the bike as Luc steered it back between the two heaviest lanes of traffic.

The next three minutes on the highway seemed like an
hour. Cars were honking at us now as we cut them off to
keep up the pace, and the honking continued behind us
as the men in black must have done the same.

I knew the exit was coming up in another quarter of a
mile. Luc veered in front of two lanes of cars to go from
the left-hand passing lane toward the ramp that would
take us down to the route that led to the village. As he
leaned to the right to make the exit, both bikers behind
us followed suit. We were hugging the right side of the
pavement so closely that I feared we would slam into the
road sign announcing Mougins.

Then, as though turbocharged with an extra measure of
juice, Luc jammed on the brakes, leaned sharply to his left
with me hanging on tight, and turned the Ducati a full
one-eighty, as on a dime, regaining the shoulder of the
highway to continue northbound.

One of the bikers wiped out completely in an effort to
copy Luc's move. I saw him hit the ground and skid
along, trapped beneath the deadweight of the heavy motorcycle, which slammed with him into the base of a tree.
The other guy swerved off the ramp to avoid a car coming directly at him. The last time I looked back, he had
come to a stop beside his fallen mate, whose screams I
could hear over the roar of Luc's racing engine.

Eight

Luc must have seen the accident in his rearview mirrors. His whole body, which had stiffened with tension somewhere early along the route, relaxed against me. He took his place in the line of cars—as though it was an ordinary ride—until we reached the next exit, on the far side of Mougins.

"Stop now," I said, practically screaming into his helmet as we turned onto the tranquil road a mile north of the village. There were brasseries and small shops and endless places with parking lots in which Luc could have pulled over to explain to me what set him off.

"Home" was the only word I understood when Luc responded.

I was sitting upright behind him, distancing myself as far from his body as one could on a motorcycle. It was another five minutes before we finished the circular climb up to the center of town, and Luc nosed the bike down into the alleyway to park it beside the door to his property, right where I had found the stack of bones.

I ripped the helmet from my head and was off the bike before he had it positioned. "That was insane. That ride was terrifying and unnecessary and totally insane, Luc. Do you see how I'm trembling? Can you make any sense of this to me?"

I turned away from him and pushed open the heavy door. By the time he'd locked the Ducati and followed me inside, I was sitting on the old stone wall that overlooked the valley. Gaspard, the sloppy basset hound, was cuddled beside me offering solace.

"Are you all right, Alex?" Luc came up behind me and put his hands on my shoulders. "I apologize for alarming you."

"Alarming me? Alarming me would have been telling me you had a hair-raising ride home this afternoon. I wasn't alarmed, Luc. I thought we were going to die—at your hands or theirs, whoever they were. What have I walked into here? What is it you aren't telling me about your life?"

He sat down beside me, much to the dog's obvious delight, and pulled the band out of my hair, combing his fingers through it, pulling at the blond wisps that had curled up under the heavy helmet.

I reached for his wire-rimmed glasses and took them off, folding them and putting them in his shirt pocket.

"I have no explanation for what's going on, Alex. Only that you'll have to trust me. You arrived Friday and everything was as calm as the sea was today. It all started in the middle of last night. I don't know why that is, and I certainly don't know how to make it stop."

"Could it be personal?"

He took my chin in his hands and made me look at him. "You're my personal life, Alexandra. You and only you. Do you understand that?"

"I'm trying to. Does Brigitte?"

"I don't think of you as the jealous type."

"I'm not."

"She was my wife. She's the mother of my children."

"She's also the reason you fired Lisette Honfleur," I said. "And Lisette's dead."

"Then let's try business. I know you don't think of my work as having the gravitas of yours, darling, but this is serious business in France. Chefs have killed themselves over losing a Michelin star. No reason others wouldn't kill to get one."

"You'll have to help me with all this," I said, scratching one of Gaspard's long ears to avoid making eye contact with Luc. "I know we can't talk about it at dinner because we'll have guests."

"And right now I'd really like to go see my kids."

"Sure. That means tomorrow. I want to understand everything that's going on with the restaurant here, and what the status is of the plan in New York. Don't worry," I said, switching to the other ear. "I'll feed the dog while you're gone. But you really do need to tell me about the guys on the motorcycles."

Luc stood up, reached for his glasses, and cleaned the lenses with the sleeve of his shirt. "I don't know who they are."

"Why do you think they were chasing you?"

"Didn't you notice them?"

"Before the highway? No, I didn't."

"They were parked directly across the street from the staircase down to L'Ondine. On their bikes, faced out, like they were waiting for someone to appear just as we were leaving. I mean, I didn't think they were waiting for us, until I pulled out of my space and turned onto La Croisette."

"And they came after us?"

"Immediately. I zigzagged through a couple of the back streets that I don't usually take—a very indirect route to get back here—and they were along for the ride. I reached the boulevard and they were still behind me. I put on some speed and so did they."

"So instead of stopping, instead of pulling over into a gas station where there would be people around, you could have gotten us both killed by driving through the traffic like a maniac."

What was unspoken between us was the story that I had told Luc about my first love, Adam Nyman. He had been killed in an accident on the highway driving from the hospital at which he was doing his residency to Martha's Vineyard, the night before we were to be married at the home we'd just bought. I'd never known whether it was speed or exhaustion or being forced off the road by another car that sent Adam to his death, but I had a lingering fear of losing control on the road.

"I had a split second to make the decision to accelerate, Alex. I saw something in the man's hand when the one on the lead bike tried to get on our tail."

"Something?" I asked. "Do you know what you saw?"

"I was looking in the rearview mirror. He pulled a pistol from his jacket so I could see it, then shoved it right back in and charged the bike."

"A pistol? You actually saw a gun in his hand?" It was my turn to stiffen and sit upright.

"Yes, I did," Luc said. "No mistake about it. And the only thing between the gun and me, Alexandra, was your back."

Nine

It was eight-fifteen when Luc called from his office to ask me to meet him at Le Relais. After brooding for a couple of hours, I showered and changed into a navy blue sweaterdress with white piping that showed off my newly acquired tan.

I pulled my suitcase from the back of the closet and—despite my promise to Luc—took out my BlackBerry. I felt too disconnected from events in the office to ignore Mike completely. The phone had gone dead, of course, so I plugged it in to charge during the time we were at dinner.

I left the house for the short walk to the restaurant, intending to bypass the main entrance and go directly into the bar. I hadn't counted on the mild night to have attracted a crowd to the outdoor tables on the terrace.

As I got closer, a woman called out and waved to me. "Alex! Come join us."

It was Gretchen Adkins, a Wellesley classmate married

to a Parisian, who'd been at the party the night before. I walked to the short hedge that separated the terrace from the cobblestone street and greeted the couple.

"I can't sit, Gretchen. I'm late to meet Luc."

"He's got his hands full inside. Just have a drink with us. We're waiting on another couple." She was kind and warm, and loved to gossip. It was comforting to see someone from home, and I would have liked to catch up with her, but I learned months ago that Luc had a reason for me not to sit with his clients.

"They buy you a drink," he chided me gently one night last fall, "and I end up buying them dinner. People mean well when they invite you to sit with them, but when the bill finally comes, most of them figure they deserve something for entertaining you while I was hard at work."

"Let's plan lunch before I leave next week. I'm really running late," I said. "Did you enjoy Luc's bash?"

"Wasn't it just divine?" Gretchen said. "Of course I paid for that good time today. Wicked hangover, and I didn't get out of bed until two. The phone rang all day with people dying to know how to get on the list for next year."

I blew kisses to her and kept on my way, interested that she hadn't heard anything about a corpse dressed in white or the scandalous news from New York.

The bartender must have seen me approaching and alerted Luc, who opened the door and bowed his head to me, taking my hand to kiss it and welcome me inside.

This was the showmanship that Luc Rouget thrived on. He looked dashing in the crisp white chef's coat with his name embroidered in green thread that was exactly the same shade as the paint trim in the dining room. He wore clogs as his father had decades earlier, long before Mario Batali popularized them as the celebrity chef footwear of choice. Regulars and first-time diners seemed to watch all his movements, curious to see whom he favored and whether any glimpse of his mercurial temper would flash.

Every table in the bar, except for the four-top in the far corner, was occupied. The crowd was more youthful and hip, on most nights, than the guests interested in the full experience of the haute cuisine served next door.

Luc escorted me to the table, and I slid into the brown leather banquette against the wall. He called to the bartender, asking for *deux coupes*, and within seconds there were two glasses of champagne on our table.

"Are the kids okay?" I asked.

Luc hovered over me, leaning one arm on the door frame between the rooms, but he had his eyes set on the action in the restaurant. He would lavish most of his attention on the high rollers who were paying through the nose for the hard-to-get reservation.

"They're fine. They don't know anything yet."

"And Brigitte?"

"What's to say? She hasn't seen Lisette in years and doesn't want to be part of any investigation involving her death. She's taken the boys out of school for two weeks while she goes to Normandy tomorrow, where her mother is."

"I take it you're not happy about that."

Luc looked down at me and nodded. "I'd prefer they be here. I'd like to be with them, especially before I head to New York."

"I know that," I said, sensing tension after his meeting with Brigitte. "Did you have an argument with Brigitte? I mean about taking the kids with her."

"Brigitte never argues. She's used to getting her way."

She left Luc a few years ago for reasons he had never articulated. He wasn't over her, and maybe never would be. I expected photographs of his two sons to be all over his home—Luc adored them—but I had no clue why he still kept a picture of Brigitte in the single drawer of the table beside the bed.

"Have you spoken to Jacques Belgarde?"

"Not yet."

"Not even to tell him about the guy with the gun?"

Luc glanced at his watch. "Trust me. He'll be in before the kitchen closes. He's got a better nose for black truffles than most pigs, and we're serving some tonight."

"Why don't you sit down with me?" I said, tugging at the sleeve of his jacket. "You look so anxious."

"Shortly, darling."

The headwaiter crossed the threshold from the dining room. "Monsieur Rouget, the guests at table six would like to see you."

"Problem?"

"Not at all. A little stroking perhaps," he said with a wink. "They knew your father. I think they just want to reminisce."

"Papa's my lucky charm, Alex. I'm bringing him to New York for the opening. His old customers will come out in droves," Luc said, the spark returning to his eyes. "This is a world he created, and he's electric at making it work."

"So I've heard."

"As soon as Jim—my wine guru—arrives, I'll bring him in and we'll order. Think of something fabulous the kitchen can create for you."

My thoughts were everywhere except on the dinner

menu. I opened my evening bag and took out the small notebook that I carried everywhere. My list-making habit was almost obsessive, and within minutes I had worked up a full page of questions I wanted to ask Captain Belgarde about Lisette and his findings. I was still jotting down ideas when I heard Luc's voice, and stuffed the papers away.

He reentered the bar, followed by a tall, stocky man who looked more like a fullback than a wine merchant. Luc motioned him to the seat beside me, and I slid over to let him in as he put the two bottles of wine he was carrying on the table.

"Alex, this is Jim Mulroy."

"Happy to meet you," I said.

"My pleasure. Luc's talked about you a lot." He rubbed his palms together and smiled at Luc. "Open these up, will you? I think I've found something unusual for New York."

While he examined the labels, Luc signaled to the bartender to come over and uncork the bottles. "Bordeaux?"

"Don't say it." Jim held up both hands. "Pretentious, stodgy, dull. Your young customers think it's old-school and over-branded. Taste this, my friend."

"Domaine de Jeuget. Never heard of it."

"I don't know how I got so lucky. Three hundred fifty years this family's had the vineyards. Just a small estate, Luc. It's not a château. The old guy who runs it took me down in the cellars. I'm telling you, there are cobwebs on everything except the barrels, and they probably predate Napoléon."

Jim sniffed the cork before handing it to Luc.

"Fresh and alive, isn't it?" Jim went on. "There are no chemicals, no manipulation. He does it just like his father and grandfather did before him, keeps it in barrels for thirty months. No oakiness, but a nice subtle aeration."

Luc poured a bit into a glass. "How much does he produce a year?"

"Six, maybe seven thousand bottles of St. Julien."

I was watching this dance between them and admiring Jim's enthusiasm. "Is that a lot or a little?"

"It's a minuscule output." Luc laughed at me. "Think of Mouton Rothschild. They put out something like one hundred and seventy thousand bottles of their best wine each year. They're farming close to three hundred acres."

"Versus three acres for Jeuget," Jim said. "It's graceful, isn't it? Smell all those violets that make up the aroma, and the minerals, too."

He tilted his glass toward me and I took a whiff. It just smelled like red wine.

"I get the picture, Jim," Luc said, explaining to me. "The major importers won't deal with this, Alex. There isn't enough product. They can't buy enough of it to ship to all their clients. They can't get a bulk price."

"Let me order five hundred cases for New York. You can charge anything you want for it, anywhere from one to two hundred bucks a bottle."

"What's the typical restaurant markup on wine?" I asked.

"Four, maybe five times what we pay for it," Luc said.

"Starting up a first-rate place in Manhattan these days, with labels you can't get anywhere else?" Jim said. "The sky's the limit. What do you say?"

"I think you've got a point." Luc was leaning back in his chair, swirling the glass. "Let me talk to my partners."

"But fast. This stuff is going to go like lightning. There isn't much of it, and it's got soul, Luc."

I laughed at Jim's enthusiasm.

"This will round out your cellar. It's what you're missing—a really profound Bordeaux."

"But five hundred cases? I haven't even opened my doors yet."

"What you can't use, I promise you Ken Aretsky will take off your hands. He's got the best wine list in the city."

Ken was a longtime friend of mine—one of Manhattan's legendary restaurateurs. He owned an upscale midtown eatery called Patroon and had become Luc's unofficial adviser in navigating the difficult waters of the modern-day business of fine dining.

"It's easier for him. I'm doing classic French cuisine, so all my wines have to be from over here. Ken's got superb American fare—steaks, pork, fish, lobster—so he can draw from the California vineyards just as well. You understand, Alex?"

"I do now."

"So where are we storing all this wine, Jim? Have you figured that out yet?"

"Solved."

"Not some warehouse in the city, is it? Nobody's got the right conditions."

"Try this. It's subterranean and it's secure, for starters. Everything a good bottle of wine loves. Dark, no vibrations, and a steady temperature of fifty-five degrees."

"How pricey?"

"If you've got more than a hundred cases, it's only a dollar twenty-five a month per case."

Luc looked intrigued. "Hard to believe, Jim. What is it?"

He reached for his glass. "A 1962 bomb shelter, in the boonies of Connecticut. Vintage Cold War paranoia built by a rich man on his estate. No more boxes of food rations, just lots of great wine. I'll take you up to see it when you're over next."

Talk of the new business venture had made Luc more vibrant than he'd been since the party last night. He was eager to get started when the headwaiter returned to take our order.

"You know what you want, darling?"

"I was thinking about veal."

"Forget the menu," Luc said to me before addressing the waiter. "Tell the chef Alexandra would like veal, however he wants to prepare it. Something very special, no?"

"Make it two," Jim said.

"And I'll have a carpaccio of tuna. Salad for all of us," he said.

"Monsieur Rouget," the waiter said, instead of turning away to place the order. "What would you like me to do about table three?"

"Nobody has arrived yet?"

"No, sir."

"A seven o'clock reservation for four," Luc said to Jim, "at one of the best tables in the house. A no-show, and not courteous enough to call to break it. Looks bad to leave one empty in the front. That's my prime real estate."

"I've got two parties having cocktails on the terrace, neither of whom was able to book inside tonight. Shall I seat one of them?"

"By all means. I'll go schmooze when you've got them inside. You have a telephone number for the no-shows?"

"Hotel du Cap, Monsieur Rouget." The waiter bowed his head and left the bar.

"That was another thing that got my father noticed in New York," Luc said to Jim and me, warming up as he talked. "He couldn't abide no-shows. Thought it was the height of rudeness when part of the attraction to other customers was filling every table and turning them over if he could. So Andre would wait till midnight, then call the offender, asking whether he wanted the kitchen to stay open in case their party was still planning on coming in."

"Ouch," I said. "I guess he didn't see many of those folks again."

"You'd be surprised. I think the harder he made it for people to get what everyone else wanted, the more they came crawling back anyway."

Luc was in his element and I was happy to see him beginning to relax. The three of us ate and drank, and told stories about our favorite food experiences. Jim seemed almost as excited as I that Luc was coming to New York to re-create Lutèce—named for *Lutetia*, the Latin word for the ancient city of Paris.

I could have set my watch by Luc's prediction that Jacques Belgarde would show up at nine o'clock. He came into the bar alone, and saw us as soon as he entered.

As he made his way to the table, Luc tried to explain to his guest that we needed to cut the evening short. Jim Mulroy didn't ask any questions. He got up to excuse himself and practically bumped into Belgarde, who clearly wanted to be introduced and find out about the man who was with us.

The captain reached into his inner jacket pocket and pulled out a piece of paper, which he unfolded as he spoke. "Were you in town last night, Mr. Mulroy?"

"I just arrived at five o'clock today. I've come from Lyons."

"Then you missed Luc's soiree, too?"

"My misfortune, yes."

"Maybe next year we'll both be favored with an invitation," Belgarde said. "And you, Alexandra, it looks like your colleagues think they've got a big case on their hands."

He handed me a printout that he had downloaded from his computer. It was a news headline from a French site much like CNN, with a photo of Mohammed Gil-Darsin featured in a perp walk—a uniquely American tradition for the high-profile criminal.

Baby Mo looked the camera directly in the eye. His hands were cuffed behind his back, the collar of his dark trench coat stood up, almost as though styled for the photo op. There was none of the head-hanging or sense of shame that such moments usually engendered.

Two first-grade detectives from Manhattan's SVU—Mercer Wallace and Alan Vandomir—gripped his arms, one on each side.

The text above the image was in bold caps, three inches high. I held it up so Luc could read it, too. L'AFFAIRE MGD!

"That's unbelievable," Luc said.

"What is?" I asked.

"You couldn't do that to a man in this country. Photograph him in handcuffs before he's been convicted of a crime. It's—it's indecent."

"So is first-degree rape."

"I'll owe you the caviar for sure," Luc said, shaking his head as he crumpled the paper. "I tell you, the French won't be happy with your justice system."

"Who cares?" Jacques said. "Bébé Mo isn't French."

"He certainly is. He's spent half of his life in this country. His father's been good to your men, Captain.

He probably spends more money bribing them for favors than they make in salary."

"Watch your step, Luc. My guys like to eat as well as you and I do. And the Gil-Darsins—uh—they're African, after all. They're not French."

"You mean they're black, is that it?" I asked.

"I said African, didn't I?" Jacques buffed the nails of his right hand on the edge of the tablecloth. "Don't make me out to be a racist."

"Mo's mother was French," Luc said, talking to Jim Mulroy and me. "Her father owned a cocoa plantation in the Ivory Coast, and she fell in love with a local young political leader. Radical stuff in those days, sixty years ago. The Côte d'Ivoire was a French colony then. It didn't gain its independence till 1960."

"That explains why we couldn't extradite him if the plane had actually taken off for Paris. He's a French national."

"Exactly. It's the vast family wealth of Bébé's mother that launched Papa Mo's political career, though she didn't live to see him become president."

"What happened?" I asked.

"She was killed by rebel forces there when her son was only three or four," Luc said.

"Living dangerously, that lady was," Jacques said. "And now Bébé Mo's a problem for the Americans, not for me. I've got my own fish to fry."

In just a few short hours, I could see that the case involving MGD would be like a Rorschach test, everyone coming to the story with his or her own point of view, bringing to it preconceived notions of race, class, power, and sexism. My colleagues at home were no doubt being assaulted by journalists voicing each of these positions.

"Do you have any news about Lisette?" I asked Belgarde.

"I do, *madame*. But it would go down better if I had a drink."

Jim Mulroy, clearly puzzled by the different threads of conversations, said good night to the three of us as Luc told the captain to pull out a chair at our table. He called the waiter over and told him to get Belgarde whatever he wanted from the kitchen. He walked to the bar and came back with a double shot of single malt Scotch.

"What's the story?" I asked again.

"The body's at the morgue in Nice. They're going to do an autopsy tomorrow. It's just as I thought this morning, at the pond. They suspect she was murdered." He winked at me and lifted his glass in my direction. "The big city *flics* thought I was pretty smart, actually, to know so much about drowning—pink foam and all that—so I'm grateful to you, Madame Prosecutor. *À votre santé*, Alexandra."

I nodded back at him.

"Of course, it will take weeks to get the toxicology results. They'll have to see if she had any drugs or alcohol in her system."

"That's true, Jacques. The tissue analysis can take quite some time."

"They haven't found a car yet, so they have no idea how she got to the pond. No purse, no ID, not even shoes, unless they're under all those lotus blossoms—so if it hadn't been for you, Luc, we'd still be struggling to figure out who she is. Just that all-white outfit, like she was heading for your party."

"And I assure you she was not. I printed out the guest list for you. It's behind the bar, next to the cash register." Luc walked over to get it.

"You were right, too," the captain went on, "about the stones in the pocket."

"Sorry?"

"That woman you told me about who killed herself. That Fox woman."

"Woolf? You mean Virginia Woolf?"

"Probably so. If you hadn't mentioned the heavy rocks she put in her pockets, I might not have looked there."

Belgarde leaned forward and opened his left hand. Displayed against the rough skin of his thick palm was a small object, two inches long and an eighth of an inch thick. Its cardboard casing had shriveled—soaked in water it seemed—and the laminated paper that covered it had curled up on the ends.

Luc put the list of names on the table between us as I leaned in to look at Belgarde's offering. It was a matchbook—a tiny box, really—the fancy type that restaurants gave away to advertise.

The captain held out his pinky and straightened the paper with his fingernail. In spring green print against a sharp white background was the single word LUTÈCE. He flipped it to show the other side—Luc's name in all caps—as he belted back a slug of Scotch.

"Now where do you suppose Lisette got hold of this, eh? You're not even in business yet in New York, are you?"

Luc had on such a poker face that even I couldn't gauge his level of discomfort.

"It's just a mock-up, a prototype," he said, waving his arm around behind him. "My staff has been handing them out here for weeks, and at the party last night, we gave them away with cigars after dinner. I've got my friends distributing them at the newsstand in the square and at lots of the bars in Cannes. It's just to start up some buzz."

"It's done that, my friend. I assure you. Even the investigators want a word with you."

Luc put his hands on his hips. "For this?"

"A dead girl isn't the smartest way to advertise, do you think?" Belgarde looked from Luc to me as he put the glass to his lips. "You're very quiet this evening, Alexandra. Any more tricks you want to pass on to me?"

"I made my views about your attitude pretty clear this morning."

"All a matter of style, *madame*, and there are those who believe I have none."

"Je suis d'accord."

"So you agree with that, Alexandra. Understood. But your accent is a bit leaden," he said, turning his attention to Luc. "They're more interested in the fact that your ex—it's Brigitte, isn't it?—that your ex felt it necessary to leave town before letting the detectives get the story of her contretemps with the late lamented Ms. Honfleur. Such bad advice you gave her, my friend."

"You know better than that, Jacques. I didn't advise her to do anything. I couldn't advise her. She's a stubborn woman."

"Apparently that didn't stop you from trying."

"It's my sons I went to see. You want me to arrange for the investigators to talk with Brigitte? Let me just get my boys out of the house."

"The officers were quite surprised to find neither she nor your children were at home."

"Where? At Brigitte's? When?"

"Eight o'clock. Just over an hour ago."

"Let me call her," Luc said, holding his hand out to

the bartender for the portable phone. "They're not leaving till morning. I'll tell her what they want. See if we can get her to be reasonable."

"What they want, actually, is that you stop communicating with her for the moment."

"She's the mother of my children, Jacques. She's my—she was my wife for fifteen years."

"It's okay, Luc," I said. "I'll go back to the house and you two can work this out."

"Awkward for you, Alexandra, I'm sure," Jacques said. He was chewing on a piece of baguette, amused at the thought he was stirring something up between Luc and me.

"Not the slightest bit, Captain." At least I hoped it wouldn't be, if I could wiggle my way out of the banquette, sucking in what was left of my spirit. "I'm so glad Luc's devoted to his family."

"Let me walk Alex home, Jacques. I'll be back in ten minutes. I need to tell you about something else that happened today."

"Just don't let me starve while I'm waiting."

"Of course not. Your dinner is on its way." Luc took my hand to guide me out.

"Very generous of you, Luc," Jacques said. "You know, one of those big-city detectives made a very rude observation. He thinks if you hadn't been so stingy on the alimony, Brigitte might have been able to hire a housekeeper with a little more class."

We were almost out the door, but Luc turned to take Jacques Belgarde's bait.

"I defended you to him, my friend. Told him how generous you are to my men." Jacques's mouth was full now, with whatever delicacy the waiter had placed in front of him. "But he says the housekeeper gave you up in a flash. Didn't like the way you raised your voice at Brigitte, Luc. Didn't understand why you demanded she get in the car with the boys when it was almost their bedtime and leave town so quickly tonight."

Ten

We were ten steps away from the restaurant door when Luc started to speak.

"Save it for later. I can get myself home from here, and I have no interest in what went on between you and Brigitte. Truly I don't. You go duke it out with Jacques."

"Wait up for me, darling. I can explain everything."

The prosecutorial part of my brain had grown tired of explanations over the last ten years. I'd have been out of business if people didn't find it necessary to give reasons for bad conduct and behavior.

"I'll be awake." I was way too wired to sleep.

"That's my angel."

"Look closely, Luc. I've traded in my wings and halo." I was beginning to question everything Luc tried to tell me.

This time when I reached the bottom of the alley, the heavy door opened easily. Gaspard lumbered to his feet to greet me and escort me through the garden and alongside the pool to the threshold of the house. I left him in the kitchen and mounted the winding staircase that took me up to the bedroom.

I undressed, got into my robe, and put on some music, then climbed onto the bed with Luc's laptop to Google Baby Mo and the facts of his arrest.

As soon as I pressed enter, dozens of hits popped up, starting with all the French news sources before I scrolled down to see the American, European, and African sites.

I took a blank notebook from Luc's desk—the kind in which I usually recorded the spectacular meals and memorable wines from my travels with Luc. It was inevitable that I would have questions for Mercer Wallace and my colleagues on his team, and maybe some ideas as well. I wanted to jot them down as I read through the press accounts.

Some long-distance Monday-morning quarterbacking of the MGD affair—even though it was only Sunday evening—would be a pleasant distraction.

I read the first story from the leading French news site. The impression that I got from scanning it was complete support for Mohammed Gil-Darsin. It described him as one of the most distinguished economists in the world, educated at the Sorbonne in Paris, with a graduate degree from the London School of Economics. He was, after all, a resident of France, with a distinguished heritage and a brilliant future as the next president of the Republic of the Ivory Coast.

The second story was even stronger, headlining with the question: BÉBÉ MO—VICTIME DE COUP MONTÉ?

I didn't know that phrase. My legs were crossed and I was working the keyboard, searching for the Larousse French-English dictionary. *Monter un coup.* A setup. A frame. Could it possibly be, as the journalist suggested, that this woman knew that the wealthy man in the expensive suite had political ambitions, and had she been hired to bring them to a crashing halt with this claim? I wondered whether the cops gave any thought, as some of the French did, to the idea that this crime report was a scam by political rivals out to ruin Gil-Darsin.

I wanted to see how the American news sources were handicapping the case. I went to the *New York Times* website and entered MGD's name. The first story had been filed within an hour of his arrest. The reporting was cautious and recapped the same facts that had been given to me by Mike. The victim was described as a hardworking immigrant from Guatemala, a single mother who had sought asylum in the United States with her child after the civil war that had ravaged that Latin American country in the 1990s.

My fingers were typing as fast as they could move. I went to a CNN story, predicting turmoil in the powerful World Economic Bureau in the aftermath of this scandal. The WEB chief's arrest would result in a power struggle for control of the agency, amid rumors that he would have to resign if the prosecution moved forward. Deputies in line to compete for the position—from America, Great Britain, and Japan—all refused to engage in speculation about the character of the accused.

The *Daily News* had already interviewed a coworker of the accuser, who described her as a deeply religious woman. The sidebar story—MGD'S CROSS TO BEAR—OR BARE?—was illustrated with a large crucifix that observers said was always visible against the black collar of her uniform. The implication was that a woman of faith wouldn't fabricate a claim. I fretted about how Pat McKinney would deal with that issue.

Gaspard barked at something or someone near the house. I sat bolt upright and listened, but he quieted down, so I assumed no one was entering. I got up to stretch and reached for the BlackBerry.

I climbed back onto the bed and looked at the tiny screen. I had accumulated 246 messages since Friday, when I left New York. Even if a third of them were spam, there were people looking for me on what I had hoped would be a quiet spring weekend.

There was a red star on the voice mail icon. Luc wouldn't have to know I had reneged on my promise to him, so I hit that button and listened to the recorded voice tell me that I had twenty-two messages in my mailbox.

I had gone too far to stop myself now. Lack of curiosity would be a lousy trait in a prosecutor.

The first messages were frisky. Joan Stafford called me on Friday night to test whether my pledge to keep the phone under lock and key had been successful and to ask me to call in with all the social gossip. Nina Baum, my Wellesley roommate and best friend, who lived in Los Angeles with her husband and young son, bet that I would never be able to fulfill the promise, and urged me to stay grounded against the fantasy of the Mougins lifestyle.

There were six calls on Saturday—a couple of old friends who were in town on business and some invitations to upcoming dinners. Nothing had any urgency until I heard Mercer Wallace's voice at three o'clock this morning, which would have been nine a.m. in Mougins.

"Alex. Mercer here. Look—I know you're on vacation with Luc and the last thing I want to do is bust into that, but would you call me when you pick this up? It's kind of

urgent. New case. I could use your eyes on this one. Just
a call, please, so I can run some of the facts by you."

Mercer never hit the panic button. He was "grace under pressure" personified, calm and dignified even when
doing the dirtiest job in the NYPD, which is what the
Special Victims Unit mandate was. The understatement
in his tone was in sharp contrast to the hour of the call.

His next message was ten minutes later, still unruffled.
"Scratch that last one, Alex. Mike just told me you're out
of the loop for the week. I apologize for hunting you
down. We're doing fine."

The next five calls were from Mike Chapman, all made
shortly before he reached me on the beach this afternoon. Unlike Mercer, there was no subtlety to Mike's
approach.

"Rise and shine, blondie. Get your ass out of bed.
Where the hell are you two, anyway? This is 911, Coop.
Urgent. Mercer needs you."

He waited about fifteen minutes before dialing again.
"Ignore me all you want, kid. I'm down with that. Just
call Mercer pronto."

As fast as I hit the erase function, the next message
loaded. "Pat McKinney knows as much about how to
deal with a rape victim as Al Sharpton would. Don't blow
this one on me."

Someone must have cautioned Mike to back off me
for an hour. Then another call. "This will rattle you,
Coop. McKinney showed up at the office with his lover.
He's making this case a team project—benching you and
sticking Ellen Gunsher in as a DH."

Pat McKinney was involved in an affair with an assistant who'd been nicknamed "Gun-Shy" for her reluc-
tance to take cases to trial. She was the daughter of a

television journalist who'd been the kind of celebrity Battaglia liked to court until her career imploded because of a series of on-air temper tantrums. Gunsher had failed in a number of other positions, but the chief of the Trial Division had left home for her last year and sought to inject her in every possible new position in hopes of a fit.

"I'm warning you, Coop, you can't taunt an alligator till you cross the creek, you know that?" In Chapman's fifth call, he was imitating Ellen Gunsher's Texas drawl, using the tired aphorisms with which the clueless prosecutor regularly peppered her conversations. Mike knew they would get under my skin, as they always did. "McKinney gets a hold of Baby Mo, and that half-breed Frenchman will think a West Texas rattlesnake has its teeth in his dick."

I smiled instinctively but realized at the same moment that one of McKinney's goals was to elbow out the talented members of the Sex Crimes Unit by taking advantage of my absence. That would give him complete control of the case.

I heard Vickee Eaton's voice next. She was Mercer's wife—also a detective—and one of my closest friends. She worked at DCPI, in the office of the Deputy Commissioner of Public Information, with access to inside scoops since she would be providing the minute-by-minute updates to Commissioner Keith Scully. She was not-so-subtly leaning on me to help her husband, and that meant more to me than just about anything.

Now there were friendly calls from the women and men who worked with me in the unit. Catherine Dashfer, Ryan Blackmer, Marisa Bourges, and Nan Toth, each giving me the heads-up that a big case was on the table. Like the district attorney, I had developed an aversion to being the last to know when something happened in my professional orbit, and my good friends always covered my back. These were interspersed with a robocall from a political candidate, the new dry cleaner in the neighborhood surfing for business, an invitation to the resort season trunk show at Escada, and my local bookseller reminding me that the novels I had ordered were in stock.

I deleted them all and held the phone to my ear again. More of the same. Nothing I couldn't ride out from this side of the ocean.

The voice on the next-to-last message was Rose Malone, Battaglia's executive assistant. As close as she and I were, she was also my barometer to read his moods. The fact that she was working on a Sunday was unusual enough, and the edge in her voice meant she was calling on orders from him, not as a favor to me.

"Alex? It's Rose. The Boss would like you to phone in immediately. We're in the office—it's Sunday afternoon around three. He knows you're in France but he needs to talk to you." There was a long pause. "Mr. Battaglia said he's got only one question for you. He won't tell me what it is, or I'd let you know, of course. Please get back to me."

I slumped down against the thick pillows. Ugh. Now I was sorry I'd made the decision to take my phone out of the bag. One caller to go and then I could shut it off and figure out what to do.

"Alexandra Cooper?" Paul Battaglia had placed the call himself. I hadn't been sure he knew how to do that, since he'd been spoiled for so long by Rose's efficiency. I sat up straight, as though he was in the room with me. "There's just one thing I want to ask you, young lady. Do you really think you can hold on to your job by ignoring everyone's efforts to reach you while the goddamn sky is falling down over here?"

The sound of the receiver hitting the phone cradle as Battaglia hung up on me was jolting.

I got to my feet and walked to Luc's desk to use the landline to call New York.

"Rose? It's Alex."

"I'll put you right through to him."

"Is it—?"

She didn't take the chance of displeasing him further by talking with me.

"Alexandra?"

"Yes, Paul."

"I got a mess on my hands and it's your bailiwick. The mayor and most of the media want to know what you figure went on and I can't—"

"Last I knew, neither you nor the mayor thought too much of my opinion. The archbishop seemed to have had your ear at the time."

Battaglia didn't like to be reminded of the few missteps he had made in his long career. I knew he wouldn't respond to my cheap shot about the last major case I'd worked this winter. He'd rather ignore it.

"Mercer Wallace and his team would like some guidance from you," Battaglia said. "And so would I."

"I'm happy to help."

"This case is more complicated than it looks on the surface. I've got the feds interested in the World Economic Bureau implications, the French president pushing me to let the perp out on his own recognizance, the West African leaders—at least those with democratic governments—screaming 'foul,' and the Latina Women's Caucus holding a rally in front of City Hall to empower the victim. I've got the country's pioneering sex crimes unit, but nobody's here to run it, Alex. When did you make this a part-time job?"

"I'm yours 24/7, Paul. I get it."

"Rose has you booked on an eight a.m. flight out of Nice in the morning. You'll connect through Paris on the one fifty-five p.m., which will have you at Kennedy at four thirty-five. Port Authority cops will meet you and bring you to the office."

"Excuse me?" I could hear Luc talking to the dog in the garden below the window. I was doing a slow boil at Battaglia's presumptuousness.

"Talk to Rose. She's got all the details. And I told them not to charge you for changing your flight."

The district attorney put me on hold and Rose picked up. "I'm so sorry, Alex. He left me no choice."

"Don't be silly, Rose. I know it's not your doing"

"There'll be e-tickets for you at the airport."

I held my tongue, instead of saying to her that I hadn't yet decided whether or not I would change my plans. I wanted to get off the phone before Luc came upstairs.

"Thanks. Talk to you tomorrow." I hung up, put Luc's laptop back on the desk, and started to make myself comfortable on the bed.

Luc seemed pleasantly surprised to find me awake. "Everything calm, darling?"

"Guess so."

He took off his clothes and went into the bathroom to shower. By the time he slipped into bed beside me, I had dimmed the lights and propped myself up on the pillows so that we could complete the conversation that Jacques Belgarde had prompted with his mention of what had happened at Brigitte's house.

Luc took my face between his hands and kissed me—first my forehead, then on each cheek, and then my mouth. He was ready to make love, but I was in another time zone altogether.

"Did you tell Jacques about the guys on motorcycles? About the gun?"

Luc was nuzzling my neck. His muffled answer sounded like yes.

"What did he have to say about that?"

He picked his head up, so that our faces were just inches apart. "He assumes they were just ordinary thugs, looking to steal your jewelry or my sexy motorcycle."

"But you saw the gun."

"Maybe a gun, maybe a black glove, maybe a—"

"Maybe what—a baguette pointed at you? You were terrified, Luc, and you scared me to death, too. Something spooked you for real."

He rested his elbow on the bed and held up his head with it. His other hand was stroking my hair. "Can we discuss this tomorrow?"

"After we talk about what happened between you and Brigitte today?"

He rolled over onto his back, clearly deflated by my cold response to his touch. "Okay, Alex, if that will make you happy."

I didn't know what would make me happy at this point, or any time in the immediate future.

"Tomorrow won't work for me, Luc. I just spoke to Paul Battaglia. I'm going to fly home in the morning."

Eleven

I was in my seat in the business-class section of the Air France flight, about to depart from Charles de Gaulle Airport. I had been texting and e-mailing all morning, confirming that I would meet the team in the office as soon as I got into Manhattan, which I expected to be after six on Monday evening. The BlackBerry vibrated again and I saw Joan Stafford's name flash. I pressed to answer and held the phone to my ear. "Are you crazy?" she asked me without saying hello or greeting me.

"You have two minutes before they close the door on this plane for takeoff. I am neither crazy nor entirely stupid. You're my pal, Joanie. You're supposed to slobber over me with love and support. Don't lay any more guilt on me than I'm already lugging around."

"I spoke to Luc this morning. He's *désolé*, Alex. I thought you two had a deal."

"I envy you the writer's life. You make your own schedule, your work is portable, nobody's well-being depends on your output. But that's not the kind of job I have."

"You promised him—"

"It's not like I cheated on him, Joan," I said, drawing a sidelong glance from the man settling in next to me. "Yes, I used my phone. I blew off Mike and Mercer and Vickee and all the peeps I trust in that job. And then Paul Battaglia himself called."

"He doesn't own you, Alex. You're entitled to a vacation. If Battaglia has a primary challenger next year, I'll bet he'll step down. How old is he already? He'll be a lame duck by then."

"I work for the man, Joan. I can't just twiddle my thumbs for eighteen months till the next election. He'll stay in this job till he's ninety."

"I still think Battaglia's lame, whether he's a duck or not." She was laughing as she talked. "Do you have any idea what Luc planned to do on your birthday?"

"We talked about a quiet dinner at the house."

The announcement came on that all electronic devices would have to be powered down in two minutes, when the doors closed.

"Obviously dinner, Alex. I didn't mean that. What's happened to your sense of romance? Do you remember that day I took him shopping after you two came back from the Vineyard last month? Do you understand the man has been looking at rings?"

I closed my eyes and gritted my teeth.

"Are you still there? Can you hear me? Great big shiny diamond rings, girl. His money, my uncommonly good sense of taste and style. Luc's madly in love with you."

The butterflies in my stomach were fluttering wildly.

"Don't go there, Joan. If you're really my pal, back off this subject. Way too premature."

"Is it the commitment thing? Swear to me it's not that."

"I don't know him, okay? The last forty-eight hours have proved that beyond—"

"Don't give me 'beyond a reasonable doubt,' babe. Forget the law in your brain and flex those underused muscles in your heart."

"You're spoiling Luc's surprise, Joan, if that's what it was supposed to be."

"Well, clearly the Hope diamond won't be jumping out of your birthday cake if you're spending that evening alone. Forget I said anything."

"Forgotten."

"He told me you're bent out of shape about Brigitte."

"Not true."

"What are you hoping to find at our age? A guy who's a forty-year-old virgin with no prior love life or involvements? No ex, no kids—maybe even an orphan so you won't have in-laws either? The Dalai Lama's been off the table for quite some time."

"How well do you know Brigitte?"

"Total pain in the ass."

"Would you trust her, Joan? I mean between Brigitte and Luc, who—?"

"Luc, of course. How can you even ask that?"

"Because if he's so over her, why does he keep her photograph in the drawer of his night table?"

"What were you doing going through his drawer?"

"I wasn't going through it. I was looking for some nail clippers, okay?"

"He probably hasn't cleaned it out in months. What is it, like a family shot with the boys?"

"Like Brigitte on the beach in Cannes. Topless."

The man next to me coughed and lowered his newspaper to look at me again.

"Get over it. Everyone in France is topless, especially those fat old tourists from Eastern Europe you'd rather not see, even when they have clothes on."

The flight attendant signaled me to turn off my phone. "Gotta go. I'll call you tomorrow. We're taking off now."

By the time we climbed out of Paris and through a cloud cover that blanketed the view for the first half hour of the route, I found a comfortable position, reclined my seat and covered myself with a blanket.

Hurtling across the ocean miles above the earth gave me a surfeit of hours to think about my personal situation. When I was immersed in the work that I found so challenging and rewarding, it was easy to put off analysis of my emotional state. Until this weekend, all my time spent with Luc was joyful and loving, and I often fantasized about leaving behind the high pressure of my prosecutorial position for more intimacy with him. Neither one of us had talked about marriage yet, but Joan had succeeded in delivering a shot across the bow of my unsteady ship.

I was a natural for a life of public service because I had been encouraged by my parents to use the opportunities they'd bestowed on me to "give back" to others less fortunate. But it would have been more logical for me to have put down roots in the medical community from which they both came.

My mother, Maude, was the daughter of Finnish immigrants; she was raised on a dairy farm in New England and later moved to New York to study nursing. She had the skills and compassion of a superb RN, and that talent—

along with the deep green eyes, a winning smile, and great
long legs —attracted the attention of my father.

Benjamin Cooper—my father—was the son of Russian
Jews who fled political oppression there, the first of their
three boys to be born in America. It was during his medical internship that he fell in love with Maude, who converted to Judaism when she married him.

He was a young cardiologist in private practice when he
and a partner fashioned a half-inch piece of plastic tubing
into a device that was adapted for use in almost every operation involving the aorta. The Cooper-Hoffman valve
revolutionized cardiac surgery and changed the financial
circumstances of our family. Unlike both my parents, my
two older brothers and I were raised in the upscale West-
chester suburb of Harrison. The trust fund they set up for
each of us enabled my first-rate education at Wellesley College, where I majored in English literature before deciding
that I wanted a legal career, which I prepared for at the
University of Virginia School of Law.

"Something to drink?" the attendant asked me as she
passed through the cabin.

"Just water."

"A newspaper?"

"Yes, please. *Le Figaro* and also *Le Monde*." I wanted
to see how the French press—from the far right to the
left—was reacting to the news of Gil-Darsin's arrest.

"I'll be right back with *Le Figaro*. I just gave this gentleman the only copy of *Le Monde* I had left after first
class devoured them."

Now my seatmate looked up again. "The news is interesting today, no?" he said in heavily accented English.
"You're welcome to the paper when I'm finished."

I forced a smile. The last thing I wanted was to be a

captive audience for a lecture from a Frenchman about MGD for seven hours of air travel. "Thanks. I'm hoping it will put me to sleep."

"You're going home to a big scandal. You've heard?"

"No. I haven't followed the news. Just visiting friends." I reached for my tote to take out sunglasses to make my unwillingness to engage more obvious.

The man put the front page in my lap, patting the photograph of the perp walk. "Disgusting what you Americans do. This kind of thing wouldn't be tolerated in France before someone's convicted of a crime. You've ruined the career of a brilliant economist."

The attendant returned with a copy of *Le Figaro* and passed it over to me. Not surprisingly, the same photograph was displayed, with a caption calling for the WEB chief to step down immediately.

"I heard you say on the phone—forgive me—that you know Paul Battaglia. That you work for him."

"You must have misheard me. I've got a friend in his office."

"He's known all over Europe for his work. Sounds like a fine man. You should tell your friend to convince him that he must do the right thing, or he'll lose the respect of the world."

"The world?" I asked. "Really? Well, I'm just a stay-at-home mom with three kids, so I don't have much to say to the district attorney."

I knew from experience that that description of my life was likely to shut down our exchange. He leaned back in his seat and I rested my head against the window, closing my eyes again.

I couldn't help but think about Mercer and Mike, and what these last twenty-four hours had been like for them.

Mercer Wallace, five years older than I and whip-smart, had earned the coveted gold shield with daring undercover exploits in his early days on the job, then continued to be promoted because of the brilliant detail work he had put into a series of homicide investigations.

But like me, he didn't thrive on murder cases. The department valued them as the most important crimes and the most elite units, but Mercer preferred the more sensitive matters of a special victims detective squad. He surprised the top brass years ago by asking for a transfer to the Manhattan unit that corresponded to my prosecutorial bureau, after solving a serial rape case involving more than seven teenage girls who'd been brutalized on East Harlem rooftops and in project stairwells.

Mercer's work, like mine, was a specialty that combined his investigative talents with a measure of compassion that allowed him to earn the trust of the most traumatized survivors—victims of sexual assault, domestic violence, and child abuse. The feature that Mike Chapman relied on most—no need to take up any time hand-holding the dead—was what made special victims work so satisfying to Mercer and me.

Mercer's mother died in childbirth, and he'd been raised in Queens by his father, Spencer, a mechanic for Delta Air Lines assigned to LaGuardia. He turned down a football scholarship at Michigan to join the NYPD. His second marriage was to Vickee Eaton, with whom he had a four-year-old son named Logan. There was as much heart in Mercer as his six-foot, six-inch frame could hold, and he had covered my back in court and on the street more times than I could count.

My relationship with Mike Chapman was more complicated, both professionally and personally, in style and in substance. Mike's father, Brian, had been one of the most decorated officers on the force throughout the twenty-six years he'd served. He raised his family—Mike had three older sisters—in the then working-class section of Yorkville in Manhattan. His great pride was his only son's success as a student whose knowledge of military history ranked him near the top of his class at Fordham University, guaranteeing the father that his son wouldn't be risking his life every day on the city streets.

But Brian suffered a massive coronary two days after turning in his gun and shield, and although Mike Chapman stayed on course to get his degree, he enrolled in the police academy immediately after graduation because he admired his father so deeply. Even in his rookie year he distinguished himself with arrests made in the drug-related Christmas Day massacre of a Colombian family in Washington Heights. His only interest was in working homicide, and he fast won a place in the Manhattan North squad, which was responsible for every murder case on the island above 59th Street.

I met Mike my first year as a prosecutor. All the men and women who'd taught me the ropes—evaluating case merits and witness credibility, giving the job every ounce of one's intellect and intuition, learning when it was essential to visit the scene of a crime and how to interrogate the vilest of criminal types—all of them required of us the most professional responses.

Then I was introduced to the Chapman modus operandi. Mike trusted no one except the closest of his colleagues, had a sixth sense about people that was rarely off target, was able to keep an emotional distance from his victims and their families, and without ever breaking the law he had a keen ability to go a bit rogue, a bit wild cowboy, and constantly tried to push me to take that ride with him.

Somewhere along the line, Mike Chapman had become my closest friend. Maybe it was because even though I had fiercely loyal bonds to Nina, Joan, and the girlfriends who kept me grounded, there was no one else with whom I'd spent so many days and nights who understood the pressures of the job and what it meant to live with such extraordinary responsibility—the fate of victims and perps alike—while going about the ordinary business of daily life.

Mike's intelligence was often unexpected by adversaries or upper-crust witnesses who figured the blue-collar background limited him in some fashion. His dark humor, whether appropriate or not, undercut almost every situation in which we'd found ourselves. His courage was a constant reminder to me of my own irrational phobias. And then there were his good looks—at about six-two, he was three or four inches taller than me, with a thick head of jet-black hair, strong features, and a ready smile.

It was an attraction that confused me as much as it delighted me. There were times I had felt the pull of a romantic entanglement, but I knew that it wouldn't work because of the jobs we had. If I gave any thought to dating Mike—even though he'd never suggested as much—I knew that Battaglia would relieve me of my position. He wouldn't allow the impression that a top detective was closing cases or eliciting confessions because he was sleeping with a supervising prosecutor.

Mike's one great love—an architect named Valerie Jacobson—died in a skiing accident two years back, and he had slipped into one of his darkest moods as a result of her death. I thought he was beginning to come out of that depression, but there was so much of himself that he kept encased in an impenetrable shell that there were times I was the last to know what went on inside his head.

I ate a bit of the snack that was offered and read a few news articles. In the feature section of the paper was a photograph of a woman, strikingly pretty and dressed to the nines as she exited a restaurant near the Champs Élysées after dinner on Saturday. The subject looked vaguely familiar to me—a light-skinned black woman, tall and too thin to be anything but a model. It wasn't Iman, but I looked down for the caption because I thought I recognized her from similar single-name runway fame. Kali. Of course, Kali. Her magnificent face had graced scores of magazine covers. KALI BLESSÉE! the headline read.

The French word *blessé* seemed oxymoronic to me. It caught my eye because the Anglo-Saxon meaning was so benevolent—to sanctify or make holy—so I scanned the piece to see what good luck had befallen the glamorous woman. It took me a second to recall that the translation here was "wounded." I read on.

The supermodel Kali, also Ivorian, was the wife of Mohammed Gil-Darsin, as this article made clear. I was dumbfounded to learn that. The piece quoted her closest friends who had been with her Sunday morning when she got the call about her husband's arrest. "Her screams pierced the air like a wounded animal," the reporter claimed, when Baby Mo's lawyers told her the story.

The wounded wife. I had spent countless hours in the presence of women who sat in the front row of a courtroom behind husbands charged with rape, murder, child abuse, and every other brutal act. Some obviously believed in the men they stood by, others were advised by counsel to suck it up through trial because jurors would be impressed that the women loved their spouses enough to disbelieve the charges, and yet a few more had been known to stick close first, then lash out later at the offenders, after the verdict was delivered.

I had heard those shrieks of wounded wives, had seen them scratch and kick at Mercer Wallace as their husbands were handcuffed and taken away. I'd been cursed by them in just about every dialect under the sun, on my way out of station houses or into the courtroom, even stalking me through the streets when I left the office at night.

My seatmate saw me staring at the photo of Kali. "You know her in the States?"

"She's very famous, actually. Very beautiful."

"Show that to your police, will you? They think a man who gets into bed with a woman like that any night he chooses wants to get it on with a peasant who takes out the trash? An illegal immigrant, I heard today, from Central America. Gil-Darsin's got filet mignon at home, but he's forcing down a helping of rice and beans on his way to the plane? It's too ridiculous to believe."

For some, it always comes down to the physical appearance of the accuser. If she's too good-looking, then she must have asked for it. If she's homely or overweight, then what sane man would bother with raping her?

"It happens every day." Not just with the rich and famous, the prominent and powerful, but in every variable of human interaction one might imagine.

"What did you say?" he asked.

I didn't have the energy to take him on. I turned my head away, pulled the blanket up to my chin, and slept for most of the rest of the flight because I expected long hours of work ahead.

The descent into JFK was smooth. We taxied to the gate as everyone turned on cell phones and waited impatiently for the plane to dock and doors to open.

I stayed in my seat while those with connecting flights crowded the aisles to make their exit. I hefted my small tote onto my shoulder and started the long walk to retrieve my luggage from the carousel and get to Customs. I knew Rose had dispatched one of Battaglia's security team to meet me, so it was likely that I would be whisked through the process.

As I approached the queues separating citizens from foreigners, I had my passport in hand and looked on the far side of the customs agents for familiar faces but saw none.

Off to the left, in the last line marked U.S. PASSPORTS ONLY, I saw the striking figure of Kali—all six feet of her—with oversize dark glasses, dressed entirely in black, arguing with a government official. Two men behind him, probably private investigators from the defense team, looked like they were trying to pull strings to get her through.

Kali must have been in the first-class section of my flight and one of the passengers to reach the checkpoint earliest. But she had chosen the wrong line and was meeting resistance from the agent.

I was summoned to the booth next to her and extended my passport.

The agent stood up to look at my two bags and then the dates stamped on my arrival in France. "Not much time for shopping, was there?"

"Not a minute."

"I take it you've got nothing to declare?"

I laughed. "This is a first, but I don't." It was also the first time I hadn't stopped to buy Battaglia the Cuban cigars—Cohibas, still contraband—that he loved so much and counted on whenever I traveled.

He waved me on, and as I closed my tote, I could see that Kali was agitated. She was arguing for an exception despite her foreign passport, in order to move through more rapidly. The louder she got and the more the two private eyes tried to lean on the customs agent, the firmer he stood, pointing to the back of the line.

The automatic doors swung open, and against the waist-high metal fencing were relatives and friends waiting for passengers from around the world. Behind them were dozens of black-suited limo drivers, holding up placards with names of clients they'd been hired to meet. I stood on tiptoes to look for one of the men from the DA's Squad—an NYPD unit assigned to our offices who had the detail to guard Battaglia.

Instead, I spotted a large cardboard placard on a wooden handle, raised above the heads of the greeters.

Below the logo of the *New York Post* was the mug shot of Gil-Darsin and the bold headline: MOMO'S MOJO: DNA ENTANGLES WEB HEAD.

I walked through the groups of drivers directly to Mike Chapman, who was holding the jerry-rigged sign. "Welcome home, kid. The DA's all puffed up like a peacock 'cause he got you here when the rest of us couldn't make you budge."

"He's got a special way with words, Mike. Just charmed me right back to the office." I reached up and kissed him on the cheek. "Thanks for picking me up."

"Never learned to travel light, did you?" he said, taking my oversize duffel and large wheeling bag from me.

"You might want to dump the sign. Madame Gil-Darsin will be coming through right behind us. She's having her 'Do you know who I am?' moment with customs."

"Sweet. She might do better if they don't know."

"I take it the DNA match is today's update?" I said as we headed for the exit.

"Confirmed by the lab this morning. The *Post* hasn't tweaked yet to half how good the guy's mojo is, Coop."

"What do you mean?"

"We just picked up the surveillance tapes from the hotel. He had another woman with him for a nooner that same day. The card swipe clocks her arrival, and she left—hair all tousled and clothes messed up a bit—just after two p.m., a few hours before he jumped the bones of our vic."

"You know who she is?"

"They're working on it. We should have her ID'd by morning. Meanwhile I'm fielding all the calls from the senior set. Everybody wants to know Mo's secret."

"Secret what?"

"The man is fifty-eight years old. He had a tryst at noon and was loaded for bear again at five. Don't you listen to those ads, Coop? If it lasts more than four hours, give your doctor a call."

"Beside the Viagra jokes, is any serious work getting done on this case?"

"Wait till you see the war room McKinney's set up," Mike said, grabbing my arm as we reached the curb, then letting go to point out Kali, being rushed to a waiting limo by the pair of bodyguards who'd met her inside.

"Any real progress?"

"Hey, Sunday's take from the media and the defense sympathizers was that a sexual assault could never have happened. MGD was rushing to meet his daughter and catch a flight. The accuser must have made the whole thing up. The old 'he said, she said' crap. Today's DNA results level the playing field, don't they? Now he can't claim nothing happened or that he wasn't there with her, can he? The perp's legal eagles have to shift their argument to consent."

"Here's where it really gets ugly, Mike. Now the defense will want us to believe that she asked for it."

Twelve

"You must have come lights and sirens all the way from Paris," Pat McKinney said when I entered the conference room with Mike shortly before seven o'clock Monday evening. He was standing at the head of the long table, flanked by the team of prosecutors and investigators he had patched together to work on the case. "Welcome back."

"Thanks."

"You want to take over the hot seat? I'll step aside."

"You're in charge, Pat."

The lawyers and cops seated between us were studying the interplay. McKinney ruled by fear, often mocking the young assistants who reported to him. I never understood why Battaglia tolerated that kind of leadership, so I worked hard to keep our personal animosity from spilling into public view.

"I guess that's it, Mr. Chapman," McKinney said. "You wanted to play taxi driver and bring Alex to us, but now I think we don't need your services any longer."

Mike didn't have a real role in this investigation or any reason to argue with McKinney. "I got places to go, people to see," he said, with his hand on the doorknob.

"Sit yourself down over there," Mercer said to Mike. He pointed to an open chair next to June Simpson, one of the best senior prosecutors in the Trial Division. Someone had convinced McKinney that neither he nor his girlfriend Gunsher could handle a trial that was difficult to any degree, and although June didn't have a sex crimes background, she was a great choice for the team.

"Getting crowded in here, don't you think?" McKinney said.

"I want Mike in this," Mercer said, his deep voice underscoring the sense of control he exercised when he was in charge of matters on the police side. "I want his ideas, his experience—"

"Of course," McKinney said, "a team misogynist to give us some balance on the victim's story. Now, why didn't I think of that?"

Ellen Gunsher laughed, June Simpson and the two paralegals cringed, the Sex Crimes assistant—Ryan Blackmer—just looked wide-eyed at McKinney, and Mercer smacked his palm on the table, causing everyone to jump.

"Catch you later, Detective Wallace," Mike said, waving to Mercer as he backed out the door. "And, Pat, if you think leaving your wife for some stolen moments with the yellow rose of Texas here is a gift to the women's movement, you're not firing on all cylinders."

"Okay, children," I said. "Let's all get in the sandbox and hunker down together. Looks like we have a long haul ahead. Mike, why don't you stay and—?"

"I'm on again at midnight. Mercer can pick my brain whenever he chooses. I'm outta here."

Mercer didn't need to speak his contempt for Pat McKinney. His expression said it all.

"June, would you ask my secretary to call the DA?" Pat said. "He wants to be in on today's briefing."

As June Simpson stepped out, I walked to one of the open spots at the table, sat down, and introduced myself to the paralegals I hadn't met. Mercer passed me the case folder he had prepared for me with copies of all the police reports, medical records, employment history, and media clips.

"Was the victim in today?"

"Yeah," Mercer said. "We had her all day yesterday, what with the first report to uniform, then interviews with the outcry witnesses at the hotel."

"Treated?"

"Sexual assault forensic examiner at Bellevue. Plus a victim advocate who explained everything to her. That's when I got called in."

"Does she have a name?" I asked.

"Blanca. Blanca Robles," Mercer said.

It was illegal in New York for law enforcement personnel to release identifying information about a rape victim to the public. The American media wouldn't tag her by name. It was the first time I'd heard her name, and I rolled it off my tongue. Within hours, the European press would print it, and if they could come up with a photograph of Blanca, they would use that as well.

"Who interviewed her today?" I wanted to hear Ryan's name. I wanted to know it had been anything except a group session.

McKinney barged right in. "Ellen and I talked with her. Ryan sat in. One of the paras took notes. And Mercer, of course. I didn't get the idea to bring June in on this till just a couple of hours ago."

"Five on one? Not the way we usually make our witnesses comfortable."

"You know how it is on these major cases, Alex. Nothing goes according to plan. I needed to explain the process to her and tell her what we expect of her this week. The tabloids are hounding her like crazy. They've already found out where she lives. The Witness Aid Unit is working with Safe Horizon to relocate her." McKinney was talking as though he did this kind of victim advocacy all the time, rather than his administrative duties.

"The interview. Pedigree and case facts. Ryan did that, right?" Rape cases were like no other kind of crime. You were asking a woman to reveal facts about the most intimate kind of trauma forced on her, when often she had never spoken of such acts to anyone outside her personal relationships. There was an art to doing this work well, and while we hand-selected and trained our unit assistants, not all prosecutors had the manner to bond patiently—yet firmly—with rape victims and get the full story of what occurred.

One side of Ryan's lip pulled back. He wanted to answer me but didn't dare with McKinney driving the discussion. "I let Ellen do it, actually," Pat said. "Woman-to-woman kind of thing."

"Ellen? Really?" I looked across the table at McKinney's lover. "I didn't think you'd ever spoken with a rape victim before."

"She's done some of the most difficult work in this office, Alex. She's—"

"It's not the same thing, Pat." The gender of the cop or prosecutor didn't matter a fraction as much as his or her sensitivity to the specific issues, an ability to connect to the victim and earn her trust in eliciting nuanced details. "Did you use our screening sheet to get the background and pedigree?"

"I didn't know there were screening sheets until Ryan gave me one. But I'd already started my questioning, so it was too late," Ellen said.

The screening tool had been developed when the unit was founded by my predecessor, and it had been fine-tuned over the last two decades. It provided a pretty thorough means of getting information from a witness, including prior arrests, psychiatric history, drug use, any other history of sexual assault—which sometimes colored the way a victim responded to the incident at hand—and a detailed primer that resulted in giving the assistant DA an arsenal of facts before the case debriefing even began.

"We can get whatever information you want tomorrow if you think it's so important, Alex. Blanca's a damn impressive witness, I can tell you that," Pat said. "No question about what happened in that hotel room. Are you skeptical already?"

"Of the accuser?" I asked. "Not at all. I've just come from a part of the world which views these crimes and our system very differently. The French are up in arms about the arrest."

"What else do you need to know?" Ellen asked. "I mean, she's obviously a very religious person. She's widowed, with a teenage daughter. Soft-spoken and demure. Wait till you hear the story of what happened to her in Guatemala during the civil war there. It'll break your heart."

"Do you know whether she's ever been the victim of a crime before?"

"Tomorrow, Alex," McKinney said before Ellen could answer.

"What do you have on her medical history?" I asked, seeing a reference to a special housing situation in the police reports.

"*Mañana*. Get it? Everyone on this team has been working like a dog, so don't come in here punching holes in the air like you could have done it better."

"Good job, then, to all of you. That's what I should have said first." A half-assed job was more likely the reality, if I knew Ellen Gunsher's work, but Blanca Robles had certainly convinced everyone who met her after the assault that it had occurred. Now we needed to get her in to the grand jury and through the gauntlet that had been stirred up by the frenzied media. "I look forward to meeting her."

"Thanks, Alex," Mercer said. "We all know what it's like when a case breaks and you're a million miles away and all you want to do is come back and work it from the inside with your buddies. I'm glad you're here."

June Simpson came back into the room. "Mr. Battaglia needs fifteen minutes."

"Let's take a break," McKinney said. "Back at the table at seven-thirty, all your answers at the ready for the Boss."

Paul Battaglia wouldn't micromanage cases in his office—not even the big ones—but he was ruthless about the need to know any bit of intelligence that might connect to something he could use to manipulate a political situation. Ready with answers was exactly what everyone in the room needed to be.

My office was on the same corridor as the conference room. I nodded to Ryan, and he and Mercer ambled out to follow me there.

I went to my desk and sat down. I had missed only two business days, and my secretary had stacked the mes-

sages from Friday—a quiet day while I was in flight—
along with the enormous pile from today, mostly related
to the MGD case.

"I hated to break up your vacation, Alex," Mercer
said.

"Don't even think about that. You know I'd go crazy
over there second-guessing everyone anyway," I said,
smiling up at him, "except you and Ryan. Blanca's
good?"

"Real good. She had the docs in tears yesterday afternoon, telling them her life story."

"Did you get everything you need from her?"

"We didn't press too hard on Sunday. Her coworkers
believed her, and they've known her for three years.
Steady employment record. It wasn't like some woman
walking in off the street with no one to vouch for her.
The medical team and advocates all thought she presented well."

"I mean Ellen's workup today."

Ryan Blackmer had a great sense of humor. "May I be
heard, Your Honor?"

"Sure."

"It was the most pathetic interview I've seen in my six
years here. Gunsher has no ear for fine-tuning, doesn't
understand that in a rape case it's all in the details."

"Did she let you get into it?"

"I've pranked her too many times. She iced me out."

"Well, that changes in the morning," I said. "You're
with me."

"Awesome."

"Did Gil-Darsin say anything at all?"

"Mike took him off the plane. He was sitting in the
first seat on the aisle. Looked up when Mike showed the

attendant his shield, sort of grimaced, and went along without a scene when asked to step off. Gracious, pleasant, not a word."

"Miranda?"

"They read him his rights in the Air France boarding area. Drove him back to the city. Mike tried to schmooze him along the way but got nothing. When they reached the SVU offices and advised him he could make a call, he woke up his lawyer."

"He already had a lawyer?"

"The suit who handles all his business matters. White-collar crime type, not street stuff. Good mouthpiece. I think his name's Krovatin."

"Gerry Krovatin? He's first-rate. I've never gone up against him before. It'll be a real challenge."

"No, no, Coop. He's conflicted out. Runs all the WEB matters internationally, so he can't rep Baby Mo on this caper."

"Well, that gives us some breathing time."

"Rethink that one, Alex," Ryan said, "because the black panther is roaming back in your sights. You want to see Ellen Gunsher's knees wobble like jelly, you should have been at the arraignment when Lem showed up."

The picture was coming into focus now. It was one thing for Mercer to want my help, but clear to me that Battaglia picked up the phone to order me back when Lemuel Howell III entered a notice of appearance with the court.

I let out a low whistle. "What a smart move. The Ivorian economist and rising political star represented by one of the top-tier trial lawyers in the country, who happens to be African American. Lem won't just play the race card, he'll have a whole deck of tricks up his sleeve."

Lem had been one of my first supervisors in the office,

dubbed the blank panther by Mike Chapman not because of his skin color, but because of his sleek elegance and smooth moves, inside and out of the courtroom. He'd been nicknamed Mr. Triplicate by his adversaries. It wasn't just the trio of Roman numerals after his name, but his habit of rephrasing all his arguments three times. I didn't need to read the arraignment minutes to know that Mohammed Gil-Darsin had undoubtedly been railroaded on the flimsiest of evidence, gossamer threads of lies, and unsubstantiated wisps of a complaint.

"You understand why the district attorney reeled you in, Alex," Mercer said. "He knows you have a great track record against Lem, not to mention he's soft on you."

"Soft on me? Are you crazy? Lem just thinks he taught me everything I know, and that if he pulls the right strings he can control me like a marionette."

My phone rang. I checked to make sure it wasn't Battaglia's hotline to me, and picked up the receiver. "Hello?"

"Bring your crew over to Brenda's office." It was Mike Chapman, who was obviously still in the building. "There's breaking news on the telly."

"What—?" I tried to ask about it, but Mike hung up on me.

Brenda Whitney was the DA's press secretary. Her office was also on the eighth floor, and she had the difficult task of herding the unruly reporters whenever a media frenzy outbreak occurred. No assistant DAs were allowed to talk to reporters, so policing that rule and trying to prevent leaks was as important a part of her job as actually pitching stories or writing press releases.

"Mike's in Brenda's office watching TV. Something's up."

Ryan didn't wait for me to clear the corner of the desk before leaving the room. Mercer put his arm around my shoulder and walked me slowly down the hall. "You must be exhausted. It's after midnight your time."

"I slept on the plane."

"Things okay with you and your man?"

I didn't answer.

"You want to talk? Grab some dinner?"

"That would be nice."

He squeezed me tightly to his side before letting go and opening Brenda's door. She was at her desk and would probably be there all evening. Two of her staff members were in cubbyholes at the rear of the room. Mike was seated with his feet up on an empty table, using the remote control to switch channels on one of the televisions that lined a shelf in the press room.

"Who's talking?" Mercer asked. "I didn't think Lem would waste any slingshots after the evening news cameras shut down."

"It's not Lem," Mike said. "It's Alex Trebek."

I hadn't given any thought to the time of evening because of the long travel day. But we all knew Mike was addicted to betting on the Final Jeopardy! question at the end of the half-hour show. I had been with him at dinner parties and bars, morgues and murder scenes, and no amount of good taste or restraint ever stopped him from turning on the set to take all comers for the night's big question.

Trebek was squared off in front of the oversize blue box as he announced the Final Jeopardy! subject. "That's right, gentlemen," he said to the three male contestants, "tonight's category is baseball. Major League Mishaps. Let's see what you good sports know about our national pastime."

"From the looks of those brainiacs I'd guess they know as much about baseball as I know about physics," Mike said. "What do you say, Mercer? Blow the bank and go for a hundred bucks?"

Our usual ante was twenty dollars. "You still dipping into your mother's change purse when you take her to church? Where'd you come up with a Ben Franklin?" Mercer asked.

"I'm feeling flush. I collared an international horndog this weekend and got my favorite blonde back in town to boot."

"I'm in," I said. The three of us were rabid Yankee fans who went to scores of baseball games, though I took a lot of grief for my pinstripe enthusiasm from Red Sox Nation neighbors on the Vineyard during the summer.

Ryan never flinched. He was as naturally generous with his spirit as with his income, bolstered by the fact that his wife ran the legal department of a large pharmaceutical company. "Me, too."

The board scrolled back to reveal the answer. "The only batter in major-league history killed by a pitch," Trebek said, turning to the three men, who were frowning at the words on the big board.

"Double or nothing," Mike said.

"So much for your poker face. Not happening, Detective," I said. I blanked on this one, while Mike clearly knew the answer.

The *Jeopardy!* clock was ticking along with the theme music. Mercer was shaking his head and Ryan wasn't playing either.

"Who was Ray Chapman?" Mike asked.

"Chapman? Foul ball," Mercer said. "You can't use the family tree to cheat us out of our money."

LINDA FAIRSTEIN

"Poor guy wasn't good-looking enough to be a County Cork Chapman. Not related, so show me the wad of money."

The first and third contestants hadn't even ventured guesses. The second man had scrawled, "Who was Doc Powers?" on his podium screen.

"I'm so sorry," Trebek said. "Powers died off the field two weeks after slamming into the outfield wall chasing a fly back in 1909. No, the correct answer is 'Ray Chapman.'"

Mike muted the volume to tell us that Cleveland Indians shortstop Ray Chapman was hit in the head by a Yankee pitcher at the old Polo Grounds in 1920. "Never regained consciousness. That's why the spitball was banned from baseball."

"I should have known better than to go against you in this category," I said. "C'mon, let's see what Battaglia has up his sleeve."

"Baseball? You know a lot about baseball."

"Mishaps, Mike. You're the king of mishaps."

"I'll wait here for you guys. I'm buying dinner."

"Did I hear him right?" Ryan asked.

"Sorry, I've got plans," I said, hoping Mercer would get the hint so we could have a quiet meal together and I could get his thoughts on what was going on in my life.

"I saw that pathetic glance you just threw him. You were gonna lean on Mercer's great broad shoulders to whine about me breaking up your love life. Get over that, kid. Finish up with Battaglia now. I'm buying the chow tonight."

We left Mike with Brenda and returned to the conference room. Paul Battaglia and Pat McKinney had their heads together at the far end of the table. Everyone was present except June Simpson.

"Let's get started. June's on a call. She'll be right back in," McKinney said.

"Good evening, everyone. Welcome back, Alexandra," Battaglia said, standing to face the group. As always, he ignored city laws about smoking inside office buildings and spent most of the day with a lighted cigar plugged between his lips. "I want to thank you for everything you've accomplished these last forty-eight hours. I have supreme confidence in the team we've put together—led by Pat—and relying as well on Alexandra and Ryan. We've got the country's premier sex crimes unit, so they'll be the face of this case to the world.

"How did Ms. Robles hold up today?" Battaglia asked.

Ellen Gunsher took the lead. "Quite well, all things considered. She wasn't expecting to become the center of a media maelstrom."

"No victim would," the district attorney said. "What's the answer to the question the *Times* keeps coming back to us with? I know we've still got a case whether she's in this country legally or not, but what's her immigration status?"

"Blanca was granted asylum nine years ago. She's Mayan, Boss, and her village was destroyed by the Guatemalan Truth Commission—an intentional policy of genocide against certain ethnic groups like hers."

"She witnessed the murder of her parents and two siblings," Pat said, interrupting Ellen Gunsher. "I mean she literally watched them being slaughtered like pigs, Boss. She was gang-raped by a militia unit that burned her family's farm to the ground. I couldn't even stay in the room for some of her story."

"You told me this morning she's a very religious

woman," Battaglia said, addressing Ellen again. He wanted that information, but wouldn't expend the emotional energy to empathize with most victims. "What parish? Where in the city does she worship?"

"I mean she wears a crucifix, Boss. I didn't ask which church she belongs to," Ellen said. "I'll ask her tomorrow."

Tomorrow was always the wrong answer to give Paul Battaglia. He didn't care about Blanca's faith. He was more interested in the political currency of the information. If the woman was part of the flock, then the archdiocese would be checking up on her well-being in the hands of my colleagues. There would be a district leader with whom to exchange promises of favors for embracing the accuser against such a powerful perpetrator, and a state assemblyman who might later weigh in on a particular vote if his constituent was well supported. The district attorney wanted to make those phone calls tonight, not tomorrow.

"Is that housekeeping position she has a union job?"

"I think so," Ellen said.

I'd learned long ago and trained all my assistants never to be short on the details that would engage Battaglia's interest. He'd leave the case management to his legal staff, but the politics that arose out of these situations was what he thrived on.

"Find that out first thing and let me know. I'm not looking for any rallies on the courthouse steps by thousands of hotel workers in this city."

"Sure, Boss. In the morning."

"Have you made her safe?" Battaglia asked.

"Yes, we've put her up at—"

He held his arms straight out. "I don't need to know

where. I just want to be able to say she's out of harm's way. When do you go to the grand jury?"

The criminal procedure law of the state of New York dictated the timeline the case had to follow. At Gil-Darsin's arraignment this morning, the People had requested remand without any opportunity for bail. There were apparently millions of dollars at his disposal—his own, Papa Mo's fortune, and the great wealth of his supermodel wife—the defense had argued. But the judge agreed that as a foreigner bound for a country with no extradition treaty with the United States for sexual assault, the powerful WEB head would remain incarcerated.

The NYPD—not the district attorney—had started the clock running by arresting Gil-Darsin late Saturday night. The arraignment had occurred at ten a.m. today—Monday—and by Friday of this week, 120 hours after our filing of the felony complaint charging first-degree rape, our team would have to present the evidence, the testimony of Blanca Robles, to a grand jury composed of twenty-three citizens, who would then vote a true bill—an indictment—if they believed her story.

"We need most of the day tomorrow to go over the facts more carefully and make Blanca comfortable about telling her story to the jurors. Alex can help with that." Ellen spoke rather tentatively, but I nodded to reassure her that I was on board. "Then we expect to go ahead on Wednesday afternoon. Get a vote and be ready to file immediately. The next court date is Thursday. If we go in before the judge with an indictment in hand, I can't imagine that he'll change the bail conditions, even with Lem Howell pushing for it."

"Sounds good." Battaglia had a dozen questions

about issues external to the crime itself for Mercer Wallace and the prosecutors. Was the Eurotel management cooperating with the police investigation? Had any other victims called in to the hotline set up by Brenda Whitney's office? Were the preliminary DNA results reliable enough to put before the grand jurors? Yes. No. Yes. The answers came as quickly as he asked them.

"I know it's tempting to leak when your favorite reporters lean on you," Battaglia said, the cigar held firmly between two fingers as he pointed around the room at each of us. "But this has to be a completely clean operation. I'm the only one talking to the media, is that understood? You get any inquiries from the UN or the French government or the WEB offices, nothing is too minor to bring to my attention."

The door opened, and Battaglia stopped talking till he saw that it was June Simpson coming back in to rejoin us.

"You're up against just about the best lawyer in the business," Battaglia said. "He'll be doing everything you can't do, including trying his case at impromptu press conferences in front of our office doors or WEB headquarters. Any overtures from Lem yet, Pat? Any sense he wants to sit down with you and hammer something out?"

"Nothing but silence, Boss. My guess is he's figuring all this media circus will freak out the victim and we'll never get her prepped to testify by week's end. He doesn't have to say a damn word."

"Maybe Lem will try to use Alex to soften you up. Let me know the minute he reaches out to you, young lady, okay?"

"Unlikely to happen," I said. I could feel the color rising in my cheeks. Lem had always played favorites, and I was one of them. He was inappropriately tactile, even in the most professional settings, rubbing my arm or my back, suggesting a physical intimacy that had never existed.

"I want somebody on this team designated to report to Rose every hour. I want updates with whatever you've got," Battaglia said, then jabbed his cigar in the direction of Ellen Gunsher. "And answers tomorrow morning on everything I asked you about Ms. Robles."

June Simpson was standing with her back to the closed door and her arms crossed.

"I'm not sure we'll be getting the answers you want. And certainly not tomorrow."

Every head in the room turned to June.

"That was Blanca Robles who called?" Pat McKinney asked.

"Sort of. That was Blanca Robles who called—but from the law offices of Byron Peaser. I think our victim's been hijacked."

There was a collective groan from the group assembled at the table. Peaser the Sleazer had long been the nickname of the greediest ambulance chaser in the city, a negligence lawyer who handled civil suits that lined his pockets with at least a third of the millions of dollars he sought for his victims.

"I thought this woman told you she wasn't looking for money," Battaglia said, facing off to Pat McKinney.

"That was yesterday, Boss. She told me this was all about justice, not money."

"And tomorrow?" Battaglia directed the question to June Simpson.

"Peaser says he's calling the shots. He'll bring Blanca in to meet with us, but he's demanding to sit in on the interviews. He wants to vet all the questions we ask her."

"No way," I said. "He'll get his turn after we're done in criminal court."

"I'm telling you, Alex, Byron's going to make this difficult for all of us. He's taken her out of the safe housing we placed her in and relocated her as of an hour ago. Won't tell me where. He'll bring her in here only if we play by his rules," June said. "What do I tell him?"

"Now she's *his* victim, too," I said. "I wonder if she realizes that."

"What are you going to do?" Battaglia asked me.

"Tell Peaser to have Blanca here at nine. I can play hardball every bit as well as that sleazebag."

June stepped to the side as Battaglia headed for the door. "Whoever you choose to be the messenger for those updates," he said, talking to no one in particular, "make sure he knows I like an occasional bit of good news. Best to lead with it if you've got it."

The door slammed behind him. "Now that the DA has brought you back for this, Alex, you damn well better get it right," Pat McKinney said, "or you might as well book your return trip to France. You and Monsieur Gil-Darsin."

Thirteen

Mike was sitting at our usual corner table, his back to the window that fronted Second Avenue, when Mercer and I entered Primola, one of my favorite Italian restaurants on Manhattan's Upper East Side, a little after nine-thirty in the evening. He was working his way through a double dose of vodka.

"Buona sera, Alessandra," the owner, Giuliano, said as we came in. He seated us and called out to the bartender. "Fenton, a Dewar's on the rocks for Ms. Cooper, *subito!*"

"I'll have what Mike's drinking," Mercer said, holding out a chair for me.

Ryan had opted to go home to put his daughter to bed, so Mercer and I drove uptown together. He used the time to fill me in on everything I needed to know about Blanca Robles. That was obviously more important than a conversation about my stalled love life.

We were such regulars at Primola that none of us needed the menu to order. I'd skipped the meal service on the flight and was starving for some comfort food, trying to forget the fact that it was three-thirty in the morning back in Mougins.

"I'm switching over to club soda after this one," Mike said. "Gotta work tonight. I slept all day."

"I slept all day, too." The restaurant was midway between my apartment and Mike's, but our homes might as well have been in different cities. My father's trust—not my public service salary—allowed me to live in the high-rent high-rise district in the East 70s, on the twentieth floor of a building with dazzling views and great security.

Mike's tiny studio apartment was southeast of the restaurant, a walk-up in an old tenement building in the East 60s. He'd dubbed it "the coffin" years ago, for its darkness and small size. There was a brief period when Valerie had tried to decorate it and organize the hundreds of books on military history that were stacked against every wall, but when Mike was overwhelmed with grief at her death, disorder reclaimed its space.

Mercer and Vickee were practically suburban. After Logan's birth, they moved to a large, handsome house in Douglaston, Queens, a tree-lined neighborhood that was convenient to work but looked nothing like the city streets from which our cases came.

"Hungry?" Mercer asked me as Dominick approached to take our order.

"Starving. I'll have the linguine with white clam sauce, please."

"I'll have that, too," Mike said. "Along with an order of chicken parmigiana."

"The chicken's the size of an entire dinner plate," I said. "That's two enormous entrées."

"I'm paying. What do you care?" The garlic bread

Mike was inhaling might actually serve him well if he was called to a murder scene during his tour. If the smell of a body was any stronger than the garlic, I'd be surprised.

"Chicken parm for me, too. Salad on the side," Mercer said. He reached out and the three of us clinked our glasses together. "To Blanca Robles. Here's to truth, justice, and the American way."

"Cheers," I said. "I'm so sorry she's in the hands of Byron Peaser."

"When did this happen?" Mike asked.

"Tonight. It's a real game-changer."

"She's entitled to a civil suit."

"Of course she is. But they've got no problem with a statute of limitations. The criminal case tolls all their deadlines. It complicates things terribly for us."

"How so?"

"McKinney specifically asked her if she was contemplating a lawsuit and she said this wasn't about money, that the thought hadn't crossed her mind. At the very same time, someone in her circle of friends was making calls to the Sleazer. Remember, he had a massive recovery for that Guatemalan cabdriver who was shot reaching for his wallet when cops thought it was a gun."

"So she changed her mind," Mike said, slathering more butter on the already toasted bread.

"I can live with that, but it's always a sticking point for jurors. June says Byron won't tell her how much he's going to sue Gil-Darsin for, but it probably won't be less than fifty million dollars."

I thought the vodka was going to come out of his nose. "That could be the most expensive blow job in history."

"And you know what the lawsuit does to the prosecution's case?" I asked. "If I'm the one who stands before that jury for the closing argument, I need to be able to convince them that Blanca Robles has no motive to lie."

"You can still do that."

"The Court of Appeals reversed me in one of the toughest date-rape cases I've ever tried. The civil suit was filed the day after the conviction, and the court held that my witness had a reason to lie for every dollar she asked for in her suit."

"Fifty million reasons to lie," Mercer said.

"So at the same moment I start working on building my relationship with Blanca, I've got to tell her we think she's made a major mistake and try to separate her from Byron as quickly—and as far—as possible."

"And that's before you got Lem Howell triplicating all over you," Mike said, nibbling on thin strips of fried zucchini and doing a fine imitation of Lem's voice. " 'Mendacity, veracity, audacity'—he's just warming up his tongue for this jaunt. So on a lighter note, Coop, how's Luc?"

"Thanks for asking. I think he's fine."

"You think?"

"I mean he's nervous about opening the restaurant over here. It's such a huge step and he's got everything invested in it, financially and emotionally. And there was actually a murder in Mougins this weekend. First one in hundreds of years."

"Talk about burying the lede," Mike said. "A murder? You should have made yourself a pain in the ass to the French cops, like you do to me."

"Not to worry, Detective Chapman. That's exactly what I did."

"Who'd the grim reaper find in that little piece of paradise you're always telling us is so safe?"

"A woman in her twenties. Asphyxiated. Drowned in a huge lotus pond."

"Did Luc do it?"

I opened my mouth to snap an answer at Mike, but Mercer put his hand over mine.

"I'm just kidding, Coop. The town has a population of six, according to you. Everybody there has to be a suspect."

"There are no suspects. And I'm Luc's alibi," I said with a smile.

"Rock solid. Especially since you skipped out of town a week early. I'd be all over you if it were my investigation. Did you know the vic?"

"No," I said, hesitating a second. "But Luc did. She used to work for him."

"Now I know why you responded to Battaglia's call. Use that 'get out of jail free' card while it's still in your hand and head for home. Leave your lover to swing on his own rope."

My drink was at my lips, but I put down the glass. I spoke calmly and evenly, with a semblance of the same smile still on my face. "Here's the thing, Michael Patrick David Chapman. Listen up. I have made a career out of helping women who have been victimized and abused. I like doing it. I like helping them get out of relationships that are unhealthy. I like restoring their self-esteem. If I heard any one of them being talked to—talked at—in the manner in which you constantly hurl—"

"See, Mercer? Every now and then I just laser in on that sweet spot that gets her dander up. Like a drone zeroing in on a single terrorist target in the mountains of Afghanistan. I have this knack—"

"Let her talk, Mike."

"It's been more than ten years. If she had something to say about this, I'd have known it by now, don't you think?"

"If I heard any woman being abused and humiliated, in front of her coworkers and friends, no less," I said, trying to finish my little speech.

"You know I worship the ground you walk on, Coop. What the hell happened to your sense of humor? Did it get lost in the Bermuda Triangle on the flight home?"

"He loves you, Alex. Everybody on this planet sees that except you. C'mon, girl. Say your piece and let's get back to business. The dude's got a sick sense of humor and we all have to put up with it."

"Whoa, Mercer, we're not talking love here. You know, Coop, you like it mighty fine when I'm riffing on McKinney or Gunsher, when I'm pulling Lem Howell's leg, when I'm playing with your posse of sex crimes vixens— ragging on Catherine or Marisa or Nan. Now you're suddenly off the table? Off the charts? Off the wall?"

I flopped back in my chair and starting drinking the Scotch. I had no idea what had made me bristle at that particular moment, other than the vision of Luc swinging from a rope because I had used the first excuse offered to run away from his problems. I never doubted Mike's respect or affection for me. We had flirted with each other for years without ever crossing the line and becoming intimate. On my part, it was an eyes-wide-open acknowledgment that we could never remain professional partners if we had a sexual relationship. With all the dark humor as an overlay, I wasn't even sure that Mike had any interest in taking our friendship in that direction.

Dominick arrived with my bowl of pasta and plates for Mercer and Mike. I thanked him and prepared to dig in.

"Look at me, Coop," Mike said, running his fingers through his thick black hair and staring at me with eyes almost as dark. "I apologize. From the heart. Really I do."

"What did you say?"

"I apologize. From the heart."

"Say it again."

"You heard me."

"I appreciate that."

"But do you accept it? My apology, I mean. Ten years of teaching you everything I know about murder and street mooks, ten years of covering your ass in every conceivable situation including the dim-witted ones you got yourself into, ten years of making you look like a rock star in the courtroom when you didn't know your opening from your closing—but then, the occasional insult? I apologize for all of it."

"Okay, okay, okay. You really nailed me with that one. I accept, all right?"

He had pushed his pasta aside and was working on the chicken parm, his appetite no more diminished for upsetting me than it would be if a corpse fell off the chair behind him.

"Good. Because there's nothing to say it won't happen again."

"Especially if I tell you that you now have marinara sauce all over your chin."

Mike picked up his napkin to wipe it off. "I bet the French don't even need napkins. I bet they don't drip stuff like this on themselves ever."

"So does Luc think this murdered girl has something to do with his business, since she used to work in the restaurant?" Mercer asked, determined to change the subject.

"He hopes it doesn't have anything to do with his

business or his personal life, but it's his ex-wife who caught Lisette stealing from his restaurant, so Luc had to fire her. That mixes in both elements. He's the only three-star restaurant in Mougins, which is the source of a lot of animosity in his professional world."

"What's the big deal with these stars?" Mike asked. "I thought Michelin made automobile tires. What do they know about food?"

"The Michelin brothers started making tires more than a century ago. In 1900, they published a guide that would help travelers find mechanics, gas stations, and tire dealers. They thought it made sense to throw in locations for good food and lodging for their customers in France."

"Clever idea," Mercer said. "Who does the ratings? People like us?"

"That's the Zagat system," I said, referring to the enormously popular series of American city guides developed by a husband and wife team in New York, using restaurant patrons to rate the cuisine and decor. "Michelin has always used professionals—trained inspectors who remain anonymous to the chefs—to rank food and service."

"Everybody gets a star?" Mike asked.

"Oh no. If a restaurant isn't deemed worthy of patronage, it simply isn't mentioned in the guide. One star means a really good cuisine in its category, two stand for excellent dining, worth a detour, and three stars—very few of them every year—mean exceptional cuisine that's worth a special journey."

"And Luc has three?"

"There are more than fifteen thousand restaurants in France, and only twenty-six of them received three stars last year."

"That's impressive," Mercer said.

"And backbreaking. You won't believe the kind of attention that goes into every aspect of producing a great dining experience. You'll get it firsthand when things start up over here."

"What's the timeline for opening Lutèce?" he asked.

"Luc and his partners have bought the property—an elegant town house, just like his father created the first time."

"In the East Fifties?"

"Eighty-First Street, actually. His partners claim the Eighties are the new Fifties," I said, talking between delicious bites of pasta.

"My mother claims the same thing. Eighty-seven with the spirit of a fifty-year-old."

"Your mother's amazing," I said. "Anyway, the space is furnished and decorated, and sometime in the next month, as soon as they've hired enough staff, we'll all be invited to tasting dinners. Luc's big season in Mougins begins now, so Lutèce won't really have an opening until late fall."

"So who found this woman's body?" Mike asked, clearly fascinated by the homicide in Mougins. "It wasn't Luc, was it?"

"He didn't kill her. He didn't find her. It was a night watchman."

"Didn't I tell you? That's when it all happens."

"I don't mean a cop on night watch duty, I just mean an old guy who was hired to check the park outside of town as security."

"Hey, that's what night watch is," Mike said. "When patrols were organized in the first American cities—New York, Boston, Philly, Baltimore—it was a motley crew of constables and marshals who tried to keep people safe from gangs and criminals. Even when the NYPD, the oldest force in the country, was established in 1845, it modeled itself on military organizations. Patrolmen were hired to work all day. And then, one man was hired to keep everyone safe at night—a single night watch—the sleepless sentinel who looked over the city from sunset to dawn."

"Check your watch, Detective," Mercer said. "Coming up on your tour of duty."

Mike called out to the waiter. "Dominick, let me have a double espresso. Make it two. That ought to jolt me into action. You guys want anything?"

I shook my head. "Counting on catching up from my jet lag tonight."

Most of the detectives in Homicide, Special Victims, Major Case, and other elite squads pulled night watch assignments several times a year. Because manpower in the precincts was low, the day and evening shifts were fully staffed, but often there were not enough officers to cover the midnight tour.

The result was a patchwork quilt of senior detectives and supervisors who responded to every homicide or serious crime that occurred between twelve and eight a.m. They worked the case, made the arrest—as Mike had with MGD—and then passed the investigation back to the squad that had the original jurisdiction to complete all the follow-up.

It was just after eleven when Giuliano presented the bill to Mike, who had to be signed in by eleven thirty p.m. I went downstairs to the restroom to freshen up, and by the time I got back to the table, Mike was standing outside the glass-paned front door, talking on his cell phone.

"I'll drop you at home," Mercer said. "Mike left your bags with the doorman on his way up from the office."

"Thanks."

Mercer pushed the door open as Mike held the phone to his ear and scratched notes on the napkin he had carried out of the restaurant. "See you there," he said to whoever was on the other end of the line, then shut off his phone.

"What's the body count?" Mercer asked.

"Just one, so far."

"I'm taking Alex. Which way are you headed?"

"Over the bridge to Brooklyn."

"What have you got?" I said, walking toward Mercer's car.

"Must be your karma, Coop."

"Why?"

"It's not exactly a lotus pond, but they just pulled out a floater," Mike said. "A young guy in a well-tailored sports coat and slacks. Throat slit ear to ear. Facedown in the Gowanus Canal."

Fourteen

"Byron Peaser with Ms. Robles. We're here to see Alexandra Cooper." I overheard the husky voice of the elderly lawyer who was talking to my secretary, Laura Wilkie, and walked to the door to greet him.

"I'm Alex Cooper," I said, extending my hand.

I'd convinced Pat McKinney that it was necessary to trim the size of the team getting the facts from Blanca. Too many people in the room would make it far more difficult for her to be put at ease, yet working alone with a witness was not smart either, in case the facts were inconsistent in different tellings or she later chose to recant any part of the story.

"Call me Byron," he said. The limp handshake, thick bifocals, and even thicker Bronx accent made a first impression that must have disarmed jurors who perhaps sympathized with him and therefore with his clients. "This here is Ms. Robles. I spoke with June Simpson last evening and she told me to ask for you. I'm representing Blanca now, so I came along for the interview."

"Why don't you both step into my office for a minute? Detective Wallace is here, and Ellen Gunsher is waiting for us in the conference room. I want to settle a few matters first."

Peaser stepped back so Blanca could follow me in. She smiled when she saw Mercer leaning against a file cabinet, and I liked that about her.

"Good morning, Blanca," Mercer said.

"Good morning to you, Detective."

Her English was good, which meant it was unlikely that the event in the hotel room involved a failure to communicate between the London-educated Gil-Darsin and Blanca Robles. There was less Mayan in her speech than there was Bronx in Peaser's.

"I understand from my colleagues that you speak English very well, Blanca. I just want to make sure that you're comfortable going forward without an interpreter. We'd be happy to provide one for you."

"She's got no problem with the language," Peaser said. "I can assure you."

"Here's the first thing that's going to happen, Mr. Peaser—"

"It's Byron, please. Mr. Peaser was my father." His shtick was going to be hard to take. And he wanted to establish the "first-name basis" bit with me to show his client how close we were. I wanted to address Blanca by her given name and get her in the habit of doing that with me and the team, but the lawyer was another matter altogether.

"I prefer to wait till we've gotten to know each other, Mr. Peaser. The first thing you both need to understand is that when I ask Blanca a question, I need the answer to come from her. Can we agree on that?"

"Go ahead, dear. Did you understand what Alex asked you?"

"Yes, ma'am. I've been in the States for lots of years now. I don't speak everything perfectly, but I understand what you're asking me and I don't need anyone to translate for me."

"Did you have any trouble getting in the building this morning, now that you've been moved out of police protection by Mr. Peaser?"

"I've got a security team, Alex. Ex-cops, you know. We've got Blanca and her daughter in a safe place, and we made arrangements to bring her through the rear entrance of the courthouse. I've been doing this for more years than you've been alive."

Peaser had obviously greased someone's hands to get that backdoor access, but I was glad they had avoided the unruly gaggle of reporters and photographers waiting outside the Hogan Place building entrance for a glimpse of the victim and a photo op.

I explained my role in the office and my experience working on sexual assault cases. It took me ten or fifteen minutes to go over what we expected of Blanca this week, repeating some of the things she had heard from McKinney and the group yesterday.

While she listened to me, I jotted down my observations about her. I had been told she was not well educated, but she was smart enough to be paying careful attention to what I was saying. Every time Peaser interrupted me, I shut him down with an admonition.

I would need to ask her height and weight. Somehow the initial news reports conveyed the impression that Blanca was slight and petite, but she was much larger than I'd imagined. I reached for the arrest report in my folder. Gil-Darsin was only five feet, six inches tall and a bit chubby. I looked up at Blanca again. She was easily two inches taller than the perp, with a sturdy build. The defense would certainly make an issue of what she had done to resist the smaller man's advances.

"At some point, Blanca, you're going to need to tell me exactly where you're living now."

"I can do that—"

"Best if we keep it under my hat for the time being," Peaser said. "I'll be in charge of her whereabouts."

"That's not going to work, sir. For the purpose of the criminal case, Blanca is the state's witness. We don't plan to go to you every time we need something from her. Talk it over with her, Mr. Peaser, but before she leaves this building today, I want the address at which she's staying."

Blanca looked at her lawyer, who put his forefinger to his lips as though to silence her.

"In a few minutes," I said talking directly to the victim, "you and I are going to go to the conference room with Mercer and with Ellen Gunsher. I know you talked to both of them yesterday, and I'm sorry I missed that meeting. We're going to go over everything again in more detail, because we expect that you'll testify before the grand jury in a day or two. Is that all right?"

Again she looked over at Peaser before she nodded.

"Do you have any questions for me before we get started?"

Blanca Robles slowly shook her head.

"I do, actually," Byron Peaser said.

"Yes?"

"How many hours do you expect to keep us here today?" he asked. "You see, as soon as we're done, I'd like Blanca to come back to my office."

"To sign papers for the civil suit?"

"We took care of that last night."

Shit. "Did you give any thought, Mr. Peaser, to holding off on that for a while?"

"She's entitled to sue the bastard, you know."

"I'm aware of that." I couldn't wait to separate them so we could explain to Blanca what she might risk by making her civil claim this very week. I stood up and gathered all my case papers. "And I expect she'll be with us most of the day, Mr. Peaser. You, of course, are free to leave now. We'll take very good care of her."

"No, no. I'm here to sit in on the interviews."

"That won't be possible."

"Whaddaya mean?" Peaser asked, replacing the goofy smile with a sneer. "I'm going to be with my client all the way through this. That's what she wants—isn't it, Blanca?"

The young woman didn't speak.

"The grand jury is deemed a secret proceeding by law, as I'm sure you know. You can't accompany Blanca into that forum, and these meetings are preparation for her testimony there. So either my secretary will make you comfortable at an empty desk so you can make calls or do work, or you can go back to your office and Detective Wallace will bring Blanca to you at the end of the day. You are not driving this train, Mr. Peaser, so take your hands off the controls. Which will it be?"

"Neither option is acceptable to me, Ms. Cooper."

I walked around my desk so that my back was to Peaser but I was directly in front of Blanca Robles. "Yesterday you told Mercer and the lawyers that your first interest was seeking justice against the man who assaulted you. Is that still the case?"

She hesitated and unenthusiastically said, "Yes."

"If we're successful in proving Mr. Gil-Darsin's guilt—and the only person who can do that is you, Blanca—then not only does he face a serious prison sentence but we've also done all of Mr. Peaser's work for him."

"What do you mean?" she asked.

"I thought I talked you through all this, Blanca," Peaser said, but the puzzled look on the woman's face belied his lame effort.

"Basically, the civil jury would learn that the man was convicted of terrible crimes at our trial, and they would just have to set a dollar number on the award to you," I said. "They would learn that he'd been found guilty in this court, and they would have to decide only how much money to give you, and that settles how much money Mr. Peaser puts in his pocket at the end of the day. Has he explained that to you?"

Blanca tilted her head to try to look around me at him, but she couldn't see him.

"Not exactly. Not yet anyway."

"Yes, I did, Blanca. I started to tell you that last night. We'll get to it," Peaser said, sounding arch and angry. He looked as though snake oil would begin to ooze from his every pore.

"So here's the choice you have to make today. You can go off with Mr. Peaser to his office and do whatever he has planned. In that case, I can't promise you when we'll be ready to take you into the grand jury. We'll need all of today to prep you, at the very least. And if we haven't obtained an indictment before Friday, Mr. Gil-Darsin will be released from jail and probably be on his way home to France."

Blanca gasped. "But that's not possible."

"If you stay and work with us all day, then I don't expect it will be a problem," I said. "But Mr. Peaser is not part of our case. He has no role, no participation in what we're doing here. Mr. McKinney—I think you met him yesterday—and Detective Wallace are in charge of the criminal matter.

"I'm not your lawyer, Blanca. I'm the state's lawyer. I can't make you millions of dollars, like Mr. Peaser thinks he can. But the district attorney has put together the best possible team to see that justice is done in your case. And if you meet us halfway, if you simply tell us the truth about everything we ask you, we'll be the most spectacular advocates you could ever have at your side. Do you get what I'm telling you?"

Her dark brown eyes were tearing up. "Yes, Miss Alex. Yes, I do. But I don't know who to trust in this. I'm very frightened."

"Of course you are. Everyone who walks into our offices has good reason to be scared and nervous. We're all here to help you get through this, I promise."

An unexpected knock on the door startled me. Laura opened it and poked her head in. "Excuse me, Alex, but can you step out here for a minute?"

I gave her a look that rudely must have conveyed my wonder at what could possibly have caused an intrusion at exactly this moment. "What—?"

"It's Mike. He says he's got to see you immediately."

"You want to deal with him, Mercer? I'm not in the mood for some slimy souvenir from the Gowanus Canal."

"Let me talk to Blanca while you go about your business. Mike asked for you, not me."

It was a smart idea for Mercer to work his magic on the victim. I could tell from her smile when she entered the room that she liked or respected him, and he would probably be more off-putting to Byron Peaser than I had tried to be.

I walked out, and Laura told me Mike was waiting in the empty office vacated by my former deputy. Ellen Gunsher was at the far end of the hallway. She held up her arm and tapped on her wristwatch. I spread my fingers to tell her we'd be with her in five minutes.

"Good morning, Detective Chapman," I said as I pushed open the door.

"Hey, kid. I'm sorry to break up your meeting. I know you've got to get your indictment. I just wanted you to see this before I take it over to One PP."

"See what?" I asked. "Headquarters? What's that got to do with me?"

One Police Plaza was just a few blocks from the courthouse.

"Commissioner Scully wants a briefing on the floater in the canal."

"Why?" I asked. "Who was the guy?"

"We don't have a clue. That's why Scully will probably go public if we can't ID him in the next few hours." Mike reached into his blazer pocket and pulled out a manila envelope with his gloved hand.

"I found this in his pocket after they fished him out of the water." He removed the small matchbox and held it up so I could see it. The shiny white background was slightly mottled from submersion in the water, but the spring green letters were sharp and clear.

LUTÈCE was written on one side of the small box, then Mike flipped it to show me Luc's name on the other.

Fifteen

"There are thousands of these boxes that Luc had made," I said, practically shouting at Mike. "What's the big deal that this dead man had one in his pocket? Why do you think it would upset me? Why would you think Luc is involved?"

"Take it easy, Coop. Nobody's accusing Luc of anything. But don't you think this is going to raise a few eyebrows at headquarters?"

"I can't imagine why it would."

"Don't yell at me, kid. I'm on your side. It's not my case, remember? As of eight a.m., it got handed over to Brooklyn Homicide. I'm just the messenger."

"Keith Scully won't even know what Lutèce is."

"Are you joking? It was hands-down the best restaurant in the city for a couple of decades. If you walked the beat in the Seventeenth Precinct, you still know that presidents and kings and captains of industry made it their clubhouse at lunchtime and dinner. Maybe I never got to taste the crumbs, but you know how many security details I worked there over the years? Keith, too. He didn't get to the top being stupid."

"That's the old place. That Lutèce has been shut down since 2004," I said, my arms flailing in the empty space as I started to pace around the room. "How would Keith have a clue? There is no Lutèce at the moment."

"Which is why it's even stranger if you give it some rational thought," Mike said. He put his hands on my shoulders and forced me to sit down. "How many of these little boxes could there be, Coop? The restaurant doesn't even exist yet."

"I told you it's about to open. These are—they're—" I paused, flustered that I couldn't even think of the word that Luc used to describe them. "It's a prototype. He and his partners had hundreds of them—maybe thousands of them—made up as a promotional thing. They're being passed out in restaurants and bars and who knows where else."

"In France, Coop, or here in New York?"

I looked up at Mike and took a deep breath. "I don't know. For sure around Mougins."

"Want to see if you recognize the dead guy?" Mike said, pulling up the photograph on his cell phone. "It's not exactly his yearbook picture, so it may be hard to tell."

A slit throat and time in one of the world's foulest waterways wouldn't do much to turn anyone's features into a money shot. I stared at the man's head from several angles before I answered. "I've never seen him. Was there anything else in his pockets?"

"Not a thing."

"So someone took everything out—wallet and cash

and identification—but either left this in place if it was actually his, or planted it there."

"It's not your case, Coop. Spinning wheels in that anxious little brain isn't going to help anything. I'm just giving you a heads-up."

"I'm grateful for that." I'm not sure I really was grateful. I felt like I'd been standing in quicksand since the earliest hours of Sunday morning, and now it had covered my ankles and was pulling me down as it aimed to swallow my kneecaps.

"Is Luc involved in any trouble that you know of, any business problems at all?"

I shot Mike a glance, confident he would recognize the mix of pain and anger I was trying to express, without my saying a word.

"I'm not being funny, kid. I'm not being mean to you," he knelt in front of me and put one hand on my knee.

"I know that." I focused on the phone, which was the only thing still left on the old wooden desk. "I don't think that he is. It's a huge undertaking, opening a business like this in New York. It's very risky."

"Does Luc talk about it with you? Would you know if there was a problem?"

"I just arrived in Mougins on Friday, so we never got around to discussing business. We weren't even together for forty-eight hours before the woman's body was pulled out of the pond. And that was after I found the bones."

"What bones?" Mike stood up in front of me.

"Old ones. Some kind of joke, the cops think, from the catacombs in Paris."

I knew I needed to tell Mike that the same type of

matchbox was recovered from the floater in the pond, but I couldn't make myself do it. I didn't want Luc to be dragged any deeper into the quicksand beside me.

"You mean there are people with worse senses of humor than me?" Mike asked.

I smiled and nodded.

"Now I know you're in a bad way, Coop. You didn't correct my grammar."

"That's a full-time job," I said, as I got up and walked to the desk. It was three in the afternoon in Mougins. Luc was probably in his office. "Who's going to handle the case for Brooklyn Homicide?"

"You have to forget I was even here today. Don't ask questions like that. Read the story in the tabs like everyone else. You don't know about the matchbox, you've never seen a photo of the corpse. Play dumb, kid. It could be a refreshing change."

"Don't worry. I'm not going to burn you with the brass at One PP. I'm thinking about Luc and all the pressure on him now. He's trying to figure out how to spend so much time away from his kids, whom he adores, and he's already put a ton of money into this deal."

"And you should be back in your office with the team. There's as much pressure on you as there is on Luc. I'm almost sorry I came by," Mike said. "No good deed, as the saying goes."

"Thank you. I really mean that. Go on your way and just give me a minute to compose myself. Tell Mercer I'll be right there."

Mike watched me for a few seconds, then turned to leave. "I'll talk to you later."

When he closed the door, I waited twenty seconds, then lifted the receiver and dialed the DA's office switchboard. "Hi, Mona. It's Alex Cooper. Would you please give me a line for an international call, and charge it to me personally?"

She asked for the number, so I slowly recited the country and city codes for Mougins.

The door opened and I swung around. Mike charged at the desk and grabbed the phone from my hand, slamming the receiver into its cradle. "I told you to play dumb, Coop, not be completely stupid. Do I have to cuff you to a chair till the evening news breaks the story, or can you just sit tight on this little secret for the rest of the day like I've asked you to do?"

Sixteen

I didn't need a distraction of this magnitude to interfere with navigating the MGD case work ahead of us. I needed more focus than I was struggling to regain at that moment.

When Mike escorted me back to my office, I was pleasantly surprised to find that Blanca Robles had made the right choice. She'd told Byron Peaser she would see him at the end of the day. To my mind, that reaffirmed her commitment to prosecute Mohammed Gil-Darsin and let the civil suit be secondary to the criminal trial.

Mercer and I led Blanca down to the conference room where Ellen Gunsher and Ryan Blackmer, backing me up as a witness from the Sex Crimes Unit, waited for us. June Simpson was out of the picture because of my return. Since Ellen had started the questioning yesterday, it made sense to leave it in her hands. She and Blanca exchanged greetings and she got to work.

"I'm going to ask you to go over exactly what hap-

pened when you entered suite twenty-eight-oh-six, is
that all right?"

"Again?"

"Yes, once again. When you testify before the grand
jury, both Alex and I will be with you. I'll ask all the questions, and you'll know exactly what they will be before you
go inside. No surprises. That's why I want to be sure we
have all the details correct."

"Mr. Peaser told me there are a lot of people in the
room. You know how many?"

"There are twenty-three grand jurors," Ellen said, going on to describe the amphitheatrical shape of the room.
"But only jurors. There's no judge, and there's no defense attorney to cross-examine you."

"Twenty-three people?" Blanca seemed startled by
that large a number. She looked up at the ceiling and
made the sign of the cross. "Is he there, too? This man
who attacked me?"

"No, no. He's in jail. After you testify, he has to appear before the judge on Friday."

"But I don't have to see him, do I?"

"No, you don't," Ellen said, as Blanca crossed herself
again. "Do you mind starting your story from the beginning, from the time you were sent upstairs to clean the
suite?"

Blanca spoke clearly, making eye contact with each of
us at different points in her narrative. She explained that
the door to the room was ajar, and she had just seen a
man from Food Services removing the table tray, which
confirmed her belief that the guest had vacated.

"I knocked on the door a couple of times and called
out 'Housekeeping.' We always do that, announce our-

selves, in case the guests are still there. I didn't hear any-thing, so I went inside."

As she spoke, Mercer unfolded a diagram of the large suite. "The hotel sent this over to my office last night." He spread it out so that we could follow Blanca's story and see where each act transpired.

"See this corridor here?" She pointed at a long, narrow hallway that led into the enormous bedroom suite. "I was just at the end of this the first time I saw the guy. He was coming out of the bathroom. Right here. And he was naked. Totally naked."

"What did you do?" Ellen asked.

"I—I kind of froze."

That would be the first point of attack for the defense. Blanca was putting them ten feet apart, with nothing separating her from the exit. Why didn't she back up and out, why didn't she turn and walk away?

"Who spoke first?"

"Me," Blanca said. "I did. I remember calling out '¡Dios mío! Oh my God! I'm sorry. I'm so sorry.'"

"Then what?"

"He told me not to be sorry. He started walking toward me and told me again there was no reason for me to be sorry."

And why didn't you move when he walked toward you? I wanted to ask. *That was your chance to get out of the room. I don't expect he would have chased you into the common hallway stark naked.*

"Is that when he grabbed you?" Ellen asked.

"Yes, exactly. That's when he grabbed me."

Why are you putting words in her mouth? Did he "grab" her or motion to her or command her to come to do what he wanted? It's Blanca who has to tell the story. Grabbing, pushing, pulling—and forcing—would be the most critical words in her narrative, and she needed to be the first person to use them.

"He grabbed you by the arm?"

"Not yet. First he grabbed—you know—he put his hand on my breast. He told me I was beautiful."

"What did you do then?"

"I—I told him to stop. I told him I could lose my job for what he was doing."

So far MGD had made no threats or used any force. We had a misdemeanor unconsented touching of a breast at most. Blanca Robles was concerned about her job, not about her physical safety and well-being.

She paused and lowered her head. When she raised it, both eyes had filled with tears. "That's when he grabbed me and pulled me toward the bed. He just pulled me and threw me onto the bed."

Blanca's hand gestures were getting very dramatic now. I wanted Ellen to stop and break down every conclusory description offered by the witness to a second-by-second account. How did this smaller man overpower such a large, strapping woman and get her the distance—maybe twenty feet—from the vestibule of the room to his king-size bed?

"That's when he pulled down your stockings and penetrated?"

"Exactly that."

I leaned forward. "I'm sorry to interrupt, Ellen. Can we just get a few more specifics?"

Blanca turned her tear-filled eyes to me. "For how long would you say the man had his hand on your breast?" I asked.

"Maybe a couple of minutes."

That was a stock answer that witnesses gave when they were uncertain about time. "Why don't you look at the clock on the wall, Blanca? Use the second hand to count out two minutes for me."

Within thirty-five seconds, Blanca spoke up. "That's way too long already. So maybe I meant seconds. It wasn't a couple of minutes. Five seconds, ten seconds? That's how long he touched my breast."

"I don't want you guessing, Blanca, like you did the first time you answered and said 'a couple of minutes.' Guessing doesn't help either of us."

"It's not a guess. It was seconds—maybe ten—but no more than that."

That made much more sense. "Then what did he do?"

"He grabbed me and he—"

"What part of you did he grab?"

She gave me an empty stare.

"Can you show me?"

Blanca Robles stopped to think about it. I flipped through the case folder for the medical records. The body chart prepared at the hospital showed no finger marks on her wrists or forearms.

"I'm not exactly sure. Maybe he just pushed me."

"Did he push you? Or did he grab you?" I asked. "Do you understand the difference between the meaning of those two words?"

"Yes, I understand," she said, closing her eyes to re-think it. "Pushed. The man pushed me."

"So, you don't think he held on to you with his hand?"

"I'm not remembering that so good. I think he just got behind me and pushed."

Lem Howell would have a field day with the visual of getting Blanca Robles from the hallway onto the bed. I looked to Mercer for backup, but he signaled me to ease up on the witness.

Ellen Gunsher picked up the narrative and got through the entire crime. The encounter lasted less than twenty minutes from the time Blanca entered the room—a good sign that it was not likely a consensual affair—but still leaving many points that needed to be firmed up before eliciting her sworn testimony.

How did he get her from the bedroom to the bathroom and onto her knees? If he held her down with one or both of his hands, what was she doing with her hands? And—the argument that Lem would undoubtedly tease the jury with—why didn't she bite him when she had the opportunity to end the attack?

There might be perfectly logical answers to these questions, but Ellen hadn't coaxed them out of her witness yet, and I wanted to know them before Blanca took an oath to tell the truth to the grand jury.

"Now, there's something you said yesterday, Blanca, that we have to go over again. You explained to me, just like you told Detective Wallace on Sunday, that you left the room before Mr. Gil-Darsin did, isn't that right?"

Blanca's thick eyebrows met over her nose as she frowned at Ellen Gunsher. "I did."

"And you told us that you hid yourself at the far end of the twenty-eighth-floor hallway until you saw him leave the room and get on the elevator, right?"

Blanca eyed Ellen distrustfully. "So?"

"Well, one of the detectives talked with a guest from that floor who checked out just two minutes before Gil-Darsin. He was in the room opposite the place you said you were hiding," Ellen said, pointing to the diagram. "And he says there was no one there—no one in the hallway at all when he left his room. Now, he could be wrong—"

"No, no, no," Blanca said, moving forward in her chair and waving her right hand back and forth. "What I told you? I made a mistake. I was very, very nervous and what I told you is a mistake."

The expression on Ellen's face froze. She stared at Blanca and then continued. "So you were mistaken on Sunday, when you talked with the detectives?"

"Yes. I've been wanting to correct that with you today."

"And you were mistaken again yesterday when you told all of us the same thing? When did you first realize you had misspoken?"

"I knew it yesterday," she said, crying again and wringing the handkerchief she took out of her bag. "But I thought you'd get mad at me if I changed my story. I don't want you to be mad at me, okay?"

Mercer moved his chair closer to Blanca Robles. "Nobody's going to be mad at you for what you tell us, so long as it's the truth."

"As God is my witness, Mr. Mercer, everything I'm telling you is the truth," she said, making the sign of the cross on her chest before stretching her arms out on the table and putting her head down. She sobbed as I watched her tears flow. "You believe that pig over me?"

"Calm down, Blanca. Everyone is with you here because we believe you. Do you remember what you did when you left the room after you were attacked? That's what we need to know," Mercer said.

"How about a fifteen-minute break? You'll feel better after that," Ellen said, standing up as she checked the time on her watch. "Maybe Laura can get some coffee ordered in."

This was the worst possible moment to give Blanca a

breathing spell. She had just been caught in a significant inconsistency about the moments after the crime occurred. She was on the ropes, and I wanted to keep her there to find out whether it was just a mistake occasioned by her trauma or an intentional lie.

"I'll ask Laura to call out an order as soon as we're finished here," I said. "Let's let Blanca explain what happened."

Blanca picked her head up from the table. "I'd really like some coffee, Miss Ellen."

"Right away," Ellen said, walking to the door and opening it. "Alex, you want to show her where the restroom is?"

"Sure."

Ellen stepped out and I shook my head at Mercer and Ryan.

"I bet you haven't even had a chance to meet with your priest yet, have you, Blanca?" I asked.

She wiped her tears with the tissue I handed to her.

"Not yet."

"What church do you go to?"

" 'Scuse me?"

"What's the name of your church?" I asked, walking to the row of windows that faced out on Centre Street, over the courthouse steps.

"Why you want to know?"

"Perhaps I can take you there for an hour or so at the end of the day," Mercer said. "It might help you to talk with your priest."

And perhaps I could get one of the answers Battaglia wanted, so he could go to work on the archdiocese to prove his bona fides. The crucifix, the comments relying on God as her witness, the religious gestures—Ellen was convinced of Blanca's credibility in some measure because of those things.

Blanca's eyebrows came together again as she tried to figure what Mercer really wanted. "I don't have time for no church."

"I don't make it there every Sunday either," Mercer said with a smile. "When's the last time you went? Maybe we can get you back. Maybe you'd like that."

She waved her right hand over her shoulder. *"Dios mío.* I haven't been to church since I left my country. I carry my religion here," she said, now patting her heart.

Mercer looked over at me and shrugged. So much for Ellen's reliance on the depth of Blanca's faith.

"That crucifix you're wearing," I said, "is very beautiful. Have you had that for a long time?"

"My boyfriend bought me this, before he left to go back to our country. He likes me to wear it 'cause he says it will keep other men away from me," Blanca said, fingering the handsome cross as she answered. "I guess it didn't bother so much this pig in the hotel room. I guess it didn't do me no good after—"

Her sentence was interrupted by the sound of two gunshots that rang out from the street eight floors below. They startled me, and I turned to look down at the crowd that had gathered on the sidewalk directly beneath our windows.

I glanced back to check on Blanca, who didn't even fidget while I trembled with fear that someone in our small universe at the courthouse—a cop, a lawyer, a court officer, a witness—had been hurt.

Mercer rushed toward me. "It's okay, Alex. It's—"

I looked down again to see someone staggering to get back on his feet, falling again as the man being wrestled to the ground by onlookers got off a final shot before the gun was kicked out of his hand.

Seventeen

"I bet you didn't get a chance to read your e-mails yesterday, did you?" Ryan asked, smiling at me as I watched the gunman and his victim brush off their clothes and reposition themselves in the crowd.

"Laura only printed out the ones related to this case."

"So you obviously didn't get the 'Please disregard the sounds of gunfire in front of 100 Centre Street between eleven a.m. and one p.m. on Tuesday. The crew of *Law and Order: SVU* will be filming here at that time.'"

The mayor had lured scores of movie and television companies back to New York because of the exorbitant fees they paid for the privilege of filming scenes on city streets. The blocks around the courthouse were frequently peopled by Detective Olivia Benson and her crew as they brought down perps and unsubs far faster than Mercer and I could ever work. And the "please disregard" messages about shootings, stabbings, car bombs, and police sirens had become as commonplace as Rose's reminders not to block the parking space reserved for Battaglia's car.

I turned to Blanca and laughed. "See? I'm more nervous than you are. That was just a scene for a television show, but I nearly jumped out of my own skin."

"It's a good thing you don't live in the projects like me, 'cause if you got scared every time you heard gunshots, you'd have a mental breakdown."

No doubt there was truth in what Blanca said, but in that moment she also demonstrated a *froideur*—a chilled aloofness—that would have served her well when confronted by the naked Ivorian in his hotel room.

"Would you like to use the ladies' room?" I asked.

"Yes, please."

"Come along with me."

I stopped at Laura's desk and asked her to unlock the executive restroom for Blanca before she called out for coffee and snacks, while I reported to Battaglia. I continued on into the executive wing, stopping at Rose Malone's desk to get the morning report on the district attorney's mood as I delivered my updates.

"Good morning, Alex."

I could barely see Rose behind the stacks of papers she had set in front of her. "Hey, Rose. Have I come at a bad time?"

"The Boss went out to a meeting at the Federal Reserve. I figured I'd get some filing done. He's pretty chipper today. About to announce the indictment of a hedge fund guy in a case they sneaked out from under the feds."

Battaglia was always happy to bring down a big target, especially when stepping on the toes of a rival prosecutorial agency.

"I'm just reporting in on the MGD investigation."
Rose shifted to her computer to take notes. "First, the
complaining witness is in with us for the day—that's Ellen, Ryan, and Mercer along with me. Forget notifying
the archbishop for the time being—no organized religion—the crucifix is a prop and she's never been to
church since getting to America. Two, we got rid of Byron Peaser for the moment, but he's greedy for a big
score, and it's hard to know where he's pushing our vic.
Three, she lied about her movements after the assault.
Pressing her on that to see if it's trauma-related or intentional. And four, if you can push anyone at the State Department to get her asylum records unsealed, I'd really
like to see what she said on that application."

"I'll stick this under his nose the minute he's back."

I thanked her and went back to check with Laura
about my messages, which she handed to me. "There are
three about pending cases, which I forwarded to Catherine to answer for you. And a long one from Lem Howell, appealing to you on MGD's bail situation."

"Let me guess. Pat McKinney's being unreasonable,
unmovable, and un—?"

"Un-Cooper-like in his dealings with Mr. Triplicate.
Lem wants to hear from you," Laura said, chuckling as
she balled up the paper and threw it away.

"Did Blanca say anything to you?"

"No. I let her into the restroom, then came back here
to wait for her. She did ask to use your phone."

Laura did better overheards than most detectives. "So
who'd she call?"

"First one was Byron Peaser. She told him that she'd
lied about something and you were unhappy with her.
Then she asked me how to make a long-distance call. I

connected her to the operator and she had a conversation in Spanish with someone. Sorry, couldn't get that."

I flipped through the phone messages and checked my watch for the time. "Nothing personal for me?"

"Two of your girlfriends. I'm not supposed to tell you, but birthday plans are afoot, Alex."

"Can you subtly get the word out to skip the festivities?" I asked. "I'm not being crabby, Laura. I simply won't have the time."

"Understood."

"No calls from Luc?"

Laura shook her head. I was churning inside, worried that the Brooklyn detectives had reached him and shut him down about calling me.

Mercer, Ellen, Ryan, and Blanca had regrouped in the conference room.

"Coffee will be here any minute," I said.

"Then let me pick up where we left off," Ellen said.

"I have a few questions before you do. Blanca," I asked, "who did you call from my office?"

"'Scuse me?"

"You used my phone just now to make some calls. Who'd you talk to?"

"*Dios mío*. My daughter, okay? I called my daughter."

"I see. And that's all?"

"Yeah. Something wrong with that?"

"Not at all. She's in the place Mr. Peaser moved you to, right?"

"Yeah."

"You called him first, didn't you?"

"Don't I got no privacy rights?" Blanca was in a huff.

"Not in a government office you don't. And the long-distance call, who was that to?"

She leaned back in her chair and closed her eyes.

"The truth, Blanca," Mercer said, trying to keep her steady and calm. "That's all she needs to hear. Remember that the switchboard will have the number that you called."

She bit her lip as she opened her eyes to speak. "My boyfriend, okay. I wanted to talk to my boyfriend. Can you understand that?"

"I certainly can." She had no idea how sincere my response to her was on that point.

"He's home in Guatemala, isn't he?" Ellen asked, looking down at her notepad. "Hector Escobar. You told me Hector went back to your village because his sister was dying."

Blanca leaned forward, rocking her body back and forth, her feet planted firmly in front of her.

"That was true, what I said."

"But there are no phones in the village, so how were you calling him?"

"That was true about last year, Ms. Ellen."

"You mean it was true that he went home to help his sister last year?" Ellen asked.

Blanca had shut me out, trying to convince Ellen that she had been candid in the earlier sessions.

I stood up beside Ellen and pounded my forefinger on the table. "Today, Blanca. Right this very minute, where is Hector Escobar?"

Blanca wasn't talking to me. "I never wanted to lie, Ms. Ellen. But I need you to believe me."

"Mercer," I said, still glowering at Blanca, "would you please go down to the seventh-floor switchboard room and get the number that Blanca called? Try dialing it yourself, will you?"

Blanca had prostrated herself on the conference table again, this time without crossing herself. The tears flowed as readily as the lies. "Hector's in prison, okay? Federal prison. Arizona."

"Charged with what?" I asked.

"Some kind of scam. Like credit cards. I don't know 'xactly, but he's been away for seven months."

Illegal scams. Large enough to get the attention of the feds. "Scam" was the last word we needed connected to a woman who would be accused by the defense of trying to scam the future presidential candidate of the Republic of the Ivory Coast.

"And you wanted that break twenty minutes ago because you knew exactly what time Hector has phone privileges, didn't you?"

Another penalty flag on the field for Blanca Robles. I pictured Lem practicing his bail argument in front of a mirror—watching the rhymes roll off his lips—barely able to stop at his customary three. Scam, sham, flim-flam. Damn.

Without picking her head up from the table, Blanca appealed to Mercer. "I don't want this lady in here with me anymore. She's very mean."

Mercer pulled his chair up beside her. "Alex is doing her job, Blanca. We can help you only if you tell us the truth."

"But I *am* telling you the truth about how this man attacked me. That got nothing to do with Hector and his problems."

"I'd like you to sit up and look at me, Blanca," I said. She continued to ignore me.

"You listen to Alex," Mercer said, and she lifted her head from the table.

"You're here because everyone on this team believes you and believes what you told us about your attacker."

"Then why do you keep talking about my lies? They don't have anything to do with my case."

"They have everything to do with your case, Blanca. Because the most important evidence we have is *you*. You and your word. Only two people were in that hotel room, and only one of them is telling the truth about what happened. Gil-Darsin has a lawyer—an extremely good lawyer. When he questions you at the trial—"

"You just said he won't be there."

"This week is the grand jury, not the trial. In several months, when there is a trial, his lawyer will get to question you in detail. He'll take the twenty minutes in that hotel room and he'll keep you on the witness stand asking you questions about it for hours, maybe for days. Ellen explained this to you yesterday, didn't she?"

Blanca took several deep breaths while I talked.

"I didn't get that far," Ellen said.

"The lawyer will be allowed to ask you about every action in the hotel room. And Gil-Darsin will feed him his own version of events, too."

"But they won't be true! That man is disgusting. He'll say anything to get out of this."

"Probably so, Blanca. But his lawyer can also ask you questions about other things in your life. His lawyer will claim you'll say anything to earn yourself twenty million dollars, or whatever amount you sue him for. Maybe the judge will let him ask about your boyfriend."

"Why? I didn't go to jail. Hector did."

"Well, was he living with you when he was arrested? Did the federal agents question you? Did Hector put any of the stolen money in your name?"

Both Blanca and Ellen were unhappy.

"Not ready to tell me? A subpoena will get me all the answers I need," I said. "Did you know, Blanca, that your phone call to Hector was taped today?"

I thought fire was going to come out of her mouth when she opened it. "I can't believe you would do that to me, Ms. Alex. I want Mr. Peaser here."

"We didn't do that to you. Every call to a federal prisoner—except when he's talking to his lawyer—is taped by the prison authorities. We can find out everything you've said to Hector since you were assaulted. Every word."

The angry woman slumped back in her chair.

"How about your application to the U.S. government for asylum, Blanca? Did you tell the truth to them, when you were under oath?"

"Of course I did," she said, slamming both hands on the table.

"You're sure about that? 'Cause if you did, you'd be the first witness I've ever worked with who did."

"What do you mean?"

"I mean that I know the circumstances that made you leave your home. They're detailed in the police reports. I know how you and your family were tortured and mistreated, and how justly you deserved asylum in this country."

"So why should I lie about that?" She raised her head, thrusting her chin at me, besting me with her life's tragedy.

"Because just about every person who comes here for asylum, no matter how good the reason, tries to make his or her story a little bit worse. Everyone knows that his neighbors and his relatives and his friends are looking for

exactly the same thing, and so each one tries to embellish—"

"Embellish? What this means?"

"Exaggerates, Blanca. Each one tends to exaggerate
just a little bit, to get an advantage over the next person.
It's not a great big lie, because the Truth Commission
did terrible things to your people. We know that happened. But suppose I came from your village, and suppose my cousin was applying for asylum, too. We were
both raped by the soldiers, let's say. And our fathers were
made to disappear. She knows half the town is looking to
escape just like we are, so she tells the Americans that her
brother was killed, too, and that all her animals were
slaughtered. Not true—she didn't even have a brother—
but all the rest of what she said can be verified, so she
takes the chance on these facts. I want to leave the village
just as much as she does, so when I hear what testimony
she gave, I exaggerate my own story. I say both my sisters
were killed and—"

"I had no need to do that, Ms. Alex," Blanca said,
lowering her voice and her head. "The worst things happened to me. Worse than anybody's life. I told Detective
Mercer all of them."

I spoke softly, respecting the atrocities she had survived. "And they are exactly the same things you told the
government lawyers, under oath?"

"Yes, ma'am."

"So, when the State Department releases a copy of
your affidavit to me—"

"When is that?"

"Maybe by Monday, maybe earlier. When I get
those papers, there won't be any surprises for Mercer
and for me?"

Blanca's arm darted across the table and swept Ellen's notepad and pen into the air, so that they landed on the floor with a thud. "Those papers are sealed up, no? What do those papers have to do with my getting raped the other day? Are you crazy?" Her anger was on full display. "What happened to me in my country don't have nothing to do with this man. This Gil-Darsin man."

"Listen to me, Blanca. If you think you've seen my temper yet, I can promise you that you have not. I don't care if you exaggerated to get asylum here. You wouldn't be the first person to do that. I don't care if you lied about Hector because you were afraid we'd think badly of you because you have a boyfriend in prison. But the judge *will* care about those things, and so will the jury. And the judge is allowed to tell the jurors that if you have lied to them, they can either disregard the lies and convict this man for what you tell them happened to you when you walked into his hotel room, or—"

"That's what I want them to do. To—how you call it?—to disregard these other things."

"Or the judge can tell them that because you lied about other things—things that have nothing to do with Mr. Gil-Darsin—they don't have to trust you at all. They can throw out your entire case because you've lied to so many people—even under oath to the government. Do you understand me? Do you understand how important it is for you to tell the truth?"

Blanca Robles was not only angry. She was stubborn, too. Large teardrops formed in each of her eyes and clung to her lower lids for seconds, before rolling down her cheeks. They were the first sincere tears I thought I had seen today. She stared straight ahead and refused to answer.

"You get what Alex is telling you, Blanca?" Mercer asked. "She's giving you another chance. She wants you to start all over again from the beginning, in your own words. It doesn't matter what you told me and Ellen and the other cops on Sunday and yesterday. It doesn't matter what you told Mr. Peaser. You've got answers for everything, including why you went into that other room in the hallway after you were attacked. You've just got to give us every one of those answers truthfully—not what you think we want to hear. That's the only way this team can take you into the courtroom. You good with that?"

Blanca Robles slowly nodded her head. "I'll talk to you, Detective Mercer, and to Ms. Ellen. But I don't like you," she said, pointing a finger at me.

"Then pretend I'm the judge," I said. "Ellen will ask the questions and I'll just listen."

There was a knock on the door. I stood up to open it. Laura was there with the delivery order, which would make for a good late-morning break.

She put the cardboard box in the middle of the table and Mercer started to pass the coffee around.

Laura motioned me to follow her. I stepped outside the room. "Any calls?"

It was almost six p.m. in Mougins, and now Luc would be about to start the dinner service at the restaurant. If he hadn't phoned yet, it would be hours before he would be free again.

"Nothing you're hoping for. But you've got a visitor, Alex. Lem Howell's here, and he says he's not leaving until he talks to you."

Eighteen

"Alexandra Cooper," Lem said, smoothing his pomaded hair as he watched me approach him down the long corridor. "I can always gauge your level of excitement about seeing me by the pacing of the click of your heels on the tiled floor. And I would say that you are either delighted by my unexpected appearance, or I have gotten your very easy-to-get goat by showing up here today."

"It's the goat thing, Lem. I'll walk you to the elevator."

"What did I teach you about keeping your cool, young lady?"

"If I ever had cool under your watch, I lost it to global warming. About face, sir."

I didn't break stride until I had passed Lem and made the right turn to the elevator bank. He followed after me, linking his arm in mine when he caught up to me. I brushed him off.

"On closer examination, Alexandra, I'd say you look jet-lagged, harried, and maybe even a wee bit heartbroken."

"You usually do better than one for three. Yes, I am jet-lagged and extremely tired. I'll even give you half-credit for harried. But who's feeding you the heartbroken line, Lem? I thought you'd be delighted to know that I'm madly in love."

"Well, you are keeping that factoid well hidden beneath those large circles under your sweet green eyes. My mama would be encouraging you to put some tea bags on them to reduce the swelling. The tannin in the tea calms it right down, soothes the skin, and—"

"Who's spreading the heartbroken story?"

"I'm just saying you did that round-trip elopement to France in record time. Did they take the Concorde out of mothballs to get you back here? It can't be you flew home for this loser of a case, so I'm thinking you and Luc had a spat."

"Think harder next time," I said, reaching out to press the down button. Of course—Baby Mo had been an occasional guest at Luc's restaurant. Doubtless he knew people in Mougins, and Lem must have told him I spent time in that part of the world. I needed to tell Battaglia about that remote connection before the news reached him some other way.

"Let's talk about Mr. Gil-Darsin," Lem said.

"Call me."

Lem didn't budge. "Now's the perfect time."

"You know I'm busy. And I know the reason you wormed your way in here is to try to eyeball the accuser. Cheap trick, Lem."

The elevator doors opened and three young assistants stepped off with their files, headed down the wide corridor to the Appeals Bureau offices.

"I hear she's a sturdy girl, Alexandra. Not so easy to push around."

The doors closed and my adversary still hadn't moved, so I pressed the button again.

"Save it for the jury, Lem. What's the bail situation you wanted to discuss?"

"Your office went overboard, asking for Gil-Darsin to be remanded without bail. This isn't a homicide."

"No, Lem, it's a rape. Or as you said to the court, it's '*only*' a rape. He's facing twenty-five years and he lives in a country that refuses to extradite rapists to America." I paused to look at Lem. "You want to tell me what your client says about how his DNA wound up on the floor of the hotel room? Oh yeah, and on this woman's uniform?"

"I don't want to say anything right now."

"This is a rare moment indeed. Lem Howell with nothing to say. I thought for sure you'd go with a love story, Lem. That is so your style. Housekeeper walks into the room. Ivorian diplomat is taken by her earthy good looks and, wait now—a triplicate—the sadness, the horror, the despair she carries everywhere with her in those deep pools of brown eyes. They bond instantly—or wait, maybe she was even the aggressor. Of course she's the aggressor—she's bigger than he is. And after all, he wasn't even sated by the lover who left his room at two p.m."

Now I had Lem's full attention.

"The lover?"

"Yes, Lem. We know about her. The girlfriend. The hotel says she's a regular whenever Gil-Darsin is in town. A Frenchwoman living in New York, working at an investment bank. She's on all the surveillance tapes. We'll have her name shortly."

He took a step toward me, so that we were standing nose-to-nose, and took hold of my wrist with his right hand.

"One thing you've always had is perspective, Alexandra. Don't lose it here."

"Was it about money, Lem? You haven't tried that one yet. Going for that hooker approach?" I said, with a laugh. "Maybe he ordered up a prostitute dressed as a French maid and got confused when the housekeeper came to the door."

"You'll never get past the grand jury, Alexandra. You don't begin to know what problems Blanca Robles has."

"I was working for you eight years ago when you assigned me the case of the nun who was raped in her convent uptown. But for that young woman, Lem, every witness who ever walked through those doors has problems."

"Not like this."

"Crazy women get raped, too, remember? The patient in the psych ward at Met Hospital? You were the first person to take her seriously. Liars and prostitutes and junkies and full-on whack jobs are victims, too. They cart all their baggage into this office with them and we sort through it till we find the truth."

"Blanca lives on the margins. She'll play you for a fool if she sucks you in. She's been doing that all her life. Talk to her neighbors, talk to—"

"What happened to the high road, Lem? You always insisted to the young lawyers you trained that we take the high road, and there you go, ferreting around in the gutter for all the garbage you can find."

I tried to wriggle my wrist free of Lem's grasp, but he was holding me tight.

"Screw the high road, Alexandra. You're going to look like a chump when the smoke clears. Be more reasonable. Come up with a price tag for bail and I'll surrender my client's passport until you sort this out."

"And an ankle bracelet for good measure?"

"Shame on you. Think of that image, young lady. A black man out of Africa in shackles? It's a vulgar image. It likens my client to a slave. I say the passport and a hunk of change."

"You're not giving me anything to work with, Lem. Are you just going to stand on the courthouse steps and throw enough dirt at Blanca until she backs off? Put a lock on Baby Mo's zipper so he saves some for his wife?"

The elevator doors opened again and Pat McKinney practically walked into me. "Slow dancing in the hallway between calendar calls, Mr. Howell? I'd prefer my assistants take a more professional approach to plea negotiations."

Lem dropped my arm. "I was giving Alexandra a hard time. You're familiar with that tactic, Pat, aren't you?" He glided onto the elevator as swiftly as though he'd been waiting for its arrival. "See you in court, Ms. Cooper. Don't forget those tea bags."

Nineteen

I tried to catch up with McKinney as he headed around the corner toward the conference room. "Where are you going?"

"Ellen called. She says you're making Blanca flip out. She wants some help."

"Look, Pat. That's how Mercer and I work. We've got to clean up the stuff that's extraneous to the case so it doesn't compromise what she's going to testify to under oath in the grand jury. She'll settle back down. You can't have her lie tomorrow and then double back on it when she's being prepped for trial."

McKinney stopped short of the conference room door and put his hands on his hips. "You let Lem be all up in your face like that time after time. Did you at least get anything out of it?"

"Nothing. But about Blanca—"

"As far as I'm concerned, Alex, you could have taken a rowboat back from France and we'd still be in the same position on this case without what the district attorney refers to as your expertise. I'll be sitting in for the next few hours. It's kid gloves in regard to Blanca from this point on, you get that?"

He opened the door and Ellen Gunsher couldn't conceal her pleasure at seeing him. Blanca and Mercer were drinking coffee and snacking on something. They hadn't resumed working in the ten minutes I was out of the room.

McKinney picked up my pad and pen and moved my things to the far corner of the table, out of Blanca's direct line of sight. He let Mercer remain beside her, and he set himself up next to Ellen.

"Here's what we're going to do, Blanca," Pat said. "Ellen will be the one asking the questions, today and in the grand jury. The detective and I may have some additional things we'd like to know, but it will be mostly Ellen, and it will be only about what happened when you went into Mr. Gil-Darsin's room to clean it. Are you okay with that?"

"What about her?" Blanca tilted her head in my direction without making eye contact with me.

"Alex is here as an observer. That's all. We want you to be comfortable."

Blanca looked at me head-on and smiled. I may have aggravated her for the first hour, but she knew she had won the second round.

"Remember what I just told you," Mercer said. "All the words have to come from you. We can't suggest them to you. We can't change them. Nobody's here to judge what you said or what you did, we just want the truth."

So there had clearly been discussion advising Ellen not to put words in the accuser's mouth. Maybe that would help this time.

"I want you to tell us everything that happened from the minute you showed up at the hotel for work on Saturday," Ellen said. "In as much detail as you remember."

"I don't have to talk about my boyfriend? Or how I got asylum?"

"No, you don't. Just about Saturday."

Blanca Robles began with the time she arrived at the Eurotel to start her workday. The time clock backed up her arrival, and video captured her in the neat uniform in which she began her rounds. In the two hours that followed, we got an exquisitely detailed version of the day's events, now including an entry into the room adjacent to MGD's before she was summoned to clean his suite.

I made notes about slight inconsistencies—what most prosecutors liked to call the hallmarks of truth—and areas of inquiry for Ellen to consider.

We took another break at two p.m., when we were working Blanca Robles hard through the occurrence of the assault. Then while everyone stretched and left the room to freshen up, I retreated to my office and closed the door.

I'd had no calls from either Luc or Mike, and I was uneasy about being kept completely in the dark. I couldn't think of any reason not to call the restaurant to see what Luc was up to. Surely the Brooklyn homicide detectives would have contacted him by this time.

I used my cell phone to dial Le Relais, and waited for the hostess to answer. When she did, I counted on the crackling noise in the connection to make my voice indistinguishable from any other American calling to speak with Luc.

"Good evening. Is Monsieur Rouget there?"

"No, *madame*. He's not here at the moment."

Eight o'clock in Mougins was the height of the dinner service, and his absence would have been remarkable.

"Has he gone home?"

"No, *madame*. Monsieur Rouget didn't come to the restaurant this evening. I haven't seen him today."

"*Merci*, mademoiselle. Thank you very much."

"Is there any message?"

"No, thank you."

I hung up and dialed Luc's house. After five rings, I put down my phone.

There was a knock on the door and Mercer let himself in. "You ready to finish up with Blanca?"

"Sure."

"Let's get her through this one, beginning to end. Then you and I can make a punch list of what we need to run down."

"Have you heard from Mike?"

"Nah. He must be sleeping off last night's job."

"Did he tell you?" I rubbed my eyes and looked at the floor.

"About the matchbox? Yes, he did, Alex. Just stay focused on what we're doing here. Don't tie yourself up in knots over this."

"You think Blanca's telling the truth?" I asked.

"It's not her strong suit. But she's holding her own on the twenty minutes in the hotel room. Nothing shakes her off that story. And the DNA doesn't lie. We know there was a sexual encounter, and so far Blanca's the only story in town. C'mon back in, Alex. We'll wind this down shortly."

Everyone settled in around the table again when Mercer and I got to the conference room. Blanca had reached the part of the narrative where she retracted her original statement about cowering in the hallway as she waited for MGD to leave. Instead, she returned to the adjacent suite where she had left some of her cleaning equipment, as the computerized record of the swipe of her key card would ultimately confirm. Minutes later, confident that her assailant had departed, she reentered his suite.

Ellen wasn't bothered by that fact, but Mercer didn't like it any better than I did.

"Why did you go back into his room?" he asked, as gently and non-accusatorily as he could.

Blanca was silent.

"I mean, weren't you afraid he might still be in there?"

Most victims would go to any extreme not to be confronted by their rapist again.

"He was in a hurry to leave. I knew that."

"But suppose he'd forgotten his phone, say, or his briefcase, and returned to get it. Didn't that possibility frighten you?"

Blanca cocked her head but didn't answer.

"Did you touch anything in the room?" he asked.

Blanca had reentered the crime scene before reporting the attack. It was impossible to know whether she had compromised any of the physical evidence, intentionally or not.

She hesitated before answering. "No, I didn't touch anything. It made me sick to see the bed where he attacked me. I just looked around and then I left."

"There are two bathrooms in the suite, Blanca," I said. "Did you go into either of those, to see whether they needed to be cleaned?"

She shook her head from side to side. "I told the police no. I never went into either one of them."

So she went in for the express purpose of changing the

linens—sheets and towels—but now says she didn't do that. In his softest voice, Mercer asked, "Did he leave any money for you—like a tip—on the dresser or night table?"

That idea had not even occurred to me. What if the exchange had been sex for money, and Gil-Darsin had promised to leave cash in the room? That would be a strong motivator for Blanca to return, and a reason for her to get back at him by crying "rape" if he had skipped out without paying.

"Are you accusing me of taking money, Detective Mercer? Is that what you think? I'm telling you again this isn't about the money," Blanca said, working herself into a real huff.

"I was talking about a tip, Blanca, for your housekeeping services."

"And one more thing—and I don't mean no offense to you personally, Detective, but this is 'xactly how I feel. Nobody—*nobody*—could pay me enough to put my lips on a black man. You understand me?"

Everyone around the table froze. Class, power dynamics, and international politics were all in the mix— and Blanca Robles had just thrown in a wild card that would offend almost every juror in Manhattan.

"Blanca—we need to talk about this," Pat said.

There was a knock on the door and Laura poked her head in the room. "Mickey Diamond just called from the courthouse steps," she said, referring to the veteran crime reporter for the *New York Post*. "He wants to know if Battaglia will comment about the four o'clock press conference."

"What conference?" Pat McKinney asked as Mercer walked to the window and looked down.

"*Law and Order* filming downstairs again?" I asked.

"This time it's a reality show," Laura said. "It's called *The Evening News.*"

"What now?"

"Mickey says Byron Peaser's taking center stage any minute. He's waiting for Ms. Robles to come down."

Blanca rose to her feet, picked up her purse, and gave us all a very self-satisfied smile.

Pat McKinney reached out his arm toward Blanca. "What's this about? We've done everything possible to protect your identity and keep the wolves away from your door. You're not appearing at any press conference, no matter who's calling the shots."

"Peaser's filed his lawsuit against Gil-Darsin," Laura said. "Fifty million dollars."

"*What?*" McKinney was practically screaming. "Before we go to the grand jury?"

"Blanca called Peaser from my office this morning," I said. "She told him we'd caught her in some lies. This is a stunt to hold Battaglia's toes to the fire, to keep the pressure on him to get an indictment sooner rather than later."

"I don't want you out there with him, Blanca. There's no reason for you to go public at this point. Do you understand me?" McKinney said.

"Mr. Peaser's my lawyer, Mr. Pat. He believes in me," she said, scanning the room as she stared each one of us in the eye. "He's the only one looking out for my good."

Twenty

Pat McKinney came back from Battaglia's office in less than ten minutes. "I can't get an audience. He's in with the rackets guys gearing up to release the hedge fund story."

"So what's the plan?" Mercer asked.

"Let's all be available to brainstorm with him at nine a.m. tomorrow. Answer all his questions, and take Blanca into the grand jury in the afternoon."

"You think she'll come back?"

"He's got to bring her in. She's his meal ticket. I agree with Alex that he's just grandstanding to push us forward."

"We could slow this down," I said. "Take a week or two to make sure we have all the documents we need to support Blanca's story. Baby Mo can obviously make substantial bail—even a million or more—and we take his passport away. Where's he going?"

McKinney's head whipped in my direction. "Lem gets

his hands on you for five minutes and you roll over like a spineless jellyfish."

"It's got nothing to do with Lem."

"How did Papa Mo escape the revolution in the Ivory Coast? Somebody did him the courtesy of sending a private jet, and he's never looked back yet. Any fifteen-year-old can buy a passport in Times Square, and our perp is airborne over the Atlantic. The press would crucify Battaglia if MGD skipped town."

"I hear you," Mercer said. "Nine tomorrow."

"I'll call Peaser myself," McKinney said. "You got the first outcry witness locked in?"

We were all walking out of the conference room.

"Yes," Mercer said, referring to Blanca's colleague from room service, who was the first person she asked for help after the assault. "And the security team from the hotel who called 911. Everybody's on board."

Laura stepped into the hallway from her cubicle and motioned to me. I broke away as the group finished their conversation.

"I've got Mike on hold. Can you pick it up at your desk?"

I handed my files to Laura and ran for the phone. "What's up?"

"I thought I'd come in early today. Caught up on my sleep and I'm ready for a little action."

"What do you know about Luc?"

"Steady, girl. They've had one conversation with him, which I only know 'cause one of the guys in Brooklyn South owes me a few. Luc was very cooperative, very open with them. Don't get your nose all out of joint."

"Do you know where he is?"

"What? Now I've got to babysit your lover?"

"Sorry. I'm just rattled by all this and I don't like being cut off from him when he might need me most."

"You got a pair of jeans in the closet?"

"Always." We had all been called out to crime scenes and grimy station houses at the unlikeliest times, and could occasionally sneak off to Yankee Stadium for an afternoon game. "Where to?"

"Grunge up, Coop. Checking into the Adonis of the Gowanus before the sun sets. We're going fishing."

Twenty-one

"It stinks," I said.

Forty-five minutes later, in jeans and a baseball cap that covered half of my face from the curious eyes of the Harbor Unit cops, Mike and I were walking along the edge of the Gowanus Canal in Brooklyn.

"Kind of that dead-rat-on-a-wet-doormat stench, don't you think? You are so not an outer-boroughs girl, blondie, but it's good for your soul."

On the ride over the Brooklyn Bridge, I'd brought Mike up to speed on the difficult day with Blanca Robles. Mercer seemed glad that I was going off with Mike for whatever distraction that offered, and Mike tried to assuage my concerns about the homicide investigation involving the unidentified man floating in the canal last night.

"This place is an environmental disaster. How could it be good for anything?"

"You're on probation once you leave Manhattan. Don't piss off the locals."

The water in the canal was speckled with dark slimy spots. Aside from the usual city trash—broken bottles, used condoms, and empty syringes—there were dead crabs and tiny mollusks lodged in the algae along the canal walls.

"I thought you were off the case once the Homicide Squad picks it up in the morning."

"You wanted inside information, Coop, so I made myself indispensable."

I turned to Mike and threw my arms around his neck. "I'm so grateful to you. How'd you do it?"

"Unhook yourself, okay? I hate clingy."

We continued on the walkway that lined the rotting wooden bulkheads while Mike talked to me. Off to our side was row after row of deserted warehouses, and across the canal was a series of barges and boats secured to the shore.

"First of all, the autopsy result is in on Lisette Honfleur, the dead girl in Mougins."

"What does that have to do with anything?"

"Try the matchbox in her pocket, for starters."

"I meant to tell you about that this morning, but—"

"I may administer a little truth serum tonight, in the form of your favorite cocktail, to see what else you've held back. I just figured I ought to know if there were any similarities between that killing and my floating Adonis."

"Lisette's throat wasn't slit."

"Nope. But they've labeled it a homicide pending the toxicology results. The docs think she was pretty high—she's got a long history of drug abuse—tossed in the water by one or two people and held under till she stopped breathing."

"That's it?"

"I'm working off the tidbit that the autopsy revealed that she had a Bronx wallet."

"Filled with—?"

"Enough cocaine wrapped in little plastic baggies to snort her way to heaven with half the people in that quaint French village."

Some Bronx-based cop had come up with the catchy euphemism for the vaginal vaults of female drug mules who concealed contraband there because they knew that body cavity searches were terrifically unpopular with the courts.

"But your guy didn't have drugs on him."

"Like you said to me this morning, it's strange that he didn't have anything at all except the matchbox in his pocket. That's what someone wanted us to find. And that's what someone wanted us to link to Luc. So I called the team and suggested they use one of the unmanned submersible drones."

"The whats?"

"You heard me right. Drones. ROVs. Remote-operated vehicles."

"What happened to police scuba divers?"

"Hey, the only human ballsy enough to go into this creek is Katie Cion," he said, referring to our favorite Emergency Services detective. "Machines first."

"Katie would never say no to you." We were making our way around rusty oil barrels and corroding lengths of pipe. In the distance I could make out the blue-and-white coloring of two of Harbor's smaller power boats. "How does it work?"

"It's about so big," Mike said, holding his hands a foot apart. "The drone weighs sixteen pounds. It's got lights and sonar and a camera that's connected to the computer—which is manned on the boat—by an umbilical cord. Color video images get sent back to base. Mostly, the drones are used to sweep the harbor when there's a suspicious boat under a bridge or a floating package near the Statue of Liberty that might be carrying a bomb. It's primarily a counterterrorism thing."

"You think it can see anything in this muck?"

"Of course it can."

"What did you tell them to look for?" I asked.

Mike ran his fingers through his hair and gave me his best poker face. "They can look for anything they damn well please. I'm just trying to make myself relevant so we get a little feedback on where this investigation is going."

"Thanks for—"

"Park yourself on a barrel, Coop. Let me see what they're up to."

I sat down and scanned the horizon while Mike approached the Harbor team. I knew that some of the areas around the canal had been gentrified in the last five years, and that art galleries and coffeehouses and commercial properties had been installed. But this was one of the sorriest stretches of urban blight imaginable.

After a few minutes of conversation, Mike returned and sat beside me. "The drone is down, and so far, it's not a pretty sight. Just a lot of sludge, sort of like black mayonnaise."

"Why did you pick this area as the starting point?"

"The canal's a bit under two miles long. You got five east-west bridge crossings over it, but they're too well trafficked to have been the drop-off point. We know where the body was found, and it's more likely moving in this direction—toward Red Hook and away from Carroll

Gardens. It's rougher this way—fewer people, lots of deserted buildings, more barges in the water. The Harbor guys figure the tides and all that, put it together with the information we gave them, and they make the call where to look."

"They can't search the whole thing. It'll be dark in an hour."

"The drones don't know dark, Coop. It'll be fine."

"Why does it smell so awful here?"

"Take it back four centuries. Gowanus was the chief of the Canarsie Indian tribe that owned all the land around here—the western tip of Long Island. They sold the land to the Dutch—the earliest recorded property sale among settlers—for a tobacco plantation and mill. Close your eyes and imagine that this was all marshlands and creeks, full of fish and wildlife."

"And you know this because—?"

"August 27, 1776. The Battle of Brooklyn. First major battle of the American Revolution following the Declaration of Independence. The redcoats forced Washington's troops to retreat right across the Gowanus Creek. You're looking at history, kid."

"Military history, of course. Then how did it get to be so disgusting?"

"Like everything else that came with the other revolution—the industrial one. This spot was the hub of Brooklyn's navigational business. Some genius decided to drain the marshland and dredge the old creek—deepen it into a canal—so ships could cut right through here to Upper New York Bay." Mike was using his arms to explain the geography.

"For commercial reasons?"

"Exactly that. Next came the factories and ware-

houses, gas refineries and tanneries, chemical plants full
of pollutants—and all of the sewage flowed right down
into the canal. Raw sewage, Coop. That's what's blowing
up your nostrils."

A few quick shakes of my head did nothing to relieve
the horrible odor.

"C'mon. They'll give us a call if they come up with
anything. I'll buy you a drink."

I stood up and gave a last look in the direction of the
Harbor Unit crew. Two of the guys were leaning over the
sides of the boats, using pool skimmers to pluck things
out of the dark water. I turned away and walked with
Mike.

"This canal makes a pretty ideal dumping ground," I
said. "You wouldn't even smell a corpse decomposing."

"That's why the mob has used it for most of the last
century. Body parts submerged in suitcases, guns buried
deep in the mud, wiseguys shot up like Swiss cheese and
weighted down with bricks. Legend has it that Al Capone
did his first murder right here."

My head was somewhere else. Luc Rouget had nothing
to do with mobsters, and the elegance of his professional
lifestyle was the flip side of this dark urban cesspool. I expected he knew no more about its existence than I did.

"I learned another thing about the canal today," Mike
said.

"What's that?"

"In colonial times, the six-foot tides of the bay forced
saltwater into the creek. That gave it the perfect brackish
mix that bivalves thrive on. For Dutch farmers living in
Brooklyn in the seventeenth century, their largest export
item to Europe was Gowanus oysters. Four to six inches
long, sweet and succulent as they could be."

"Out of these waters? Now you're joking."

"I have it from an unimpeachable source," Mike said. "The detective who called Luc asked him if he'd ever heard of the Gowanus Canal, and Luc gave him the back-story on the oysters. Much as I wish he'd never heard of it, he knows all about this place."

Twenty-two

"I'll take you up on that drink," I said, putting the baseball cap on the car seat between us and shaking out my hair. "But can't I talk to Luc now? Can't I phone him?"

"Has he called you?"

"Not the entire day."

"Don't look so glum. He's trying to keep you at arm's length from trouble."

"I don't want to be at arm's length. I want to help him."

We had driven only three minutes from the canal when Mike braked the car and parked it on Conover Street.

"Here?" I asked, looking at the faded paint on the facade of the bar, sporting a yellow-and-red neon sign that said SUNNY'S. "We're drinking in Red Hook?"

"Don't turn your nose up at this joint. It's an institution. They've got a bar and I've got a crush on the barmaid, and they've got a TV and you've got a crush on

Brian Williams. Even Steven. See what the world is saying about Baby Mo and drown your French-fried sorrows at the same time."

"Is there a bar in this city that you don't know?" I asked, opening the car door.

"Mostly the ones your yuppified friends hang out in. I first came here with my old man, back when this hood was all longshoremen and wannabe wiseguys. Now that there's a fringe group of so-called artists who are threatening to make Red Hook chic, Sunny probably doesn't know what hit him."

Sunny himself greeted Mike inside the door and led us past the pack of thirtysomethings at the bar to a small table in the corner. Mike was out of luck—the bartender was a long, lean guy with spiky hair—and nobody was paying attention to the television screen. It looked like we had walked into a 1950s movie set, down to the Pabst Blue Ribbon stained glass lamps that decorated the small tabletops.

Mike walked to the bar, asked Sunny to flip the channel to NBC, and came back with our drinks.

"Cheers!" he said. "Here's to Gowanus Canal oysters. Maybe Luc just knows about them 'cause they were such powerful aphrodisiacs."

"Talk about something else, will you?" I lifted the glass so that I could get the stench of the canal out of my brain.

"Food, sex, history. I've exhausted my repertoire. I'm done."

The local news ended and the commercials were a lead-in to Brian Williams. His first story was about a car bomb in Afghanistan, and the second was a long piece on a kidnapping off the coast of Somalia.

"This is good for Battaglia," I said. "We're not the top story tonight. He'll be criticized for whatever decision he makes in the morning—grand jury this week or not. Every reporter thinks he or she's got the inside track on how a case like this ought to be handled; only none of them has ever been in the hot seat with a witness who's under a magnifying glass."

"Yeah, well, I'm the guy who took Mo off the plane, so try and make me look good at the end of the road."

"You absolutely had to do that, Mike."

"But that started the clock running for Battaglia. You could have vetted everything she said before we cuffed him, if he wasn't sitting on the runway, headed for home. That's what you usually do."

"Blanca is so good at storytelling I don't know what to think. One minute, she's got you all balled up when she talks about the massacres in Guatemala, and in the next breath she's so facile at lying you just want to tear your hair out."

"And when we return," Williams said, "we'll have the latest on the MGD scandal that has garnered worldwide attention for the powerful World Economic Bureau leader."

I stood up to walk to the bar, to better hear the television. "For once, Brian may be wrong. I think I've got the latest."

"What's that?" Mike asked as he followed me.

"Blanca's last shot of the day was to tell us she doesn't 'do' black men. Can you imagine me summing up on that point? That she couldn't possibly have consented to Baby Mo's advances because she's a racist?"

Mike gave me his best grin. "I can see the defense case coming. Forget the jism all over the floor and wall and on her uniform. Lem Howell just shows up with ten of his blackest brothers to swear they've been done by Blanca. No contest."

When Brian Williams returned, he introduced the local reporter who covered the courthouse, and the visual was Byron Peaser standing at a microphone on the steps of 100 Centre Street, with Blanca Robles at his side.

"For the first time today, Brian," the reporter said, "the world gets to see the woman who has accused Gil-Darsin of this violent sexual attack."

"I can't believe she actually did that," I said. "When I left, Pat McKinney was giving her a pretty stern admonition about going public before she testified. And now she's defied him."

"So much for all the safeguards of her privacy and security that everyone was concerned about."

"Ms. Robles," the reporter went on, "was introduced by the lawyer who filed a civil suit on her behalf today, seeking fifty million dollars from Gil-Darsin, whose political ambitions now seem to be derailed. She spoke only seven words from the podium, Brian, telling us emphatically: 'I am the victim. I was raped.'"

"Thank you for that update," Williams went on. "It certainly sounds like her lawyer is taking a stab at getting the court of public opinion on her side. Gil-Darsin, of course, is still on Rikers Island and still hasn't issued any statement, anticipating his next appearance before a judge later this week."

"Okay if I shut Brian down?" Mike asked.

I nodded, grabbing a bowl of peanuts from the bar counter and returning to our table.

"Are you hanging out with me until you start your

tour tonight?" I asked. "Afraid I'm going to burn up the phone lines to France?"

"I'm hanging out with you because I think you're in overdrive and need a little adult supervision. And besides, the next show after this is *Jeopardy!*"

I was cracking the peanut shells with my teeth.

"Don't break any bicuspids," Mike said. "I get lucky and win tonight, I may buy you a real meal."

"I'll settle for a second round, as long as you're buying."

My elbow was on the table, my head in my hand, as I gave Mike all the details of today's interview. He kept one eye on the TV screen, and when Alex Trebek announced the Final Jeopardy! category, he walked over to turn up the volume and then came back to me.

"Famous Misnomers," Trebek read the large letters on the single blue square to the three contestants. "Famous Misnomers is tonight's category."

Mike opened his wallet and took out a twenty, our usual wager. "This could be tricky."

Two contestants were neck and neck with about eight thousand dollars each. The third one had less than one thousand.

"Don't worry," I said. "I'm in. My money's in the car."

Trebek read the answer as it was revealed on the screen. "The Rembrandt painting actually named *The Company of Frans Banning Cocq and Willem van Ruytenburch* is mistakenly called this."

The two women contestants both looked as stumped as Mike, but the guy tied for the lead put his head down and started to write a question.

194

LINDA FAIRSTEIN

"Total fraud," Mike said. "They should have said the category was art. This one has your Wellesley art history bullshit all over it."

I laughed for the first time in hours. "Double or nothing?"

"Hardly."

I sipped on the second Scotch. "What is *The Night Watch*?"

"*Night Watch*? Like my duty assignment?"

As Trebek was congratulating the man with the correct answer, an image of the colossal painting flashed on the screen.

"These are the citizens who defended the ramparts of Amsterdam—but the painting actually depicts them in daytime, off duty. It was just so dark a canvas that it was given the wrong name for centuries. It wasn't night, and they weren't on their watch."

"I'm glad you're enjoying the peanuts because that may be all you get tonight," Mike said as I picked up his twenty-dollar bill and pocketed it.

We were almost done with our drinks when Mike's phone rang. He put a finger in his left ear to block out the noise and held the phone to his right one.

"Chapman here."

He listened to the caller for more than a minute. Then he responded. "Yeah, I can do you that favor. I know the place. I can head over there before I sign in. Call you back."

"What?" I asked.

"I always hate it when my vic turns out to have a better name than the one I gave him."

"You mean Adonis of the Gowanus isn't Adonis anymore? They've ID'd him?"

"Luigi Calamari," Mike said. "Louie the Squid. No wonder he winds up dead in the most toxic waterway in the world."

"How did they make him?"

"Three distinctive tats on his back. He's in the NYPD computer system. Got locked up once for gun possession. They found his brother this afternoon, who just ID'd him."

"Thank God he's not French," I said, leaning back in my chair, relieved that there wasn't an obvious connection to Luc.

"That's the good news."

"Is there something bad?"

"He's a waiter, Coop."

"There's a million waiters in this town."

"He was just fired from one of the most exclusive restaurants in the city 'cause he has a problem sniffing white powder."

"So?"

"His brother says he didn't care about losing his job. He'd already lined up another one at a swanky new place called Lutèce."

Twenty-three

We were in Mike's car, headed back to Manhattan, and I was arguing with him because my anxiety had been ratcheted up another few notches.

"It's not possible, Mike. You don't understand the restaurant business. Luc would never hire an Italian to be a waiter."

"Doesn't that smack of Blanca not putting out for black men? Listen to yourself, Coop."

"That's not what I mean. Go to any of the great French restaurants. La Grenouille, Le Bernardin, Daniel—"

"I can't afford to."

"They're all staffed by Frenchmen. And I do mean men—you rarely ever find a woman working in them. And French for the language, the ambience—the chefs are French, the sommeliers—most of the staff. That's how they all communicate with one another."

"Except for the Mexicans chopping onions."

Mike was right about that. The lowest guys on restaurant staffs were always the latest pool of immigrants in the city. And the bottom of the totem pole was currently Mexican.

"But not waiters."

"So according to Luigi's brother, Coop, their mother is French. The whole family is trilingual. Seems to be there's a French connection after all."

I was staring at the skyline of Manhattan as we drove onto the Brooklyn Bridge. All the lights were glittering against the deep blue backdrop of the night sky.

"Have they called Luc to ask if he knows this Luigi person?"

"Not yet."

"What's the favor you told the detective you were going to do for him?"

"Save the lazy bastard a trip to Manhattan. Go talk to the manager who fired Luigi. Find out why and when. And where he was living. His brother didn't know that."

"What's the restaurant?"

"Tiro a Segno. Ever been?"

"Never heard of it."

"It's Italian for 'shoot the target.' Otherwise known as the New York Rifle Club."

"Is it a new place?"

"Try 1888."

"That's a well-kept secret, then. Am I in?"

"I told you I'd feed you tonight, one way or another."

"Is it as good as Rao's?" I asked. The East Harlem eatery was one of my favorite places in the city, but scoring one of its twelve tables was harder than winning the lottery.

"Nothing's that good. But Luigi didn't work at Rao's,

so those roasted peppers and lemon chicken are gonna
have to wait for another day."

"Where is this place?"

"Five minutes away, hiding in plain sight. Right on
MacDougal Street in the Village. Three brownstones
next to one another, with a discreet little sign out front.
You've been past it a thousand times. You'd just never
get by the 'members only' thing."

"But you did?"

"Remember a couple of years ago when I had the detail bodyguarding the prime minister of Italy?"

"Silvio Berlusconi."

"Yeah. That guy. The one who liked teenage girls a
little bit too much. This was his favorite place to come
whenever he was in town."

We were off the bridge, and Mike was maneuvering
through the narrow one-way streets—some of them still
cobblestoned—from Tribeca up to Greenwich Village.

"It's a private club?" I asked.

"Very much so. Prospective members have to be nom-
inated by a current member, and there's a tight quota on
non-Italians. Enrico Caruso belonged. So did Fiorello La
Guardia."

"I wonder if Paul Battaglia does. He's never mentioned it."

"He withdrew, Coop. Every distinguished Italian-
American businessman—or -woman—wants it. But once
Battaglia ran for office the first time, it didn't help to be
part of something so ethnically exclusive."

Mike parked the car in a spot that said NO STANDING
and threw his laminated NYPD plaque in the windshield.
We walked to the door of 77 MacDougal Street and he
rang the bell.

Seconds later, a well-dressed young woman—
Ferragamo from the scarf around her neck to the gros-
grain ribbon on her shoes—admitted us to the entryway
and politely asked who we were with.

"We're not with anybody," Mike said. "I'm a detective, and I'd like to talk with Sergio Vico."

"Mr. Vico is in the dining room, Detective. Can this
wait until after the dinner service?"

"Give him my card. He might let somebody else take
the orders for a while."

She glanced at the business card and seemed more at-
tentive when she saw the word "homicide." "Certainly,
Detective. Allow me a minute."

It barely took that long for Sergio Vico to come out
to greet us. He was as tall as Mike, with a thick mane of
silver hair and a broad smile. He was dressed in a tux and
looked as elegant as a movie star.

"Detective Mike," he said, putting both hands around
Mike's and shaking it firmly. *"Come stai?"*

"I'm good, Sergio. Everything's fine."

"Are you working tonight?" he asked, with an accent
that oozed Roman charm. "Bringing us the governor,
maybe? Someone important?"

"Just got a friend of mine here. The workingman's
Sophia Loren. Meet Alex Cooper."

"It's a pleasure, Ms. Cooper."

"I need to talk to you, Sergio. Can you give us twenty
minutes?"

The manager glanced down and took note of our
jeans. "I'm afraid I can't seat you in the dining room,
Mike. And it's my busiest time of the evening. Perhaps
you can come back in an hour or so?"

"It's about a murder, Sergio. I'd like to get started now."

"Something to do with Tiro?" Sergio asked, losing his smile.

"A former employee of yours. Luigi Calamari."

"Has he done something?"

"Got his throat slashed, Sergio. He's dead."

"Then we should talk, certainly. Downstairs, perhaps, in the basement?"

"That will be fine."

He started to lead us through the dining room. "May I offer you something to eat or drink while you're here?"

"Good idea."

Sergio stopped one of the waiters and spoke to him, while Mike and I took in the large dining room. Well-heeled regulars—probably a hundred of them—looked us over in our scruffy clothes as though we were truly interlopers.

"New decor," Mike said. "The place used to look like half a pizzeria, with garish frescoes of the Bay of Naples and the Tower of Pisa."

Now there were Roman columns throughout the room and a large wooden fireplace, topped by a bust of Leonardo da Vinci. After the odors of the canal, the divine smells of garlic and oregano were like the most precious perfumes in the world.

"This way, *prego*," Sergio said, leading us to an exit at the far end of the room. We went down single file and through heavy double doors at the bottom of the steep row of steps.

Just as Sergio pushed the second door open, I recoiled at the sound of a gunshot, and flinched again when another followed immediately.

"Coop, it's a rifle club," Mike said, putting his hands on my shoulders to steady me. "You knew that coming in."

"It's a restaurant." I was flustered, and upset for the

second time today by the sound of gunfire. "I didn't think there'd be shooting in the restaurant."

"Forgive me, Ms. Cooper," Sergio said. "I thought you knew about us."

"Not really, no," I said, as we walked along the back wall of the room.

Two men in business suits were standing together, each holding a rifle, one of them instructing the other how best to aim for the target.

"I thought it would be quiet down here, Mike," Sergio said. "Sometimes the members come down to take a few shots between courses. I'm sure these gentlemen will be done in a few minutes."

"What do they do with their guns during dinner?" I asked.

"I assure you that all the rifles are kept under lock and key. Our club is a very old one, *signora*. We used to have a hunting estate on Staten Island—stocked with pheasant—but that was sold off long ago. It's all just target practice now, right here in this room. Our members enjoy excellent food, the best wines, their cigars—despite the mayor—and shooting."

"And you never had a case out of here, Coop, so it's less dangerous than any other joint in town."

Sergio seated us at a table, and apparently our conversation spoiled the concentration of the marksmen. They headed off to an adjacent room to store their guns before going upstairs.

"Some wine, Mike?"

"We've had our cocktails."

"Then I've ordered you some pasta, and that rack of veal you enjoy so much."

"That'll hold us."

"Now tell me about Luigi. What happened to him?"

"I'm working midnights all week. Got a call last night that there was a body in Brooklyn. Emergency Services pulled the guy out of the water," Mike said, deliberately leaving the exact location vague. "Dressed in a suit. No wallet, no money, no identification."

"But you know it's Luigi?"

"He's got three distinctive tattoos. And because he was arrested once for possession of a handgun, things like tattoos and birthmarks and nicknames are all entered in the NYPD computer system. Once they had his name, the police report from the old case showed he called his brother from the station house. So the cops got in touch with the brother and he came to the morgue this evening to make the ID."

"That's too bad. I liked the kid. He's only what? Thirty-four, thirty-five years old? Smart boy, nice looking," Sergio said, giving Mike the most sincere expression he could muster.

"A real Adonis. Except for the gaping hole in his neck where his throat used to be. His brother says he worked here."

"He did. For three, almost four years. Luigi was good. Very charming, very popular here."

Then why did you fire him? I thought to myself. But Mike would go at his own pace.

"You two get along?" Mike asked.

"Very well."

The double doors and ceiling were obviously soundproofed to keep the noise from the basement out of the dining room. I didn't hear the waiter coming until the door creaked open and he appeared with a large tray topped with food and setups. Sergio waved him over to the table.

Mike was ready to put away everything served to him. Despite the spectacular aroma, with the combination of my nerves, my concern for Luc, and my overindulgence in Sunny's peanuts, I had no interest in eating.

Sergio chatted about the eighth-century Italian bow-and-arrow marksmen groups that had been the first Tiros, until the waiter left the room. Mike was already twirling his Bolognese and devouring it.

"You hired Luigi?"

"Yes, yes, I did."

"You supervised him every night?"

"Exactly that. He was my best guy on the floor," Sergio said emphatically.

"Did he have any problems?"

"Problems? Here at work? Not so. I take you upstairs and you ask any of the important people here—especially the ladies—they loved him. Worked well with everyone else, too."

"No petty theft?"

Sergio dismissed Mike's question. "We're a club, not a restaurant. We don't do anything with cash around here."

"Drugs?"

"Why? You find drugs on him? We don't tolerate that here," Sergio said, shaking a finger at us.

"Story goes you and he fought about his drug habit."

Sergio shrugged again. "That's not true. Is this going to be in the newspapers?"

"I don't write the headlines," Mike said, before asking another dozen questions about possible sources of tension between Luigi and Sergio. They all drew negatives from the very cool, dignified manager.

"You found him in the water, you said?" Sergio asked. "At the beach?"

"Not exactly the beach, but close. You know where he lives?"

"In Brooklyn, with his girlfriend. She's got a place there."

"You know her name?"

"The other guys do—they'll tell you. She's a painter, you know? An artist."

"Okay." Mike was halfway through the rack of veal.

"That's why I asked if you found Luigi at the beach. The girl lives on a boat somewhere out there."

"That's helpful. Give me more stuff like that, Sergio." Mike said, pushing back from the table. "I'll go a round with you while you think."

The older man stood up and disappeared for three or four minutes.

"What's the point, Mike? Am I supposed to be swooning over your manliness now?"

"Relax, Coop. Take a bite of proshutt and chew on it. I'm trying to bond with the guy. And I always like to see how my witnesses handle their weapons."

Sergio returned with two rifles. He handed Mike some bullets, and I watched as they both loaded their guns—.22-calibers—then stepped to the line in front of the row of targets.

I hated guns. Mike had tried to get me to learn how to shoot at the police range in the Bronx after a few life-threatening situations, but I had less fear of a handgun being used against me than I saw value in trying to master its control.

"Why don't you choose the target, Detective?"

There were six of them against the wall—two with the traditional multicolored bull's-eyes, two depicting charging wild boars, and two with the ever-popular image of the late Osama Bin Laden.

"I'm old-fashioned. Let's go for the bull's-eye," Mike said. "So if this guy wasn't stealing and wasn't snorting coke, why'd you fire him, Sergio?"

Mike squared his stance against the target, his left foot on the painted line and his right six inches behind it. The butt stock of the rifle was high up on his chest, his cheek pressed firmly against it. He looked through the open sight and fired, landing his shot four circles away from the bull's-eye.

"Perhaps you winged your perpetrator, Detective, but I'd guess he's still on the loose," Sergio said, chuckling at Mike's performance.

Mike ejected the shell casing and reloaded. Sergio took a bladed stance, his weaker shoulder turned to the target, like a baseball player in the batter's box. He lifted his arms to raise the rifle, barely creasing the lines of his tux, then aimed and fired. The round landed only an inch from dead center.

"Nice shot," Mike said.

"I'm here every day, Detective. I get more practice than you do."

"Why'd you fire Luigi?"

"Fire him? I didn't fire him," Sergio said, reloading as he talked. "Luigi quit."

"Sounds like he had everything going for him," Mike said, raising the rifle to shoot and missing the last circle of the target completely. "Why would he quit?"

"Maybe you would do better with the boar, Detective?" Sergio said, getting even closer to the center of the eye with his second shot. "Luigi had a better offer, Mike. I tried everything I could to keep him here."

"Where was he going to work?"

"I don't know the name of the place. I don't even

believe it's open yet. I heard that it's French, which makes sense because Luigi was actually born in Marseille. His mother was French, and his father Italian."

Mike's third shot was the best, catching the edge of the outer ring of the bull's-eye.

The sound of the gunshots was making me edgier and edgier. The rifles recoiled slightly on the shoulders of both men, jerking them to the side, and the noise in the confined space was magnified so that it sounded to me like cannon fire.

"Have you ever heard the name Luc Rouget?" I asked.

I could see the expression on Mike's face as soon as I opened my mouth to speak. If he could have smacked me over the head with the rifle, he would have done it.

Sergio smiled again. "Certainly, Ms. Cooper. Mr. Rouget has been a guest here many times."

I took a deep breath. "Recently?"

"Several times a year he comes. You know him? Quite a distinguished reputation he has back in France. He has something to do with this?"

Why had Luc never brought me to Tiro a Segno? Never told me he'd been here.

Sergio took a final shot and seemed to have nailed a bull's-eye.

"I can't top that," Mike said, surrendering his rifle.

"And which member sponsored Mr. Rouget to come to dinner?" I asked, with as much personal interest as professional.

"I'm so sorry, *signora*. I wouldn't be permitted to tell you that," he said, making sure both rifles were empty as he got ready to store them. "I'd never have lasted this long at Tiro if I told secrets."

"And I'd never have lasted so long as a cop if I didn't

know how to get answers out of people without having to bully them by asking the district attorney to issue a grand jury subpoena," Mike said, talking loud enough for Sergio to hear him in the next room.

"But a subpoena for what?" he said, returning to lead us upstairs. "Luigi hasn't been here in a month—maybe longer."

"Even his brother's singing to the squad that there was bad blood between the two of you."

"*Stupido*. I don't know his brother. I'm not going to disrespect one of our members for nonsense you hear on the street, Mike."

"Let's just keep it a secret between us for the time being. This member who wined and dined Mr. Rouget has something to do with the restaurant business?"

Sergio had one hand on the door to the staircase. "Not that I know."

"What kind of business then? Something legit?"

"All our members are legitimate, Detective."

"Then I'm surprised they let that portrait of Mussolini hang in the bar for so long before they canned it."

Sergio's hand was over his heart. "Insult me, Detective, and you insult my heritage and my culture. That portrait was removed before you were born."

"So what kind of job does this friend of Mr. Rouget's have?" I asked. Maybe there was some business link that brought Luc to this place for dinner.

"A CEO, Ms. Cooper. The chief executive of one of the largest fragrance companies in this country."

"If you just tell us his name," I said, knowing we could get the rest of the answers from Luc, "we'll get out of your hair and there's no need for us to reveal you as our source."

Sergio looked from my face to Mike's, for an assurance that our word was good on that promise. "Rather sexist of you, Ms. Cooper, to assume this CEO is a man."

I was startled.

"Mr. Rouget's friend is one of Tiro's most distinguished members. Her name is Gina Varona," Sergio said, opening the heavy door and holding it back for me. "And now, I must invite you to leave."

Twenty-four

I waited in the lobby of the club until Mike came out of the kitchen. I said the name Gina Varona aloud six or seven times, but it didn't sound the least bit familiar to me. I couldn't wait to get home to begin Googling her, hoping she was twice Luc's age and had a dowager's hump.

Mike approached me as though he was about to break into a trot, sweeping past me and going out to the street. "C'mon, kid. I got a little nugget of gold."

"About Gina? Tell me she's old enough to be Luc's mother."

"You worried about your love life or the body count?" Mike asked. "Luigi's pals just gave me a piece of the puzzle."

"What's that?"

Mike took my elbow and steered me in the direction of Bleecker Street. "I'm putting you in a cab to go home."

"And you?"

"One of the other waiters says Luigi's girlfriend lives on a boat, all right. It's a houseboat."

"So?"

"So it's not an oceangoing vessel, Coop. The broad makes collages of crustacean legs, okay? Friggin' tiny dead crab parts glued up on painted pieces of driftwood."

"Sounds disgusting."

"I bet I know where she gets the little bastards. There are five or six houseboats moored all along a section of the Gowanus Canal, this guy says. Luigi's was behind a truck lot on Bond Street. Probably illegal, which is why there's no official address for it."

"You're going—?"

"To give the Harbor cops and my drone a little direction. Get the Brooklyn DA's office working on a search warrant for the houseboat. And don't even ask, 'cause you've got a big day with Blanca tomorrow."

At the corner of the busy street, Mike hailed a cab and I got in. He told the driver to take me to my home on the Upper East Side. Then, with the door still open, he leaned inside and picked up my hand.

"I know it's been rough for you, Coop. Just hold it together another couple of days. No whining, okay?"

I took a deep breath. "Why can't I call Luc now?"

"Just between us, I spoke to him today."

"You what?"

"Real short. But he's good and I explained that it's best he keep off the phone with you until a few things are resolved."

"Can I start the meter running?" The cabdriver was more impatient than I was.

"Sure," I said, turning back to Mike. "What else did he say?"

"Trust me for another twenty-four, will you? I didn't give him a chance to say anything—that wasn't the reason for my call. You get some sleep. I'll phone you in the morning if we come up with good stuff."

He let go of me and slammed the door. The driver took off and I belted myself in.

Then I speed-dialed Joan Stafford at her home in DC. "Joanie? Is it too late to talk?"

"It's not even ten o'clock. Where have you been?"

"Just on my way home from work. I'm in a cab."

"What have you heard from Luc?"

"Nothing at all, Joan. How about you?"

"Same here. But then, I'm not the one who skipped town on him."

"Hasn't he even called Jim?" Joan's husband was one of Luc's closest friends.

"Jim's in Moscow on business. How about I come up on Saturday and at least we can spend the evening together?"

"Forget my birthday. We'll celebrate another time," I said. "But would you do me favor?"

"Sure. If you do one for me."

"Deal."

"What's yours?"

"Call Luc. I mean, it's too late now. But call him in the morning and feel him out on what's going on. He wasn't even at the restaurant tonight. And he didn't answer the phone at the house."

"Maybe he's with his boys."

"They're in Normandy, with Brigitte's mother," I said.

"So maybe he's in Normandy, too. I get it. You don't want to call there because you don't want to deal with Brigitte?"

If that's what Joan wanted to think, it was okay with me. "Exactly."

"Fine. I'll call in the morning. Ready for my favor?"

The driver was weaving erratically up Park Avenue. I told him that I wasn't in a hurry to get home.

"Sure. What is it?"

"So I think I figured out what might be behind the whole Baby Mo case, and I really think you should tell Battaglia and your colleagues about this. Your boss is getting slammed in the international press, you know."

"So I hear. And now my beloved friend, best known for writing fiction, is going to enlighten us before we head into the grand jury tomorrow. Shoot me."

"You know the French think this is all a conspiracy, don't you? A setup."

"*Oui*, Joanie. *Un coup monté*."

"So you get it?"

"We just can't figure who framed the sucker," I said, hoping the sarcasm in my voice wasn't too off-putting. "There's no sign of his Ivorian presidential rival anywhere in the Eurotel. No Ivorians anywhere, actually. And President Sarkozy didn't leave any fingerprints. Totally disinterested. The guy in line to take over the WEB position worldwide seems as bored with Mo's sexual escapades as any good economist would be. Who's your perp in all this treachery?"

"Hold on, Alex. I'm serious," Joan said. "Kali. His wife, Kali."

"Of course," I said, stifling a laugh as the cab screeched to a stop at a red light. "Kalissatou Gil-Darsin. Who was, by the way, in Paris at the time this happened. Motive? Coconspirators? I bet Battaglia will just fall in my lap when I tell him you solved this for us."

"Who has a better motive than his wife? Are you kidding? Think of it, Alex. Suppose she knew about all this womanizing that's obviously been going on forever. There she is, one of the most magnificent, most desirable women in the world, and her husband's chasing every piece of tail there is. First young journalists in France, then coworkers, then the mother of the journalist. I mean, c'mon, Alex."

"So Kali set up the maid?"

"Well, not personally. But she's the mastermind behind all this. She hired thugs to do it. Who was in that room next to Baby Mo's? The one the maid went in and out of, before and after? Do your guys know the answer to that?"

"How do you know about the before and after?"

"That maid's lawyer was all over the news tonight. Even she made a statement. I'm so serious, Alex. Kali knows his weakness, his Achilles' heel, better than anyone. He's been embarrassing her for years with all his affairs and his harassment of women, whether it's at conferences or in his own offices."

"You've got a great imagination, Joanie."

"Don't dismiss me. You promised you'd tell Battaglia."

"As soon as I figure out why Kali would want to humiliate herself so publicly by creating an even bigger scandal than whatever has been going on with MGD for years. She could have just divorced him, Joan. Or killed him. I'd do that before I'd spend the twenty or thirty million his legal fees are going to cost."

"Well, this is the angle that intrigues me—a conspiracy, a frame, a setup. Jim has all his sources from the African bureau at the newspaper working on it."

"Very helpful," I said. "Excuse me a minute, Joanie.

Sir, there's a driveway on the left halfway down the block that you can pull into."

"You still there?"

"I'm almost home."

"Someday I'm going to solve one of your cases and you're not going to know how to thank me."

"Driver—stop!" I called out as he raced past the entrance to my building. He braked to a stop fifty feet beyond and I handed him the money and waited for change.

"I'm home, Joanie. Call you tomorrow," I said, and shut off my phone as I got out of the cab and stepped onto the sidewalk.

I walked toward the mouth of the driveway that cut through in front of my building. Three teenagers came running from the opposite direction. I pulled my bag up on my shoulder and hugged it close to my body. But they weren't interested in me and continued running ahead, toward the better-lighted avenue.

As I turned onto the pavement beside the drive, a man came forward out of the shadows and tried to block my path. I stepped to my right but he grabbed the sleeve of my jacket and tugged me back toward him.

I clutched my bag even tighter as I yelled out the names of a couple of the doormen, hoping that one of them would be on duty. "Oscar! Vinny!"

"Don't scream, Ms. Cooper," the man said, as I wrenched my arm away and stumbled backward, almost falling to the ground. "Don't scream."

He was older than I and taller, unshaven, with dark, wavy hair and dressed in sweats. He didn't look like a mugger and he didn't have a weapon.

"You want money?" I asked. He started to extend his arm to me and I called out for the doormen again.

"Don't be a fool, Ms. Cooper. I just want to talk to you."

I took a step toward him and kicked him in the knee-cap. I was aiming higher but was too tired and off-balance to lift my leg. He doubled over and I ran past him, grabbing the revolving door and spinning myself inside to the safety of the attended lobby.

Twenty-five

"We didn't hear you or we would have come out," one of the evening doormen said, looking to the other for support. "We thought you knew that guy."

I was out of breath and wanted to be out of sight, not in the glass-fronted facade of the apartment building. I went straight to the elevator and pressed the button. "What gave you that idea?"

"He came to the door to ask for you several hours ago. Then he went away and came back with coffee." I had stepped into the elevator when the doorman said, "He told us he was a friend of Mr. Rouget's."

I held the door open, my head pounding as I tried to think why any friend of Luc's would intercept me at the door to my home. "I don't know the man. If he shows up again, call 911."

"Certainly, Ms. Cooper."

Once inside my apartment, I bolted the door behind me, turned on the lights, played the three messages on my answering machine—one from my mother and two from friends—and poured an inch of a single malt Scotch that was on my bar, to drink neat.

I dialed Mike's cell.

"Yeah?"

"Where are you?" I asked.

"Still in the car. On my way to the canal. What's up?"

"Some guy was waiting for me outside the apartment, like for hours."

"Did he get lucky?"

"Very lucky. When I kicked him I missed my target. I'm serious, Mike. He came at me and tried to grab me. Knew my name and had been hanging around waiting for me. Told the doormen he was a friend of Luc's."

"So he probably was."

"That's crazy. Luc would have given him my number."

"Maybe not. I told Luc today I didn't want either of you calling each other so your numbers wouldn't show up on phone records, in case things went far enough for a prosecutor to ask for those," Mike said. "Did this guy scare you?"

"Not as much as what you just said does," I said, sipping on the Scotch.

"Lock the door, pour yourself a double—"

"I'm ahead of you. Just wanted to make sure Luc didn't mention anything about sending someone to talk to me."

"Not a word. I'll call you in the morning."

I undressed and took a steaming hot shower, scrubbing the smells of the Gowanus off my skin and out of my hair. I slipped into an aqua silk nightshirt and set myself up on the bed with my laptop.

I punched Gina Varona's name into the search engine,

and dozens of stories queued up instantly. I clicked on the third one, which was a ten-month-old profile that ran in *The Wall Street Journal*.

Forty-five years old, born and raised in Philadelphia, first in her family to go to college—Yale undergrad and Harvard Business School. It was totally a puff piece about Varona's meteoric rise in the cosmetics and then fragrance industry. Brilliant, creative, consensus-building, outside-the-box thinker.

Two things were missing from that piece. Balance— there simply had to be some bad news about her somewhere—and a photograph. She was reading too good to be true and she was bound to be better-looking than I had hoped.

I opened a second article on a fashion blog. There she was—Gina Varona on the red carpet at the launch of a new perfume named in honor of Britain's popular young princess. I enlarged the shot to full-screen size. Varona was a sexy brunette with wavy hair that swept her shoulders and a full figure that was attractive and well-toned.

The annual philanthropy issue of *Town & Country* blubbered over her, too. She'd been photographed in her SoHo loft—a stone's throw from the rifle club—and at her Vero Beach oceanfront villa. Twice divorced, no kids, two large black standard poodles, and a staggering amount of money donated to hospitals, wildlife conservation, and the Boys and Girls Clubs of Italy.

I didn't usually develop an immediate dislike for people other than child molesters and rapists. I knew it was jealousy that had me wound up about a woman I'd never met. I logged off and got comfortable in bed, organizing my notes and thoughts for the morning meeting with Battaglia while I finished my drink.

I turned off the light at midnight and slept fitfully until my alarm rang at six-thirty.

I worked out for half an hour before showering and dressing, brought the newspapers in from the hallway to see how the reporters were handicapping our progress in the MGD affair, and brewed a pot of coffee.

It was almost seven-thirty when the house phone rang. "Good morning, Ms. Cooper. You've got Mike Chapman coming up."

I grabbed an extra mug and then met Mike at the door. He was wearing a hooded sweatshirt, which looked filthy, and carrying a large shopping bag, which seemed to be ripping off from its handles. "What'd you get?" I asked him.

"Breakfast, for starters."

He came in and went straight to the dining room table, setting down his load while I put out plates and poured the coffee. He took a smaller brown bag from within the top of the big one and unwrapped an enormous fried egg and bacon sandwich on a club roll with a side of home fries. Then he helped himself to a glass of juice from the refrigerator.

"You got something in there for me?"

"I didn't want to tempt you out of your Raisin Bran routine. You always work better when you're regular."

I poured my cereal and sat down at the table with Mike, swiping a slice of crisp bacon from his sandwich. "Let's go. What happened?"

"First of all, that little drone is amazing."

"You found Luigi's houseboat?"

"Absolutely."

"And the girlfriend?"

"Nowhere to be seen. There were three houseboats in

the same area." Mike had half an egg and some bacon well into his mouth as he tried to describe things to me. "One of them belongs to this so-called environmentalist— you know, solar panels for electricity and a composting septic system—he's trying to bring back the canal all by himself."

"Environmentally insane, living there."

"The other two are these artist hipster types, one of whom is Luigi's girlfriend. Three hundred square feet of crab collages, covered with blood."

"But you actually got in?"

"Had to," Mike said, washing his mouthful down with juice.

"Please tell me the Brooklyn detectives stopped to get a warrant."

"First of all, you could see the blood through the window. Second, the damn houseboats are illegal. They'd have to be permitted by the Building and Fire Departments, and that isn't going to happen for any of these dumps. It's like a mini–trailer park sitting on a sludge pond, into which city dwellers deliver a million pounds of raw sewage a day. Third, the occupant of this particular shithouse has been murdered, and his roommate hasn't been seen since the weekend, when she was sunbathing on the roof of the damn place."

"Did you take anything out of there yet?"

"Not really."

"That's not the answer a prosecutor wants to hear, Mike."

"I couldn't find anything much to take. No weapon, nothing relating to Luigi that was laying around in plain sight. But there's no question it's where he got butchered. Crime Scene's on the way over. They'll do all the blood and print work and get it to the lab."

"How about the drone?"

"Worth its weight in gold. Harbor moved its operation to this area off Bond Street and plopped the little ROV down again, and doesn't she flash back some images from underneath the Squid's hideaway."

"You mean, something hidden on the outside of the boat?"

"Let's just say that if Lisette Honfleur had a Bronx wallet loaded with coke, then Luigi had a Brooklyn suitcase, and he didn't need to carry it on his person 'cause he had the most foolproof safe around—the most polluted waterway in America."

"Drugs?"

"How about twenty pounds of pure cocaine—street value at least three million hot dollars."

"But where?"

"In a few lengths of PVC piping attached to—"

"Whoa. PVC?"

"Polyvinyl chloride. It's a synthetic resin, Coop. Looks kind of like a thick rubberized tubing."

"What would that do?"

"Cocaine and heroin come from halfway around the world wrapped in PVC all the time, clipped under the keel of cargo ships or freighters. The team recognized the packing right away. They've confiscated tons of piping like that from foreign vessels, filled up with every illegal substance you can smoke or stick up your nose. It's the perfect protective material for drugs underwater or just about anywhere in the universe."

"So they sent divers down?"

"Yup," Mike said, adding more ketchup to his fries. "I expect Commissioner Scully will have to give them combat pay for that kind of work. They were submerged for a couple of hours unbolting the PVC from the houseboat."

"There's more coffee if you want," I said. "I've got to get downtown and be ready for Battaglia."

"I'm outta here," Mike said, dropping his plate in the sink. He walked back to the dining room and reached into his shopping bag.

I was rinsing the dishes when I turned my head to check what he was lifting out onto the table.

"I didn't want you to eyeball this on an empty stomach," Mike said.

I was curious why Mike had turned his back to me and gloved up. When he stepped out of the way, I could see the yellowed human skull that he had set down on the newspaper where my plate had been.

"I didn't think anyone would miss this old guy for an hour or two. Is he speaking to you, Coop, or what? 'Cause your mouth is wide open, like you're gonna talk back."

I had no words for this. Not only was it like the others I had seen in France, but now there was a stain—dried blood as red as wine—that had dripped down the hollowed cheekbones of the ancient skull.

Twenty-six

"Any chance I can have five minutes alone with the Boss?" I asked Rose Malone when I reached her desk at eight forty-five on Wednesday morning. I had to tell Battaglia about the murder in Mougins and its connections to the Brooklyn homicide investigation, since the latter would now be ramped up with the identification of Luigi's body and the findings on the houseboat. He'd crucify me for keeping this news to myself.

"Pat McKinney's already in there with him. Ellen Gunsher, too." Rose knew me well enough to read my expression. I didn't even want to mention in their presence that Baby Mo had been a customer in Luc's restaurant and a social acquaintance for many years.

"Why don't you stay on when this session is finished? I'll hold off his next meeting."

"Thanks. Mercer and Ryan are in my office. I'll be back with them in two minutes."

I crossed the hall to get the two people I trusted most

in this mix to brainstorm with us. Rose waved us right in when we returned.

Paul Battaglia was standing at the head of the conference table at the rear of his enormous office. He was talking on the phone with a cigar dangling from the side of his mouth. He was shouting at one of the reporters in the press room about the coverage in this morning's tabloids.

On one side of the table, closer to Pat McKinney, was the *Post* with its snappy FRENCH WHINE headline, remarking on the complaints of the European press about the American criminal justice system. Nearer to Ellen Gunsher was the *Daily News* with THE MAID OR THE MO? caption, painting Battaglia's dilemma, like the Lady or the Tiger, in choosing which of the parties to champion.

The district attorney slammed the phone back in the cradle. "I guess it's open season on me. It's MGD's sperm that's all over the Eurotel, and it's the housekeeper who can't keep her facts straight, but somehow I think this whole fiasco winds up blackening *my* eye. Where's your victim? Is Oprah coming back to TV to do a morning special featuring the maid who couldn't keep her mouth shut?"

"I spent half of last evening bargaining with Byron Peaser," McKinney said. "He's producing Blanca here this morning, with a million conditions that we're still—"

"Conditions?" Battaglia said, walking across the room, flapping his wings like an ostrich trying to get airborne. "What the fuck is he thinking, that he can impose conditions on us? When she walks in the door, slap a bright green grand jury subpoena in her hand."

"I'm trying to mollify the old sleazebag, Boss. The only issue left to decide is whether we try to make our

180.80 deadline," McKinney said, referring to the Criminal Procedure Law section that mandated a grand jury vote within this week to keep bail conditions the same.

"Or what? Gil-Darsin gets out and we never see him again?"

"If you sit down with us, Boss, we can lay out where we stand and give you our opinions on which way to go."

Battaglia made his way to the head of the table. "Since when did this office become a democracy? Five of you each think you get a vote? Are your names going to be on that ballot with me next year when the editorial writers all claim they know this game better than I do?"

"If you're worried about the Ivorian vote in Manhattan, Paul," I said, "there are exactly one hundred twenty-three registered voters here who were born in the Republic of the Ivory Coast. I don't think they'll riot for Baby Mo."

"If you go for the indictment today, who's putting Ms. Robles in the jury?"

"Ellen is," McKinney said, sneering in my direction. "Alex will be with her to oversee the presentation, but the victim doesn't much like Alex."

"What did you do to her?" Battaglia asked.

"Tried to get at the truth."

"But you did it so heavy-handed," McKinney said. "You're the one always telling people how compassionate to be with rape victims."

"Of course that's true. But the first time the witness lies—I'm not talking about mistakes that everyone makes, or confusion as a result of trauma—but when she outright lies, then our most critical task is to find out whether that fib is a stand-alone, or whether lies permeate the entire underpinning of the story."

"And what did all those hours together lead you to conclude, Alex?" Battaglia said.

I hesitated for fifteen seconds, fully aware that the district attorney had summoned me back from France to lead the charge on this case. "That I just don't know what to believe."

"Why not?"

"We all know something sexual happened in that room between MGD and Robles. But she's the most facile liar I've ever confronted. One minute she's staring me directly in the eye and I'm ready to fight to the death for her, and the next time she answers a question, it's a complete fabrication."

Battaglia's annoyance with me was palpable. He put his elbows on the table and templed his fingers. "Mercer?"

"I think you have no choice but to indict the man," Mercer said. "I'd like more time to get some background info on Blanca checked, but Alex says Lem Howell isn't offering that option."

"Ryan?"

The bright young lawyer leaned forward, pleased to have his say in a top-level powwow. "I hate to disagree with Mercer, but she's not ready for prime time, Boss. Let MGD out with an ankle bracelet, hold his passport, and—"

That was all of Ryan Blackmer that Battaglia wanted to hear.

"Ellen. Are you ready to go?"

"'Bout as ready as a prairie dog heading out to meet an armadillo."

"Save those little bits of Texas for home, missy. Got it?" Battaglia had been ridiculed in the media the last time Ellen spoke at a triumphant press conference, when dozens of guns had been confiscated by cops working with her unit. The Gunsherism—"If bullfrogs had side pockets, they'd have pistols, too"—wasn't meant to turn the serious moment into a comedy show.

"Yes, sir."

"Pat?"

"Full speed ahead. Ellen's ready for a bare-bones presentation. Less margin for error that way."

"Bare bones" was the leanest way to put the legal elements of a case before the grand jury. Only the essential facts were elicited from the witness—nothing requiring long answers or extraneous information.

"She's still got to be telling the truth, Pat," I said. "A single lie under oath at this point will undermine the entire case going forward."

"So what do you want today, Alexandra?" Battaglia asked. "Right this minute."

"More information. I want to know what Blanca swore to in that asylum application. I want to know what lies she told to get into this country. Have you heard anything back from your request to the State Department?"

"Monday at the earliest," the district attorney replied.

"It's irrelevant," McKinney said. "The whole damn thing is irrelevant."

"I'll give that to you, Pat, for the purposes of the grand jury," I said. "But doesn't it bother you just a little bit, in getting to these facts, that she's capable of lying under oath?"

"Everybody seeking asylum does it."

"Fair enough."

"What if one of the jurors asks about why she got asylum?" Battaglia countered.

"That's why you've got your bureau chief in there, Boss," McKinney said, waving a hand in my direction. "She's their legal adviser. If they ask any questions when Ellen is finished, then Alex tells them it's none of their business. She'll keep them in line."

"What else do you want?" Battaglia asked me.

"The recording of Blanca's call to her boyfriend in federal prison after the attack," I said. "I want to know exactly what she told him about it. I want to know if she talked to him about getting millions out of MGD."

Pat McKinney shook his head. "Ellen's questions don't even touch the fact that she has a boyfriend. The jury won't know about him, so they won't know he's in jail."

"What if the facts she told him—which are on tape by the way—are different from what she told the police and all of us?" I asked.

"The feds can get that tape to us by the weekend," Pat said. "I'm all over that."

"How about the prison authorities just play it for us from Arizona or wherever he is?" I asked. "We've got three Spanish interpreters on staff."

"So far, I'm not having much luck finding anyone in the business who speaks the Mayan dialect they used in the call, Alex. Our Spanish interpreters can't understand a word Blanca said when they talked to each other."

"Do you have all the surveillance tapes from the hotel?" I asked Pat McKinney. "The hallways, the front desk, the entrance?"

"All? What do you mean all? I've got what we need for today." He looked to Ellen for confirmation, but she'd been deflated by Battaglia and her eyes stared blankly ahead.

"You'd hardly know that unless you had every tape from the time period in question. I would have asked for them from every camera that might have caught any of the players—including the security team—and MGD's girlfriend."

"I'm satisfied with what we've got," McKinney said. "If Blanca changes her mind again, we'll go back for more. Besides, before you got here I was filling the Boss in about Blanca's argument that she wouldn't ever be sexually involved with a black man. It's hard to get around that one. It's horribly racist, but it makes her position clear."

"Did you have that conversation before I came in the room by plan?" Mercer said. He didn't volunteer much in meetings with Battaglia, but when he spoke, he got everyone's attention.

"Well—no, I—uh—well, it was just a new fact the Boss didn't know."

"Do you have something to say to that, Mercer?" the district attorney asked, getting up to ground out the tip of his cigar.

"Bullshit," Mercer said in a firm but quiet voice. "Most respectfully, sir, bullshit."

Pat McKinney threw back his head and pursed his lips. Whatever he'd been trying to sell to Battaglia before we walked in had just been compromised.

"You think she's lying about that?" Battaglia asked.

"Her prejudice? I just think it's ugly. And personally, I think she threw that line in out of the blue yesterday, as though Mr. Peaser put it in her head as one more reason to find in her favor."

"You know what her boyfriend looks like?" The DA turned to Pat McKinney.

"The jailbird? No idea."

Mercer stood up, took some photographs from his jacket pocket, and passed them to Battaglia. "They're called mug shots, Pat. You could have had them pulled up in a flash, like I did."

"This is Blanca's convicted felon?" Battaglia said, squinting at the picture.

"Yeah. He's from the same town she is. Got those Mayan features, but I'd say there's been some chocolate sprinkled into his family tree over the last few generations."

McKinney still had fire. "The other thing I was telling the Boss just now is that last night Byron Peaser gave me another factoid in Blanca's favor. She's been HIV-positive for eight years and on a battery of medications. No way in hell she'd volunteer to have sex with a stranger."

"Welcome to my world, Pat. Just when you think you have all the answers," I said, "you enter the dark realm of special victims work. You know how many women who are already HIV-positive think that giving blow jobs doesn't put them at risk? You know how many others just figure they're already infected with the worst thing a man can pass along to them, so why not have sex? If that's your ace in the hole, so to speak, Pat, it's a losing argument."

"Two people alone together in a hotel room for twenty minutes. Everything in the world's at stake for both of them. One is shielded in all the privileges our Constitution allows," Mercer said, "and that leaves only the other one to tell a story—out of both sides of her mouth, in this case."

"So what do I do?" Battaglia asked, standing and pacing in the middle of the long room.

"We put her in," I said. "We get an indictment today and file it tomorrow."

"But you want more time, Alexandra."

"Yes, Paul. My head's in the same place as Ryan's. And like Mercer, I don't believe Blanca's bullshit and prejudice. But Lem won't budge. No hint of a story from MGD that would flat out contradict his accuser. Won't agree to an ankle bracelet to monitor his guy. So like Pat and Ellen, I think we've got to get her under oath—she's never wavered on the story about what happened in the room with Gil-Darsin. If you can take the heat that goes with riding this whole thing on Blanca's back, then we go in today and continue to work around the clock to sort out every detail that's dangled before us."

Pat looked at me, seemingly shocked that I had agreed with him.

"Glad you're being sensible, Alex," he said.

"I'd rather take our time like Ryan says, but it's not the sensible choice, with all of MGD's resources and the fact that Lem Howell hasn't proferred any plausible scenario on his client's behalf. But I'm not the one who's going to be hit with the RUSH TO JUDGMENT? headlines. That's all on the Boss's head."

"I'll put my armor on," Battaglia said. "You think you can get this done today? We can do the filing and press conference by tomorrow or Friday?"

"Absolutely," McKinney said.

Battaglia dismissed us as quickly as he was able. We all gathered our notepads and started toward the door. I took an extra minute to shuffle my papers in hopes I could have a private word with the district attorney.

"Ryan Blackmer," the DA said to me. "I like that kid.

He's not afraid to say what's on his mind. I hope he's wrong this time."

"Ryan always says what's on his mind. It should be refreshing," I said, "after all the ass-kissing you get."

I didn't need to drop McKinney's name in that sentence. Battaglia had already picked up the phone to ask Rose to get his mole at WEB headquarters on the phone.

"Listen, Paul, I think you ought to know some other stuff that's going on."

"'Stuff'?" he asked me. "Is that a term of art?"

"Sorry. You're right. There was a woman murdered in Mougins this weekend."

"I take it you have an alibi." The side of Battaglia's mouth drew back in a grin. It wasn't even ten o'clock, and the second cigar was already lighted and filling the space between us with smoke.

"And then a man's body was found by Night Watch in the Gowanus Canal."

"Saw it in the tabs. Had his throat slit. So?"

"Well, he was a waiter. It's complicated but, uh—" I searched for the right words as I fiddled with the buttons of my gray-striped suit and tugged at the collar of the silk blouse. "There may be a connection to Luc Rouget in all this."

Battaglia covered the mouthpiece with his hand while he continued to hold for the person he had called. "What does that mean exactly?"

"I don't know, Paul."

"Well, what does Luc say? What kind of connection?"

"I—I haven't been able to speak to him in a day or so. I'll let you know as soon as I do. The woman who was killed in Mougins used to work in Luc's restaurant, several years ago. I'm sure it's total coincidence, but I just thought you should know."

"I don't believe in coincidence, Alexandra. You're well aware of that."

"Then you should know that the Gil-Darsins live in Grasse, Paul. It's the neighboring village of Mougins," I said, struggling to keep my eyes steadied on the DA's face. "They've been customers of Luc's restaurant—for years, Boss, for many, many years."

I thought the look from Paul Battaglia's eyes was going to burn through the lenses of his glasses. "Go on."

I didn't know where to go. "There may be no significance in all this. I wouldn't say they were close. But Luc's father, Andre, was a good friend of Papa Mo's."

Battaglia grunted. "The great dictator. The thief who took the ivory out of the Ivory Coast. Lives like a king in France but left his people penniless. Go on."

Someone spoke into the phone on the other end and I took a deep breath. Battaglia released the mouthpiece and answered. "Just a minute, Mr. King. I'm getting rope-a-doped by one of my lawyers here."

He was already leaking information to James King, the straight-arrow, brilliant former IRS head who would be in the running to succeed Gil-Darsin at the World Economic Bureau.

"Don't leave me hanging, Alexandra," Battaglia said, wagging the cigar as he talked out of the side of his mouth.

"That's all I've got, Paul. I just wanted you to know." I could save the news about the matchbox in Luigi Calamari's pocket for later. And the bloody skull. I wasn't supposed to have known about either of those things yet anyway.

"Tell Luc to stay in the kitchen, will you? You look like the cat that swallowed the canary, young lady. I don't want you slinking back in here later to tell me something else you wanted to say to me right now but it got stuck in your gullet."

"Whatever happens, Paul, you can count on me not to slink."

"Another minute, Mr. King. I just want to make sure we're on a secure line," Battaglia said, before turning his attention back to me as I moved toward the door. "I hope this—this nonsense didn't have anything to do with your visit to Tiro a Segno last night. I hear you didn't even wait long enough for the pasta to get al dente."

Twenty-seven

I walked to the window bank at the end of the hallway that faced the short side street, Hogan Place, which was the actual entrance to the DA's office. The bank was halfway between Battaglia's suite and Laura's desk and offered me the privacy to make a call.

"I am so steaming mad," I said into my cell phone to Joan Stafford. Of course someone at the private club to which he had once belonged had given me up to the district attorney.

"Whatever happened to 'good morning,' Ms. Cooper?"

"So far I can't say that it's been very good. Did your mother ever tell you that she had eyes in the back of her head when you were a kid? Knew everything you did, no matter where you were? I feel like that all over again with my boss."

"Then you should have asked him where Luc is," Joan said. "All I can figure is that he's off chasing the one-armed man."

"What now? Didn't you reach him?"

"Better take me off your payroll, girl. The bad news is that he's not answering his phone at all, as irresistible as I think I am. The good news is that I called that she-devil, Brigitte, and he's not with her."

"So what do you think?"

"Didn't you ever see that Harrison Ford movie—with the one-armed man?"

"Are you talking about *The Fugitive*?"

"Precisely."

"Oh, Joanie, just when I need you to be sensible, here you go writing fiction again."

"Think of it, Alex. Suppose the French detective—*le flic*—actually thinks Luc's a—what do you call them these days?—a person of interest in the murder of Lisette Honfleur."

"No one could possibly think that."

"Say he's Inspector Clouseau. Completely incompetent. He thinks that."

"I'll give you completely incompetent," I said.

"So he leans on Luc, freaks him out. Wants everyone in town to believe Luc is guilty to sort of make him crack. Then Brigitte turns on him, 'cause she doesn't want the kids involved. I'm telling you Luc's running around out there like a fugitive, chasing the one-armed man who's really the killer."

"And I called you to calm me down. What was I thinking? I'll talk to you later."

"No, no, no, no, no! Don't hang up on me. Where's Mike? I bet he'd agree with me."

"Joanie, I adore you, but I've got work to do. I don't think Mike's all that into Luc, if you know what I mean.

Anyway, we're about to be disconnected." I turned off the phone and stormed back to my office.

"Don't even stop at your desk," Laura said, holding up both hands to stop me. "The whole team's in the conference room with Byron Peaser and Ms. Robles. Better get yourself down there if you don't want to miss any of the fireworks."

I reversed direction and walked down the corridor.

From behind me I heard Ryan Blackmer's voice. "Wait for me, Alex."

"Are you making yourself useful?" I asked, forcing a smile.

"Checking the hotline."

"Any messages about Gil-Darsin?" The Sex Crimes Unit had long had a dedicated phone line to take calls from victims or witnesses, many of whom were hesitant to notify the police but trusted the reputation of our pioneering office. Whenever a major case broke and there was a likelihood that the offender might have a recidivist history, the press secretary added our hotline number to the media releases.

"Nada."

"So we're still at one vic," I said, continuing down the hall.

"Hold it a minute. Don't you think it's strange? Okay, so the guy's a womanizer and all that. Plenty of stories to support how he comes on to every woman in his orbit. But rapists don't just start with violent behavior when they're fifty-eight years old, do they?"

"Never had a novice that age before."

"It's one thing to seduce someone, but it's a different animal to come raging out of the bathroom and assault a complete stranger. The hotline is stone-cold. That never happens when you've got a serial rapist."

"I'm with you on that."

"And I've called every Eurotel where Baby Mo is likely to have traveled on WEB business. No reports, no complaints, no violence. Affairs, yes. Attacks, no. Only that whack job in France who waited eight years to decide that after she held hands with him during a professional interview, maybe he thought he had a green light."

"That'll go nowhere," I said. "She's beyond the statute of limitations."

"She's beyond belief, is what she is. So why didn't you make that argument to Battaglia?"

"I just forgot, Ryan. Sorry, I know how strongly you feel about slowing this down."

"Are you okay, Al? It's not like you to forget to tell the Boss something like that."

"Tired. Stressed out about doing the right thing on this."

We were a dozen feet away from the conference room when I heard Byron Peaser ranting at someone through the closed door.

"She didn't know it was there, don't you understand that?" Peaser shouted.

Ryan opened the door for me and we went back inside. Peaser was having a standoff with Pat McKinney, and I didn't want to get in the way of that.

"Look, Byron, Detective Wallace just got a call back from Citibank about the subpoenas he delivered last night. They told him there are five accounts in Blanca's name. Five bank accounts—I'm asking her to explain that."

Blanca Robles, dressed in a black suit that Peaser probably bought her for the occasion, started to answer. "I swear I didn't know—"

"Hush up, now, Blanca. You see, Pat," Peaser interjected, "that scumbag boyfriend of hers must have forged the signature cards and opened these accounts in her name. Whatever criminal enterprise he was up to, we simply don't know. Just another jerk taking advantage of this poor woman."

I couldn't believe McKinney was letting Peaser give answers—or suggest scenarios—to rescue Blanca. "I find it works better, Pat, if we have Mr. Peaser wait outside."

Peaser threw up his hands, obviously aggravated by my appearance. "So Ms. Torquemada comes to join us again, in case my client needs a little more waterboarding. You didn't get your fill of questions yesterday?"

"We go where the truth takes us, sir," I said. "Maybe Ms. Robles doesn't like that, but it's pretty much the way we operate here."

"Well, is it taking you to the grand jury or not?" he asked, pounding his fist on the table.

"Two p.m. sharp, Byron," Pat said. "If you'll step out and let us get back to work with Blanca, I've reserved half an hour and we'll be the first case of the afternoon session."

Peaser picked up his briefcase, gave me his best "drop dead" expression as he passed me, and left the room.

Ryan Blackmer stood next to me, whispering in my ear as the team took their places around the table. "I'm never going to say 'I told you so,' Al, but there's a new piece of garbage under every rock you pick up with this broad."

I nodded my head while Ellen reminded Blanca Robles about what the remainder of the day would entail.

"I'll give you another rock to look under, Ryan. Will you cut a subpoena for the IRS for her tax records this afternoon, and don't tell McKinney that I asked you to? It'll take a good two weeks for them to come back, but at least we'll know if she's playing any games on that front. And you are welcome to a huge 'I told you so'—in the middle of Times Square—if you're right about this."

We spent the rest of the morning prepping Blanca for the questions, exactly as Ellen had scripted them. Unlike a trial, there would be no surprises for the witness in the grand jury. Now that she had gone public in a televised press conference, the usual jitters occasioned by facing twenty-three grand jurors in an amphitheatrical setup would be less of an issue.

Mercer kept Blanca company while she ate lunch. The rest of us further refined the questions down to the barest bones possible to make out the charges.

At quarter of two, we walked upstairs to the grand jury waiting area. Row after row of uniformed cops with gun cases and drug arrests picked up their heads when our small army came in. The photo of Blanca Robles on the courthouse steps was on the front page of both tabloids, and a buzz rippled through the witness benches as the warden went inside to make sure there was a quorum.

A few minutes after two, Ellen Gunsher went inside the jury room. I entered behind her and walked up the third tier of steps, to perch on the windowsill behind the foreman.

Ellen spoke from behind the table at which her witnesses would be seated. The court reporter was next to her, taking down every word.

"My name is Ellen Gunsher. Today I'll be presenting

to you the case of the People of the State of New York against Mohammed Gil-Darsin."

Baby Mo's name was an instant wake-up call to the jurors jaded by dozens of cases heard throughout the last three weeks of their monthlong term. Newspapers rustled as they were put away, muffins and sodas were deposited in totes and backpacks, and everyone gave Ellen his or her undivided attention.

"I'd just like to remind you that in the event you have read any accounts of this matter in the papers, or heard any stories on the news, you must put aside all that information. When I submit this matter to you, I will ask you to vote solely based on the evidence you hear today from the witnesses who appear before you."

The jurors all nodded their heads, although it was unlikely that any of them could be held to that standard, any more than it was possible to enforce the fact that the proceedings within the jury room were deemed by the law to be secret. By day's end, most would be bragging to family and friends that they had heard the evidence about the scandal between the infamous MGD and the housekeeper.

Ellen walked to the door and admitted Blanca Robles, who followed her to the front of the room. She appeared to be appropriately nervous—which jurors always liked—and scanned the faces in the room. If she was counting the number of black men, I figured she'd be disappointed to know there were seven of them.

She remained standing while the foreman, who had a heavy Spanish accent, administered the oath.

Ellen spoke next. "Would you talk in a loud, clear voice and tell the jury your name, your age, and in which county you live?"

The pedigree questions were short and simple. There was no other mention of Blanca's personal life. Information about her imprisoned boyfriend was outside the scope of the direct examination.

On to the work history. Where was she employed, for how long, and in what capacity? Had she ever met or known Mohammed Gil-Darsin before Saturday?

"Would you tell us exactly what happened from the time that you entered Mr. Gil-Darsin's room on Saturday evening?"

Blanca had taken direction well. She made eye contact with the foreman—most likely because she identified with his Latino accent—and crossed herself before beginning to speak.

She told her story even more convincingly than I'd thought possible, playing to the audience with every exaggerated gesture in her. Gil-Darsin grabbed and pulled and pushed her, his naked, erect thing rubbing against—

"Do you mean his penis, Ms. Robles?" Ellen asked, needing to establish every element of the crime.

"Yes. As God is my witness I can't say that word in public."

Some of the jurors were riveted on her expressions and movement, while others focused on the wall clock above Blanca's head or stared into their coffee cups. The language of sexual assault wasn't easy for most people to stomach.

"Then he put it in my front—"

"Do you know what a vagina is, Ms. Robles?"

"Of course I do. Is there he put it," she said, clasping her hands together in front of her and murmuring something under her breath.

"What did you say?" the court reporter asked.

"I was just praying."

I walked to Ellen's side and whispered to her. She nodded and said, "Please strike that last question and answer from the record. I'd like to ask the jurors to disregard what the witness said, please."

Ellen got her back on track with a handful of leading questions. There was no adversary to object to them.

"Did the defendant put his penis in your vagina?"

"Yes."

"Did the defendant put his penis in your mouth?"

"*Dios mío*, yes," Blanca said, as tears rolled down her cheeks and the expression on her face looked like she had swallowed a fistful of lemons.

Ellen moved through the outcry, meeting the police, being subjected to a hospital examination—and within six minutes, the witness had completed her testimony. It was merely the outline of the crime, but enough of a legal foundation on which to send a man to jail for the next twenty-five years of his life.

If Blanca Robles's case was to make it to a trial six months from now, Lem Howell would likely take these six minutes—and all the flesh that had been left off the bones for this presentation—to skewer the woman for the better part of three days in a courtroom.

"Thank you, Ms. Robles. You may step out."

Before she could push back from the table, the hands of three jurors shot up in the air. I followed Ellen to the first one and listened as the ponytailed guy in a flannel shirt and jeans asked her, "What about the lady's lawsuit? I know what's in the papers isn't evidence, but I got some questions about her lawsuit."

"As your legal advisers, sir," I said, "we must tell you that lawsuit is not relevant to this proceeding. There is a separate forum—the civil court—in which that matter will be decided."

Grand juror number eight seemed displeased by my response. I guessed he had the blue-collar reaction of a pox on both their houses—the wealthy African son-of-a-thieving-dictator and the hoping-to-win-the-lottery maid who might have been too melodramatic for this guy.

We crossed the room to reach number thirteen, a retired high school principal in her late sixties. "You didn't ask her if she screamed. I want to know whether she screamed when she says this guy attacked her."

"I'm going to decline to ask that question, ma'am," Ellen said. "There is no legal requirement that any victim of a crime has to scream."

"I'd still like to know why the girl didn't scream," she said, a little louder than was necessary.

Behind her was the assistant foreman of the grand jury, an African American businessman in his early forties. "So, what did Mr. Gil-Darsin say about this?"

"I'm going to excuse Ms. Robles and call the next witness. You understand, of course—and I know you've been charged on the law earlier in the month—that the defendant has no obligation to say anything at all," Ellen said.

Ellen excused the witness, who lumbered from the table like she was carrying all her troubles on her broad shoulders. Ellen opened the door to let her out and to bring Mercer in before the jury.

Mercer's imposing presence always made a strong impression on jurors. There was a subliminal message sent by his size and manner and deep voice that he was a force for right and good and justice. If there were hesitant jurors, he would likely put Blanca's case over the edge, just by his appearance.

He raised his hand and swore to tell the truth. "Mercer Wallace. Detective first grade. Manhattan Special Victims Unit."

He wore a navy blue suit with a yellow silk tie and pocket square, and all eyes were on him as he told the group how long he had been on the job and when he was awarded the top grade in the department and assigned to the elite SVU.

"On Saturday, April 23, did you meet with the complaining witness in this case, Blanca Robles?" Ellen asked.

"Yes, I did."

"And during the early morning hours of Sunday, April 24, did you arrest the defendant in this case, Mohammed Gil-Darsin?"

"Yes, I did."

"Did you advise Mr. Gil-Darsin of his rights?"

"Yes, I did."

"Did he make any statements to you concerning Ms. Robles or the allegations against him?"

"No, he did not."

I could see the assistant foreman shaking his head from side to side. Although defendants had the right to remain silent, the average citizen hated the fact that they did.

Mercer described being present for Crime Scene's examination of the Eurotel room in which the encounter occurred, and the fact that Baby Mo's semen was on the wall, floor, and maid's uniform.

He was out of the room within three minutes' time.

Ellen Gunsher moved to the front and read the charges to the grand jurors from the Penal Law. Then she and I stepped outside while they deliberated.

When cases presented few issues, the vote could take a matter of only seconds, signaled to the waiting prosecutors by the foreman's buzzer that rang on the warden's desk. These deliberations would take longer, jurors being certain to bring press accounts into the conversation although they had been admonished not to.

"Can I send Blanca downstairs?" Ellen asked.

"Keep her right here. If they want her back for any more questions, let's have her standing by."

I could hear raised voices from within. Probably one team of doubters, led by the retired principal who wanted her rape victim to be screaming, taking on the law-and-order jurors who wanted to vote a true bill.

Mercer, Ryan, and I went out in the hallway and paced together. Fifteen minutes of waiting turned into twenty-five.

"Maybe we got a runaway jury going on," Ryan said.

"Forty-five minutes in," Mercer said, "then I'll start to worry. This is nothing for a case with all this media coverage."

"Remember the old chief judge, court of appeals?" I asked Mercer. "Before your time, Ryan, but he once bemoaned the prosecutorial control at this stage in the case, saying a Manhattan grand jury would indict a ham sandwich if asked to."

"Well, maybe they're not biting on your croque monsieur, Al."

"Don't get smug yet," I said, yanking his necktie.

Now the loud voice I heard came from the waiting room. I poked my head back in to see Blanca Robles facing off with Pat McKinney.

"They don't believe me? They taking so long because

they don't believe me? I'll get Mr. Peaser and we'll go to the other court."

Pat held the woman by the arm and tried to restrain her as she came our way.

"I didn't say that at all. Please, Blanca. I was just trying to explain why it sometimes takes them longer."

"That's because she was in the room," the angry woman shouted, pointing at me. "If they didn't care about what happened to me, it's because you poisoned them, Alexandra Cooper."

Mercer blocked the door and worked on calming his witness as only he could do. "Alex is on your side, Blanca. You wouldn't be here if all of us didn't agree about this. You've got to trust us—"

The sound of the buzzer startled everyone and quieted the commotion.

As Mercer went into the jury room, I hurried over to the warden's desk to retrieve the slip on which Ellen had written up the charges.

When Mercer returned thirty seconds later, he handed the paper to Ellen and gave me an instant thumbs-up. I read it over her shoulder. Mohammed Gil-Darsin, head of the World Economic Bureau and aspiring president of the Republic of the Ivory Coast, stood indicted for the crimes of rape in the first degree and criminal sexual assault—known by the crude name "sodomy" until recent changes in the law—both committed by forcible compulsion.

There would be little likelihood of a judge any longer releasing Baby Mo on bail.

Twenty-eight

It was six-fifteen when Laura said good night and Mercer told me that Mike wanted to have dinner with us to talk about things.

The grand jury vote was not a matter of public record until the filing of the indictment with the court, so Battaglia would have no shot at a press conference this evening. The papers would be signed by the foreman at two tomorrow afternoon, and then an arraignment in the higher court would take place on Friday.

"I don't want to hang out tonight. I'm whipped."

"I'm all spiffed up with nowhere to go," Mercer said.

"Take your wife to dinner. She's hardly seen you this week. Let Mike quiz her about *her* love life, 'cause I'm off duty as of right now."

"Vickee's got a girls' night out, and I think Logan prefers the babysitter's cooking to mine. Who said anything about your love life?"

"Mike won't talk to me about the cases. I get that. It's just—I'm not up for being a punching bag tonight."

"I'll give you a ride uptown. You've got a few miles of snarled traffic that might make you change your mind," Mercer said, turning off the light switch and closing my office door behind us.

It was one of those rare nights I could leave all my folders behind on my desk. I was looking forward to a quiet evening alone. I daydreamed about drawing a hot bath and sipping Scotch in the tub while I tried to let myself relax. I needed to make sense of what a train wreck I'd made of my romance.

We took the elevator down and walked around the corner to Mercer's car. In just a few minutes, with local radio news telling us the FDR was jammed, Mercer began the slow crawl up the Bowery to the East Side. We passed the time talking about everything except what mattered most to me. Mercer was sensitive, as always, to my mood.

My cell rang and caller ID showed it was Mike's home phone. "You can pick it up, Alex," Mercer said. "I'm fresh out of interesting gossip. He's not interrupting anything."

"He's going straight to voice mail, my friend. Mike's interrupting my attempts to get in touch with my saner self."

"That's a Herculean task, Ms. Cooper, right at this very moment."

Now the text function began to vibrate. "Whoops. I love it when he gets desperate and has to communicate with me silently," I said, pressing the button to open it.

I looked at the message and laughed out loud. We

250   LINDA FAIRSTEIN

were stopped at a red light and I held the screen up in front of Mercer: C>~~~~~~.

"Keyboard sperm," he said, also chuckling at the image Mike had sent, a Sex Crimes Unit shorthand detectives often sent prosecutors when DNA results came in. "I hope he's trying to tell you something professional, not personal."

"Fingers crossed on that count," I said, pocketing my phone.

"You're not even answering the text? C'mon, see what the boy wants."

"I'm not having dinner with you guys, period. I'm ordering in from Shun Lee and that's the end of it. I don't want to talk to Mike or text him or take any of his crap tonight. Over and out."

Mercer's phone rang next.

"He's relentless," I said, as Mercer answered it.

"Yes, indeed, Detective Chapman. I am holding one beat-up blond hostage in my car, and she wants absolutely no part of you," Mercer said, pausing for the reply. "Oh, it's me you wanted?"

He listened while Mike explained something to him, then spoke again. "Okay, so dinner's not happening?" Another pause. "Yeah, I've got the lab report with me. Sure thing. Alex can run it up."

I assumed I looked as exasperated as I felt.

"Don't roll your eyes at me, girl."

"I'm sorry to break up your dinner plans, but—"

"Not a problem."

"But I'm not running anything up to Mike."

"When he goes in tonight, the lieutenant wants the DNA report on that rape-homicide we're working together. That was a professional sperm symbol Mike e-mailed to you. I picked up the lab papers today on my way in, when I stopped for the certified copy of Baby Mo's results."

"It's too creepy in Mike's apartment. It's still like a shrine to Valerie. He's got to get her clothes out of there. I'm not going up."

"Ancient history. Vickee took care of that a couple of months ago."

"Really? You guys are great. That was a sweet thing to do."

"And just because I'm asking you to, you're going to take that gray envelope out of my briefcase and go up-stairs. I don't care if you don't go inside, I don't care if you don't want to see him. Just slip it under Mike's door while I stay double-parked, then I'll drop you at home. The dude's been doing double-duty for you all week, Alex."

"Guilt me, Mercer. Just lay it on." I slouched down in my seat. "I'll take the papers upstairs, okay?"

"I promise to wait for you," he said, turning up the radio so I could listen to Smokey Robinson tracing the tracks of his tears. The ride from there was chatter be-moaning a Yankee season without Posada and trying to schedule a May weekend on the Vineyard for Mercer, Vickee, and Logan.

Mercer stopped the car in front of a fire hydrant close to the dilapidated brownstone where Mike lived. I got out with the folder and opened the door to the vestibule. Instead of his name on the plate next to the bell for 4A, the typed tag read COFFIN. I pressed it, and thirty seconds later the buzzer went off, admitting me to the hallway.

I grabbed the banister and started trotting up the steps. With each flight, the cracks and chips in the paint seemed to be longer and deeper.

I reached the fourth-floor landing and stopped to catch my breath. Mercer was right about Mike's concern for me this week, and all he had done on my behalf.

I knocked and said, "It's me, Mike. I've got your papers."

The door opened. Luc Rouget smiled at me and took me in his arms.

Twenty-nine

"Ssh, ssh, ssh, ssh, ssh," Luc said, wrapping me inside a great embrace, kissing me all over the top of my head. He kicked the door shut while he tried to stop my crying. "Everything's going to be all right."

"It can't be. That's a foolish thing to say, Luc." I was unable to stop the meltdown. "What are you doing here?"

He stroked my hair and held me close. "We'll talk about it, darling. Just calm down and—"

"Calm down?" I said, looking up at him. "I had no idea where in the world you were. I've had every horrible thought—"

"Just stop thinking, then, Alex." He lifted my chin and kissed me, long and lovingly. I gave in to him, letting the tears stream down my cheeks, kissing him again and again.

"When did you get here?" I suddenly realized there was barely enough room in Mike's apartment for two of us to be inside with him. I took a step back. "Where's Mike?"

"He's been a prince throughout all this," Luc said, dabbing at my mascara-streaked face with his handkerchief. "I owe you an apology for the way I talked about him on Sunday."

I bit my lip, laughing at myself. "Great. And I've been an absolute bear to him tonight. Blew him off completely."

"He'll recover."

"Did you send some guy to my apartment the other night, to talk to me? Did you really do that?"

"It was before I had a chance to talk things through with Mike. I was desperate to get word to you. Just one of my old friends. It was a stupid thing to do. Sorry, Alexandra."

Luc took my hand and started to lead me over to the bed.

"Don't even think about that here in this apartment," I said.

"Give me a little credit, darling. I was just going to get you off your feet to talk."

I went over to one of the two stools in front of the kitchen counter. I could hardly handle the idea of being in Mike's apartment to meet with Luc about anything.

Luc took the other stool. "It's the police who kept me from calling you, Alex. You understand that, don't you?"

I couldn't look him in the eye. I didn't answer.

"What? You think I didn't want to?"

"I'm so confused. What are you doing here?"

"The Brooklyn detectives asked me to come over. You understand there was a man who was killed," Luc said. "Mike told me you—"

"Luigi Calamari? Do you know him?"

"I don't know him. I mean, I met him where he used to work, in a professional capacity. I don't know him outside of that."

"But you've hired him to be at Lutèce?"

"I didn't hire him. I've got a manager and partners who do all that work on the ground over here. I didn't know anything about Luigi until I got the call from the police."

I looked away from Luc. A photograph of Valerie on the table next to Mike's bed caught my eye. She was standing on a steel beam, thirty stories above the city, on the framework of a building she had designed. I wanted a share of the courage she possessed till the very end of her life.

"Listen to me, Alex. I'm as confused as you are."

"That couldn't possibly be. Your head would be spinning like mine is," I said, closing my eyes and shaking my head. "You'd be as dizzy from it as I am right now."

Luc stood up and put his arms around me, resting my head against his chest.

"I am dizzy, Alexandra, but not because of you. I'm quite clear about that."

"I spend half my professional life trying to sort out lies people tell me—even the people who come to me for help. Now I feel like my personal life reeks of the same deceitfulness."

"I'm not lying to you, darling. I never will."

I broke away from him and pushed the stool out behind me. "Why are we here, anyway?" I asked. "Let's go to my place."

"We can't, darling. At least I can't, for now."

"What do you mean, you can't?"

"Look, Mike picked me up at the airport this morning and drove me to the detectives' office in Brooklyn. They know all about Lisette, Alex. They've spoken with Belgarde in Mougins. The matchboxes, the skulls, the murders—they think there might be a connection."

"To each other, yes—but to you, Luc?"

"Not to me."

"And Mike?"

"They wouldn't let him stay for the interviews. They said it's not his case. So he came home to sleep for the day—he said he'd been working all night. Then at four o'clock this afternoon, when they had finished with me, Mike came back to pick me up."

"Then let's go," I said.

Luc pulled me back to him and kissed me again. As good as it felt in the moment, I was seized up inside with doubt and dread of the days to come.

"I can't stay with you tonight," he said.

"But that's crazy."

"Mike convinced them to let us have dinner together—with him as the chaperone. But all the cops think it's not wise for me to stay at your place. Not for me," Luc said, drawing back with his hands on his chest. "But that there's no need to drag you into this investigation right now."

"I'm already there. Where are you staying?" I asked.

"The Plaza Athénée."

The elegant boutique hotel on East 64th Street at which Luc always stayed. "Fine. Then I'll just throw some things in a bag and go with you."

"Darling, it's the same problem. If there's any negative media, neither the cops nor I want you drawn into it."

I threw up my arms in despair. "I feel like I'm talking

to a perp. If you didn't do anything wrong, why is everyone worried about the possibility of negative press?"

"Be sensible, Alex. I'm well-known in my business—and someone is obviously trying to bring me down, on two continents. There could be news stories about this and they won't be pretty."

"Paul Battaglia's getting so much bad publicity about Baby Mo that there won't even be room for a footnote about us. I wouldn't worry."

"Come here, darling. This half hour of stolen time is Mike's gift to us. He didn't tell the cops he'd let me see you alone for a while at his apartment. He simply promised he wouldn't let me go to yours. Just let me hold on to you, Alex. It may be the last chance we have for the next several days."

I walked to Luc and put my arms around his neck. For the next three or four minutes, I got lost in his kisses, comforted by the expression in his soft blue-gray eyes.

I jumped at the sharp sound of a rap on the door.

Mike pushed it open and I stepped away from Luc.

"Break it up, you two. Think *Casablanca*—1942. This is just about the moment when Rick tells Ilsa, 'We'll always have Paris.'"

I could feel the color rising in my cheeks. I swiveled to the sink and ran some cold water to rinse my face.

"Thank you, Mike," Luc said. "Thank you for giving us this time."

"I got one question for you, Luc. Do I need to change the sheets?"

Thirty

I used the bathroom to freshen up, and when I emerged, Mercer had joined us in the cramped apartment. Mike had summoned him to watch *Jeopardy!* before we left for dinner.

Trebek was just announcing the final answer. "The category, folks, is Popular Phrases. Popular Phrases. Are your wagers all in?"

The three contestants had scribbled their numbers, having been neck and neck with one another in the first two rounds of the show.

"Twenty bucks is our rule," Mike said. "Double for foreigners."

Luc smiled at Mike and put his arm around me. "Whatever you say."

"And the answer is," Trebek said, reading from the board, "This was the period of origin of 'bootlegging'— the practice of concealing illegal liquor in the top of one's boots. Bootlegging."

"Got it?" Mike asked.

"I think we all got it," Mercer said. "Prohibition."

"The Roaring Twenties," Luc said. "That always sounds so American."

"Let me see your green," Mike said, pointing at Mercer's pocket. "You, blondie?"

"Same."

"Then you three would be losers, just like those three," Mike said, pointing to the screen. The contestants' answers were displayed one at a time. "What is the Civil War? That's the ticket, guys."

Trebek and Chapman were on the same page. Mike started turning out the lamps on the two tables. "You're thinking rum runners and stuff. I mean there were bootleggers in Prohibition, but the whole thing started with Confederate soldiers during the Civil War—sneaking moonshine into camp in the legs of their pants."

"Let's feed these people," Mercer said, handing his money to Mike.

"I'm not hungry," I said. "Can't I just—can't we just—maybe take Luc's stuff over to the hotel and hang out for a while?"

"No can do, blondie," Mike said. "I'm responsible for tailing you two, and that stop isn't on the agenda. Besides, it's a working dinner. A little something to get your mind off Baby Mo."

"Working on what? Where?"

"My favorite saloon."

"That leaves way too many choices," I said.

"Top of the line, Coop," Mike said, holding open the door. "Ladies first."

I glanced back over my shoulder at Luc. He seemed remarkably calm under the circumstances. I was glad about that, although it unnerved me a bit as well. I couldn't help but wonder why he wasn't more stressed about the summons to New York by the Brooklyn detectives.

Mercer reversed direction and made his way to Fifth Avenue. Luc and I were in the backseat. It felt to me like the only things missing were two pairs of handcuffs.

"You want to tell me what's going on?" I asked.

"The '21' Club," Mike said.

"We're going to '21'?" I looked to Luc for an explanation. "Working?"

The classy restaurant that had attracted a tony crowd of society and business figures, celebrities and movie stars for close to ninety years had indeed started life as a saloon—a speakeasy in Greenwich Village opened by two cousins shortly after the passage of the Eighteenth Amendment in January 1919, which marked the beginning of Prohibition.

"Meeting some people there," Mike said.

"My partners, Alex. My business partners. You need to understand what's been going on, what's involved in getting Lutèce off the ground. There must be something mixed up in all this that will help the police get their work done."

"This is about as hiding-in-plain-sight as we can go," I said.

"I planned it that way," Mike said. "Can't fault a guy for being transparent, out in the open. Luc's got nothing to hide, let's meet in public."

'21' had been a fixture in the world of fine dining and fancy booze for as long as any New Yorker could remember. The upscale "speak"—quite different from low-down dives known as "blind pigs"—had bounced around from location to location, until it settled in at 21 West 52nd Street on New Year's Day 1930.

While we were driving downtown, stories about the fabled restaurant raced through my head. Hemingway bragged about making love to the girlfriend of the notorious killer, Legs Diamond, in the kitchen one night, while the joint was being cleaned. Jack and Jackie Kennedy dined in the front room the night before his inauguration. The owners' nephews flew to Havana with a million dollars in cash to buy Cuban cigars for the restaurant when news of the embargo was imminent. Babe Ruth, Joe DiMaggio, Prince Rainier of Monaco, Clark Gable, Greta Garbo, Bogart and Bacall—who became engaged there—and just about every foreign potentate and president of the United States had all found their way to '21.'

Mercer squared the block and parked behind the row of limousines that stacked up nightly to wait for the high-rolling clients inside. He, Mike, and I had managed our fair share of evenings in the east room—known to regulars as Siberia—stopping in for a late-night burger or the divine steak tartare—always in the care of a bartender who knew a great pour, especially after all the well-dressed swells had headed to the theater or their homes.

"Can you imagine the consistency of a place like this, to be thriving after so many generations?" Luc said, as we got out of the car. "You offer good food and wine, and you make the customer feel like he's a member of an exclusive club, and there's your recipe for great success."

The entrance of the building was as distinctive as its history. Still standing were the double-wide iron gates, as decorative now as they were useful during Prohibition—then the first line of defense to keep cops and agents from getting in to search for liquor. Down three steps to another iron-grilled door with a brass bell, from the days when patrons were admitted only if they were known to the owners.

Topping it all off, on the balcony over the door, on the front steps, and inside the entrance, was the vibrant array of more than twenty jockey statues, each dressed in the color of the stables he represented. As far back as the 1930s, many wealthy horse breeders were such loyal patrons of '21'—Vanderbilts, Mellons, and Phippses among them—that they donated jockeys as tokens of appreciation for their private tables and all the privileges that went with their status.

"Welcome back, Monsieur Rouget," the gentleman by the door said as we entered. "Always nice to have you with us."

"Thank you, Shakur. Good to be here."

We followed Luc to the maître d's stand, where he was again met with a personal greeting. "Your guests are seated inside, Monsieur Rouget. They came a bit early."

"Thank you, Joseph. But I was hoping for something very quiet when I reserved. We have some business to discuss."

"Certainly, monsieur," the man said, making notes on the side of the large paper on his podium—a layout of the main-floor rooms with all the tabletops represented on it—as he nodded and winked at Luc. He held up a finger to ask for a minute's time as he walked away. "I hope you don't mind, sir, but I was just dressing the room with Ms. Varona until you arrived."

"Dare I ask?" I said, controlling my instinctive dislike of the woman I'd not yet even met. " 'Dressing the room'?"

"Just an old trick of the trade, darling. You try to put

the best-looking women at the most visible tables. It's quite good for the restaurant's image, and even better for the beverage orders from the men who can see them."

"No wonder that big round table in the window at Michael's is always filled with such fine-looking babes at lunchtime," Mike said, referring to the media-hot restaurant on West 55th Street. "Window dressing."

Joseph came back from the dining room. "I have the six of you at table two, sir. It was always your father's favorite. But I'm afraid we're so crowded tonight that I have couples close to you on both sides."

"That won't work," Mike said. "I want you to be seen, Luc, but not heard."

"We've got private rooms upstairs, of course. But they're for very large parties."

"How about the wine cellar, Joseph?" Luc asked. "Is it occupied tonight?"

"No, as a matter of fact. Would you be comfortable there?"

Luc turned to Mike. "That's up to you."

"I'm okay with it. We'll let Joseph take the three of us downstairs. Why don't you sit with Gina for a few minutes. Work the room, if either of you know anyone here. Then let Joseph bring you down. That way you get to show your face, but there are no ears listening to us in the cellar."

"Warn me now if there are any hunting targets down there," I said, still unsettled by last night's experience.

"Just great wine, I expect," Mike said. "We'll take it."

"Very well, then," Joseph said, leading us through the main dining room.

If you could stop yourself from gawking at the swells on the banquettes here, it always paid to look up at the barroom ceiling. Starting with the first trophy given by a wealthy client—a model of British Airways's "flying boat" from the 1940s—captains of corporate America gave for display their most identifiable products—football helmets, racing cars, sports trophies, Hyster forklifts, miniature blimps, and even a model of President Clinton's Air Force One plane—all hanging overhead, claiming a place in this living museum of presidential perks and rich boys' toys.

Mercer was directly in front of me as we walked toward the swinging doors that led to the kitchen, so I had no opportunity to turn my head to try to catch a glimpse of Gina Varona.

We passed completely through the working area of the kitchen—sous chefs and line workers never looking up from their stations as they prepped their dishes at the height of the dinner hour. Off to the right near the back was a narrow entry to a staircase. At that point, a waiter took over from the maître d' and guided us down.

The corridor at the bottom was long and narrow. We came to a massive door, which the waiter stopped to unlock. He pointed to the entry of the wine cellar, advising us to watch our step over the wooden strip that protruded from the floor.

The room was cool and a bit damp. Straight ahead was a long banquet table that looked like it could seat twenty people. The waiter apologized that it had not been readied in advance, but I explained that we hadn't booked the room earlier.

Around the table, from floor to ceiling, were bins and bins of wine, bottoms pointed out, with a brass plaque identifying each of the patrons who stored their supply within this storied vault, or a red-and-white label on the bottom of each bottle. The captions read PRIVATE STOCK, and many had, below that, the owner's name.

"How big is this cellar?" I asked.

"There's a series of rooms, madam. These were three brownstones put together when the restaurant was first built—we're actually in the basement of nineteen right now, not twenty-one—and there are thousands and thousands of bottles here. If you'll excuse me," he said, "I'll be back shortly with your setups. May I take a drink order?"

"That would be great."

"Sparkling water all around," Mike said.

The waiter excused himself.

"Business first," Mike said, observing my frown. "Then cocktails."

"Now that we're alone, Detective, what have you found out about this Gina Varona broad, and why do I have to have dinner with her?" I asked. "I'm sure I'll need a drink."

"You'll need whatever is best for Luc, and that's to let him and his partners put everything on the table for us."

"Have you talked to this woman yet?"

"Not a word. Cool your jets till they get down here, okay?"

Mercer was studying the labels on several of the bottles of wine. "Château Lafite Rothschild. 1908. Domaines Barons de Rothschilds. What would that one fetch?"

"Probably seven, eight thousand dollars," I said. "The owners buy wine at one price, then charge whatever the traffic will bear at a place this classy. It accounts for a lot of a restaurant's profit when they can sell the high-end labels."

Mike was quick to shoot back. "And you wouldn't know it from swill."

"You're right about that. I think I can tell the difference between a five-dollar bottle and a thirty-dollar bottle, but after that, I wouldn't have a clue." I followed the passageway into the next room, staggered by the size of the collection.

The door creaked open again, and although I couldn't see him, I recognized the waiter's voice as he spoke to Mike and Mercer.

Mike said something, but I couldn't hear him.

"Were you talking to me?"

"Yeah. I told you not to wander too far away."

"Don't worry. I'm not going to smuggle any Romanée-Conti out of here."

"You'll get lost, girl. This whole place is booby-trapped," Mike said, coming in my direction.

"Right," I said, laughing at him. "That's my idea of '21.' Danger everywhere."

"Sealed up forever in a wine cellar with me."

"Haven't you had enough of Poe's entombing to last you a lifetime?"

"I'm not kidding you, Coop. There's contraptions all over the place," Mike said. "It's ingenious. And it's the only reason there was never an arrest made at '21' all throughout Prohibition, despite the fact they were serving the best hooch in town."

Mike was leaning against the wall, arms crossed, with Mercer coming along behind him, still fixated on the labels and plaques. "It all started at the front door. The agents looking to raid the place were stopped first by the huge iron gates. If they got past those, the doorman was a lookout, using the peephole to see who was outside."

"But they still had to let the agents in, didn't they?"

"Not before the doorman pressed a buzzer that went straight to the bartender, while three other alarms signaled clients on each floor. The waiters collected all the glasses, while the barkeep pulled a switch. Every liquor bottle behind the bar was on a collapsible shelf. One flip and all the whiskey in the whole place was flushed down into the basement, where it drained out below the building's foundation. The place may have reeked of alcohol, but there wasn't ever a trace of the stuff inside the restaurant that anybody could prove in court."

"Are you making this up, Mike?"

"First heard it from my dad, and then found out it's been a legend in law enforcement all this time. They teach the '21' system of foolproof-design deception at the academy, for today's sophisticated drug raids."

"Mercer? Is he—?"

"Mike's always right. You know that."

"So what else?" I asked.

"All kinds of secret spaces. There were several closets with metal hooks for waiters' uniforms. But if you took a table knife," Mike said, pulling out his pen to represent the knife, "and placed it so that each end of the knife touched a hook—bam!—it completed an electric circuit, and the back of the closet swung open to reveal a narrow room lined with liquor."

"Very clever."

"But this cellar is the masterpiece. It had to be practically the size of a warehouse to hold all the wine—two thousand cases of it, at least—and the booze. So the architect created a secret door in the brick foundation of '21,' which gave access to the vacant building next door—19 West 52nd Street. The door was made of exactly the same materials as the adjacent wall, so it seemed invisible. And it had to be thick enough so that when the cops tapped on it, it didn't sound hollow. It had to mesh so tight to the other wall that if the feds blew cigarette smoke into it—looking for cracks with an air draft was the typical test—it wouldn't be a giveaway."

"So far so good," I said.

"This door to the secret caves here must have weighed two tons. The main challenge was to make a locking mechanism that wouldn't jam up, that could work from either side of the door—in case there was a siege and the owners took cover inside here—and that wouldn't be visible to the raiding agents."

"How did it work?"

"The builders put a plate on the inside of the door. It could only be activated by inserting a long thin metal rod through a tiny hole in the brick wall. When the rod hit the plate, it all clicked and the lock was released by a rolling mechanism."

"But wasn't the hole obvious to everyone?" I asked.

"Nope. The genius who designed it had them cut dozens of holes in the wall, even though none of the others went through to the plate. They just looked like defects in the brick. The door to the wine cellar is impenetrable," Mike said. "If the lock ever broke, they'd have had to tear down the entire building—or dynamite the wall—just to get inside here."

I started to retrace my steps to the first room. "Then it seems a doubly odd place to plan a dinner party."

"It turned out to be a very useful location for married men to tryst with their lovers after Prohibition ended. A private dinner at '21,' when this space was furnished a bit more cozily, was the perfect alibi for anyone who could afford it—including Mayor Walker, back in the day—who liked to entertain showgirls down here while his wife covered the home front."

"Just when I thought I was learning a lot about the restaurant business," I said to Mercer.

"There's a dark underbelly to this city, no matter where you go, Alex."

Mike must have heard the same noise I did—footsteps in the hallway. He moved toward the door just as Luc entered, followed closely by a woman and man.

"Sorry to keep you," he said. He held out his hand to Gina as she came into the room. "This is Gina Varona. Gina, I'd like you to meet Mike Chapman and Mercer Wallace—they're both detectives. And you've heard me talk about my fian—my dear friend, Alexandra Cooper."

Luc almost tripped over the word "fiancée," but he managed to catch himself. Gina lifted her hand and waved at the three of us. I hoped that the smile I returned was not as cheesy and forced as it felt to me.

Varona was a bit shorter than I am. I regretted not having stopped to change out of my courthouse clothes and put on some makeup. She was carefully coiffed and painted, in a cream-colored knit dress that accented her dark hair and petite waist.

"And this is our third partner," Luc said. "Peter Danton."

Danton nodded his head and said hello. I guessed him to be in his mid-forties, about my height, and he was dressed—like Gina Varona—to kill. His tailored suit fitted the sleek lines of the body he'd so obviously been sculpting with his personal trainer.

"Pleased to meet you," Danton said. "Especially you, Alexandra. Luc talks about you all the time."

He extended his arm to shake with Mike and with Mercer. That's when I noticed he was missing the top half of the first two fingers of his right hand.

Thirty-one

We faced off on opposite sides of the long table. Mike in the middle—flanked by Mercer and me, and Luc between his two partners.

"I'm sorry it took so long," Luc said to Mike. "If you were hoping people would see me, they did. There were five or six clients—old friends—in the room. I made the rounds, and Gina introduced me to a man named David Columbia."

"You might as well have invited Liz Smith to join us for dinner," I said to Mike. "David writes The 'New York Social Diary.' The news that Luc is here will be viral in David's column by midday. Are you sure that's what you want?"

"Yeah. Let everyone in town know that you're here on business, Luc. Takes the heat off the cops—and you."

I was more worried about the killer or killers being drawn to Luc by the announcement of his arrival in New York. Surely Mike had considered that angle.

"What's happening here right now isn't official," Mike said. "You don't have to talk to us. You don't have to answer our questions."

Peter Danton laughed. "I know. We have the right to remain silent."

"Actually, you don't have any friggin' rights at all on my watch. You wanna help us, you talk. You want the body count to climb and the Health Department to put a PLAGUE sign over your about-to-be-brand-new front door, stay mum," Mike said. "Mercer and me—we got a thing about Coop. Personally, most of the time she makes decisions with her head up her ass. Professionally, both of us would rather work our cases with than without her."

"Could I just—?"

Mike put his hand on my arm to tell me he wasn't finished. "She says Luc's the real deal, that's all I need to know. You in? Tell me something about yourselves, then about where this business operation stands. Ladies first."

Gina Varona had no shortage of self-confidence. She leaned forward and clasped her hands together on the tabletop. She wore no rings of any kind, but her diamond studs matched the large round diamond necklace that showed off her décolletage. She looked Mike directly in the eye and began to speak.

"I assume you've done enough homework to know who I am," she said. "I live downtown, when I'm not traveling, in SoHo. Two dogs, Detective, which I find much easier to keep than my men. I was the CEO of a company called the American Fragrance Design for the last twelve years."

"Was?"

"That's right. There was a buyout by a larger European conglomerate. I stepped down at the end of last year."

"Fired?" Mike asked.

"Hardly, Mr. Chapman," Gina said, sneering ever so slightly. "An irresistible golden parachute. It's still airborne."

"What's that supposed to mean?"

"It means all my benefits and a fifteen-million-dollar bonus for moving on," she said, flipping her hair off her shoulders. "I was restless, ready to try something new. Luc was looking for backers and it sounded interesting to me."

"Why's that? Can you cook?"

"Kibbles 'n Bits, Detective. That's my entire repertoire."

"How long have you known Luc?" I asked.

She turned her head to look at him. "My goodness, what would you say? Almost twenty years?"

I resisted the temptation to ask if they had ever been intimate, and whether that was why he hadn't ever mentioned her name.

"Twenty years? Really? How did—?"

Now Gina was talking directly to me. "I met Luc through Brigitte, originally. When I first worked in the cosmetics business, she'd done some modeling for my company. She and I hit it off, got along well. So we spent a lot of time together hanging out in France on some shoots and business trips. Got to be very good friends."

Of course, Brigitte would have been the perfect model—elegant, serene, almost anorexically thin, and beautiful. La Belle Brigitte—an aperitif that Luc had named in her honor—was still on the menu in Mougins, though his ex-wife was no longer around.

"See, if you knew Coop a little better, you'd realize she's probably stuck on whether or not you and Luc ever hooked up," Mike said, like he had been reading my mind.

"That's ridiculous. That's not even—" I tried to protest, but Luc talked over me.

"Alex, darling, you should have just asked me. I'd have told you all about Gina."

Gina Varona leaned back, tilted her head, and looked down at me as though I were a child. Perhaps I'd been acting like one.

"Ask what? I'd never heard of Gina until last night. Now I find out you've been having dinner with her right here in New York. What was I supposed to ask?"

"Business meetings. Certainly dinners. But you knew that. You knew I was lining up partners and trying to get backers for Lutèce, Alex. I would have told you their names if you'd asked me. What difference would that have made?"

I shrugged my shoulders. The waiter reappeared with several large bottles of sparkling water and poured a glass for each of us.

Mike waited until he left the room. "You gotta excuse her, Ms. Varona. Coop would go nine rounds in the ring with Muhammad Ali if something dear to her was at stake. She'd come out bloody and bruised with her tail whipped, but she'd never walk away from a good fight."

I waved Mike off. "Back to you," I said.

"So, how'd you get together with Luc on this plan?" he asked.

"I'm in the South of France quite often, actually."

"Visiting Brigitte?"

"I do that, too. I'm the godmother of their older son,

so I see her and the boys as often as I can. But also, Detective, there's a small town called Grasse. It's the perfume capital of the world. I'm there on business several
times a year. And it's just a few kilometers from Luc's
restaurant."

I knew that was true. Exotic, expensive perfumes and
the home of Papa Mo, Gil-Darsin's father.

"Luc told me that he was going to try to open Lutèce
here in New York. I didn't know the restaurant in his
father's day, but I was a regular when the great Soltner
ran it. I already had word that I'd be transitioning out of
my job with this big financial windfall, so what better
than to shift gears and back my friend in his venture?"

"He's a lucky man," Mike said. "Do most restaurant
owners have backers?"

"If you're not talking about a mom-and-pop operation or a corner pizzeria," Luc said, "the model these
days is to have help on the business side. It's prohibitively
expensive to start up a serious place like ours. It's a total
crapshoot."

"How much cash are we talking about, to get something like Lutèce going?" Mercer asked.

Peter Danton and Gina Varona both looked at Luc.
He thought for a minute before answering. "For us?" He
cleared his throat with a cough. "The real estate alone
was four million dollars. The build-out has cost another
three million. That's before we talk about staffing and
salaries and all the licensing."

Mike and Mercer were dumbfounded. "Eight to ten
million, at least? And I'm happy with a hot dog at PJ
Bernstein," Mike said. "Are you kidding me?"

"But you don't have that kind of money, Luc," I said.
"I'm staggered."

He rested his glasses on the table in front of him and stared at me like he was seeing me for the first time. "That's right, Alexandra. I don't have anything like the amount of money I need. That's why I'm relying on Gina and Peter. Do you understand that this has been my dream—for, for most of my life? Do you understand what this project means to me, in my heart?"

I was trying to discern whether it was passion that was driving Luc's speech, or disappointment in my business naïveté.

"When my father opened Lutèce more than fifty years ago, Mike, he had this idea to make it the best restaurant in New York—more likely, in the world. He had a great imagination and spirit to go with his style. The first thing he did was buy a town house. Do you know how many restaurant owners in New York own their buildings, too?"

"No idea," Mike said.

"Fewer than one percent. One percent, do you see? A brilliant investment. Most places go broke having to pay rent to a landlord, raising it lease after lease. There are only a handful of great places today whose owners had the good sense to buy the real estate. Ken Aretsky at Patroon, the Kriendlers at the '21' Club, the Massons at La Grenouille, the Pellegrinos and Stracis at Rao's. So at the same time, my older siblings and I—we all lived above the shop," Luc said, smiling briefly when he recalled one incident. "Mother had to take my roller skates away because I was tearing up the hallway in the apartment and diners complained that the chandelier was shaking so violently they feared it would fall."

"I'm sure—"

"Let me finish, Detective. My father insisted on the

most elegant appointments. He was the first restaurateur
to serve on bone china, to use Christofle silverware and
crystal wineglasses. No frozen food, nothing canned. He
flew in fresh Dover sole from England and Scotch salmon
every single day. It was he who discovered a twenty-
seven-year-old chef—the great Soltner—working in a Parisian restaurant and the very next day, offered him the
big job in New York.

"I think the reason I never got sick as a child is that
our apartment was kept at sixteen degrees Celsius—the
ideal temperature for wine—which was stored in our closets. It took him five years to get the restaurant going—
selling off everything he and my mother owned—stocks,
bonds, paintings by Degas and Rouault. A guy named
James Beard was giving his first cooking lessons in our
kitchen upstairs. Opening week, lunch was price-fixed at
eight fifty—and the public screamed so loudly about it that
my father had to cut it down to six dollars. But he did all the
work and he paid for every bit of it by himself, and it paved
the way for all the great restaurants that followed Lutèce."

"None of that would be possible today," Mike said. "I
get your point."

Luc took a deep breath and a long drink of water.

"So the way it gets done now is with backers," Mercer
said, trying to take the conversation down a notch.

"That's the only possibility," Luc said, ticking off
names of the hottest places in the city. "Danny Meyer has
Stephen Ross, Jean-Georges Vongerichten has Phil Sua-
rez, Daniel Boulud has Lili Lynton."

"Other women have done this?" Mercer asked.

"I may not be as brilliant as Lili, gentlemen—she was
a financial analyst before she got into this crazy business—
but I'm hungry enough to want to follow in her foot-

steps," Gina said. "Boulud operates thirteen restaurants, eight of them in New York."

"But that's not your goal, Luc," I said.

"ETB, he calls it." Gina Varona patted Luc's shoulder and laughed. "Expansion to bankruptcy. I've got my eyes on the rest of the world, but Luc's happy to keep what he's got back home while replicating his father's success here. It's refreshing how sensible he is."

"Just how much money are you willing to put into Luc's dream, Ms. Varona?" Mike asked.

"I figure I'm good for five million." Neither one of her false eyelashes blinked.

"And I'm impressed. That should score you a reservation any time you'd like," Mike said.

"Vanity restaurant investments won't make me a dime, Detective. I'm backing Luc because I've watched him run the classiest operation on the Riviera. He's got the knowledge and style, and he's always in his place— which customers count on. We've got Andre Rouget's blueprint for a classic winner, and the three of us have figured out exactly what it's going to cost to open Lutèce, to run it, and then for it to throw off some income. I plan on getting every nickel back—with interest."

"How long do you figure that will take?" Mike asked, drumming his fingers on the table.

"Restaurants have a generally short life span," Luc said. "Unless you really get lucky—like my father and some of the other greats."

"Not that I don't trust Luc to get it done for me," Gina Varona said. "But I'd like to see the cash within the next five years."

"Phew," Mike said. "I guess the prices will be pretty steep."

"As J. P. Morgan used to say, Detective, 'If you have to ask how much it costs, I guess you can't afford it.'"

"I'm a Shake Shack kinda guy myself."

Peter Danton stood up, stretched, and started to walk around the end of the table to come behind us. As he moved, I saw him point to the floor with the forefinger of his good hand.

Mercer and I were watching him. Luc nodded in return.

"I'm getting to you in a minute, Mr. Danton," Mike said. "What's with the sign language?"

"It's restaurant speak, Mike," Luc said, laughing. He jiggled the knot in his geometrically patterned silk tie. "All dreamed up in the forties by the owner of the Stork Club. If he played with his necktie, it meant there'd be no check for the diners at that table. If he touched the tip of his nose, it meant the people being served weren't important."

"And Mr. Danton, here, pointing his finger at a spot on the floor?"

"All he's trying to tell me, Mike, is that somebody ought to bring some cocktails to this table."

"Point well taken. I'll get the waiter. Just one more thing, Ms. Varona."

"You must be smelling blood, Detective. Isn't that what Columbo used to say when he was homing in on the killer? 'Just one more thing'?"

"I'm light-years away from a killer at this point. Don't get nervous yet."

"I rarely get nervous. Just when my money's on the line."

"The girl who was killed in Mougins last weekend. Did you know her? Did you know Lisette Honfleur?"

Gina Varona put her hand on Luc's forearm. "Lisette? Isn't that the bitch who had the fight with Brigitte?"

Luc started to answer, but Mike spoke over him. "That's right. You remember that fight?"

"I wasn't there. I mean I wasn't in town at the time. But Brigitte told me about it later. Or wait—maybe it was you, Luc, who mentioned it. Didn't you tell me that they fought over—?"

Luc interrupted whatever Gina had been about to say. "Brigitte caught her stealing from us," he said. "Don't you remember? Lisette was stealing cash from my office."

"Oh. Oh, I thought—" she said, stopping abruptly.

"What is it, Ms. Varona?" Mike asked. "What were you about to say?"

"Never mind, Detective. Luc's memory about something like that would be much more accurate than mine. I really don't know why Brigitte and Lisette had a fight."

Mike looked annoyed. I could tell he thought she was holding something back, encouraged to do so by Luc. "But you do know why Luigi Calamari left his job at the Rifle Club, don't you?"

"Now that, Detective, would be in the category of *two* more things you wanted from me, and I only promised you one. Let's see how I feel about that subject after I've had a drink."

Thirty-two

Mike summoned the waiter to take an order from us. While he went around the table, Mercer tried to lighten things up with some general conversation.

"So where did people eat before there were restaurants in this city?" he asked Luc. "I mean, folks who were working in offices or foreign travelers."

He had hit on one of Luc's favorite subjects, something he had made a study of for his entire life. "Pretty grim fare, actually, served at boardinghouses and taverns and English-style chophouses scattered about. The first actual restaurant was created in a French pastry shop on William Street in 1827. It was called Delmonico's—the only place in town to have an à la carte menu and an actual wine list. The Delmonico brothers introduced a whiff of elegant European dining into the rough-and-tumble of this city. The restaurant moved uptown from time to time, as the population did, but it remained the gold standard in the business for almost a century."

"And the food came from—?"

"This city was blessed by nature, Mercer. My chefs today are envious of what this environment—forests and wetlands and rivers and ocean—provided every day. Venison from the plains of Long Island, fruits and vegetables from New Jersey, and the most amazing array of fish that filled the Fulton and Washington Markets every morning.

"Bear meat was plentiful, woodcocks covered the land that later became Central Park, and the thing that New York was best known for—like Boston for lobster and Baltimore for crab—was oysters."

"No kidding," Mike said. I knew exactly what had caught his attention.

Luc held up his hands and spread them apart. "Oysters grew as large as dinner plates in these waters. The inlets of New York Harbor, Long Island Sound, the Raritan River—they produced the largest and sweetest oysters in the world. I've told Alex there were oyster saloons all along Canal Street, just north of your courthouse, in the 1830s—all the oysters you could eat for six cents. They were as abundant and fresh as the waters at that time, until the harbor became polluted and the supply depleted."

"And today?" Mike asked. "Where do you get oysters from? I don't mean for France, but when you open here."

"Any place but New York," Luc said, giving that idea the back of his hand. "Hog Island oysters from Point Reyes Peninsula, Island Creeks from Duxbury, Alex's favorites from the Tisbury Great Pond—nature's perfect food, naked and delicious."

"How about from the Gowanus Canal?"

"Once upon a time, Mike."

"Do you know it?"

"Like I told the Brooklyn detectives today, I know the history. Used to be, you could get the best oysters in the world from that water. Such a specialty they were pickled and shipped to France. But that, Mike, was four centuries ago. And no, I've never been to your—may I say?—stinking canal."

"What's that mob expression?" Gina Varona asked. "Sleeping—?"

"With the fishes," Mike said.

"And there was my poor friend Luigi," she said, interlocking her fingers together and staring at the ceiling of the wine cellar, as though she were in church, "sleeping with the oysters."

"You don't sound too broken up about it."

"Devastated, my dear detective. I just don't wear my emotions on my sleeve like your friend Alexandra. But I know once we Italians get into the mix, you cops are bound to think the mob had something to do with it. Ethnic profiling and all that."

This time two waiters appeared. One placed a cocktail in front of each of us, while the other set down on the table an array of appetizers, traditional fare from the fabled bar upstairs—'21' Club mini-burgers, crispy chicken wings, jumbo shrimp cocktail, and a large charcuterie.

"Nobody's mentioned the mob," Mike said, dredging a shrimp in the sauce and moving it to his mouth without a single drip. "You know something we don't?"

"I liked Luigi. He was a good kid. He was hardworking and smart." Varona was pulling hard on her Knob Creek bourbon. "I guess you learned from your visit last night that I knew him from Tiro a Segno. Sergio called to tell me you were there. Luigi didn't have any ties to the mob. He wouldn't have lasted a day at Tiro if he had."

"And we hired him," Luc said. "I told the detectives that, too, today."

"Hired him for what?" I asked.

"To work at Lutèce. To help us put a waitstaff together."

"You knew him?"

"I met him through Gina," Luc said. "She took me to dinner at her club expressly for that purpose. Luigi was great at his job, really well connected to guys in the business, and he spoke French as well. He seemed perfect to me."

Luigi Calamari—the second murder victim—was linked directly to Luc, just like Lisette Honfleur.

"Why would his brother tell the cops that Luigi was fired from his job?" Mike asked. "Why would he say his own brother had a drug habit?"

"The kid was clean as a hound's tooth," Gina said. "I assume they'll autopsy him. The doctors will make that clear."

I guess Mike hadn't told Luc yet that there were several kilos of cocaine glued to the underside of Luigi's houseboat. Or about the skull on the kitchen table.

"It was you who convinced him to leave the Rifle Club?" Mike asked.

Gina Varona smiled again. "I made him an offer he couldn't refuse. That's why he left, Detective. Plain and simple matter of economics."

"So who hated him enough to slit his throat?" I asked, knowing full well there was another business—the lethal one of importing drugs—that had exposed Luigi to a violent death.

"If I think of anyone, I'll give you a buzz," Varona said.

What did Luc possibly see in this woman, except her deep pockets?

"What about you, Mr. Danton? Where do you come into all this?" Mike asked, stirring the rocks in his vodka with his finger.

"And I thought Gina was doing so well you'd forgotten about me," he said. "Where would you like to begin?"

"Tell us about yourself," Mike said, gnawing on a chicken wing.

Peter Danton was drinking a glass of red wine. "Let's see. I'm married, with one daughter away at boarding school in Connecticut. My wife and I live on the Upper West Side. I'm forty-three years old."

"How long have you known Luc?"

He turned his head to Luc. "What would you say, my friend? Maybe fifteen years or so."

"About that."

"You in the restaurant business, too?"

"That's where I started out, Detective, but it was a little rough for me. I actually thought I wanted to be a chef—you know, one of the greats. So I went to Le Relais to do a *stage* there when Luc's father, Andre, owned the place."

"A *stage*?" Mike asked, imitating Peter's pronunciation of the soft "a."

"It means a training session, Mike," Luc said. "Like an internship. I was studying with my father, too, that summer. Peter and I became friends."

"You stayed in the business?"

"Till I had my accident," Peter said, holding up his

hand. "I was working in the kitchen at the time, in one of Bobby Flay's restaurants. The meat cleaver and I had different ideas about how difficult it was to prep a dinner. I'm a lefty—swung too fast and hard and I severed the tips of these two fingers on my right hand."

Mike was the only one eating the food. I wasn't hungry any longer.

"This is quite common," Luc said. "You won't find many chefs who don't have scars and nicks, fingers chopped or cut, or who haven't scalded themselves with boiling water, burned their hands pulling something out of the oven. Those are occupational hazards of being a chef."

"It's why Luc prefers working the front of the house, as they say. Anyway, it got me out of the kitchen faster than lightning," Danton said. "But I never lost my love for the business of entertaining, for being in great restaurants, for wanting to create that unique kind of hospitality that an exclusive restaurant does. Luc's a master at it. I think it's in his genes."

"What's your game, Mr. Danton?" Mike asked. "What kind of work do you do?"

"We have an art gallery, actually. My wife, Eva, and I own it together. It's on Columbus Avenue."

"What do you specialize in?" I asked.

"African art. Contemporary African art."

My thoughts flashed to Mohammed Gil-Darsin. "Any country in particular?"

"No. Anywhere on the continent. Sculptures and paintings, primarily. Ethiopia, South Africa, Ghana—there are fantastic artists working everywhere over there."

"The Ivory Coast?" I asked.

"Sure. We've got a great inventory of Senufo masks. Are you interested, Alex?"

"I'm not in the market right now. I was going in the direction of current events, Peter. Do you—uh, do you know Baby Mo?"

"No, I've never actually met him," Danton said, lifting his glass for another sip. "And I suppose that's a good thing, at the moment. His wife has shopped with us, I know that."

"Kali?"

"Yes. She's one of Eva's favorite customers. You'll have to talk to Eva about her. She might have some insights that will help you with your big case."

"And how long have you known Gina?" Mike asked.

"Maybe ten years or so. We both met through Luc. I was staying in Mougins with him and Brigitte, stopping over for a few nights on my way back from Nigeria, and Gina was there on business. We had dinner together one night, and I guess that's how it all started. We have so many of the same interests."

Why hadn't I met either of these people on my trips to the South of France? On second thought, I was beginning to feel grateful that I hadn't.

"Are you putting money into Luc's venture here, too?" Mercer asked Danton.

"A great deal of it. We're determined to make this work."

"How much?"

"So far, I've invested three million with Luc."

I stared across the table at my lover. My head was reeling at these numbers, and I was feeling more and more like I had been sharing a bed with a total stranger.

"I gotta tell you, Mr. Danton," Mike said. "I had no idea there was that kind of money in African art. I mean, I look at those masks and statues, and then I see the souvenir shops at an airport in a third world country, and it looks like they were all made yesterday from the same cookie cutter."

Danton smiled and took another drink of wine.

"You get me? It's all women with drooping breasts and men with these enormous erect penises. No offense, Mercer, 'cause I know it's your roots and all that, but I can't imagine how those carvings sell for very much."

"Then I guess you'd be quite surprised, Detective. It's really the emerging market in the global art world. Eva and I have done quite well," Danton said, rapping his knuckles on the table, knocking wood.

"Hey, I'm surprised every day of the week. That's murder for you. My job is a surprise, every time I walk into the squad room," Mike said. "So exactly how are you involved in Luc's business, Mr. Danton?"

"Basically, I've done everything he's asked me to. I think because Gina and I are here in New York, Luc's relied on us to get the project off the ground. I found the real estate, and together we bought the building. Luc insisted on a town house, like the original Lutèce."

"Not too rough an assignment, on a budget like the one you've got."

"You'd never believe it, Mike," Luc said. "All the restrictions the city places on us. For a building to be zoned commercial for a restaurant, it has to be within one hundred feet of a main avenue. But in order to get a liquor license, it's got to be five hundred feet away from a church or a school. Not so easy on the Upper East Side."

"Sounds like more restrictions than they place on where a convicted sex offender can live when he gets out of jail," Mercer said.

"Probably so. Then the building out of the restaurant

takes another couple of million—all the flues and duct-
works to create a kitchen that can serve hundreds of
meals a day, keeping the food fresh and preserved. The
decor and furniture, and the equipment, from refrigera-
tion and professional ranges to what the table is set with.
Fine dining is all about air and light and sound and comfort, before you even get to the food."

"Tell them about the licensing, Luc," Gina Varona
added.

"*C'est fou*. The city regulations could make you crazy.
The Department of Buildings has all these guidelines you
have to pass, then it takes months to get a liquor license.
The Fire Department has to check the equipment and
installations. Worst of all is the Department of Health."

"The new rating system that Mayor Bloomberg
started in 2010?" I asked.

"Exactly. This—this ridiculous ABC grading of restaurants. I tell you, five or six years ago, the city collected
about ten million dollars in fines. Last year, it was close to
fifty million dollars." Luc was red in the face, jabbing his
finger at his chest. "You think I could kill someone,
Mike? I tell you it would be a restaurant inspector.

"My friends are all telling me it's killing business.
These kids—these new inspectors—they walk into the
best restaurants right in the middle of service. They see
three drops of water on the kitchen floor in front of the
sink, they announce it's conducive to vermin, and they
shut the place down for two weeks. You know how much
that costs one of us?"

"What else?" Mike asked.

"Okay, so Gina mentioned the mob. You'll never get
them out of the food business. They still control all the
linens in restaurants."

"Table linens?"

"It's a multimillion-dollar business for them," Luc said, holding up his white napkin. "Every piece of table linen in this city runs through one company. Try to buy or rent from some place cheaper, you'll be dead. And garbage is worst of all."

"What about the good old City Department of Sanitation of New York? It's free."

"Don't even think about it, Mike. You get a visit from one of the private carting companies when you're setting up shop, and they tell you how much they're going to charge you per week to take your garbage away. The price makes you want to gag, and all you can say to them when they hand you the bill is '*Merci beaucoup*.' Roughly translated that means 'Thanks so very much, because I'd rather pay you this outrageous sum than to have both my legs broken.'"

"It sounds like more tension in a restaurant than I'd ever stopped to think about," Mike said.

"You haven't even gotten to the staff yet," Peter Danton said. "Front of the house versus back. Managers, captains, sommeliers, bartenders, and servers out in front. And then the guys who never touch the table—the sous chefs, line cooks, prep cooks, dishwashers, porters, all working behind the scenes. Think of how many people it takes to get all that exquisite food from the market onto the dinner plate. Don't even try to imagine the rivalries between them."

"You're understating it if you describe it as tension, Mike," Luc said, downing his drink. "The better word for it is rage."

Thirty-three

It was after ten o'clock when we left '21,' Gina Varona and Peter Danton going their separate ways, and Mike and Mercer driving Luc to his hotel on their way to take me home.

"Don't look so discouraged, darling," he said, getting out of the car and kissing me on the top of my head. "There's a lot to sort out here. We'll get there, I promise. The detectives don't need me tomorrow, so I'll probably go up to the restaurant and do some work. Will I see you, Alex?"

"Better ask our keepers," I said, slumped against the back door of the car.

"I'll be in touch with you," Mike said to Luc.

"Listen, Mike. I don't know how to thank you for everything you've done for me these last two days," Luc said, leaning into the front passenger window of the car.

"It seemed like the right thing to do—for you and for the blonde in the backseat," Mike said. "She'll figure out how to express her gratitude. Have a quiet night, Luc."

We watched him enter the lobby before Mercer started up the car for the short ride to my apartment.

"So where's your head, Coop?"

I didn't answer. I couldn't.

"You've been hanging out with some high rollers. You got any vibes?"

"They're not like the friends of Luc's we've spent time with in Mougins. Truly. I mean I met Luc through Joan and her husband, who's the most grounded guy I know. I'm as shocked as you are by the amounts of money involved."

"Who'd you think was putting up the dough for the restaurant, Coop? The tooth fairy?"

"I knew his father was kicking in to help him, and that he was using a lot of his own money as well. Luc told me he was taking a big loan from a bank. He mentioned that he had silent partners, but I never asked who they were."

"Any of your old man's Cooper-Hoffman heart device money about to disappear into crab cakes à la Gina Varona? Maybe a Gowanus bivalve? Bivalve replacement surgery?"

"No. And I'm not amused."

"Luc ever asked you for any dough?"

"No."

"You really think it's about love and not your money?"

"Ease off the girl," Mercer said.

"You take all the pleasure out of a late night ride, m'man," Mike said.

"What do you guys think?" I asked.

"About what?"

"Luc's caught in the middle of these two murders. I'm heartsick about it. I know him well enough to believe he's got nothing to do with either one, but I hate that all this deadly stuff is spinning around him, close enough to leave a permanent stain."

Neither man spoke.

"I hear you. What did the Brooklyn detectives do with him today, Mike? How do you think that went?"

"Hey, Luc was great. Very forthright, answered all their questions, didn't seem to have anything to hide."

"They asked him about Luigi? I mean he identified the guy from the morgue photos?"

"He did."

"I hope he told them how he knew Luigi. I mean, from his dinners at Tiro with the perfume queen," I said, taking a swipe at Gina Varona.

"Luc actually told them he'd seen Luigi more recently."

I picked my head up. "Really? When was that?"

"In Mougins last weekend. In fact, Luc was kind of surprised when I told him you hadn't recognized Luigi when I showed you his photo. He said he'd been a guest at your dinner in white on Saturday."

Thirty-four

The three of us were standing in a corner of the well-appointed lobby of my building. "No, you are not coming upstairs to discuss this with me tonight. What is it, Mike? Are you going to tell me that you don't believe me? Because if you do, that's all the crap I'm going to take from you ever again. If that's what you want to say to me, do it right here in front of the doormen and my neighbors. Tell me right now why you don't believe me."

"I believe you."

"Don't sound so lame when you say it. What's your problem? Do you think I'm lying to protect Luc?"

Mike was slow to answer. "That possibility crossed my mind."

"Get out of here. Mercer, take him home. I'm not kidding, Mr. Chapman. Get out of my building. Get out of my personal life."

"Alex, he's just baiting you."

"I'm not baiting her, Mercer. She's gonna marry the guy. Of course she'd lie for him."

"I'm not going to marry Luc. I wouldn't lie to protect him or you or Joan Stafford or anyone else. Where do you get your ideas?"

Silence.

"Did Luc tell you that? Answer me, Mike. Did he tell you I was going to marry him? It's not happening. I don't know the man who was sitting in that room with us tonight. I don't want to go to a ball game with him right now, no less marry him."

"Oh, Jesus, don't start to cry on me."

"I'm not crying. I wouldn't give you the pleasure of thinking you could say something that would upset me."

"Let's take this outside," Mercer said. The man with the wheaten terrier who was waiting for the elevator was staring at us like he expected me to throw a punch.

"I am telling you," I said to Mike, ignoring Mercer for the moment, "that I had never seen the guy in that photograph before. Maybe the slit throat threw me off, okay?"

"Maybe if you saw him done up all in white, like with the sheet from the morgue over his body. Maybe he'd look a little spiffier in white, like he was dressed for your dinner in Mougins."

The couple entering the lobby dressed in evening clothes had opera glasses and programs in their hands. She frowned when she heard mention of the morgue.

"I left that party before Luc did. Could be Luigi and I weren't there at the same time."

"Could be you had such stars in your eyes you didn't see anybody but Luc."

Mercer put his arm around my back and started to

guide me to the front door. He had left his car parked at the end of the driveway. "Hollering in this fancy building is going to get you evicted, Ms. Cooper. A little fresh air will do us all good."

"Have you got any photographs of Luigi in the car? In your case folder?" I asked.

"Everything but his prom picture," Mike said.

We approached the old Crown Vic from the rear and Mercer popped the trunk. Mike reached in and grabbed his Redweld, stamped with the word HOMICIDE across the top.

"You've called the airlines and Immigration to see what his passport shows?" I asked. "Checked his travel history?"

"Believe it or not, they got DAs as smart as you in Brooklyn, Coop. You're not the boss of everyone, you know."

"I hope they're smart enough to add Gina Varona and Peter Danton to their travel search list. France, Africa, who knows where else."

"I'm on Night Watch all week. They'll get me an update when I start working tonight."

Mercer was still the peacemaker. "Mike's working overtime for you, Alex."

I looked away. "I guess that gives him double the justification to pile in on me. Is it that I haven't thanked you properly for all you're doing? You've overwhelmed me, Mike, with your kindness to Luc. You actually think I would lie to you guys?"

" 'Course not," Mercer said.

Mike handed me a blowup of the picture he'd shown me from his cell phone Tuesday morning. I held it at every angle. "No go. I don't know this man."

"Try the ME's version of dress for success."

The wound in Luigi's neck had been carefully sutured. His hair was combed and his eyes closed, although his expression was not to be confused—as people often said—with that of someone who was sleeping. A clean white sheet was pulled up over his chest.

"This man and I were not at the same party at the same time."

"Here's a dozen photos his brother brought to the squad. Luigi Calamari at his nephew's birthday party, Luigi in a tux for his cousin's wedding, Luigi in sunglasses and a shirt opened down to his navel—looks like it was taken at the beach."

"No, no, and again no. Good night, Detective. I can't thank you enough for everything you've done for me— for us—today."

"Sounds anything but sincere, kid."

"Must be the company I'm keeping." I turned to walk twenty feet back to the revolving door of my building.

That's when I heard the shouts and saw two men running from the entrance of the drive coming directly toward me out of the darkness, one of them screaming my name.

"That's her!" the voice called out. "Ms. Cooper!"

"Get her," the second guy yelled.

I froze in place as Mercer caught up with me.

A bright light went off—flashing twice, maybe three times—as Mercer pulled me against his chest and Mike took after the two men, who turned and ran.

Thirty-five

"So they got you," Paul Battaglia said, shaking his head. "Right at your own front door." He had been waiting for me when I walked into his office at eight a.m. on Thursday.

The district attorney didn't like it—with good reason—when his lawyers became the headline rather than the backstory.

The *New York Post* stringer and the photographer who snapped the photos last night had convinced the editor to find room for the dreadful picture of me, cowering beside Mercer with my eyes covered against the blinding flashbulbs, on the front page. Baby Mo still owned the top-of-the-fold space, but there I was with an equally cheap caption just below: MURDER SUSPECT 'COOP'ED UP WITH PROSECUTOR?

"I apologize, Paul. There's not much else for me to say."

"It really compromises your credibility on MGD," he

said, tossing the newspaper on top of the unanswered correspondence on his desk. "I want you standing next to me when I announce the indictment this afternoon. I need you to field questions, and this outing doesn't help a whole lot."

"I can do that with you, if it's what you need. This has nothing to do with my credibility. Luc's not staying with me. I'm not harboring a felon."

"That's kind of missing the point, isn't it? They've tagged your gentleman friend as a murder suspect."

"The police haven't."

"The tabloids have," he said, lighting what was probably his second cigar of the morning. "How the hell did they get this?"

"Mike says the Homicide detectives squealed. Thought the Brooklyn DA would like it if you had a little egg on your face, in the form of me as the sacrificial lamb, since you get all the big-time publicity."

"You're off your game, Alexandra. You should be more careful."

"I'm not dating a wiseguy or a thief or a—a crooked politician," I said, causing Battaglia to scowl at me. "The man's in the hospitality business."

"Not so hospitable to have folks dropping dead all around him."

"He's aware of that, Paul. We both are."

"What time will the indictment be filed?"

"We're meeting now to proofread and edit it. We'll have it in front of the foreman as soon as they convene at two p.m. and get it right up to the clerk's office. The arraignment has been scheduled for three in front of Judge Donnelly."

"Four o'clock for my press conference. And I'll tell

Brenda to instruct the reporters that we're not taking questions about anything else except MGD. No side-show about the Gowanus Canal case."

"Understood."

"When I look your way, you talk. Other than that, you're silent as the grave."

Those were the usual rules. Battaglia had always been squeamish about details of sexual assaults. He left it for me to fill in factual blanks that supported the criminal charges.

"Yes, Boss. I'll see you later."

The whole team was arriving in the conference room, as planned, each carrying morning coffee and pastries from the cart in front of the courthouse. Mercer pulled his chair up next to mine, potential armor against the slings Pat McKinney was likely to throw.

"You've been in with Battaglia?" McKinney asked. "Boy was smoke coming out of his ears when I got here today. You know how to bring out the best in a guy."

"Still smoking, Pat," I said.

"I was thinking of going to Umberto's for lunch to-day," he chuckled, "but not if your pal, Luc, has taken over the lease."

Just a few steps from the rear of the courthouse, Um-berto's Clam House was put on the map years ago when Colombo family kingpin Joey Gallo was shot to death in the middle of his lunch, his face slamming straight down into a plateful of spaghetti alle vongole.

"Suit yourself, Pat. I prefer Midtown myself. Mercer and Ryan were planning on lunch at Sparks Steak House," I said. I knew he'd catch the reference to Big Paulie Castellano, who took six bullets to the head on his way in to a holiday dinner on East 46th one snowy night.

"Fine dining and murder often go hand in hand. Ellen, do you have the indictment ready?"

Restaurants and mob murders. Maybe that's what Gina Varona had been so defensive about last night.

"Yes," Ellen said. "I've got a copy for each of you."

Four pairs of legal eyes in the room should guarantee that there were no errors. Date and time of occurrence in the county of New York, victim and perp named, and the precise tracking of the penal code definitions that would stand up to a defense motion to inspect and dismiss. We spent the better part of the next hour scouring the document to catch every possible typo and correct two minor substantive errors.

"Will you take Ellen with you to the grand jury for the foreman's signature?" Pat asked me.

"Sure. Then we'll file it in the kitchen," as the busy court clerk's office was known, "and be ready for the arraignment at three. I assume you want Ellen to stand up for the bail application in front of Donnelly?"

Ellen grimaced. "Ugh, she's so tough."

"But she's smart and she's fair. We couldn't ask for a better judge."

Once the indictment was filed and Mohammed Gil-Darsin was formally charged as a felon, the case would be moved to a higher court—New York State Supreme—and his lawyer would be able to renew his bail application in front of this judge.

Mercer's cell rang and he walked to the window to answer it. We all paused and looked over at him. "What news from France?"

He listened again while Ryan Blackmer raised his eyebrows. Then Mercer pointed at the TV screen mounted on the wall.

I got up and flipped the dial to CNN.

"Breaking news," Mercer said. "About Gil-Darsin."

We were between cycles, and the reporter on-screen was covering an earthquake in Indonesia that locals feared might trigger a tsunami. The lead story would come up again on the half hour, and we were all riveted to the screen.

Six minutes later, a young American journalist stood in front of the gates of the American embassy in Paris, adjusting her earphones.

"It's late afternoon here, Anderson, and we're just getting word that the furor about Mohammed Gil-Darsin, the head of the World Economic Bureau, is about as fierce as the storm that's brewing in the Pacific Ocean.

"Executives of two business firms are under investigation for their alleged role in a prostitution ring that officials believe has been linked to the brilliant but controversial WEB leader known to the world as Baby Mo. The Ivorian-born French resident is now incarcerated in the United States on charges of sexual assault unrelated to today's stunning news."

"What else do you know at this time?" Cooper asked.

"There goes my last chance of slowing this case down," Ryan said. "You guys win. I guess bail's a no-brainer at this point."

"To be clear, Anderson, the early reports carry no suggestion that Gil-Darsin was an organizer or key figure in the criminal enterprise of this prostitution ring, or controlling it in any way. However, the government is looking into rumors that Baby Mo hired some of the women employed by the network, as escorts—or for sexual encounters."

"In France? Are you saying this happened in France?"

"In this country, actually, it's not illegal to trade sex for money. Soliciting or trafficking in prostitutes, however, is against the law here. This matter was uncovered in a luxury hotel in the city of Lille, where a business firm is alleged to have provided women to the prominent men under investigation, some of whom have been named today. These women were imported, if you will, from Belgium and Germany and the Netherlands."

"Hence the trafficking charge. And what's the connection to the United States?"

"The answers aren't all in yet, Anderson, but it's apparent that in some instances, corporate funds of some of the businesses engaging in this enterprise are involved. One of the first arrests today was of a high-ranking local police official in Lille, who literally flew to Washington, DC, with one of the women, when engaged by another World Economic Bureau bigwig, to have her take part in what are being called 'sex parties.'"

"Mohammed Gil-Darsin is expected to appear before one of New York's toughest judges later today. How does his name figure in this newest scandal?"

"Too early to know for sure, but it's believed that texts from Baby Mo were intercepted by investigators, in which the disgraced leader tried to hire women in the past—mostly Belgian—to be flown to meet him in New York, in Washington, and at a recent WEB conference in San Francisco, for the purpose of sexual activities."

"Thanks for bringing us—"

Mercer grabbed the clicker from me and turned off the television. "Well, I'll bet Byron Peaser is doing a happy dance right now. This will put new steam under Blanca's sails."

"I wouldn't want to be in Lem Howell's shoes, going

in front of Judge Donnelly with this just off the wires," Ryan said. "And on the outside, poor Lem's probably got to deal with Mrs. Baby Mo, too. That must be one unhappy broad."

"You know the French," Pat McKinney said. "Anything goes. She's probably copacetic with the whole thing."

"Don't be so sure," I said. As an American involved with a Frenchman, the mores and attitudes of his countrymen had always remained foreign to me. The first news image of Kali's screams piercing the air like a wounded animal had become embedded in my mind. "Madame Gil-Darsin is African. She only lives in Paris."

"Well, if I were Baby Mo," Ryan said, "I'd be thrilled to bunk down at Rikers Island for a couple of weeks, rather than face the wrath of the missus. Order in some takeout, get a delivery of a stack of classic DVDs, do a bit of jailhouse lawyering to stay safe when he's on his cot. I'm just sayin' . . ."

"I think, Alex, that we'd better tell Battaglia about this," Pat said. Then to the rest of the team, "Give us fifteen minutes with the Boss."

Rose was surprised to see McKinney and me arrive together. "Go right in."

The district attorney was on the phone with his stockbroker when we entered. He ended the call abruptly and asked what had brought us back.

Pat McKinney outlined the story about the possible involvement of MGD in an international ring of businessmen and call girls.

"Looks like I made the right call about indicting him this week, don't you think?" Battaglia said, jamming another cigar between his front teeth while he reached for his lighter. "How's this going to play with Judge Don-nelly?"

"She's not likely to be budged by uncorroborated rumors," I said.

"So gather some facts before three o'clock. Give her something to work with. Get your whole team on this, Pat, do you understand? And, Alex, I want you to write an op-ed piece for me to submit for tomorrow's *Times*."

"On a pending case?" I had written for Battaglia before. There were days I thought I could nail his voice with more accuracy than my own, but I'd never considered doing it when a charge was active before the court.

"Pending, my ass. Steer clear of the instant mess. Make it a grand riff about power and dignity, race and class, about giving women access to the system, no matter who the offender is—one of those speeches you do all the time for the ladies who lunch and their charities. What did Leona Helmsley call folks like Blanca? The little people. Make it about the little people—I mean, say it more tactfully than that—having a day in court against the rich and famous, against men in high places."

"For tomorrow, Paul? We're overloaded with work on this case all afternoon."

"Think of the trouble it'll keep you out of while you polish it up tonight. Have a draft ready before I leave here at six."

For once, I believed Pat McKinney when he told me he felt sorry for me as we walked back to the conference room.

He began handing out assignments to the team. He would call sources at the State Department and the Department of Justice to get access to French government officials, while he directed Mercer to tackle Interpol. Ellen and Ryan were responsible for revising the indictment and getting all the facts bullet-pointed for the bail application.

I returned to my desk. Laura was manning the busy phone lines and had set me up with more coffee. "Nobody from the press gets through," I told her. "Absolutely nobody. And yes, Luc is here in New York, and no, he won't be calling in today. You don't need to worry about me in that regard."

She knew me well enough not to say another word about him.

"Lem won't be trying to get me either. Some rough stuff going on in his camp, which will keep him from triplicating me about his client's bail all morning. And Mike? Send him directly to Mercer, who's using the conference room. I'm working on something for the district attorney."

I sat at my desk and scrolled through the avalanche of e-mails that had come in since the morning papers had saturated subway riders. Most of my well-meaning pals had checked in with humorous or consoling remarks. I couldn't help but wonder how Luc was feeling and what he was doing for the day, undoubtedly overwhelmed by everything that had come crashing down on his world, personally and professionally.

I searched my document file for several of the speeches I had prepared in the last few months. The office had triumphed in many cases with an uneven power dynamic— a teenage girl against a physician who had molested her during an office procedure; a mentally challenged young adult over a teacher at a vocational school; and a woman who cleaned offices late at night who had convinced a jury that the head of a world-renowned ad agency had sodomized her in a deserted corridor after he drank too much at an office party.

Each of these cases would fit into the template for Battaglia's remarks, although the timing of the piece wouldn't allow for subtlety. I channeled myself into his speaking style—rougher than mine, with fewer adjectives and all traces of feminine style made to disappear—and began to fashion a narrative.

There was no way I could concentrate. I was more attracted to e-mails and outreach from friends and certain that this was an exercise in futility, created by Battaglia to keep me out of harm's way and headlines for the better part of the day and night.

At one-thirty, with the bare outlines of a draft under way, I drifted down to the conference room to chill with Mercer for a while. Laura had called out for lunch, and I nervously ate half a turkey sandwich—still hungry because I hadn't eaten last night—while Mercer told me about his slow progress. He had made more than a dozen calls, but the small police unit in Lille had been swamped with attention from media everywhere in Europe and America.

Shortly before two, Ellen came in with the revised indictment. We went upstairs to the grand jury to get the required signature, then took the elevator to the tenth floor and filed the papers with the clerk of the court.

We returned to the conference room to gather the rest of the team. Then another elevator ride to the eleventh-floor courtroom in which Donnelly presided. The enormous double-wide corridor was packed with journalists and photographers from just about every newspaper on both sides of the ocean. Uniformed court officers marched our formidable band of MGD prosecutors, followed by

Mercer Wallace, into Part 30 of the Supreme Court of the State of New York. Every seat on every bench in the room was full, except the front row, from which Pat, Ryan, and Mercer would watch the arraignment.

Lem Howell was already planted in the well of the courtroom. On the right-hand side, next to the counsel table at which Ellen and I sat, two sketch artists had taken up positions in the jury box, at work on Lem's profile.

Jan Donnelly took the bench as soon as we were in place. Lem smiled at her and got up to walk toward her.

"Step back, Mr. Howell. Is there anything to discuss before we bring the defendant in?"

"I just thought I could give Your Honor a brief overview of—"

"On the record, Mr. Howell. We'll do this all on the record. Both sides ready to proceed?"

"Yes, Your Honor," Ellen Gunsher said. She seemed intimidated by the stature of the judge, whose stern demeanor seemed incongruous with her pretty face and warm smile, on those occasions that she chose to smile.

"Bring in the defendant."

The court officers exited through the door on the far side of the courtroom. I could hear the sound of the handcuffs jingling as they were removed from Gil-Darsin before he was brought inside. The door opened and he walked in, head held high, dressed in a suit, shirt, and tie that Lem had taken to him in his jail cell. He looked every bit as imperious as though he was about to call to order a meeting of the top dogs of the World Economic Bureau.

Lem leaned over to whisper something to him. I scanned the row behind their seats and was surprised that

Baby Mo's wife wasn't there in his support—not even as a prop, to weigh on the conscience of the judge. Knowing Lem, he was saving her for a more dramatic appearance at a later time.

The judge introduced herself to the defendant. The clerk read the charges from the indictment and asked Mohammed Gil-Darsin what plea he wished to enter.

"Not guilty." Two words, spoken firmly in his best upper-class British accent, with a twinge of his native Ivorian French.

"Please be seated, sir," the judge said. "I'll hear the People on bail."

Ellen rose to her feet, armed with a detailed list of facts in support of her request to keep the defendant remanded without bail. She did well until she ventured into today's news of the Lille-based prostitution scandal.

"Do the French authorities intend to charge Mr. Gil-Darsin with a crime, Ms. Gunsher?" Donnelly asked.

"I don't have that information at this time."

There were six more rapid-fire questions that Ellen could answer only with guesses and gossip. "Sit down then, Ms. Gunsher. Save those arguments for a day when you're more properly informed of the facts. Mr. Howell?"

"Good afternoon, Judge Donnelly. My client and I thank you for this opportunity to correct the terrible injustice of the original bail application," Lem said, grandstanding for the audience at the same time as he struck a pose for the scribbling sketch artists. "As you can see from the criminal court arraignment proceedings, my client—who commands, who deserves, who enjoys worldwide respect for his financial acumen and diplomacy—has been deprived of his liberty when he most needs it: to help to prepare for his defense in this case that apparently takes—let me see—four, *four* prosecutors to shepherd through the treacherous waters of the criminal justice system."

"What's your point?"

"Remand status, Your Honor, is generally reserved for the most heinous of criminals, for homicides and murder cases—like the one in which my dear friend Ms. Cooper finds herself entangled today."

Low blow, Lem. I fixed my eyes on the portrait of Lady Justice hanging on the wall behind the judge.

"Strike that remark from the record," Donnelly said. "Go on. Any circumstances of which the court was not aware on Sunday, when bail was set at remand?"

"First, Your Honor, my client's family was not able to be here with him at that time, which presents a very different picture of any man. But now his wife has arrived in New York. Madame Gil-Darsin—Kalissatou, as she is known—is an exceptional woman, an international superstar, and a woman of great character as well as independent means. The only reason she is not present today is that she is actually securing a lease—a twelve-month lease—on a furnished apartment on Central Park South. So we can assure you that my client will indeed have roots in this community—very expensive roots, I might add—for as long as it takes to dispose of the allegations against him."

"Is that all, Mr. Howell?"

Lem covered every angle. He went on about Blanca Robles's fifty-million-dollar civil suit, the connection to an imprisoned lover, the possibility that she had lied to police about her grounds for asylum.

"How about DNA, Mr. Howell? How does DNA

lie?" Judge Donnelly asked. "Do you care to offer any explanation about how it came to be on the uniform of the complaining witness, as well as the walls and floor of your client's hotel room?"

Unlike me, Lem never gave the slightest hint that the wind had been taken out of his sails. He bent his head in the direction of the judge and in a clipped voice said, "Not at this very moment, Your Honor. I'll save that conversation for another day, after the prosecution has provided me with their lab reports so that our own experts can advise about any improprieties. We all know that mistakes can happen."

"Very well then. You're welcome to return to me when the ink dries on your client's lease and you have any new grounds for reconsideration of his bail. I agree with you that remand on these charges, for a first offense, is a highly unusual position for Mr. Battaglia's office. Feel free to renew your application when you think it's appropriate."

"Thank you, Your Honor."

"Until such time, however, the defendant is remanded."

Mohammed Gil-Darsin stood up, appearing far less sanguine about the news than did his lawyer. Lem chatted with him and patted him on the shoulder as he sent him off to the holding pens behind the courtroom to await the bus ride to Rikers Island, then tried to make his apologies to me before we could follow the crowd out into the hallway.

"Well, at least Donnelly didn't close the door on me entirely, did she?" he asked.

"Not so hard as I'd like to do."

"How about I buy you a cocktail at the end of your long day, Alex? I think you and I have a lot to talk about."

"It's such a tempting offer, Lem," I said, holding my

arms out, palms up, imaginarily weighing each side like Lady Justice over my shoulder. "A drink with you tonight or root canal? Tough choice, but I think I'm leaning toward the latter."

We were interrupted by Mickey Diamond, who'd come forward from the press section to select for tomorrow's paper one of the sketches the *Post* artist had rendered.

"It's not my fault, Alex," he said. "I wasn't working last night. I hated what they did to you with that headline this morning."

"I know it wasn't you. Don't even think about it." It was my own damn fault—the entanglement, as Lem called it, in the two murders that had occurred, the fact that Mike had been drawn in to help Luc on my behalf, and my bickering with him last night in the driveway in front of my building.

"How's this?" Diamond said, holding several drawings in his hands. "Pick your favorite one. I'll make it up to you. Your best angle, Alex."

I laughed. "I'd prefer to be left out of it all together. Use this one of Ellen—it's very flattering. Or this one of Lem, posturing like a peacock. I'll even write the caption for you."

"They're going with the line I got already. I mean, it's not my fault. I texted it in after Lem made his crack about you to the court."

"Dare I ask?" I was so low on adrenaline that I couldn't even muster the juice to blush with embarrassment or engage my bad temper.

Diamond lifted his pad to show me. SEX CRIMES PROSECUTOR DINING IN HELL'S KITCHEN? .

Thirty-six

I made it through Battaglia's press conference without taking any personal hits, then went back to my own office to continue working on his op-ed piece.

When I showed him a partial draft of the essay at six forty that evening, he told me the language wasn't strong enough and I should stay at it. He had clearly given up the idea of placing it in the next day's paper, so I felt no need to struggle with it any longer after he left.

Mercer was still waiting for me when I returned to my desk. "I neglected to feed you last night, after all that talk at '21.'"

"I'm not very good company. I've got no focus at all."

"Mike wants to meet us for dinner."

"Didn't we just try that routine? It had a miserable ending for all concerned."

"You owe it to him, girl. This week you just do. He has some things to tell you, and he wants to pick your brain."

"There's nothing left in it to pick. It's like a flock of vultures went at it on empty stomachs. Is this with or without Luc?"

"Without."

"No surprises again? Because I couldn't bear it." I opened the door to the narrow coat closet in my office and took a look at myself in the mirror.

"No surprises."

"Do either of you plan on telling me whether Luc's on his way to Sing Sing already or just keeping busy around town?"

"Luc's fine. He had another session with the Brooklyn cops today, along with both of his partners."

I brushed my hair and put some lipstick on, but nothing was going to help the drained look my face had taken on during the week, or the despair I felt tonight.

"Let's go," I said. "Whatever's left of me, I'm all yours."

The elevator came down from the ninth floor, half-full of lawyers from one of the bureaus in the Trial Division. Two complimented us on the MGD indictment, while two others made gentle fun of the morning's headline. I couldn't wait to get out on the street, away from the office.

Colleagues were coming out of both buildings the DA's office occupied on Hogan Place—five hundred lawyers strong, with thousands on the support staff as well. Those on trial would burn the midnight oil, but others split off in groups of two and three, headed for the bar at Forlini's or an affordable dinner in Chinatown to relive the day's work.

"Hey, Mercer," Tom Curran, a senior litigator, called out. "Can I buy you a drink?"

"Rain check," the popular detective said, leading me toward his car on Canal Street.

"What's the matter? You Coop'ed up tonight?"

I waved back at the group that guffawed at his joke. "The next dog of a case that finds its way to my desk will have your name written all over it, Tom."

"Bring it on, Alex." There was nothing about a court-room contest that scared my good-natured friend. "What happened to your boy toy? Today's *Post* read like Chap-man quit the force to write copy for them. You need a backup? 'Cause I'm almost as good-looking as he is."

Tom and Mike had the same distinctively handsome Irish faces, both with thick heads of black hair and win-ning smiles.

"You'll be the first to know when I'm on the market."

"Then go a round with us at Forlini's right now."

"You heard Mercer. Next time."

"Tell you what," Tom said. "When Lem knocks you out with an acquittal on MGD, I'll throw the party."

"I've had ten better offers than that just this after-noon. See you tomorrow."

We got into the car and Mercer made a U-turn to drive uptown on Lafayette Street.

"Where to?" I asked.

"Patroon."

I was happy for the first time all day. Ken Aretsky had been a trusted friend to Luc and me and would protect me in his superb restaurant, with all the care and comfort that went along with his great food.

"I love this idea. Thanks a million." I knew Mike had a purpose—beyond his palate—in this venue. He, too, had benefitted from Ken's generosity, and he undoubtedly wanted to get the restaurateur's insights on what had been happening in Luc's world.

We cruised uptown and found parking easily on East 46th Street, right in front of Patroon. Ken and his wife, Di, one of my dearest friends, were greeting guests in the main dining room. The chic-looking crowd in the plush banquettes reflected the glow of the understated lighting from the wall sconces, showing off one of the most distinguished photography collections in any public space in the country.

Stephane, the stunningly efficient captain who had been with the Aretskys for the fifteen years since they'd opened their doors, directed us to the Humidor Room on the second floor. Although he and I always addressed each other in his native French, I didn't want to hear a word of that language this evening.

The entire level on two was a suite of handsome rooms of different sizes, all for private parties. The intimacy of this one, with its Spanish cedarwood and spotless mirrors, was one of my favorites.

"Totally my fault last night," Mike said, hands up in the air like he was surrendering to the local sheriff.

"My idea to take your quarrel out onto the street," Mercer said. "My bad."

"Gentlemen, gentlemen. Let's not all fall on our swords at one time. I've been pretty stupid about some of this."

"Damn right you have, kid. We'll regroup tonight."

"Up here?" I asked.

"No, but behind that sleek bit of cabinetry, there's a door with a flat-screen TV."

Mercer opened it and turned on the television, muting the set while we waited for Final Jeopardy!

"So my day was as busy as yours," Mike said. "And I'd need a flying carpet to keep up with Luc's partners."

"What do you mean?" I asked.

"Peter Danton for starters. The guy can't sit still. He's gone for two weeks every month. His usual flight pattern is New York to Ghana. Roams around West Africa."

"That's his business, Mike."

"Don't be so thin-skinned, Coop. I'm just laying out the facts," Mike said. "He picks up again from Senegal to the south of France, before going on to Paris and home."

"Nothing unusual about that."

"Then you got Gina Varona. South of France, Paris, Milan."

"All fashion and cosmetics."

"And friends and food, Coop. I get it."

"Do their trips overlap?"

"Rarely," Mike said. "But the Brooklyn techs got a new name from Luc today. A new player. Jim Mulroy."

"That's not new at all. I know Jim. I mean I met him on Sunday. He's the wine buyer. That's his business."

"Yeah? Well, he's been all over the place, too. And begging for a piece of the action."

"How do you mean?"

"He wants a cut of the partnership, behind Varona and Danton. His last trip was Paris, Lyons, Mougins, Bordeaux," Mike said, flipping through his pad.

"Everywhere I'd expect a wine merchant to be," I said.

"Lille, too?" This time it was a question, no doubt prompted by today's news about MGD.

"Beer country," I said, crestfallen. And then, hoping to save Mulroy from any hint of the scandal, I added an idea. "Although Lille's right in the heart of where the best champagnes come from—between Reims and Troyes."

Mike looked at his watch and then the television.

Trebek had already revealed the blue screen with the final category and was reading it aloud for the second time as the volume came on. "Presidential Shelter."

"Who knows what they mean by that one," Mike said. "Twenty only."

Stephane reappeared with a drink for each of us. We clinked glasses and Mercer toasted to a speedy solution to Luc's predicament.

"Here's your answer, folks," Trebek said. " 'These two islands were the sites of fallout shelters built in 1961 for JFK during soviet face-offs.' We're looking for two islands."

The musical timer ticked away while the three contestants scratched their heads and screwed up their noses.

"You got any fallout shelters on the Vineyard, Alex?" Mercer asked. "That would have been close to the summer White House in Hyannis."

"No such thing on my little island. I've never heard of this. Doesn't the White House have its own bunker?"

"Built during WWII," Mike said, "to protect FDR. You got it."

"So where could these be?" I asked, grateful for the diversion from the serious work of this week.

"Is that an 'I give up,' Coop?"

"Why, is your Cold War trivia as good as the real military stuff you know? And yes, I've given up on just about everything."

"What is Nantucket?" Mercer asked. "That has to be one of them."

"You're halfway there," Mike said.

Trebek was shaking his head at the three women, who seemed frozen behind their podiums. None of them were writing.

"What are Nantucket—and Peanut Island?" Mike asked.

"Now, that one comes straight from your twisted imagination," Mercer said to him.

"No takers?" Trebek said. "What are Nantucket—the island off the coast of Cape Cod, where the president and his family summered—and Peanut Island? Peanut Island, for those of you who didn't know, is a tiny strip directly opposite Millionaire's Row in Palm Beach. Nobody guessed that, did you?"

Mike turned off the television. "Yeah, Navy Seabees built the shelter at the end of '61, as we were ramping up to the Cuban Missile Crisis. Just a helicopter hop from the Kennedy home, on this little island that was meant to be a terminal for shipping peanut oil."

"Just hearing the word 'peanut' makes me hungry," Mercer said.

"Then let's chow down."

"Up here?" I asked.

"Nope," Mike said. "Follow me."

The three of us took the tiny elevator down two flights, to the basement. Patroon, too, had a wine cellar with a dining table. It was far more intimate than the space at '21,' and without all the sinister hidden doors and locked rooms. Luc and I had surprised Vickee and Mercer with an anniversary dinner for eight in the divine, candlelit space several months earlier.

"What's the point of this?" I asked. "Déjà vu, all over again?"

"Ken thought it would give us privacy. I've got to

bring you up to speed, and he said he'd help us with some answers."

Stephane brought menus down to us, but we'd eaten at Patroon so many times that we really didn't need them to order.

"I'll have the rack of lamb," Mike said. "Onion rings, whipped potatoes, grilled asparagus."

"Very good choice, Detective. Did I forget to say 'ladies first'?" Stephane asked, pointing his pen at Mike. "He just jumped right in ahead of you, Alexandra."

"He's a growing boy. And I'd like the thirty-five-day dry aged sirloin, please. Black and blue."

"Mercer?"

"Dover sole. Grilled."

"It's sublime," Stephane said. "We're serving it tonight with a caper meunière sauce. Will that be okay for you?"

"Just perfect. Mike's side dishes will do us all fine."

"Mr. Aretsky wants to send you a bottle of wine, with his compliments. He said to tell you he'll be down here shortly."

Stephane excused himself to place the order. I started peppering Mike with questions.

"What else did you find out today?"

"The lieutenant finally took me off Night Watch. He's letting me give Brooklyn Homicide a hand. I was there most of the day, with Luc."

"Thank you so much for being with him. Truly, Mike. I mean it."

"After they sent him on his way, I began making all the calls. They asked me to reach out to the police captain in Mougins."

"Jacques Belgarde?"

"Exactly."

"What does he add?"

"I'm trying to see if there's any link between Luigi Calamari and Lisette Honfleur. We know they were both in Mougins the night of Luc's party," Mike said, "and now they're both dead."

"There's the candy connection," Mercer said.

"Yeah, Lisette had blow hidden in her Bronx wallet, and Luigi had a boatload of cocaine stashed in the canal."

"Has the ME given you any word about Luigi's drug use in the autopsy report?"

"No signs of it. Gina Varona might have been right. No vascular changes in the nasal submucosa, no perfora-tion of the nasal septum like a chronic addict might have."

"And the tox results will take weeks. So what do you think Luigi's brother meant about his drug problem?"

"Could be," Mercer said, "that he knew the kid wasn't a user, but that he was up to something every bit as lethal."

"Importing it for sale," I said. "There's something I've got to ask you, Mike."

"Shoot."

"Did Luc tell you anything else about what time Luigi got to the party last Saturday? Or how long he stayed?"

"He said it was late. Definitely toward the end of the night. Probably after you left for home."

"And Lisette," holding my breath, because Luc had so emphatically denied her presence to Jacques Belgarde, even though the clothes she died in were all white. "Did you ask him whether Lisette came to the party with Lu-igi? Did Luc see her there as well?"

"No. He still insists he hasn't seen her in several years. We're working on the car rental places at the Nice airport, to see whether Luigi rented one to get to Mougins, see where he spent the night."

"They have to have been working together, Mike," I said, putting down my drink to map out the lines between the players. "Luc and I left the house for the party at about seven o'clock, to make sure everything was set up for our guests. The door to the street is never bolted, but when I got home at around two a.m., not only was the door locked and jammed with bits of bone but the larger bones were stacked up in front, and three skulls had been placed at the entrance to the restaurant."

"And did they resemble the skull I brought to your apartment from Luigi's houseboat?"

"Exactly the same type. Very, very old and discolored. From the Parisian catacombs, I'm quite sure. Belgarde has Lisette's arrest record for trespassing there."

"So the logical thought is that Luigi and Lisette were deep in something together," Mercer said.

"Something that Luc didn't have any reason to know about." Both of them ignored me when I spoke.

"Let's say Luigi had a legitimate reason for going to Mougins."

"Was Luc aware of that?"

Mike hesitated and glanced across the table at me. I'd seen that look before. He was trying to decide how much information to trust me with.

"He didn't know Luigi would be there at the party, but one of the other waiters invited him, telling him to drop in at the end of the evening, after some of the guests were gone. He said he'd come to town to try to recruit staff for Lutèce from the other restaurants around Mougins," Mike said. "Luc liked his moxie. He even agreed it would be great to steal talent from his competitors in France and have a few authentic French waiters."

"That sounds like Luc," I said. "So Luigi arrived after I left the party?"

"Probably so."

"Alone?"

"Yes."

"That could account for the Lutèce matchboxes. Luc was giving them away at the party, and the waiters were using them to light candles, too. Luigi could have taken some, maybe even given one to Lisette."

"That's an idea," Mike said.

"Lisette was dressed all in white," I said. "I wonder if something or someone stopped her from coming to dinner."

"Doesn't seem like we're ever going to know," Mercer said. "She could have been planning to go in with Luigi, but got cold feet about being confronted by Luc."

"I got another thought," Mike said. "Suppose she's the one who planted the bones and the three skulls while you were up at—where was the party?"

"At the highest point of the village, just outside the Saracens Gate."

"Explain the geography to me, Coop. Can you see Luc's house—or the restaurant—from that point?"

"No way. It's a stunning vista, but built in medieval days to keep out invaders. So you can see all the way to the Mediterranean because it was meant to be a lookout for foreign armies, but you can't see back down to the village behind the stone walls."

"So if you and the town's 'in crowd' were up at the party all evening, someone like Lisette could have made her way to the house with—let's say—a bag of bones," Mike said.

"Sure. And instead of looking to any villagers like a stranger roaming around the town," I said, "she'd have seemed to be done up for Luc's party. No one would have thought twice about it."

"And she knew the way to his house, I take it."

"No doubt. The timing works, too. When I was trying to get the door open—Lisette must have jammed it, just to make trouble for us coming home. That's when I heard laughter from the field below Luc's property. She'd delivered her gruesome skeletons and was on her way down to the parking lot."

"But who was laughing with her," Mercer said, "if Luigi was up at the party? How many people were involved, and what was Luigi really up to with his visit to Mougins?"

"Feels like the age-old double-cross," Mike said.

"How?" I asked.

"Assume for a minute that Luigi Calamari seemed like the real deal to Gina Varona and to Luc. Smart, young, handsome guy—speaks French—has experience at an upscale private club, so they want to lure him away to head the waitstaff at Lutèce."

"Got it."

"Makes sense he'd sniff around to get other experienced staff. What's to lose? You're the one who told me these French places don't like to use anyone but their own in the front of the house. Maybe Varona or Peter Danton financed his trip to Mougins, because Luc claims that he didn't know about it."

"And you believe Luc?"

"I do, Coop. I do," Mike said.

"But what's Luigi's connection to Lisette Honfleur?"

"Cocaine, obviously," Mike said, running his fingers through his black hair. "We just have to find out who hooked them up together, and how long ago."

"So you're saying Luigi worked the cross," Mercer said. "Surprises Luc at the party, to show his face and offer his bona fides about the business trip. But you're thinking he had two purposes, and the other involved a drug transaction."

"Exactly."

"And Lisette got bounced 'cause she was holding out on Luigi."

"Yeah," Mike said. "Kept her coke too well hidden."

"But the bones and the skulls?" I asked. "What about them?"

"Captain Belgarde is still convinced they were just a diversion. A hoax. Three skulls, like you said, and Luc's three stars. They were supposed to freak out all the locals. Make Luc worry that someone was out to sabotage his standing, his restaurant in Mougins."

"I'm seeing the light," Mercer said, nodding his head. "The bones were meant to take Luc's attention off what was happening here in New York."

"What do you mean?" I said. "What's happening?"

"Somebody in this partnership, Coop, is dirty-dealing. You've got blinders on, girl. You just keep looking stupefied while we get to the bottom of this. That's all I'm asking of you. Either Luc's not who you think he is—"

Mike stretched his hand out to reach mine while he spoke, but I recoiled.

"Or he's being played for a fool by someone here—

someone who's trying to turn Luc's dream into a nightmare."

"And the girl was just a casualty of the drug wars," Mercer said. "Maybe she was introduced to Luigi for his side game?"

"Importing drugs in his spare time, expecting a high-class clientele—hedge funders and young turks he'd curry favor to in the restaurant—ready to buy his stuff. He was probably looking for someone like Lisette to be a burrier," Mike said, using the latest term of art for a smuggler, a combination of "courier" and "burro."

"I'd guess she was playing hide-and-seek with Luigi that night, keeping her own stash safe and sound," Mercer said.

"Think of it, Mercer," Mike said. "If Luigi found out that night that Lisette had a criminal record—"

"How would that come up?" I asked.

"Easy. Suppose she bragged about where she got the skulls, trying to prove her mettle? Suppose she thought he'd be impressed that she'd been a bad girl—a thief, a shoplifter, and who knows what else?"

"Yeah."

"The problem is she would have been revealing that she had a criminal history. A rap sheet, a record, fingerprints on file."

"Useless to Luigi," Mercer said, "as an international burrier. With a record, Lisette wouldn't have made it past the customs line at JFK."

"So that's a reason to kill her?" I asked.

"Depends on how much she knew about Luigi's plans," Mercer said. "That could give him a motive. So could stealing his dope supply. And then he slips a matchbook into her pocket, to keep the heat on Luc—knowing all the while Luc has an alibi."

Mike tossed his head back to finish his last shot of vodka. "Also could be how Lisette knew about Luc's plans. Poker face, blondie. Just you keep a cool poker face. I'm not fingering Luc, I'm just saying he's in the middle of a maelstrom, and we've got to help him get out."

The door opened and Ken Aretsky came in. He leaned over and kissed me, and I was instantly disarmed by his warmth. Ken was the epitome of a mensch—a total stand-up guy for whom friendship and loyalty were paramount.

Mike and Mercer stood to shake hands with him. Ken was a little taller than I, slim and fit in his smart tweed jacket, with an irrepressible smile and tortoiseshell glasses that did nothing to hide the sparkle in his eyes.

"I know you wanted to talk to me, Mike. Am I interrupting anything?"

"Please sit down with us, Ken. We need your help."

"Sure," Ken said. "Where's Luc?"

"He's got lots of stuff to do," Mike said.

"He'll be okay in all this, won't he?" Ken was talking to Mike but looking at me.

"That's a work in progress," Mike said. "We're on top of it."

"What do you need from me?"

"Talk to us about how the business end of this works, Ken. Where's the profitability? How do you deal with investors? How do they make their money back?"

"Have you got all night?"

"Start talking."

"It's different for every restaurateur, Mike. Luc and I

get along well because I think we've got pretty similar interests. We're about giving our clients great hospitality and really good food," Ken said. "Luc's got the same gift his father, Andre, had. He takes an interest in the people who eat in Le Relais. It's not about his ego at all."

"But he's talking about six to eight million to start up a new place like Lutèce. How do you make a go of that?"

"Well, you certainly can't do it alone anymore."

"So Luc's got partners, right? Rich guys who throw money at him. How long will it take him to pay them back?"

"You can be sure that his team has spent plenty of time with their accountants. This all has to be managed down to the last dime, Mike, to the very last penny. It's plotted out to the price of the candle that sits in the middle of a table, or whether or not you can afford to put truffles in a reduction sauce you're using on a veal dish."

"What else?"

"The numbers guys tell you how much you're going to have to spend—and make—to turn a profit," Ken said. "It can easily take five years for an owner like Luc to earn the first dollar that's free of debt."

"That's a long time."

"Say he has a hundred and sixty seats to fill at dinnertime at Lutèce. They'll be counting on turning them over for a second seating on the high-traffic nights."

"What are those?" Mercer asked.

"Thursday, Friday, Saturday. The other nights you're lucky if you turn over a quarter of them, in this economy. Appetizers for as much as thirty-five bucks, and entrées between forty and sixty. You do the same figuring for the luncheon business. If you get lucky and fill the tables more times than you expect, it's all money in the bank."

"What's different about this economy?" Mike asked. "It always looks to me like the rich boys still like to eat well."

"I count on that," Ken said, with a smile. "Luc's very fortunate. Even though he's the new kid in town, he gets the instant name recognition of Lutèce, one of the greatest restaurants ever created, which lasted more than forty years. But when he started to plan this opening, it was before the bloodbaths on Wall Street. A lot of those over-the-top bonuses are what kept my private rooms full and my wine vaults empty."

"What's the deal with all you guys and private rooms?" Mercer asked.

"They're a surefire way to make more money."

"Why?" I asked.

"People like the exclusivity, Alex. And on our end, we get to charge the patrons for renting the room, beyond the price of the food. You reserve our Sporting Room upstairs for a dinner of thirty, let's say, and you choose the menu for your guests in advance? The chef knows exactly how much food he needs to prepare, so there's no waste, and I know you're good for some expensive wines to wash it down."

"So this wine cellar of yours," Mike asked, looking around at the elegant display of cabinetry holding the bottles, "is it modeled on the idea of the one at '21'?"

"Same concept," Ken said with a wink at me, "only mine is nicer."

"And those stories about the secret door at '21'?"

"All true, because of Prohibition. It used to be the best-kept secret in town, but now it's a familiar story. The architect ultimately revealed his design."

"How many investors does it take in today's market to create a place as classy as Lutèce?" Mercer asked.

"It depends how much money each one wants to put up. I'm not sure how many backers Luc has."

"Neither are we," I said.

"Well, we know about Peter Danton and Gina Varona for sure," Mike said. "But Luc said something to the cops today about another silent partner or two, people that were giving money to Danton and Varona in order to get a slice of the pie."

Ken shook his head. "It's a bad way to go."

"How so?" Mike asked. "Too many cooks?"

"That's the general idea. You get four, five, or six people—it's bound to happen that one doesn't get along with some of the others. There's too much at stake. In the end, it's Luc who suffers. It's Luc," Ken said, "who's likely to go under."

Thirty-seven

The three of us devoured the feast prepared in the Patroon kitchen. We'd all been working so hard that we'd existed on junk food, caffeinated drinks, and pure adrenaline. The conversation was bland. We stayed away from Luc and his situation, and the latest revelations about Baby Mo.

The restaurant was only ten minutes from my apartment. I took my place in the backseat for the short ride.

"Are things so bad you're not going to let me call Luc and say good night?" I asked. "Do you even know where he is?"

Mercer took his eyes off the road to glance at Mike.

"He's working, Coop."

"Where? On what?"

"He's at Lutèce. I dropped him off at the building when we left Brooklyn. He was meeting the designer there, and some of his suppliers. You want to call? Go ahead."

I leaned forward and took hold of the collar of Mike's blazer. "You're going to see him, aren't you? You two are planning to drop me off and go talk to Luc, am I right?"

Mercer flashed Mike another glance.

"I want to come along, Mike. It's not fair. Think how devastated he must be. It's another dozen blocks past my apartment. I want to see him, too. Just for ten, fifteen minutes. Just to say good night."

"What's the harm?" Mercer asked.

Mike twisted his neck to release my hand from his jacket. "What if—? That's the harm. What if the Brooklyn Homicide cops are tailing him?"

"So I pop in for a visit. I say good night. What's the big deal? They know we're—we're, uh—" I couldn't manage to say that we were lovers.

"You're what? What are you two anyway?" Mike asked.

I leaned back against the seat. "I'm not so sure anymore."

I knew that I loved Luc, but I couldn't articulate that fact at the moment.

Mercer continued on past 79th Street, making his way to the quiet row of town houses on the block where Lutèce was located. He double-parked near the restaurant, which had no signage and such an understated facade that it looked like just one more multimillion-dollar residence.

"It's almost ten o'clock, Coop. Take fifteen minutes and then I'll send you packing," Mike said.

I got out of the car and stepped onto the sidewalk. There was someone—an adolescent, I thought—peeking out of the window of the building to the west of Lutèce. A small dog beside him, on the edge of the sofa, was barking, probably at the sound of the car door as I slammed it shut.

On the far side of the restaurant was a twin to the Lutèce building—a common architectural feature of Upper East Side Manhattan streets. They were identical in style and feature—both of Beaux Arts limestone—and Luc told me they had been part of the dowry a wealthy Englishman gave to each of his daughters when they married American financiers a century ago.

The restaurant appeared to be dimly lit from within, but I had been cautioned that the interior space had not been completely decorated yet.

I held on to the railing as I took three steps down off the sidewalk to the front door. I knocked loudly and thought I heard footsteps within. Two workmen emerged from the twin building as I waited, depositing a wheelbarrow full of debris in garbage pails on the sidewalk before locking the front gate. They saw me and both said good night.

Luc opened the door, surprised to see me. I put my arms around his neck and kissed him. "I just needed to set eyes on you once today. I know you're expecting Mike, but I came to say good night."

"I couldn't be happier, Alex. Come," he said, taking my hand. He was wearing a light blue linen shirt open at the neck, with jeans and driving moccasins. "Come see what we've done so far. Just watch your step over these wooden planks."

I looked around, and in the soft light emanating from the back of the long space, the restaurant looked every bit as stunning—though much more formal—than the rooms at Le Relais. The trademark trellis that lined the walls behind the plush banquettes was the same soft green as in

Mougins, and small brass sconces would no doubt be filled with tiny peach-colored bulbs that would throw the most flattering light on the women sitting beneath them.

"Oh, Luc, it's so elegant."

"It will be, darling, once everything is installed."

That was when I heard voices from the darkened rear corner of the room. "There's someone here with you?"

"Yes, Alex. I haven't been able to get anything done during the day, so we're making up for it now."

As I approached the last round table just outside the kitchen door, I recognized Gina Varona. "Good evening, Gina."

"Hello, Alex. I didn't know Luc was expecting you."

"He wasn't," I said. "But I hope he isn't as disappointed as you are."

"Not at all. We were just about to leave anyway," she said. "C'mon, Josh."

The man who stood up from the table was the same guy who'd been waiting for me in my driveway on Monday night, the one Luc told me was an old friend.

"Alex, this is Josh Hanson," Luc said.

My cheerful expression had vanished instantly. "We've met."

He didn't look quite as sinister now, clean shaven and dressed in a business suit.

"The last thing I'd intended was to scare you, Alex. Luc asked me to go to your place and assure you—"

"I understand, Josh. I probably overreacted." I had no intention of apologizing for the swift kick I had delivered to his kneecap.

"You don't have to leave," Luc said to both of them.

"It's late. We've got all day tomorrow, haven't we?" Gina Varona asked.

"It's clear on my end."

She picked up her tote—Prada, of course—and finished her glass of red wine. "We'll see ourselves out."

I wasn't able to hide my curiosity. "Who's Josh Hanson and why is he here? You told me he was an old friend of yours."

"He's a friend of Gina's, actually. He's been a client of mine in Mougins for years, but it was she who first introduced me to him. Josh is in advertising. He broke away from Ogilvy and Mather and started his own shop. Kind of a big deal."

"Is he involved in the restaurant?"

"He wants to be, Alex," Luc said, seeming a bit agitated as he cleaned up the papers that they'd been examining before I came in.

"Are you thinking of bringing in another partner? I wish you'd talk to Ken about this. How many backers do you need?"

Luc was jamming the papers into his briefcase.

"It's not entirely up to me. Gina's willing to give Josh a piece. I think she's squabbling with Peter already."

"Fighting about money?"

"The damn place isn't even ready to open yet and Gina and Peter are at each other's throats," Luc said. "I'm so used to operating alone, with just my father watching out for me, that I'm ready to throw up my hands and go back to Mougins. I'm a lone wolf at Le Relais, and I much prefer it that way."

Luc took the jacket off the back of his chair and put it on. He lifted his briefcase from the table but had forgotten to clasp the lock, and the papers inside spilled out all over the floor.

"Damn it," he said. "I'd just like to take you and run

away from here. Leave all of this pressure behind. Where would you like to go, darling? Some little island in the South Pacific?"

Luc kneeled to scoop up the papers, and I could see that his hands were shaking.

I got down beside him and helped with the pickup. There appeared to be endless pages with numbers and prices and lists of distributors on them.

Luc grabbed my wrist with his hand. "You've got to help me, Alex. You've got—"

I put my other hand on his cheek to calm him. I did my best to conjure up a smile. "Don't get crazy, Luc. I'm not running away with you."

"Not that, Alex. I'm not talking about that," Luc said, keeping a firm grip on my wrist. "I need you to get me a lawyer."

Thirty-eight

"What do you need a lawyer for, Luc? What have you done?"

"I haven't done anything."

"Then what do you need a lawyer for?" My heart was pounding now, matching the rhythm of the hammer that was beating against my tired brain.

"Mike thinks I ought to get one," he said, sitting down at the table again, pouring himself another glass of wine. "The detectives in Brooklyn tell me I'm crazy not to have one."

"They're just cops, Luc. I'm a lawyer and I'm telling you that if you didn't do anything, you don't need to hire one."

"Mike and Mercer are the sharpest guys you know. You're always telling me that. Now you're saying they're 'just cops'? They think you're blind to the situation, too close to me to see what's best. There's too much going on around me that I just don't understand."

I sat down opposite Luc.

"I've got to go home, Alex. I've got to see my sons."

"I understand that," I said, almost in a whisper. I knew it was true.

"But I need someone to handle my interests here, someone to deal with the investigation, to stand up for me."

I took a deep breath. "Okay, Luc. We'll take care of that in the morning. Are the detectives okay with your going back to France?"

"They seem to be fine with it," Luc said, relieved that I accepted the idea of his leaving town, and finding him good counsel. "You know who I want to represent me, Alex? That man you introduced me to on the Vineyard last summer. I don't care what it costs. The guy you said was the smartest lawyer you'd ever known. You remember him? You know who I mean?"

I looked at Luc and nodded. "I know exactly who you mean. Justin Feldman."

"Yes, Alex, that's who I want at my back. He's wise and brilliant and strong. Will you call him for me?" Luc said, looking more optimistic than he had all week.

"I wish I could, Luc. But he died, darling. I've never known a better lawyer than Justin—he was truly a giant—but he died last fall. He can't help you with this."

Luc had every reason to be thinking of himself right now, but for me, the mention of my dear friend's name—and his sudden loss—added a profound layer of sorrow to the tension of this moment.

"Désolé," Luc said. Three short syllables, but one of the most powerful words in the French language. *"Vraiment désolé."*

I was totally disconsolate, too. I bit my lip to fight back tears.

"What will I do?"

"Let me think about it tonight, Luc. I'll have a name for you in the morning."

"I want to tell you something."

"Better to save it. Better I don't know anything else." I helped myself to a glass of wine.

"It's about Brigitte, Alex. You've got to know it."

"I think I've known it all along, Luc. You still love her—there are photos everywhere," I said, thinking of the one in the bedside table in Mougins. "There's no room for me in your life right now, and I'm beginning to accept that."

"You're wrong, Alex. Mike's right about how stubborn you are, how thickheaded. You've never believed me when I've told you that I'm way over Brigitte."

"What is it, then?"

"You want to know why she left me? You want to know why our marriage broke apart?" Luc asked, as full of anger as I was full of *tristesse*. "We split because she's an addict. She has been for all of her adult life, and it's unlikely now that will ever change. We broke up over that."

"But you never told me."

"What's to tell? I thought she had beaten it again by the time we'd met. She's been addicted to cocaine since she was a kid at university. She tried to stop for me—I've had her in the best rehabs in Europe—in Switzerland, in England, in Belgium," Luc said. "At best she's sober for a few months, then she relapses. It's going to kill her before too long if no one can get her to stop."

I tried to think of all the times we had talked about Brigitte, and whether there were hints of her addiction in the conversation.

"Why do you think I've fought so hard to be with my sons, Alex? Why do you think it has meant everything to me to be near them? To make sure to see them as often as I could? To try to keep them safe?"

"Didn't the subject come up when you divorced? It should have been easy for you to get custody, with Brigitte's drug history."

"Right after we split, Brigitte spent six months in a rehab facility in Zurich. The kids stayed with me, and Brigitte's mother moved down to help me. I thought she was heaven-sent. The boys were in their home, going to their own school, cared for by me and their grandmother, two people who loved them more than life itself. Then— boom!—it all backfired."

"How?"

"The hearing before the judge was set right after Brigitte's release. She was perfectly sober, of course. She was the model of a repentant ex-addict. As you Americans like to say, for three months she walked the walk. The judge was charmed and thoroughly convinced that Brigitte had kicked the habit. Maybe the judge was just ignorant about addiction—didn't realize it's a fight that goes on every day of a person's life."

"What backfired then?"

"The last straw was that Brigitte's mother testified against me."

"Against you? How is that possible?"

"Like coming to praise Caesar, not to bury him . . . but bury me she did. What a good father I wanted to be—tried to be. But it was all about the lifestyle and how much my work kept me away from the house. And that my business required me to be in the restaurant from five or six in the afternoon—when the boys got home from school with their homework—till one or two in the morning."

"But, Luc, all anyone has to do is see you together with those boys. You live for them. You spend the rest of every waking moment with them. They adore you, they want to *be* you. I've seen them follow you to the restaurant and pretend to be your helpers," I said, laughing at the sweet memory. "Little Mini-Mes."

"That was another strike that Grandmamma threw in. There's liquor at the restaurant, as she reminded the judge. The wine flows like water and the boys are even allowed to sip it from time to time."

"Quelle horreur!" I said in mock surprise. "French kids start sipping wine when they breast-feed. How dare she?"

"All I can say is that it worked like a charm. Brigitte was at her very best—her million-megawatt smile on display and totally pulled together for the judge. I was the dad who was working his ass off so hard to keep the boys that I wasn't responsible enough to be in charge."

"And the fight with Lisette several years ago," I said, starting to put a more complete picture together. "Did Brigitte really catch the girl stealing money?"

Luc looked me straight in the eye. "Money was the least of it. It was Lisette who was supplying the coke to Brigitte, delivering it to her anyway. When I learned about that, I cut off Lisette's access to the cash in the office, where she'd been working for me. That cash drawer was the fund that fed both their habits. Lisette threw a tantrum and broke into our house to steal money—from me personally."

"So when Brigitte found out, there really was a catfight, wasn't there?"

"A major one."

"And when Captain Belgarde asked why you'd never filed a police report about the theft," I said, "it wasn't because you were afraid of being investigated by the tax authorities."

"Not at all. If I called attention to Lisette's drug habits by going to the police, I'd be dragging Brigitte into the very same mess. We cut the girl loose instead, and off Brigitte went for another round in rehab," Luc said. "It was shortly after her return from that trip that we split up."

I was trying to put the timeline together, and more important, trying to fathom how someone measures the love of a parent for a child.

"You've got to go home, Luc. The rest of it will fall into place," I said. "You've got to know that your boys are protected in the midst of everything that's going on."

He stood up again and came around the table to me. I also stood and put my arms around his neck.

"You understand, then, if I leave this weekend?"

"Completely," I said, thinking of the 24/7 demands I still faced on the Gil-Darsin case, as new information seemed to be unfolding every day. "And do you understand that I can't go with you?"

"I don't want you to come, Alex."

"But—?"

"I think it's too dangerous for you to be there right now."

"What is it I don't know, Luc? Is this part of why you want a lawyer?"

Our bodies were against each other. I could feel Luc's heart pounding as strongly as the beats of my own were coming. "I put you in harm's way, Alexandra."

"Not intentionally, Luc. You're as helpless as I am with all this coming down on your head."

He unlocked my hands from behind his neck and stepped back. "But I know more than you do."

"Then tell me about it, please."

Luc wiped his forehead with the back of his hand. "Last Sunday, when we left the beach in Cannes," he said, choosing his words carefully.

"The men on motorcycles who were chasing you," I said. "The two men with guns."

"They could have killed you, Alex. They were trying to get to me, but they could have killed you."

"You know who they were? Let's tell Belgarde about them."

"Jacques Belgarde's a joke. It's not a case for him."

"Who were they, Luc?"

"I don't know their names. And their names don't matter for a minute, because when they're gone, there'll be two more goons to replace them."

"But Luc—"

"It's about drugs, Alex. Do you get that? Don't you remember *The French Connection,* or was that just a piece of movie trivia to you and Mike?"

"Of course I remember it, and I'm well aware that it was real," I said. Marseille, just down the coast from Cannes on the Mediterranean, had been the intersection where Turkish poppies were sent to French labs to be converted to heroin for sales in America—and the export of the deadly finished product.

"You know what that so-called connection is today?"

"No, Luc. No, I don't."

"There's a new source for cocaine that's flooding the south of France. You Americans have finally made a dent in the Colombian cartels, so now there's a different place that excels at exporting the raw material. What used to be called Africa's Gold Coast is known as the Coke Coast."

I thought of Papa Mo, the deposed Ivorian leader

who had stolen millions of dollars from the rich cocoa crop of his war-torn republic.

"West Africa is the world's new narco-state, Alex. It thrives in dirt poor countries like Guinea-Bissau and Mauritania," Luc said, completely wound up in his description of the drug trade. "Two weeks ago, five women pretending to be pregnant were stopped on the Mali border. They had concealed several dozen kilos of cocaine on their bodies."

"And the Republic of the Ivory Coast?" I asked.

"Of course, Alex. That country, too. All those isolated corners of the politically unstable African coast, with its hundreds of miles of unpatrolled shoreline. The cocaine is concealed in caravans that cross the Sahara, and in small planes that fly over the sea and land on small strips along the French border."

I needed to slow Luc down. Why was he so on top of the drug trade in his part of the world? "And you know all this because—?"

"Because of Brigitte, of course," he said, snapping at me. And then he lowered his voice. "Because I'm due back in court next week to lay this out before the judge who made the custody decision. My lawyer has done all the research to make his point, and I've spent more time studying the subject than I've done with my business plans. I need to get my sons out of her life. I won't stop at anything this time."

I turned and looked around the room for no good reason, as though an answer to my problems might be hidden behind an exposed beam or an unfinished wall unit. "But no one—neither she nor the court will let you leave the country—leave France—with your children. That will never happen, Luc. You aren't even established over here yet. You're staying in a hotel."

"Don't you think I'm aware of all this? Don't you know it's tearing my gut apart, Alex?" he said, the despair soaking through every word he said. "Here we are, standing inside the bricks-and-mortar foundation of what my dreams have been, professionally, for most of my life. In three or four months, the apartment on the third floor will be ready for the boys to live in—just the way I grew up, which was quite wonderful, actually."

Luc slowed down his delivery. "On top of that, I somehow found you, and I'm having trouble making sense of how to hang on to that slice of good fortune as well."

"Go back to the men on motorcycles, Luc," I said. This wasn't the moment to tell him that if that's what he considered his good fortune, it might be about to change. "Why were they after you? The day it happened—just last Sunday—you swore to me you had no idea what it was about."

"I didn't put it together at the time, darling. Now it's pretty clear they were after me, and maybe after you, too."

"Me? That's insane."

"Look at what happened. Lisette came up to Mougins the night before, with a supply of cocaine. But she didn't return. Not with the drugs, nor with money, if she was supposed to sell them for the dealer. She disappeared, at least in the minds of whoever gave her the drugs to deliver."

"She disappeared with the coke."

"She was dressed in white, so maybe she had told her friends—her suppliers—that Luigi had promised to get her into the party," Luc said. "Perhaps she even bragged about getting to me directly, told them my wife used to be one of her best clients."

"But your wife is gone."

"So was Lisette, for three or four years. Maybe she didn't know about Brigitte. Or maybe she just figured that there was a good chance someone at the party would be up for a little blow."

"And when she didn't return on Sunday morning, these guys figured that you had it, Luc. That you took it from Lisette, and they wanted it back—or they wanted to get paid for it. But me?"

"Hey, you're just the girl hanging on to me on the back of my Ducati. Motorcycle gear and helmet on, it's not exactly like you had 'district attorney' stamped on the back of your outfit."

I could understand what Luc was thinking. "That's why you were so anxious to leave me at the house after the chase and rush away to make sure your sons were okay."

Luc exhaled. "That proverbial rock and a hard place. Scylla and Charybdis. It was a terrible thing I did, Alex, leaving you alone while I raced to make sure the boys were safe. Because of Brigitte's drug habit, they've always been so vulnerable."

"The guys on the motorcycle were coming after you, Luc, for the coke or the cash."

"But it was you, Alex, it was your back that they had in their sights," Luc said, "because I had never told you the truth about Brigitte, and that could have gotten you killed."

Thirty-nine

There was no conversation in Mercer's car on our way to my apartment. Luc and I were in the backseat, as far apart from each other as it was humanly possible to be.

The doorman came to help me out as I said good night. Mike and Mercer were going to take Luc to the Plaza Athénée and talk to him there. I had told them Luc had more information he needed to give them, both about Brigitte's drug history and the new frontier of the West African world of narco-trafficking.

My comfortably appointed home, always my refuge, had never seemed lonelier. From my window on the twentieth floor, I could see the view south to Luc's hotel. Any other time I would have longed to be there with him, but tonight I was knee-deep in self-doubt.

I followed my usual late night routine. First I soaked in a practically scalding bath, scented with lavender oils, to remove the day's tension and debris. I poured a stiff nightcap of Dewar's before slipping into my favorite silk sleep shirt. When I got into bed, I balanced my laptop on the pristine D. Porthault duvet cover, then settled in to search for the latest news stories on MGD. I entered the search words, and dozens of brand-new articles popped up instantly. The French and British papers had head-lined the stories about Lille and prostitution, some with links to Baby Mo himself, and others naming business-men who were wealthy but not so well-known abroad.

The first three pieces were short. The fourth one men-tioned the drug trade. It made no link between Moham-med Gil-Darsin and illegal substances but said that some of the parties paid for by prominent men using this sex ring were fueled by cocaine.

The fifth piece played off the previous one. It identi-fied the disgraced French police officer who had traveled to Washington to deliver one of the escorts, speculating that both he and the Belgian hooker carried drugs as part of the expensive transaction.

By the time I reached the third page of stories, the theme had shifted to the drug connection. The *World Politics Review* cited tightened U.S. drug enforcement, coupled with a weak dollar and surging demand for coke in Europe, as leading to political and economic chaos across West Africa.

I punched in Mohammed Gil-Darsin and cocaine but got no result. I tried a variety of entries, but all that came back were the old stories about Papa Mo stealing all the money from the lucrative Ivorian cocoa trade.

Brigitte Rouget was on my mind, for no good reason. I Googled her and found a string of articles that showed her at social events, openings and parties. The latest pic-tures featured her solo, always with a champagne glass in one hand and a cigarette in the other. Jumping ahead four pages, there were endless snaps of her with Luc, both at Le Relais and other restaurants, all over Europe.

I scrolled back up the page and studied some of the photographs. In at least five of them, Gina Varona was pictured with Brigitte. One went back to Brigitte's single days—from the caption beneath—when it appeared she was an almost anorexically thin runway model at a designer show in Milan.

Maybe Gina had been into the happy dust with Brigitte. I was as creative in my search as the late hour and double Dewar's allowed me to be, but all the references were either to the fashion and cosmetics business, or to Gina's philanthropic generosity.

I moved on to Peter Danton. There were pages of stories about him, many of them in art magazines—foreign and domestic—about the gallery he and Eva owned, about their personal collection, and about his quest to hunt down the finest African art by traveling to the most remote regions of the Dark Continent.

He, too, seemed to be entirely aboveboard.

There were far too many articles to absorb tonight, so I made a note to ask Laura to download more of them tomorrow.

I was yawning now, just about ready to close up shop. I punched in Josh Hanson's name and was not surprised to find a very long string of references to his advertising position, crediting him for major campaigns for junk food that won awards for Super Bowl 2010 and the last Olympics.

Several pieces paired his name with Gina Varona, all of them related to new perfumes being introduced to the market. I added Peter Danton to the quest and came away with obligatory photos of both men—Peter and

Josh—sponsoring black tie events at the Temple of Den-
dur or soaring over some minor Alp in a hot air balloon
at a birthday party for a dot.com billionaire.

When the phone rang shortly before midnight, I assumed that it was Luc.

"Am I getting you too late, Alex?"

"Ryan?"

"Yeah. I'm just too nervous to let this fester till morning."

"It's never too late. What have you got?"

I pushed my glass away from the edge of the night
table and sat up.

"First of all, Citibank got the papers that Mercer sub-
poenaed down to us."

"At this hour?"

"Nope. I called there just before closing. They had a
rush job going on it and told me if I waited at my desk
until ten, they'd get them to me."

"Good man."

"Five bank accounts, Alex. Blanca has more than half
a million dollars collecting interest in her name. Six hundred twelve thousand and thirty-nine cents to be exact.
On a hotel maid's salary, she must be a very thrifty
woman."

"It's not possible."

"I'm looking at the statements right this minute.
That's either a boatload of counterfeit pocketbooks the
boyfriend is selling, or enough drugs to keep the rest of
Guatemala on a permanent high."

"Is it possible she never did anything else but sign the
signature card, Ryan? That the lover—the guy in the
slammer—is running the scam and she's just an ignorant
dupe?"

"Hardly. Looks like she withdrew a nice chunk of change—more than ten thousand dollars—about three weeks ago, long after the boyfriend was carted off to jail. I suppose the bank will be able to match up the time on the slip to a photograph of Blanca grinning at the camera when the teller counted out the money."

"We need to get her back into the office first thing in the morning," I said. "We need to take one more hard run at her."

"Do you think it's weird that she's got all that money in the bank but still works as a maid?"

"She knows that money is likely to evaporate the minute the feds get around to reclaiming it, Ryan. Blanca needs the day job."

"I hope you don't mind that I used your name, Alex."

"Maybe you'll have better luck with it than I do. Why?"

"This bank stuff made me crazy, so I called the IRS tonight. What's the point of waiting another two weeks for their news?"

"You got past the switchboard after hours?" I laughed.

"Got shuttled along to some bigwig in their law division who was at home in the middle of dinner. Told him I was Alexander Cooper, Manhattan DA's Office. Gave him some of that 'don't you know who I am?' crap and he folded like a deck of cards. He vaguely remembers reading the profile of me—'Coop's Crunches'—in last month's *Men's Health*."

"Remind me not to believe anything you ever tell me again."

"Believe this, Al. Blanca hasn't ever paid income tax. Not a cent."

"The jury will probably applaud her for that."

"Maybe as a housekeeper, but not with half a million bucks on ice."

"Okay, I've got a plan."

"I'm not done. I'm working on a trifecta," Ryan said.

"Why's that, Mr. Blackmer? You planning to make a run at my job?"

"Hey, Al—no way. I'm—"

"'Cause there may be an opening at the top of Sex Crimes this time tomorrow night."

"You'll be fine, Al. I'm just totally into the nuts and bolts of all this. Here's the last piece you'll want to know. I'm in Queens now, in a tiny shithole of a place off Roosevelt Avenue."

"What are you doing, Ryan?" I was scribbling notes on the only Post-it I could reach.

"Did you know the Guatemalan consulate has a mobile van? That there are so many undocumented Guatemalans in the five boroughs that this little sucker drives around night and day, trying to find these people and help them?"

"And you've commandeered it in my name, right?" The image did make me laugh.

"Actually, you're off the hook on this one. I told them I worked for Senator Schumer, and they—"

"*What*? Are you trying to get us all locked up?"

"No, no. I did work for him, Alex. Past tense. I interned for Chuck when I was in law school. They love him in Queens. He's totally the man to know out here."

"I'm afraid to ask what you're doing there. That's not where Blanca is now."

"Do you know how many Mayan dialects there are?" Ryan asked.

"Oh, jeez. You have a copy of the phone call from Blanca to her jailbird."

"So, Mayans are Amerindians, and there are twenty-
one freakin' different dialects. My global mobile consulate van has its pulse on the people of Queens, Al. We've
struck out five times, but I'm very optimistic. I've got all
night for someone to translate what Blanca said to him
after her encounter with MGD, and these folks just don't
seem to sleep. They're eating, drinking, dancing, gam-
bling. Viva Guatemala!"

I was trying to process Ryan's information.

"Talk to me, Al. You're not happy with what I've
done."

"You're amazing. Of course I'm pleased with everything, and better to find this stuff out now than on the
eve of trial. It's just that your position on this case has
been clear from the outset. I'm afraid you're trying to
squeeze the shoe onto a foot that doesn't fit."

"But—"

"Let's assume that Blanca is in on the counterfeiting
games her boyfriend has been running and that she
doesn't pay taxes. I'll even go the next step and bet she,
too, lied on her asylum application. It doesn't change the
fact of what Baby Mo did to her in the hotel room."

"Maybe it does. You know that, Alex. Maybe she's
incapable of telling the truth about anything."

That was the bottom line in all this. How could we ask
a jury to find MGD guilty beyond a reasonable doubt, if
everything his accuser said cast more doubt on her?
Maybe Blanca had lived on the margins for so long, she
wouldn't recognize the truth if it hit her squarely between the eyes.

"Okay, then you keep your global mobile van out on
the streets. I have the unpleasant duty of calling Pat
McKinney at this hour." I stretched my arm out for an-

other shot of Scotch to ready me for that task. "He needs to light a fire under Byron Peaser and make Peaser bring Blanca to the office at nine a.m."

Ryan was pumped up with his own sense of accomplishment. "As they say in the hood, she got some 'splainin' to do."

I was already making my list for the morning. "I want to thank you for all this, Ryan. You know that most prosecutors in this country would just leave all this dirt for the defense to dig up. Throw it against the wall in the middle of a trial and see what sticks. I'm so proud of you for running this all down."

"Where do you think it will go, Alex?" Ryan asked, the tone of his voice much calmer now.

"That depends."

"On what?"

"I think we have to have another shot at Blanca in the morning. Confront her with her lies and go back at her about the events in MGD's room."

"Worst case scenario?"

"We ask Judge Donnelly to hear us again in the afternoon. I have the prisoner produced. I let Lem dress me down for ten minutes. I tell Donnelly I was wrong—"

"It wasn't you, Al. It was the whole team."

"I tell the judge I was wrong and that we need to reconsider the bail status of Gil-Darsin so we can sort everything out—cool, calm, collected."

"You'll let him walk, even though you know he's a pig?"

"He might well walk, Ryan. And Paul Battaglia will have my head."

Forty

I decided to drive to work on Friday morning because I had a slight detour to make.

I left my garage at seven-thirty and drove up Madison Avenue. I wanted to stop and see the twin buildings that Lutèce and its neighbor occupied on the quiet, tree-lined street not far from Central Park, which was in full spring bloom.

There were several parking spots on the street. Many wary New Yorkers lived by the hours of the alternate-side street-cleaning signs rather than pay for garage spaces more expensive than most monthly rents in the country.

I slipped into an opening just off the corner and got out of the car.

The work crew was setting up in the restaurant. They were unloading tools and equipment from two small trucks double-parked on the street. The front door was wide open, and although I was tempted to go in to look around, I knew that I would be in the way.

I crossed to the other side and studied the facades of the matching buildings. The exteriors of both had been restored to their original elegance. That alone would have cost a small fortune.

Double-hung windows had been replaced in each, the neighbors appeared to be copying the effect of the painted trim on the sills, and the handsome silhouettes were aesthetically pleasing to the eye.

The only difference I noted was in the entrance to the buildings. Lutèce was open to the sidewalk, with black wrought iron handrails that would give customers secure footing on the steps in and out of the restaurant.

Around the adjacent residence, there was black wrought iron, too. But it wasn't a simple railing. Rather, it was an eight-foot-high gate that extended from the sides of the house itself and squared around the front of the building, where the two sides met in the middle with a formidable lock at the entrance.

The residential twin town house looked as unwelcoming as the fancy restaurant appeared to be inviting. The distinction amused me. It was not everyone's idea of home to have the daily foot traffic of hundreds of diners and the constant commercial deliveries of food and liquor and flowers and linens.

Workmen were also setting up in the town house next to Lutèce. I waited for a school bus to pass, then crossed back to stand in front of the gate.

"Excuse me," I said to one of the four men in painters' pants who were carrying buckets from their van into the building.

"Good morning, lady."

"How far along are you?" I asked. I didn't know enough about construction work to think of anything more profound.

"How far with what?"

"This building. I mean, is it going to be ready for occupancy soon?"

"It's not for rent, if that's what you're asking," the guy said. He was standing at the rear doors of the van, passing paint rollers and tarps to the other three.

"I'm a friend of the guy who bought this other building—the restaurant next door. I'm just interested in what's happening here."

"Antique white on the walls on the ground floor. Pastels in most of the bedrooms upstairs. Martha Stewart kind of colors. That's what's happening here, so far as I know," he said, his Bronx accent undoubtedly thicker than the paint.

"Who's the owner?"

"Lady, the last time I played Twenty Questions I was in third grade. I don't got the slightest idea who the owner is."

I followed him toward the gate.

"I'm just curious, 'cause I'd like to talk to him—or to her—about when they're moving in. Things like that."

"Hey, Joey," he yelled out to one of the others. "Who owns this place?"

He waited for an answer. "It's not people that's moving in, lady. It's a corporation that owns it. I'm not trying to be difficult with you."

Joey shouted back. "The name's on your pay stub."

I walked down the steps behind the guy I was talking to and went inside. The walls had been freshly plastered, and I could smell the coat of paint that had been applied yesterday.

"Look around, lady. Suit yourself."

The parquet floors had been laid but not finished. That would wait until after the paint job. There were no furnishings at all yet, and the space flowed freely from one area at the front of the house to the next.

"You guys do nice work," I said. "Do you have a card, in case we need any help?"

"Your workers would throw a fit if we elbowed in on them."

"You just never know when you need to bring in someone from the outside. I think they're running way behind schedule."

The painter reached deep into his back pocket for his wallet and removed a card for me. Then he unrolled a piece of paper—the pay stub of his check—and showed it to me. "That's who's gonna be your neighbors."

I looked at the name: GINEVA IMPORTS. I played with the letters and said it aloud a couple of times, but it didn't mean anything to me.

"Would you mind if I looked around the basement?" I asked.

"Right over there. Most people want to see the upstairs. They made it a nice space—three bedrooms on the second floor with three baths. Really spiffy. Two on the floor above that."

"Any lights down here?" I was on the staircase, and the bare bulb shining overhead only got me halfway down the staircase.

"I got a flashlight," the man said. "Whaddaya want to look at?"

I was flustered and trying to think of an answer.

"We've got a wine cellar in the basement of the restaurant, and that's where our sound system will be," I said, making up the second part. "I'm just wondering where it will abut, because of the noise late at night. I'd hate to cause any trouble after all this construction is done."

"I wouldn't give it a second thought, lady. The walls down here are like Fort Knox."

"How so?"

"We just got in to start the paint job this week," he said, running his hands over the rough stones that formed an entire length of wall adjacent to the basement of Lutèce. "They had some bricklayer come in and install this just before we started working."

The flashlight exposed the bricks, and I could see that they were heavy and real, not a veneer.

"Tell your friend his clients can make all the noise they want because the folks on this side of the wall won't hear a thing."

"I'll do that," I said. "Would you just shine that light over this middle area again?"

"You're a real stickler, lady. On second thought," he said good-naturedly, "don't be so quick to call if you need a paint job."

He directed his flashlight to the area I pointed out. I looked closely and could see that the bricks were riddled with dozens of tiny holes and that a thin metal rod hung from a hook on the ceiling above—just like at the seamlessly invisible entrance to the secret door in the wine cellar designed for the '21' Club.

Forty-one

"Where are you, Coop?"

"In my office, about to go into the conference room to do battle with Blanca Robles."

"Something change since I saw you last night?" Mike asked.

"Yeah. Everything's upside down. Blanca's cred is crumbling by the minute. Mercer and I are going to have another go at her in a few minutes."

"Is that why you called?"

"No. But I'd like you to run down some other stuff for me."

"Like what?"

"I stopped by to look at the building next door to Lutèce on my way in this morning."

"The doppelgänger town house?"

"Yes, it's a doppelgänger except for the wrought iron fence with spikes on top that would keep out the most

daring second-story man—and the secret door that con-
nects to Lutèce."

"The what?"

"Last night, when you were parked out in front,
did you happen to notice that the other building was
being renovated, too?"

"Yeah, Mercer and I were talking about it. Like what
it must cost to gut and redo a pricey home like that."

"Well, it made me curious, too. I mean, not everyone
would want to move in next door to a restaurant, with
people coming and going all day and into the night."

"Maybe that's why they have the stay-out-of-my-
house fence," Mike said.

"That's one good reason for it. But then I asked the
workmen for a quick tour. I was particularly interested in
the basement."

"Why?"

"'Cause Luc's doing one of those wine cellars, too.
Like '21' and Patroon."

"What did you find?"

"I think you need to do something I can't manage, Mike.
I think you need to take Luc back to the restaurant today
and have him show you the place, from top to bottom."

"Sure," he said. "But why?"

"Because in the basement of the adjacent building is a
brick wall—just installed last week—and I think it's got a
concealed connection to the basement of Lutèce."

"Does Luc know about it?"

"He's never said a word about anything like that."

"Wait a minute, Coop. Does Luc own the other building?"

"Not that he's told me. That would have cost him a
fortune that he doesn't have. It's bad enough he's rely-

ing on these other people for the loans to build out the restaurant. It's all smoke and mirrors to me, Mike. I'm afraid he's going to lose his shirt."

"He'll be fine. You'll be eating bonbons for a long time to come, kid."

I lowered my voice. "What I'm really afraid of is that Luc's in way over his head. I didn't know about any of this—backers and silent partners putting up millions of dollars—until the murders started unraveling things. I'm afraid that Luc's been caught in the middle of something ugly."

"Like what?"

"I'm trying to figure that out, Mike. Like a financial fraud—a Ponzi scheme," I said. "Do these people who want a piece of his business just manufacture money or what? I don't care how much Luc charges for three courses and a superb magnum of expensive wine, he'll never get out of debt with what he's got to put out to keep the business afloat."

"So you want me to check out what he's hiding in the basement?"

"For starters. And I want to see how he reacts when you find the hidden door. I mean, if that's what it really is."

"I can barely make out what you're saying, Coop."

"I'm whispering. I don't want Laura or anyone else to hear."

Mike chuckled. "You know what you sound like? You sound like Nancy Drew and the secret staircase. You're getting all twitchy on me, blondie."

"Laugh all you want, Mr. Chapman. I'll call the Attorney General's Office myself."

"For what?"

"I want to know everything there is to know about Gineva Imports—when the corporation was created, who owns it, when they bought the building next to Lutèce. Everything that's on file with the AG. Not to worry yourself about, Mike. I'll have nothing but time on my hands after I watch Blanca Robles implode. I'll do it myself."

"Wait a minute. What's Gineva Imports?"

"The corporation that owns the town house."

"You know anything about them?"

"Just a guess."

"Bring it on."

"Wordplay, Mike. Gineva," I said, spelling it for him. "Take the 'gin' from Gina Varona and the 'eva' from Peter Danton's wife. Gin and Eva."

"You probably won the spelling bee, too."

"Not my strong suit."

"What do you think they're importing, besides African art?"

"If I were an optimist, I'd say great wines. Or maybe they're just betting the restaurant will be so successful that Luc will need to double its size before too long."

"But you're not an optimist, Coop."

"That's why the whole setup makes me sick to my stomach."

"You've had a hard-on for Gina since you first heard about her."

"Women's intuition, Mike."

"Grow some testosterone."

"Well, what if they're importing something that would get them locked up for the rest of their natural days?" I said. "That's what's eating at my guts."

"Like what?"

"Think about it, Mike. Gina Varona is one of Brigitte's best friends, and Brigitte is still blowing coke. And Eva is married to Peter Danton, who travels to West Africa every month to buy art—but—well, now that part of the world is the go-to place for cocaine smugglers."

"And you're thinking that one of them is responsible for the cocaine glued to the bottom of Luigi's houseboat, right? Now," Mike said, "we just have to figure out who that is."

Forty-two

There was no stopping Byron Peaser this time. He led
Blanca Robles into the conference room and he wouldn't
leave.

It was eleven o'clock on Friday morning, and the team
was stationed around the table, ready to take on the trou-
bled accuser.

Robles and Peaser sat next to each other with their backs
to the row of windows facing Centre Street. I didn't want
her to have any visual distractions when she talked to me.

Pat McKinney sat at the head of the table, ready to
referee the match.

Mercer was at my side, with Ellen Gunsher behind
him, her chair against the wall, and Ryan Blackmer was
behind me.

"Good morning, Blanca."

The angry woman met my gaze straight on but refused to answer.

"She's not interested in talking to you, Ms. Cooper," Peaser said.

"That's no longer your choice, Blanca."

"I'll tell you what," Peaser started to say.

"No, sir. I'll tell *you* what. You're here as an observer. There are a few things that have come to our attention since your client testified before the grand jury, and we need to straighten them out right now."

I started with the money that was in the five bank accounts in her name. Blanca didn't respond to any of my questions, until Pat McKinney leaned in and told her that she had no choice but to answer if she wanted us to go forward with her case.

I asked her again whether she knew there was half a million dollars in those accounts. Her expression was deadpan as she told us no. Peaser looked like he was going to fall off his chair.

"When is the last time—the most recent time—you went to Citibank to take any money out?"

"As God is my witness," she said, "I didn't take no money out."

I asked the same question about six different ways, then took the withdrawal slip from Ryan and put it in front of Blanca Robles.

She refused to look at it and threw back her head in defiance of my questioning.

Peaser was craning his neck to try to eyeball the slip of paper.

"April third," I said. "Nine-oh-six a.m., Blanca. You withdrew eleven thousand, five hundred dollars."

"That wasn't me," she said.

"In another hour, I'll have a photograph that was

taken when you were talking to the teller. That might jog your memory."

If looks could kill, I'd be a dead woman.

Blanca let go of the handle of the purse that she was clutching on her lap with both hands and jabbed a finger on the table. "As God is my witness—"

It seemed to me that the greater the need to lie, the more she invoked the Lord's name.

"When was the last time you paid your income taxes, Blanca?"

"Excuse me, I didn't finish explaining to you about the money."

"Tell me about your taxes first, Blanca." I wanted to keep the pressure on, jumping from subject to subject to keep her off guard.

"Last year. I think it was last year, or maybe the year before. Maybe I forgot last year."

I turned to Ryan and asked for another folder. We didn't have any written report from the IRS yet, so this morning I had borrowed a file from one of the prosecutors who'd just convicted a swindler in a bribery case.

The array of numbers on the page was dizzying. I held it close to me, on the table, and Blanca leaned over in an effort to see what it was.

"What's that? That's not my taxes," she said.

Ryan jumped in. "No, ma'am. It's a government form that lists returns from everyone named Robles in New York State. You're not anywhere on here."

"Show me and I'll tell you."

"I'd prefer that you tell me first," I said, "and then I'll show you."

"Tell you what?"

"When you paid your income taxes last? Why you aren't on this list?"

Blanca's nostrils flared and her eyes widened. She pointed at Ryan and raised her voice. "You're lying. That's not what those papers say."

Ryan stood his ground. "It certainly is."

"I don't have to talk to you, 'cause you a liar."

Mercer spoke for the first time, in his deep, ever-calm voice. "What is it, Blanca? Are you the only one who's allowed to lie? Is that it?"

Her head swiveled toward Mercer. "I get confused. I don't lie."

"From the first time I met you, Blanca, I believed in you. You know that, don't you?"

"You supposed to, Detective. It's your job to believe me."

"No, Blanca. That's not what I'm supposed to do. My job is to find out the truth."

"She told you the truth about what the defendant did to her," Peaser said.

"One more interruption, Mr. Peaser, and you can wait in my office," I said.

"Pat," Peaser said, hoisting his palm in my direction. "Can you talk some sense into this woman?"

"Alex is right, Byron. We're long past the time for games."

"What did you tell your boyfriend, Blanca, when you called him in prison? What did you say to Hector?" I asked.

"I can't remember," she said, both hands firmly attached to the handle of her purse.

"Did you assure him that you were all right?"

"I did." She gave me a sideways glance, as if to see why I had tempered my tone.

"Did you tell him you were taking your attacker to court?"

"I did."

"Did you tell him anything about the man? About Baby Mo?"

"When I called my friend—Hector's not my boyfriend, you know."

"I see. He just gave you half a million to watch over while he's in prison?"

"Yeah. Because he can't trust nobody else. He's my friend."

"I see. So did you tell him anything about Baby Mo?"

"Why should I? I didn't know who the guy was. I didn't know nothing about him."

"Not even on Monday, after it was all over the newspapers and television that the man who attacked you was famous? That he was wealthy?"

"That didn't mean nothing to me."

"But did you discuss it with your boyfriend?"

"No. I didn't tell him nothing about that."

"Ryan?" I said. "Would you play that portion of the tape?"

Ryan Blackmer had the microcassette he had taken to Queens in the middle of the night. It was primed to a particular point in the conversation between Blanca and her incarcerated lover.

Ryan put the small recorder on the table and hit the play button. Blanca's voice was unmistakable. Although I couldn't make out a single word of the Mayan dialect, we listened to that segment of the tape three times.

"What were you talking about there?"

"You don't know my language, any of you. I was saying how upset I was, okay? I was very upset that day."

"Ms. Robles," Ryan said. "I found an interpreter last night. Someone from your country who understands your language. A man who told me every word of this conversation."

Blanca slammed her handbag on the table. "See? You're telling lies again. You're not allowed to do that."

Ryan fast-forwarded the tape. The next speaker gave his name, address, and date of birth, and the village he came from in Guatemala. He summarized the conversation that Blanca had earlier in the week.

The back-and-forth between the accuser and her boyfriend sounded flat and unemotional. The part that interested us most was translated by Ryan's witness. "Don't worry. This guy," Blanca had said on the call, referring to MGD, "he has a lot of money. I know exactly what I'm doing."

Ryan flipped off the recorder.

"Is that a fair description of what you said?" I asked.

"It's not fair."

"What she means is," Mercer said, "is that what you told your boyfriend?"

"I don't remember. I said that to you before."

"But these are your words, Blanca," he said. "It's your voice."

She had no comeback for that, no one else to blame. She didn't respond.

I leaned back and let Mercer take over the questioning. "All these things, Blanca—your application for asylum, your taxes, your bank accounts, your relationship with Hector— they don't have anything to do with Mr. Gil-Darsin."

"I know that. I'm not stupid."

"But if you can look me in the eye and lie about those things, Blanca—those things that don't really matter today—how can I trust you to tell me the truth about every little detail that *does* matter."

"Like what, Mr. Mercer? Like what do you want?"

Mercer took his time, slowly and clearly going back to the moments immediately after the attack—crucial points in time that the jury would have to be made to understand.

"First, Blanca, you told me you ran out in the hallway and waited for Mr. Gil-Darsin to leave the room."

"I said that. I know I said that."

"But then you changed it to tell us you went next door to number twenty-eight-oh-eight. That you opened that door with the key card, so you could go in to clean that room up."

"Yeah, that one is true."

"So even though you'd been raped, you were going to continue working and make up the adjacent room, like you were fine?"

Blanca looked to Peaser and back at Mercer. "No. No, no. I just went back to get my cleaning supplies. I couldn't work. Too upset."

"Do you remember telling me that you went to that room to get back to work?"

"Okay, so I was going to go to work there, but then I decided to go back to number twenty-eight-oh-six. To go back to twenty-eight-oh-six and change the linens, like they sent me to do originally. I didn't want to go near the bed, like I told you the other day," she said, looking to Mercer for approval—as though she remembered that it might have compromised any finding of DNA. "But I had to get the towels from the bathroom. That's part of my job."

"So you went into the bathrooms?" Mercer asked.

"Only one of them. The big one with the shower and all. Not the powder room," Blanca said. "I never went into that. Nobody used that one."

"Did you remove any of the towels?"

"That's why I went there, Detective. To clean it up."

I couldn't believe what I'd just heard. I sat up straight and my spine stiffened. I didn't want to look at Mercer or Pat, but from the movements each made, I was sure they'd caught the latest change.

"I'm sorry," Mercer said. "You went back into the room where Gil-Darsin attacked you?"

"Yes," Blanca said firmly, standing her ground like she was sure it was the right decision.

"And at that time, you went into the bathroom, too. And you took the towels out of the bathroom with you?"

So that if there was any trace evidence linked to Blanca Robles anywhere in that bathroom, it would no longer be possible for us to know whether she had actually had the opportunity to clean herself up in the moments after the alleged assault—which she had denied all along—or on this later visit to clean up the room.

"Have you told anyone that fact before right this very minute?"

"What fact?" Blanca asked.

"That you entered the bathroom of suite twenty-eight-oh-six after Mr. Gil-Darsin left the room?" Mercer said. "That you removed potential items of evidence from that suite?"

"Why do I have to tell people? It's my job, to send things to the laundry. It has nothing to do with this man assaulting me."

"And that's what you did with the towels? Sent them to the laundry?"

"Yeah. All the washcloths and towels. They went down to the basement with the linens from the other rooms."

Six days after the alleged attack and countless interviews later, and a critical new fact had just emerged. If Gil-Darsin were to claim at the trial that after their consensual encounter, Blanca had used the bathroom to clean herself up, there would be no way to refute the argument.

"Did you tell that to the grand jury on Wednesday?" Mercer asked.

"Ms. Ellen didn't ask me that. None of you did."

"Let me understand this, Blanca," Mercer said. "When you went back to number twenty-eight-oh-six this second time, did you let yourself in?"

"With my card, yes. My key card."

"Was Gil-Darsin still there?" Mercer asked.

"No," Blanca said, with a wave of her hand. "He was in a big hurry. He left fast."

She had flip-flopped again on this fact. At first she told police she had concealed herself in the hallway to make sure he had left. Then, two days ago she put herself back in the room from which she could not have known about MGD's departure, and just now, she told us that she removed property from the crime scene.

She had just given Lem Howell an opening in her story—and in the police crime scene work—wide enough for the defense to drive through in a Mack truck.

Mercer continued with a list of questions about both times that Blanca was in room 2806. Some of the answers were different than they had been on previous days—a problem for the case and a larger problem for the accuser herself.

Pat McKinney stood up and signaled to me. "Can we talk in your office, Alex?"

"Sure."

I let Ryan take my place at the table while Mercer's quietly effective cross-examination moved ahead. I stepped in front of Ellen Gunsher, who had the same stupefied look on her face that she usually did—this time for good reason.

McKinney and I walked down the hallway, past Laura, and sat around my desk.

"What do we do, Alex?" he asked. "I have to say, I have a whole new respect for what the lawyers in your unit deal with every day. There's nothing like these cases."

Pat McKinney had rarely complimented my staff before, and it might be a long time before he did it again. The fifty prosecutors who handled sex crimes, domestic violence, and child abuse dealt with the most sensitive issues imaginable in the life of the accuser. Every report teetered on becoming "high-profile"—because of the crime or the victim or the location or the vagaries of the press.

"Thanks, Pat. I don't think Blanca leaves us any choice about what to do."

"Let's go tell Battaglia. You'll appear in front of Donnelly and suggest releasing MGD on his own recognizance?"

"Okay."

"You can take the pressure better than Ellen," McKinney said. "You've made big mistakes before."

"This isn't anyone's mistake, Pat. Blanca Robles has done this to herself."

Paul Battaglia's mantra had always been to do the right thing. He drilled it into his assistants from the moment they came on board.

"Well, get ready to suck it up, Alex. Someone's got to take the heat for this one."

Forty-three

Battaglia was stone-faced when McKinney and I gave him the news. "How fast do you have to move on this?"

"I called Lem Howell, and my paralegal is processing the papers so that Gil-Darsin can be produced from the Tombs," I said.

"They didn't ship him back to Rikers yesterday?"

"No. He's still next door. Lem wanted time for him to have a visit with his wife today, so we're lucky he's still close by."

A quick walk across the Bridge of Sighs, from the short-term detention center attached to the courthouse, would bring Baby Mo back to get the news of his release.

"Stall it till Monday," Battaglia said. "It'll give me time to write something."

"I won't delay it, Paul."

When I first came to the office more than a decade ago, a colleague of mine had failed to file a dismissal on a grand jury vote reached late on a Friday afternoon. The seventeen-year-old defendant had been falsely accused by a rival gang member of participation in a robbery. That weekend, taunted by fellow inmates about his first arrest and his fierce denials, he tied two towels together and hung himself in his cell.

"What will I say?"

"I can script something if you'd like," I said.

"How much time do we have?" Battaglia asked, looking at his watch to confirm that it was now eleven thirty a.m.

"The judge wants us there at four. The press pool has asked for cameras in the courtroom, and they need time to set up."

"Can I make my remarks in here, as usual?"

"You won't be able to, Boss," McKinney said. "It's not just the locals. You'll have reps from all the foreign press here as well. By mid-afternoon, you'll have several hundred correspondents and photographers. It's got to be the courthouse steps."

Paul Battaglia crushed his cigar in the ashtray on his desk. "Tell Brenda to make sure there's a podium out there. All the equipment I need. Get to work on my comments, Alex. And be sure not to steal any of my thunder for your bail app."

"Of course not, Paul. You'll have all the best lines."

I told Laura to hold any calls or visitors. I got to work on the district attorney's statement before I crafted a few short paragraphs to explain to the court the reversal of our bail position.

I knew that Lem would be spinning the media all day about why our team was walking back the cat on MGD. This was not the time to go head-to-head with him. I needed to retain whatever dignity Blanca Robles had left herself and to think about the impact of this change on the victim advocacy community I respected so much.

At one o'clock, Laura opened my door and put a turkey sandwich and soda on my desk. "You've got to eat something, Alex."

I smiled at her. "You're not old enough to be my mother."

"But she called an hour ago, and I did promise to make sure to put lunch in front of you. I couldn't swear I'd get you to put lipstick on before you faced the cameras, but food I could do."

I blew Laura a kiss and got back to work.

Half an hour later, Ryan and Mercer came in together. They both looked distraught.

"Where's the funeral?" I asked.

"It can't get worse than this, Al," Ryan said.

I threw my pen on the desk. "Something change? I'll be out of ink before I get to the courtroom. What have you guys been up to?"

"I'm trying to keep Blanca and Byron here for as long as I can. I moved them out of the conference room, because the commotion is starting in front of the courthouse."

"Where to?"

"I've got them up on the fifteenth floor, facing the rear of the building—no access to anything or anybody. Ordered in lunch and Blanca is watching some soaps on the tube. I don't want them leaving the building until after Gil-Darsin is released. I figure the first shot at spin control goes to Battaglia," Mercer said. "Then Lem. By that time, Byron Peaser will just sound like a bag of wind."

"Why do they think they're being kept here?" I asked.

"I told them you're redrafting paperwork for her to sign. Blanca's okay with it, and Peaser doesn't want to let her out of his sight."

"Then why are you two looking so miserable?"

"If you're building the coffin for this case," Ryan said, "I just came up with the last nail."

"Let me guess. Her real name isn't Blanca Robles and she doesn't work at the Eurotel."

"She's good on both those counts. It's her application for asylum."

I looked up at Ryan and nodded. "That wasn't going to be available to us until next week. Who'd you impersonate this time? The secretary of state?"

"I thought about it, but she has such a distinctive voice."

"Thanks for your discretion."

"Look, Al, I explained the situation to one of the deputies. They'd already pulled it from the system when they got the subpoena, but it was sitting on his desk until legal got to authorize its release," Ryan said. "He read me through the whole thing."

"Okay. I'm expecting some exaggeration. I've seen dozens of these. Unless there's a bombshell, then—"

"There's a bombshell," Mercer said.

"It's got everything Blanca told us the first day we talked to her, Al. The day you were still in France. So Mercer and I just went back over all the facts again with her."

I put my elbows on the desk and started massaging my aching head. "What now?"

"The stuff about her parents and brothers—she swears that's all true," Mercer said. "And when I asked her to tell me one more time about the militia—"

"You mean the soldiers who gang-raped her?" I asked. "The story that brought everyone on the team to tears?"

"Yes, ma'am. That very one. It turns out that's the story that she made up out of whole cloth."

I dragged my hands down over my mouth, thinking of the consequences. "Blanca Robles fabricated a story of rape?"

"Completely. She admitted that to us just now."

"That woman could have lied about almost anything else and still have a chance of being believed," I said. "I could have argued to the jurors that all the financial crap and taxes and the asylum stuff in general was extraneous to the facts of the Gil-Darsin assault. But to look every one of us in the eye and make up the story of a sexual assault? We'll never be able to sell this one to a jury that's faced with convicting a man of rape in the first degree. Never."

"We just thought you and Battaglia ought to know."

"Thanks, guys," I said, picking up my pen to do the edit on both my statement and the district attorney's. "Hey, Mercer? You willing to walk the plank with me?"

"My distinct honor."

"Quarter to four? Pick me up here and take me to Judge Donnelly's part?"

"Sure thing."

I honed and sharpened my words. If ever there was a time that less was more, this would be that moment.

At the appointed hour, I dragged myself out of my office and walked through the great hallways with Mercer beside me. We took the elevator from the DA's office wing to the thirteenth floor, Part 31 of the Supreme Court of the State of New York.

As we stepped off, flashbulbs started popping, and the

reporters who were waiting to be admitted to the locked courtroom were screaming out questions.

The court officers let Mercer and me in. Directly ahead I could see Lem Howell, preening in the well, gloating at the victory we were handing him.

"Alexandra Cooper," Lem said, "I taught you well, young lady."

"If you want to claim the credit for all this, just hop right on my back. That's where everyone else seems to be."

The judge came out of the robing room, ready for the sideshow that would have media clowns jockeying for seats as the pool cameraman set up his equipment, focusing on the two counsel tables. We'd all be in high def for the evening news. Since Donnelly tolerated no nonsense, the proceeding would be mercifully short.

"Mr. Howell, Ms. Cooper—good afternoon. As you know, Mr. Howell, Ms. Cooper contacted my clerk late this morning. I understand we're going to have a change in bail status for Mr. Gil-Darsin. Has your client been produced?"

"Yes, Your Honor."

"Before we go on the record, do we have any house-keeping to do?"

"No, Judge," I said. "I intend to be brief."

"Very good. Does your client have any family members who wish to be seated in the front row, before I let the reporters in?"

"No, ma'am," Lem said, barely able to suppress an enormous grin. "Madame Gil-Darsin would prefer to greet her husband outside the courthouse—when he is a free man."

"This will be rich," I whispered to Mercer. "Lem's staged a grand reunion, played out for all the world to see. I should have figured as much."

The officers led Baby Mo into the courtroom. Lem had provided him with yet another suit from his vast collection of bespoke clothes, and a fresh shirt in cerulean blue, perfect for the television cameras.

The defendant tried to say something to me—thank you, I'm sure—but I turned my back to him to avoid the impropriety of that discussion.

"How the worm turns, Alexandra," Lem said, positioning himself between me and the bench so that he could watch the press corps jam themselves into the empty seats.

"All's fair in love and war, Lem," I said, "and don't forget that every dog has his day. That's three, isn't it? A triplicate of platitudes for you."

"Don't go bitter on me, young lady. Plenty of room for Paul Battaglia to do that. I have no agenda but to praise your fairness."

"Save it for another time, Lem. It rings too hollow today."

Judge Donnelly banged her gavel. "May I have your appearances, please?"

"Alexandra Cooper, for the People."

"Lemuel Howell the Third, for Mr. Gil-Darsin."

"You have an application, Ms. Cooper?"

"Yes, Your Honor. At this time, I'd like to request that Mr. Gil-Darsin be ROR'd—released on his own recognizance. We'd also like the court to consider asking to secure his passport, at least until the next court appearance."

"Just to be clear, Ms. Cooper, this is the same matter on which your office requested a remand of this defendant just twenty-four hours ago?"

"It is, Your Honor."

"Would you mind detailing some of the changed circumstances?"

"Of course," I said, picking up my list of Blanca's lies to read into the record.

I could barely hear myself speak over the rumble of the reporters behind me.

"Thank you, Ms. Cooper. Three weeks? Do you think you can resolve some of these issues in that time, Mr. Howell?"

"I am most certain, Judge Donnelly, that we can figure out the misunderstanding between the two parties by then."

I wanted to scream out loud at Lem's choice of the word "misunderstanding." Buried in Blanca Robles's twisted telling of the short encounter I was pretty sure there was a crime.

"Yes, Your Honor," I said. "Three weeks is fine."

"May 20," she said. "Are you able to arrange the surrender of your client's passport, Mr. Howell?"

"If Detective Wallace would be so kind," Lem said, reaching out his hand to me. "I believe the police, in their haste to detain my distinguished client, seized both his personal and his diplomatic passports."

Lem underscored his point about MGD's international prominence. Mercer passed both documents to Lem, who gave them to the clerk.

"Mr. Gil-Darsin, you'll be taken in the back by the officers and processed for immediate discharge," the judge said, with one more bang of her gavel after she announced that court was adjourned.

The defendant wrapped his arms around Lem Howell and gave one emphatic fist pump to the audience.

Reporters scrambled over one another to dash out of their seats and phone in their headlines.

I called Pat McKinney to urge him to move Battaglia

to the front steps of 100 Centre Street as quickly as he could, before the unruly crowd assembled. I wanted him to make his remarks with as much dignity as possible, before Gil-Darsin played to the cameras.

I was the last one to leave the darkened courtroom, thinking that this had been the worst week of my entire life.

Forty-four

"Every accuser," Paul Battaglia said, speaking into the bank of microphones that covered the entire podium, "every victim of a sexual assault who comes forward and reports these heinous crimes, is entitled to be met with the utmost respect by the men and women of the NYPD and my great office."

Pat McKinney and I flanked the district attorney. The rest of the team lined up behind us, with Mercer over my shoulder, while the district attorney went on to describe the background of Blanca Robles and her odyssey through the week's interviews.

"Tens of thousands of witnesses come to our office every year, from diverse and frequently difficult circumstances, many with imperfect pasts. If we are convinced they are truthful about the crimes committed against them, and will tell the truth at trial, we will ask a jury to consider their testimony to prove a crime."

He had added an important riff about the proud history and high priority of his long tenure in seeking justice for sex crimes victims and protecting the vulnerable immigrant population of the city.

". . . In this particular instance, the nature and number of the accuser's falsehoods," Battaglia said, reading the words I had written, having edited them to fit his personal style, "the shifting and inconsistent version of events she gave surrounding her encounter in room number twenty-eight-oh-six of the Eurotel . . ."

The sea of reporters packed the entire roadway. Police had blocked off Centre Street from Hogan Place to White Street with the interlocking gray aluminum partitions—ironically known as French barriers—that had replaced wooden sawhorses for crowd control a decade ago. Uniformed officers stood side by side across the length of the curb that bordered 100 Centre Street.

A single car—a black limousine that would no doubt whisk Mohammed Gil-Darsin to his temporary home in Manhattan—was the sole vehicle that was positioned in front of the courthouse.

The only people standing still, not jostling to push closer to the steps from which Battaglia spoke, were the six enormous bodyguards—who looked as though they'd been plucked from some rapper's entourage and who surrounded the sleek stretch sedan.

The district attorney commented on many of the specifics that had complicated Blanca Robles's story. He separated those misstatements that were extrinsic to the alleged assault—asylum, bank accounts, tax records, phone calls—from those that related directly to her face-off with MGD and its immediate aftermath.

". . . and my team, composed of some of the most experienced, senior lawyers on my staff, and representatives of this country's pioneering and premier sex crimes prosecution unit, has ultimately been unable to credit the accuser's version of the events of last Saturday beyond a reasonable doubt."

Pat McKinney and I stared straight ahead. The late-afternoon sun was beginning to drop behind the Family Court building, but neither the direct glare nor the breeze sweeping in from the Hudson River caused even an eyelash to flutter.

"If *we* do not believe this accuser beyond a reasonable doubt at this time, then I cannot ask any one of these prosecutors to stand in front of a jury and ask them to require that of twelve good citizens of this county.

"We will press forward with our investigation, ladies and gentlemen. We urge the full cooperation of our witness, who has come to speak to us now only through her lawyer, Byron Peaser.

"We ask again, as we have from the outset, that she participate within the structure of the criminal justice system, rather than holding forth in media interviews and sponsored appearances. We hope that you, members of the Fourth Estate, will respect our need to see that justice is done.

"For today, we are left with no choice but to request the release of Mohammed Gil-Darsin, the defendant in this case, on his own recognizance, while we continue our search for the truth. Thank you very much."

Two detectives from the DA's squad moved in on either side of Paul Battaglia and escorted him inside the north entrance hall of 100 Centre Street and toward the back way into the DA's office.

The brief statement in front of the building had been choreographed so that Battaglia would disappear before

MGD was brought down from Part 31 to the south entrance hall of the vast lobby. The podium was left in place for Lem Howell and his client.

"Let's go," I said, turning to my colleagues. We were the only ones moving from our positions.

"Don't you want to see this, Al?" Ryan asked. "Lem Howell dancing on your—"

"Not on my grave, Ryan. Don't overdo this."

"You've got to see him in action."

"I'd rather have a drink."

"We can't leave now," Mercer said. "We'll look like we're running away from something. Let's just move off to the side. Prop yourself back against that wall and take it all in."

Mickey Diamond and the guys from the local papers, who knew all of us, were trying to get our attention. "McKinney! What's the tagline?"

Pat McKinney shook his head at the group in front.

"Alex!" Diamond screamed out. "Gimme something about how it feels right now, will you? Watching this perv walk out of here, Alex. How can you stand by and just stomach the whole thing?"

"Do you think he really did it?" It was one of the other reporters waving a microphone in midair.

The five of us were no longer standing quite so tall. I leaned against the massive pillar between the two entrances and covered my mouth with my hand to talk to Mercer.

"How I feel right now isn't fit for print. What about you?"

"Right there with you."

"The bastard did something to her in those twenty

minutes in that hotel room, that's what's at the bottom of all this. He just picked the right vic, didn't he?"

"With laser precision."

A huge roar from the crowd went up as Lem Howell and Mohammed Gil-Darsin emerged from within the lobby and out onto the top of the steps.

I looked above them at the words carved into the granite of the old courthouse:

EQUAL AND EXACT JUSTICE TO ALL MEN OF WHATEVER STATE OR PERSUASION.

Mercer tilted his head back, too. "1939. A little sexist in those days, don't you think?"

I laughed. "It's better now? I hate doing what we did to that woman."

"She did it to herself, Alex. We gave her every chance, even before you got back to town. Like you said, I'm not really sure she knows what truth is."

I crossed my arms and readied myself for a speech.

Lem Howell silenced the crowd, one hand raised above his head, by speaking a single word: "Innocent."

"Good afternoon, ladies and gentlemen," he said, putting his hand on the shoulder of Baby Mo. "Since the very beginnings of this case, I have maintained the innocence of my client. Throughout this week, I have argued that there were many reasons to believe that Mr. Gil-Darsin's accuser was not credible."

The distinguished-looking WEB head had a more serious expression on his face than the one he'd worn in court just an hour ago.

"You have seen something extraordinary today—something remarkable, something so unusual that I have not seen it at any time since Paul Battaglia's first election to this job, more than five terms ago. The district attorney stood at this podium and announced—*after* an indictment was filed, after his star witness had given sworn testimony, after he had asked for the imprisonment of my client without bail—he announced that he had doubts about the credibility of the woman who testified. I tell you that we are fortunate to live in a time and in a place where this kind of justice is available to all who come before the court."

There was a movement at the bottom of the steps. The door of the limousine opened and the bodyguard closest to the side of the car pulled it back.

Those of us on the steps and some people jammed together at the front of the crowd, along with all the uniformed cops, watched as Kalissatou Gil-Darsin planted her feet—shiny black patent stilettos bearing her long legs—on the pavement of Centre Street and gracefully unfolded from the backseat of the stretch.

"My client and his family—his beautiful wife, Kali—have believed in the American system of justice, despite the unbearable indignity of his incarceration all this week."

Lem paused so the reporters who were closest could get photographs of Madame Gil-Darsin. She appeared to be at least six feet tall, dressed in a long-sleeved cobalt blue sheath that complemented her figure as well as her husband's attire. There was a shawl draped over her left arm, along with an open tote that matched her shoes.

If Baby Mo represented the world of sleaze—a charge of first-degree rape, semen in the hotel room after a sexual encounter with the maid who'd been his accuser, confirmation that a girlfriend had visited his room the night before, and his possible involvement in a ring of escorts and prostitutes—then Kali was the epitome of elegance.

The reunion of husband and wife, on the steps of the hall of justice, would be the money shot to play in newspapers around the world.

"I know you'd like to hear from Mr. Gil-Darsin," Lem said, "but while the charges are still pending, it would be unwise of me to allow him to address you—despite his strong desire to do so."

MGD nodded his head up and down.

Reporters began to rumble with displeasure at word that the defendant himself would not speak.

"How'd the semen get on her uniform?" Mickey Diamond yelled out.

"Will you comment on the news out of Lille?" a miked-up reporter with a French accent called out.

"What about the civil lawsuit?" a local TV commentator asked. "How much are you willing to settle for, to make it go away?"

I couldn't take my eyes off Kali. Her bearing was regal, and in the midst of all the tawdry comments and tacky circumstances, she never winced or evidenced a shred of emotion.

"This is not the end of the matter against my client," Lem said. "But his freedom speaks volumes about the strength—or may I say weakness—of the People's case. I want to thank you, on behalf of Mohammed Gil-Darsin, for your fair and open-minded reporting on this matter. I hope you will give my client a few days to make up for the liberty taken from him. A good weekend to you all."

Lem Howell and Mohammed Gil-Darsin exchanged handshakes and bear hugs. They took the first two steps

down, then Lem stood to the side while his client waved
to the crowd. MGD clasped his hands together and
bowed his head several times.

The defendant—I still thought of him as that, and
would continue to do so until we reached a final decision—continued down the last few stairs of the courthouse.

He opened his arms wide, facing his wife and smiling
at her, saying the words "thank you" loud enough that
they were audible to all of us, even without the microphones.

As Baby Mo stepped onto the sidewalk, just a few feet
away from her, Kali reached into her bag and pulled out
a small handgun.

Her first shot struck Mohammed Gil-Darsin squarely
in the chest and took him down immediately. The three
that followed quickly, as she stood over his body and
fired before six police officers reached her side and disarmed her, made certain he was dead.

Forty-five

"I didn't get the e-mail today," Mike said, coming into the conference room a little after ten p.m., carrying two boxes of pizzas which he dropped on the long table.

"Which one was that?" Ryan asked.

"You know. 'Ignore the sound of gunshots. They're just shooting a scene from *Law and Order* on the courthouse steps.' I don't know that anybody has ever been so sorry to be ROR'd as Baby Mo," Mike said. "Or Baby *Mort*, as they're calling him now."

The entire team—Pat McKinney, Ellen Gunsher, Ryan Blackmer, Mercer, and I—was still in shock. It was impossible to absorb that we had witnessed a homicide at our own front door, almost stage-set by the defense counsel for the photo op of his infamous client reuniting with his perfect wife.

Like any group that had gone through a traumatic event together, we were reluctant to leave one another for the weekend, even though our work was done. We kept reliving the day's events, talking about whether there were any measures that we should have taken that would have changed things.

"Where's the big cheese?" Mike asked, obviously trying to cut the tension in the room.

"Battaglia? He left about an hour ago," I said.

"I see you raided the liquor cabinet. Couldn't wait for me, Coop, could you?"

I'd contributed a liter of Dewar's that I kept in the bottom of one of my filing cabinets for special occasions. McKinney had vodka and bourbon, and we were making do with plastic cups.

"It was just a horrible sight. A cold-blooded execution, right under our noses," I said, taking another sip of my drink.

"CSU is still downstairs finishing the job."

"It took forever to clear the crowd to get Crime Scene and the morgue van in," Mercer said. "That slowed them down badly."

"Declared here, or did he make it to a hospital?" Mike asked.

"Before his head hit the sidewalk," Mercer said, while Ryan handed out slices. "Kali fired four from a Lady-Smith .38. Then she dropped it and held up her slim wrists to be cuffed and taken away. Stiff upper lip the whole time."

"Not as stiff as his is." Mike poured himself a few inches of vodka and touched his cup against mine. "Here's to Carrie Underwood."

"Why?"

"Must have been Kali's favorite song," Mike said, singing a few bars of Underwood's hit that scored with the line "maybe next time he'll think before he cheats."

"Rough justice," McKinney said. "I didn't see that one coming, for sure."

"How did Battaglia take it?"

"He's as stunned as the rest of us," I said.

"Did he get any more airtime?"

"Yeah. He couldn't do anything on the front steps, but he invited the major press reps in to his office. Said all the right things."

"And we slipped Byron Peaser and Blanca Robles out the back door," Mercer said. "Nobody had any interest in what they had to say tonight."

"Who winds up with Kali's case?" Mike asked.

"The head of Brooklyn's DV unit," I said. "She's terrific. She'll be designated a special prosecutor in this county."

"If she picks her jury right," Mike said, halfway through his first slice of pepperoni with mushrooms and onions, "those people are likely to pin a medal on Kali. You want twelve angry women in that jury box—the first wives' club—divorced, dumped, or deserted by the pricks in their lives. They'll see things just the way Mrs. Mo did."

"Most women do," Ryan said, "according to my wife and her pals."

"The sad thing is she'll be tortured while she's a prisoner at the Women's House. That's where her elegance and good looks and upper crust will work against her—in a jail cell."

"Battaglia's not asking for bail," I said. "He's releasing Kali. He figures there's a whole battered women's syndrome defense to be worked up here. Psychological abuse and all this public humiliation."

"How enlightened of him. Are we close to an election year?"

"Must be," Ryan said.

Pat, Ellen, and I began to nibble at the pizza. The alcohol was starting to calm me, and I could feel a slight buzz replacing the numbness of the afternoon's experience.

"You should all look a bit more enthusiastic than you do, guys. A day like this one gives new meaning to 'Thank God It's Friday,'" Mike said. "Don't tell me you're so miserable about MGD's sudden demise that none of you watched *Jeopardy!*?"

"There's nothing funny about today," I said, getting up from my place at the table. "Do you get that?"

"Where you going, kid? I just got here."

"It's been a long one, Mike. I'm packing it in."

"Ellen, what kind of giant lizard was King Kong supposed to fight in the original movie?" he asked.

"What? Why do you want to know?" Ellen said, wiping the red sauce from her chin.

"'Cause it was the final answer tonight," Mike said. "You know it?"

Ellen Gunsher shook her head. I announced that I wasn't playing, and neither Mercer nor Pat guessed at the question.

But Ryan Blackmer was as quirky as Mike. "What's a Komodo dragon?"

"That's it, pal. I should have known you were a detail man. Have all the pizza you want."

"Somebody leave the Scotch bottle on my desk when you're done," I said. I was ready to go home and go to sleep.

I understood why they were ignoring me. Each of us had retreated into a space from which we couldn't see the murder unfolding in front of us. Each of us was going to have to deal with it in our own way.

"Here's the really cool thing about Komodo drag-ons," Ryan said. "They've got two penises."

Mike was helping himself to more vodka. "Awesome!"

"Why do you think that's so awesome?" I asked, almost out the door. "You hardly know what to do with one."

"If that's your best shot, Coop, you ought to sit on it."

"It's a strange time of night to start getting frisky, Al," Ryan said.

I shrugged my shoulders and rolled my eyes. "I thought I was making a joke, Chapman style."

"I'm actually saving up in case they ship your man out," Mike said.

"What do you mean?"

"Luc. I mean Luc. He's looking to be a perfect candidate for the French Foreign Legion, kid. No questions asked. That's always been how they assemble their troops for combat. Cutthroats and crooks, murderers and—I don't know, maybe they've got an opening for shady res-taurateurs."

I'd been one-upped. I stopped in the doorway. "What did you find out today?"

"Nothing that can't wait until tomorrow."

"Please?"

"I'll walk you out. How are you getting home?"

"My car's parked right downstairs on Hogan Place."

I said good night to everyone, stopped in my office to get my keys, and walked with Mike down the quiet hall-way to the elevator.

"You're right about the Gineva Import company. It's owned by the Dantons and Gina Varona."

"Is it a dummy corporation?" I asked. "Or for real?"

"I couldn't get much on the phone. The Brooklyn

prosecutors will have to subpoena the records on Monday. All the AG would confirm for me were the owners and the fact that the company bought the building a few months ago."

"Which would be six months after Luc bought the one next door. Is his name anywhere involved with Gineva?"

"Not so far as the AG's filings show."

"So this whole thing gets more tangled. You know Luc wants to go back to France, don't you?"

"And he should, Coop. He's got stuff to deal with there. I'll throw this information over to the Brooklyn techs this weekend."

"Did you call Luc? Did you find out whether he knows about this?"

"Not yet. That's not for me to do."

"But what do you think, Mike?"

"I think that you think too much, Coop. Just let it be."

"I need to know."

"That'll happen soon enough. Just take a time-out for the night, will you?"

We left the building and Mike waited while I opened the door and got in my car.

"You okay to drive?" he asked.

"I'm good, thanks."

"You did the right thing, Coop. About MGD, I mean."

"I thought so a few hours ago. Hard to believe it now."

"Get some sleep," Mike said, as I started up the engine. "Talk to you soon."

At this time of night, without much traffic, it usually took less than twenty minutes for me to drive straight up Park Avenue to the Seventies and into my garage.

The bar scene in SoHo was busy, and the mild night invited young patrons out onto the streets with their martinis and cosmopolitans. Every time I stopped for a red light, I looked at the Friday night revelers who seemed to have left work behind them for the weekend.

I thought back ten years and wondered if I would ever know what it was like to have a job that didn't press on your brain—and nerves—24/7. Every now and then I thought it would be worth trying to find out.

I drove through the canyon of tall office buildings— deserted at this late hour—that lined Park Avenue north of Grand Central Terminal.

I couldn't get the day's images out of my mind's eye. Gil-Darsin himself, smiling at me in the courtroom with an air of arrogance that befitted his delight at the abrupt prosecutorial reversal. And then Kali, so serene and yet severe, staring her husband straight in the face as she took aim at his heart.

Forty-six

I was detoured over to Madison Avenue at 59th Street by a Con Ed crew working on an underground repair. When I reached the corner of 68th, several blocks from my apartment, I realized that home was the one place that I didn't want to be.

I crisscrossed Madison and took 69th Street over to Fifth Avenue, then made a left onto 64th Street.

When I pulled into the space in front of the Plaza Athénée, the doorman came out and asked whether I was checking in. I explained that I was visiting a friend and would be leaving early in the morning. He agreed to have the car valet-parked on the same block.

I had to wait several minutes at the check-in desk for a clerk to appear. It was ten-forty-five in the evening, and the chicly decorated lobby was empty.

"May I help you, *madame*?"

"Yes, I seem to have misplaced the card to my room. May I have another?"

"What is your name?"

"Rouget. My husband is Luc Rouget. Room 409."

"I'll have to see some identification, please," the young man said.

I fished in my purse for my wallet and cell phone. "Actually, my last name is different," I said, showing my driver's license to him. "But perhaps these will help."

I leaned over the desk and scrolled through the scads of recent photographs of Luc and me together—happier days—the last of which were taken at the dinner in white just a week earlier.

"Lovely, *madame*. Quite lovely. I've never seen Mr. Rouget," he said rather sharply, "so these don't really help me at all. I'll have to call up to the room."

I reached out and put my hand on his as he picked up the receiver. "Would you do me a favor?" I asked. "Would you just use your computer and Google Luc Rouget?"

He was puzzled.

"I'm trying to surprise him," I said. "I hate to do this, but it would mean the world to me. Here's my government ID."

The young man checked the photo on my New York County District Attorney's Office badge, and his entire attitude changed. "Ah, *madame*. I saw you on the television earlier tonight. You had the MGD case, am I right? What a terrible tragedy today."

He had withdrawn a blank card from his drawer and was keying in the code of Luc's hotel room.

"You should have said this to begin with, Madame Cooper. Nice to have you at the Plaza Athénée."

I tipped him, explained I had no luggage, and assured him I knew my way around the hotel.

I got out on the fourth floor and made my way to

409. I slid the card in, lowered the handle, and let myself into the suite.

The lights in the entry and living room were off, but the one in the bedroom was still on. I stepped out of my shoes, left my suit jacket on the sofa, and tiptoed to the door.

When I pushed it open, I could see Luc sitting in the king-size bed, propped up against several pillows, reading a book. He didn't look up until I was halfway across the room.

"Darling, I can't believe you're here," he said, tossing the book on the floor and reaching out for me as I climbed onto the foot of the bed. "Who let you in? Are you all right?"

"I just needed to be with you, Luc," I said, kissing him and letting him hold me as tightly as he could.

"You *are* with me. You're always with me."

"It was such an awful day. It's been such an awful week," I said, disentangling myself from his long arms and legs so that I could undress. "Can you believe that it was one week ago tonight that I arrived in Mougins?"

"And how different everything looked then," Luc said. "How different it felt."

I went into the bathroom and showered, scrubbing my hands and face and hair, as though MGD's blood had been everywhere. I toweled off and went back to Luc, letting myself be cradled in his arms. It was a time-out, just like Mike had directed me to have, and for once I was determined to enjoy the moment without thinking of any of the sinister machinations swirling around our lives.

Making love with Luc soothed and comforted me. He was strong but gentle—neither one of us in the mood for any athletics—and I closed my eyes and nestled in beside him when we had finished.

I was almost asleep when he nudged me aside and got out of bed. I heard the minibar open and close. "Nothing for me, thanks," I said, rolling over away from Luc's pillow. "I'm sated."

A few seconds later, with Luc beside me, I heard the distinctive pop of a champagne cork. I picked up my head to see him pouring into two glasses from a split that was bubbling over.

"Happy birthday, Alexandra Cooper," Luc said, offering me one glass and lifting the other. *"À votre santé, ma princesse."*

"Is it after midnight? Is it the thirtieth already?"

"It is, darling. Now you must wish for something."

I closed my eyes and thought of everything that had happened since I found the pile of bones at the entrance to Luc's home. If I could have wished away the entire last week of my life, personally and professionally, I would have done it. If I could have wished away all the problems that were stacked up on Luc's doorstep, deadlier than the ancient bones, I would have done it. If I could have wished that Blanca Robles had never had the misfortune to enter the hotel room of Mohammed Gil-Darsin before he'd departed, I would have done that, too.

"What is it? What have you wished?" Luc asked.

"I can't ever tell, Luc. Then none of it will come true."

"Can I see you again tomorrow, before I leave?"

"What flight are you on?"

"The nine p.m. to Paris."

I took a deep breath and made another wish—that this wasn't the last time Luc and I would be together.

"Then maybe during the day, if the police don't need you," I said. "Maybe they'll let us meet for lunch."

"Does Mike know you're here with me?"

"Nobody knows. It's the first thing that's felt good to me since we sat on the beach together in Cannes," I said.

It's what I want to remember when you leave here, I thought to myself.

We sipped our champagne until I was overcome by drowsiness. Luc turned out the light, and we both gave in to the emotional exhaustion that had drained us throughout these long days.

The next time I looked at the dial on the clock-radio, it was five a.m. Luc was sleeping soundly, so I slipped out of bed, took my clothes into the living room to dress, and let myself out to go to the lobby.

The doorman had the keys to my car, which he pointed at halfway down the street. I drove the short distance home and crawled into my own bed for a few more hours' sleep, certain that someone from the office would be calling me before too long to set up my debriefing about MGD's shooting.

I was awakened at nine a.m. by the loud ring on the landline on my night table.

"Hello."

"It's me, Coop," Mike said.

"Good morning."

"Is Luc with you?"

"No."

"Did you spend the night with him?"

Not exactly, I thought to myself. "Why?"

" 'Cause I'm here at the Plaza Athénée. Apparently some loopy-looking broad showed up late last evening and tried to break into his room. At least it wasn't you. You'd never lie to me, would you?"

"I have this vague recollection that you told me to

take a time-out last time we talked. I didn't spend the
night. I just dropped in to say hello."

"Where is he now?"

"Luc? He should be in his room."

"Did he tell you when he was flying out?"

"Yes. Tonight at nine."

"Did he have any plans for today?" Mike asked.

"In fact, we talked about having lunch together, once
I cleared it with you."

"I see," Mike said, his annoyance growing more obvious. "You need permission to grab a meal together, but
you figured you'd just use your own discretion about
getting laid?"

"Sorry to disappoint you, but I didn't get—"

"Excuse me. I'm sure the French have a much classier
word for it. And I get to tell the commissioner the LKP
of Alex Cooper is the suspect's bed."

Last known position. Why was anyone at headquarters
remotely interested in my LKP, and how long had Mike
been reporting on it? "Suspect in what?"

"Nothing, Coop. I misspoke."

"The Brooklyn cops think Luc is tied up in this in a
bad way, don't they? And you just keep on humoring
me."

"That's Brooklyn for you. Don't pay it any mind,"
Mike said. "What did Luc tell you he was doing today?"

"I swear to you, Mike. If he had any plans, he didn't
let me in on them."

"But you let the cat out of the bag about Peter Danton and Gina Varona, didn't you? You told Luc about
your visit to the next-door neighbors and what you
thought was going on? A little late-night pillow talk."

"I didn't say a word to him. We never talked about the

case at all," I said. I didn't want to tell Mike that we had more important things to tend to last night. "What's wrong?"

"The detectives were supposed to pick Luc up here this morning. One last go-round in Brooklyn, and then—yeah—they would have had him back here in time for lunch."

"Isn't he answering?" I said. "He's in room four-oh-nine."

"The concierge says he left the hotel almost an hour ago. Some guy was waiting for him in front in a silver SUV. Luc's gone, Alex. Your man is gone."

Forty-seven

Twenty minutes later I pulled over in front of the Plaza Athénée and parked.

Mike was on the sidewalk in front of the hotel, talking to two men I assumed were from Brooklyn South Homicide. The French and American flags flying above their heads, and the cheerful red awnings over each ground-floor window, made it appear more like a Parisian boulevard than an Upper East Side street.

He introduced me to both of the other men, and they examined me from head to toe like a doctor reading a patient's CT scan. I imagined they were thinking that this was the crazy woman Mike had been telling them about.

"You two always dress alike?" one of them asked.

We were both in jeans and collared white polo shirts, with cable-knit crewneck sweaters. "Yeah," Mike said. "She's my evil twin. Separated at birth so she could have all the advantages of a superior education. Me? I got lucky. I got street smarts instead."

"Okay, Detective Chapman. You're right. I did a stupid thing. What else do you want to know?" I asked.

"Other than this here doorman, who came on at seven this morning, Mike says you were the last person to see Luc Rouget."

"That's probably true."

"How long were you with him?"

I could feel the color rise up the sides of my neck and into my cheeks. "I'd say I got here about eleven last night, and it was five a.m. when I left."

"That could be the longest 'dropped-by-to-say-hello' in history," Mike said. "What else did you talk about? And spare us the love story."

"There was very little conversation. I was wiped out from yesterday's drama—the killing of Mohammed Gil-Darsin," I said, talking to the pair of detectives. "I—uh, I hadn't been with Luc all week, and I expected him to leave the country today. I just needed to—well, wanted to see him. We hardly talked at all."

"Did he ever tell you about our questioning of him this week?" one of the cops asked.

"No. Not a word. Mike made it clear I wasn't to speak to him."

"Not all that clear apparently, was I?" Mike was running his fingers through his hair, agitated that I had broken the rules last night.

"Did Luc tell you what he was doing today? Did he say where he was going?"

I shook my head. "We talked about maybe having lunch together, and Luc said he'd have to see what the detectives wanted him to do. That he was on the nine p.m. flight back to Paris. When I left the hotel room, he was sound asleep. We haven't spoken since."

"What do you want to do?" Mike asked the older of the two detectives.

"I'm going back to the office. My partner can hang out in the hotel room. See when Mr. Rouget hoofs it on back here. Frankly, Mike, I don't think it's any big deal. He's probably just sick of us. I've been hung out to dry by more important people than him."

"Have you checked—?"

"Been there, Ms. Cooper. All his luggage is in the room, along with his passport and plane ticket. Could be he'd had enough of us for one week. I wouldn't twist myself up in knots over this."

"Has he called or e-mailed you, Coop?" Mike asked.

I took my phone out of my pocket and looked at it, but there were no new messages of any kind.

I scrolled down to Luc's name and speed-dialed his cell number. It rang once and went immediately to voice mail.

I took a few steps away from the three men and lowered my voice, trying to sound as relaxed as I'd felt at midnight. "*Bonjour, Luc. Ça va?* I'm still hoping we can have lunch this afternoon. I'm going to go to my Saturday-morning ballet class to stretch for a bit, but call me. *Grosses bises.*" Big kisses, I'd said to him, anxious and curious about his well-being.

The younger of the two detectives went into the hotel, while the older one said good-bye to us and started walking off to his car.

Mike was leaning against my dark blue SUV, rubbing the toe of one of his loafers against the leg of his jeans to get some dirt off it.

"Want me to apologize to you again?" I said.

"Not if you have to ask."

"I am most sincerely sorry. Really I am. You've been such a great friend to me all week," I said. "What do you think we should do about this?"

"It's probably nothing. Go take your ballet lesson. Give me a buzz if Luc calls. And if you've got a Ulysses, let's give it to the snitch."

"Fifty bucks?"

"Yeah, let's put that dead president right in the mitt of this doorman."

"Why?"

"'Cause he gave me the make and model of the car Luc left in, as well as a partial plate."

"Then what are you standing here for?"

"No need for those guys from Brooklyn to get in my way. I'd rather find Luc before they do."

Forty-eight

Mike was on the phone with Lieutenant Ray Peterson at Manhattan North, the longtime commander of the Homicide Squad.

"Run it six ways to Sunday, Loo. That's what I want. The guy isn't sure of the numerals on the plate. It's a silver Lexus SUV from the GX series, 2011 or 2010. Connecticut plates. It may start with the letter K, or that's one of the first three letters, and it ends with the numbers two-two."

When Mike came on the job, at roughly the same time I was a rookie prosecutor, the infancy of computer searches was still tedious and slow. My weekend exercise routine was the last thing on my mind. It would take the NYPD system less than ten minutes to search for a license if any of the partial information Mike had given the lieutenant was correct.

We walked to Madison Avenue and bought ourselves a cup of coffee and a Danish. By the time we were back on the sidewalk, Peterson had called.

Mike listened to him, took a pen out of his back pocket, and jotted down the information on the side of the brown paper bag.

"Thanks, Loo. No APB yet. Let's see if I can figure out what's going on."

"Way to go," I said.

"Peterson says the make and model are right. We're looking for RK7-622. It's registered to a woman in Old Greenwich named Mulroy," Mike said, then repeated the name a second and third time.

"Jim Mulroy. The guy who buys wine for all the big restaurants."

"That's the name that came up in Luc's interview two days ago, of course. The wine maven who also wants a piece of the business. Do you know where he lives?"

"No idea."

Mike called Peterson back. "Would you do a people-finder on the Mulroy woman and that address in Greenwich? See if she's married to a guy named Jim? And I'll take you up on your other offer. See if any departments spot the car on the road. No interception, 'cause we've got no reason to think anything's wrong. Just what direction they're headed."

"They've got an hour jump on us, wherever they're going," I said. "Where's your car?"

"I don't have a department car this weekend. I'm off duty. Remember?"

"Mine's better anyway. The GPS actually works, it's got shocks—unlike any Crown Vic I've ever been in—and it's full of gas."

"You mind? I'll have it back to you by the end of the day."

"I'm riding with you."

"And there I was, sure you'd be acting out your tortured soul all day, doing your best black swan for the rest of the girls in the class."

I handed Mike the car keys and walked to the passenger side. "I'd rather keep my tortured soul close to you."

"What if the day doesn't have a happy ending?" Mike said, striking a more serious tone.

"I need to know that once and for all. What's the big deal if they're just going to Greenwich for the morning? Luc could still be back in time for lunch with me."

We sipped our coffee and waited for Peterson to call back. Fifteen minutes later, he did.

Mike put him on speakerphone and held a finger over his mouth, reminding me to keep quiet. "I got that vehicle going through the tollbooth E-ZPass lane on the Triboro Bridge at eight-twenty this morning, Mike. Any help to you?"

"Could be, Loo. That's the way I'll roll."

"You moving on this? You're not even signed in."

"Just a favor for a friend, Loo. No worries."

"Last time you told me that, I practically had the Vatican coming down on my head. Stay in touch, Mike."

"Will do," he said, disconnecting the call.

"We can go to my apartment and wait, you know. It's not like they're up to anything nefarious. I bet Luc just wanted to get out of the city for the morning. At least we can be comfortable."

"What? And watch Saturday-morning cartoons?" Half the Danish was in Mike's mouth as he washed it down with a slug of coffee. "I'm fine right here."

I hadn't expected another call from Peterson quite so

quickly, but about eight minutes later Mike's phone rang. The car's motor was running, and he was hands free, so that I could hear the lieutenant, too.

"Did you tell me you thought this car was on its way back to Greenwich?" Peterson asked.

"Best guess."

"Then it should have gone north on I-95, or over to the Hutchinson River Parkway. But instead it rung up another E-ZPass on the New York State Thruway, in Ardsley. What does that tell you?"

"He's going north," Mike said. "Not to Greenwich at all. Thanks, Loo."

He put his coffee in the cup holder and pulled out of the parking space. "You got a map in this car?"

"I haven't seen a road map since GPSes were invented. Why didn't you ask Peterson whether they went over the Tappan Zee Bridge?"

"Because there's no tollbooth on the northbound side of the highway on that bridge. You only pay on your way south," Mike said. "So they could be going up toward Albany, or up Route 684 toward western Connecticut. Think, Coop. Do you know anything else about this Mulroy guy?"

"Not really. He came to dinner at the restaurant in Mougins, but it was the same night that Lisette's body had been found. And Captain Belgarde broke up our conversation, so Jim didn't even stay that long. He seemed like a very nice guy to me—and Luc trusts him, at least in regard to business—but I don't know anything else about him."

"There's a gas station on 96th Street and First Avenue, right before we get on the drive. Run in and buy some maps, kid, and double-down on the java. Then we'll hit the road."

"You're worried about Luc now, aren't you?" I asked.

"I'm not worried about anything yet."

I was trying to call up the things we'd been talking about while Luc and I sat with Jim Mulroy in *le zinc* at Le Relais last Sunday night.

"Wait a minute," I said. "Something else reminded me of that guy this week. Something you said, or something I heard on TV."

"What was it?"

I was trying to make word associations, but they weren't coming fast enough. "It wasn't the baseball player named Chapman, and it wasn't the Komodo dragon. I'm thinking Peanut Island and Nantucket and bomb shelters from the 1960s."

"And Mulroy?"

"Exactly. That's exactly it," I said, snapping my fingers. "He was trying to sell Luc on the perfect place to store wine. It's actually a converted bomb shelter, and it's in some remote part of Connecticut."

"Way to go, babe. I want more. You gotta remember more than that."

"There isn't much else he talked about."

"What's the name of the place?"

"It's a horse farm. A really fancy horse farm. That's part of the name."

We were on 96th Street. I took out cash for the road maps and large coffees as Mike pulled in past the gas pumps. He braked and I ran out to the small office, returning with supplies for the ride.

Mike got back onto 96th Street, under the FDR overpass, and then to the Drive itself.

"Like Derby winners? Like Secretariat or Sea Hero or Barbaro?"

"No, no. More generic. Like Horse Tail Lane or Colt's Neck—wait, wait. I think it's Stallion Ridge. Stallion Ridge Cellars. I'm pretty sure that's right."

"Where, Coop? Where is it?"

"I don't think he said. I just remember the bit about it being ideal for storing wines. Cheap prices, because it's out of the city. It's kept at a steady temperature of fifty-five degrees. No vibrations. Dark, subterranean, and secure."

I said those last three words and shivered at the image they now conjured for me.

"Dial Mercer's number for me. Saturday morning, ten o'clock," Mike said. "He should be at home with Vickee and the kid."

The phone rang twice before Mercer picked it up.

"Yo, Detective Wallace," Mike said. "Am I interrupting anything?"

"Froot Loops everywhere. Vickee's getting Logan dressed, and I'm doing the dishes. What's up, Mike? You checked in on Alex yet?"

"Good morning, Mercer," I said. "I'm doing fine."

"Your assignment," Mike said, "if you choose to accept it, is to get on your computer and search for a place called—what is it, Coop?"

"Stallion Ridge Cellars. It should be in Connecticut, Mercer. A horse farm of some sort, with a storage facility for wine."

"Vickee's got her iPad hooked up here next to the kitchen counter. Hang with me a minute."

We were on the Triboro Bridge, taking the turnoff to the Thruway.

"Pops right up, guys. It's got its own website. State-of-the-art warehouse," Mercer said. "Whoa. Must be the black hole of the wine business."

"What do you mean?" I asked.

"Address is top secret. They don't even give it on the site. Bragging 'cause that's the kind of security they offer their customers."

"How do we find it then?" Mike asked.

"I'm working on that. Going back and going back. Most recent article is from *The Wall Street Journal*. Looks like the property was sold six months ago. It used to be part of some fancy digs called Kenner Stables. The woman who owned some two hundred and twenty-six acres—her name is Patti Kenner—sold off the part with—get this—a bomb shelter. She sold about one hundred acres to a New York corporation."

"I'm hearin' you, Mercer. Any chance the buyer is Gineva Imports?"

"You're on the money, Mike. Is that a good thing, or bad?"

"Not so good for Luc, I'm thinking."

"Try looking for Kenner Stables," I said, trying to keep my anxiety in check.

"I'm doing that, Alex. Going back a few years," Mercer said. "Hold it, hold it. Patti Kenner of Kenner Stables. Local newspaper. She held a fund-raiser for the volunteer firefighters at the horse farm. We're looking outside the town of Washington Depot in Connecticut. Do you know it?"

"Yes, yes, I do," I said, turning to Mike. "My friend Cynthia has a place nearby. I've been up there dozens of times. It's magnificent horse country, and great antiquing. Take the Thruway to 684, then onto 84 and up Route 7. We're less than ninety minutes away."

"Does it give an address, Mercer?" Mike asked.

"Just says Kenner Stables is off Route 109. There's a

picture showing a few large barns all huddled together, and a large white silo next to a smaller barn at the end, visible from the road."

"Great help," Mike said. "Turn left at the white silo. How many of those do you think we'll see?"

"A ton of them," I said.

"What are you doing today?" Mike asked Mercer.

"Whatever you need. Vickee promised we'd take Logan to the zoo on the first nice spring day, and here it is. He can't get enough of the penguins."

"I'll tell you what, Mercer," Mike said. "Fuck the penguins. Tell Logan I'll buy him one for Christmas. Call in every chit you got to find this Patti Kenner, and if you feel like a ride in the country, meet us at Stallion Ridge."

Forty-nine

"I'm Patti Kenner," the woman said. She was standing inside the gated entrance to her property, dressed in riding clothes. A tall chestnut mare from which she'd dismounted was beside her.

"This is Alex Cooper. I'm Mike Chapman." He displayed his shield to Kenner. "Thanks for coming out to talk to us."

"Happy to do it. The town police chief said your partner had called."

"Your place is hard to find."

"That's the idea, Detective."

Kenner appeared to be in her late forties. She had beautiful curly black hair with touches of gray around her face and looked especially pretty when her features relaxed into a smile.

"Not even a sign on the road?"

"You'd have to understand my great-uncle to appreciate why. Do you want to come in?"

"I'll be back for the long version. We're on our way to Stallion Ridge. The chief told us how to get there," Mike said. "About three-quarters of the way past your white silo, on the other side of the road. Also an unmarked driveway."

Kenner pursed her lips and her brow wrinkled automatically.

"This won't get back to you, Ms. Kenner," I said. "We can promise you that."

"Yes, that's one of the entrances. There's also a back way in, but it's a lot harder to find—and impossible to ride on after a rough winter. It's completely rutted most of the time."

"We've tried to get a description of what's on the property there, but nobody seems to know. Can you help us out?"

"Sure." Patti Kenner took off her riding gloves and leaned against the gate. Mike got out of the car and came around to my side to listen to her.

"My great-uncle bought the piece we're standing on in the 1940s. He'd been very fortunate with his investments and wanted to get into the business of breeding thoroughbred horses. Land in this part of the world was incredibly cheap then, so he picked up twenty acres to begin with and, over the next decade, kept adding property on both sides of the road."

I looked around the countryside, which was lush after so much spring rain, with rolling green hills in all directions.

"He wasn't always so crazed with security. Kenner Stables contributed handsomely to the local economy over the years, employing a lot of the townspeople. Everybody knew where to find us back then."

"What happened?" Mike asked.

"It was long before I was born, in the late fifties. A ring of arsonists set fire to several of the barns one night," Kenner said, pausing for a moment.

"I can't think of anything worse," I said, looking at the magnificent animal pawing the ground behind her.

"Fortunately, because there were so many farmhands on the property, not a single horse was injured. But in all the confusion of getting the animals out of their stalls and to safety, the arsonists—who were actually horse thieves—were able to steal six thoroughbreds that night. My uncle never saw those horses again."

"So down came the signs," Mike said. "And that's why you love the volunteer firefighters."

She laughed and told Mike he was right on both counts.

"Is there really a bomb shelter here?" he asked.

"That's on the part of the land that I sold off," she said.

"Tell us about it."

"After the time of the fire, as you might understand, my uncle was more than a bit obsessed about security. Not just the animals, but a bit paranoid about his own life, too. In 1962, a consortium of his bankers and insurance brokers were based in Hartford," Kenner said. "They got him all fired up about a Soviet ICBM attack. They convinced him that he'd need a safe place to store all his papers—which I don't really think was its purpose—and to protect them and their families at the same time."

"So he built one?" I asked.

"Oh yes."

"How big?"

"It's a twelve-thousand-square-foot underground bunker, behind a blast wall—"

"What's a blast wall?"

Mike answered. "Reinforced concrete that can withstand a bomb blast going off anywhere near it."

"That's right. So there's a blast wall and a twelve-ton steel bank vault door. If you get past that, the rest of the interior has walls that are eighteen inches thick."

"Well stocked?" Mike asked.

"At the time we sold it, fifty years after it was built, the food rations and water cans were all still intact. There were even gas masks ready to go."

"Do you know anything about the people you sold it to?" I asked.

"They must have more of my great-uncle's DNA than I do," Kenner said. "They're so secretive they make him look like P. T. Barnum."

"The wine cellar idea, do you know where that came from?"

"I was ready to sell off a lot of this land. And my son—who was getting his MBA at Columbia—actually brainstormed the proposal for some kind of entrepreneurial planning course he took."

"A plan to convert the bomb shelter into an upscale wine storage facility?" Mike asked.

"Yup," Kenner said, her dark eyes coming to life. "He won a prize for it at his graduation. I promised him a nice bonus if his vintage protection plan helped increase the price of the property."

"I'm sure it did," I said.

"Quite nicely."

"Do you know the buyers?" I asked.

Patti Kenner patted the top of the white wooden gate. "Good horse fences make good neighbors," she said.

"I've never met them, and I don't think they're very keen on having me come by for a cup of sugar."

"Haven't you been curious to see the wine cellar?"

"Actually, Ms. Cooper, I've never wanted to go near the shelter since the first time I went inside there as a kid. An underground bunker with a thick steel door that's the only way in—and the only way out? I even got my son to put in a separate entrance when he redesigned the space. But it's still far too spooky a place for me."

Fifty

The entrance drive to Stallion Ridge Cellars was as easy to miss as its owners wanted it to be. There was a turnoff onto a narrow dirt road with no signage and no landscaped greenery. Without the police chief's detailed directions, we would have missed it altogether.

Mike made the turn and began to drive along the road. He stopped twenty feet in and called Mercer, who was already on the way to meet us, to describe exactly how to find the place.

Both sides were fenced in with posts identical to the Kenner property and probably original to the period when the farms had been developed as one.

"You don't want to wait for Mercer?" I asked.

"I'm not expecting trouble, Coop. I'm just being nosy. Have you checked your cell?"

"Every five minutes, and not a word." I had left three more messages for Luc, trying to feign casual concern. The first was a check-in after the hour of my supposed ballet class, then having showered—wondering about a luncheon date—and the last about why there had been no contact. "Nosy about what?"

"Why Mulroy wanted to bring Luc out here."

"That's easy. Luc would be fascinated to see the wine cellar and all the great vintages that are supposed to be stored in it."

"Enough to miss a date with you?"

I didn't know how to answer that. Luc knew that he and I were walking on eggshells at this point in our relationship. "Maybe I annoyed him by surprising him with a visit last night. Maybe I annoyed him even more by slipping out this morning without saying a word."

"I say we crash their little party. I love a good wine tasting."

Off in the distance, in the direction we were headed, a small herd of horses was grazing in one of the pastures. They were all shades of palomino, and the sunlight danced off their backs as they moved away from the sound of our approach.

The path began to twist as we crested a small ridge— the first of many on the drive in from the paved roadway. Out of sight of passersby, on the far side of the slope, the plantings began in earnest. The trees may have been natural to the area, but there were well-tended privet hedges and flowering azalea bushes that suggested an intentional effort to make the property even more appealing—and more private.

The trees got thicker as we drove along, and now there were small posters warning of deer crossing. Another bend and we could see horses in a fenced field, this time off to the left.

There was still no sign of any humans, although I

could make out several pickup trucks—empty, it seemed—on different parts of the property.

The fourth ridge was by far the tallest. When we nosed over the top of it, the vista changed entirely. There was a series of barns ahead of us, exactly in the style of the Kenner stables with which they had once been paired. It was a completely tranquil pastoral scene, reminiscent of the Virginia countryside where I had spent my law school years. Real old-fashioned horse country.

And off to the right side of those buildings was the mysterious lump in the ground—an enormous swell on the earth's surface that looked like a gigantic burrowing mole had pushed up the dirt while making his home below. It was the old bomb shelter, now transformed into the ideal wine storage site known as Stallion Ridge Cellars.

"Looks like we're in time for lunch with the boys," Mike said.

Mulroy's silver SUV was parked in a gravel-covered area next to the largest barn. Beside it were two white pickups, both with the SRC logos on their doors.

Mike wound his way down the incline to the parking area.

"Aren't you surprised there's no security to ask who we are?" I asked.

"I bet there are cameras in half of those trees, Coop. If it's so high-tech and well concealed here, they don't need a guardhouse to stop the cars."

Mike got out of my SUV and stood next to it, to do a 360-degree sweep of the property. There were no unusual noises, just natural sounds of birds and the occasional neigh of a horse.

"Door's open," he said. "You got any cheese and crackers on you?"

"Thoughtless of me, wasn't it?" I said, getting out of the car. "The old K rations will just have to do."

There was a small wooden shed, low and shingled in the style of the larger barns, which formed the entrance to the bunker. Both its doors were swung back and latched on hinges, creating an eight-foot-wide opening. Bales of hay were stacked to the right and left inside the shed, giving the appearance that it was part of the horse operation.

But standing in the threshold, I could see the gleaming steel door of the storage vault. It looked so out of place in this bucolic setting. I could imagine one just like it at the entrance to the Federal Reserve Bank, protecting the billions of dollars stored there against invasion or assault.

The steel entry was open—displaying its thickness and impenetrability from all angles.

I stopped just short of the massive door when I heard men's voices from within. For almost the length of the room I could see a long passageway, lined on both sides with wine boxes from floor to ceiling.

"Move along, kid."

"Let me wait here, okay?"

"Claustrophobic?"

I nodded. "And not feeling very confrontational today."

"I'll give you a pass. I'm not planning a confrontation either. No need to let on about any of our suspicions. I'm just making like I want to glue myself to Luc so you guys have a few hours together, and I get to explore this storage facility for a few minutes," Mike said, patting me on the back. "Don't leave without me."

"I won't go anywhere, so long as you promise to come out with a bottle of nineteenth-century Lafite," I said. "Just don't channel yourself into Cary Grant."

"How so?"

"*Notorious.*" Mike knew it was my favorite movie. The tense scene in the wine cellar of the villain's mansion in Rio was one of the most exciting in film history. "Black sand—uranium—in the broken wine bottle. Nazis against Cary, and he found the right vintage at the wrong moment. Don't drop any bottles, okay?"

"That's an idea," he said, walking through the doorway. "If I see anything interesting, we can always come back with a warrant."

I watched Mike walk down the center aisle of the storage shelter until he reached the wall at the far end. He stopped for a minute, as though trying to determine where the voices were coming from, and then disappeared out of sight, off to the left.

I wedged myself between several bales of hay and sat down on a low pile near the front of the shed, where I could still feel the fresh afternoon breeze as it wafted by.

I started to play with my phone, seeing whether I could text or send e-mails. But there was no signal. Maybe Luc hadn't contacted me because there was no cell availability in the bunker. I composed a few messages and sent them, but the red "x" that popped up seconds later informed me that they couldn't be transmitted.

Almost ten minutes passed before I heard footsteps coming in my direction. I was used to the pacing of Mike's walk and the sound of his well-worn loafers. This wasn't his tempo at all. I pulled myself back against the wall, in the shadow of the loft above me.

The man who emerged was neither Mike nor Luc nor Jim Mulroy. It was Peter Danton, one of the partners who had acquired the real estate next to Lutèce, as well as this unusual wine cellar.

Danton didn't notice me, so I sat quietly to see what he was up to.

He stopped in the doorway of the shed and held something up to his mouth. It was a walkie-talkie. I suspected I was right that cell phones didn't work inside, and perhaps there wasn't even a tower on the entire property. That was another way to ensure complete privacy, even from intruders who wandered on, unable to summon assistance if they became stranded.

"Where are you?" Danton demanded of the person who answered. "Am I paying for a goddamned security system or not?"

The device crackled and he held it to his ear to get an answer.

"Yes, yes, I see it. A navy blue SUV with New York plates. The guy that drove it here happens to be a New York City detective."

More crackles and another comment.

"Yes, I told you we were meeting here at noon, but this cop isn't part of the meeting, okay? It's supposed to be Mulroy and Rouget, who came together in that silver car, and Josh Hanson, who's with me. So as soon as I can get rid of the detective, I'm going to ask you to escort him off the property. Nice and easy, but off. Is that clear enough?"

A static-filled response, and Danton shifted the phone to his right hand. As he tried to keep a grip on the walkie-talkie, I could see the two fingers that had been sliced in half.

"What other person?" Danton asked. "In the blue SUV?"

He waited for an answer.

"Find her for me. Maybe she likes horses, maybe she's

wandering around the barns. Find her and make sure she's strapped into her seat belt in the car. In the meantime, until we can regain control of the situation," Peter Danton said, "I'll go back inside, and I'll be locking the door to the vault when I do."

Fifty-one

My heart was racing as Peter Danton turned and went back inside the bunker. He pulled the door after him, and it closed as tightly as if it was the breach door on a submarine.

I slid off the hay bale and ran to the great steel handle, twice the size of a steering wheel. I turned and pulled at it, but nothing moved.

Outside the shed, I heard several trucks speeding across the gravel and stopping just in front. It sounded as though there were three different voices, as the men exchanged comments with each other.

"I think she's got light hair," the first one said. "I could see it on the tape when they drove in. Danton wants you to check the horse barns. Maybe she's out walking over to the animals."

"How about the shed?" another asked as I flattened myself against the wall, behind the tallest pile of bales.

"That's where Mr. Danton was standing when he

called me. Fan out and look for her. No need to be un-pleasant. Just bring her back to this blue car. They'll be leaving soon."

"Who's watching the surveillance screens?" the second guy wanted to know.

"There's only the three of us working today. One of you will be back on that duty after you find the girl."

I was relieved that nothing unpleasant was in store for me, and also to know that the security team was under-staffed. But I didn't feel comfortable enough to identify myself to them as long as Mike was on the other side of a locked door. And I didn't want Mercer to meet any resis-tance if he drove in before we were able to get out.

I exhaled when I heard the workmen leave. But now all I could focus on was that two of the men who meant the most to me in the world—Luc and Mike—were locked in the underground storage facility and had no reason to know that Peter Danton was unhappy to have Mike there.

I didn't want to be "found" by the searchers, so I squeezed myself farther back between two tall stacks of hay bales.

There must have been a legitimate purpose for the meeting Danton had arranged, I tried to convince myself. Both Jim Mulroy and Josh Hanson had expressed their interest in investing in Lutèce. Had Luc been lured here to see the vault, and then been obligated to sit down with the group to accept their offer to expand his team?

And what did he know about Gineva Imports? Had Gina Varona not been invited to this impromptu get-together, or was she simply unable to make it on short notice?

I saw the giant wheel on the steel door begin to spin

only minutes after Danton had gone back inside. Maybe the discussion had been aborted because of Mike's presence, and the foursome was coming out. But it was Peter Danton, this time accompanied by Josh Hanson.

Danton walked to the opening of the shed and must have seen his workers scrambling around, inside and out of the other barns.

He held the walkie-talkie to his mouth with his good hand.

"Haven't you found her yet?" he demanded.

I couldn't hear the answer.

"Just get her back to her car. I'll have the detective out to her shortly. He's just poking around before he leaves."

I was frozen in place.

Peter Danton turned and started talking to Josh Hanson. "It's time to break up our meeting. I want to get Chapman out of here before he does any more snooping. Go back in and tell Luc you've got to hurry back to your kid's soccer game. Understood? We'll deal with your cut of the business another time."

"That's fine."

"Get rid of the detective and Luc so we can move the stuff out of here if we need to. Worst he can do is come back in a couple of days looking for it, if he's half as smart as he thinks he is. I'll rejoin you in a few minutes. Just keep Chapman away from that bin behind the Domaine de la Romanée-Conti."

"Will do."

Josh Hanson went back through the open steel door, and Peter Danton took one more look outside the shed.

He pressed the walkie-talkie to find his security head. "Where is everybody?"

The machine crackled back at him.

"If the detective's traveling companion wasn't in any of the barns, then check the closest trails," he said. "She can't be that far away."

"Say that again? You've just gone back to watch the surveillance tape a second time?" Danton held the device to his ear. "You're telling me she came into this little building with the detective but never left?"

Danton turned and started to look around the small shed. "No, no. You go out with the other men and keep looking. I'm doing fine right here."

Peter Danton put the walkie-talkie in his rear pants pocket, then walked to the door of the vault. He pushed it closed and locked it, with four men still inside, to begin his search for me.

Fifty-two

"Alexandra Cooper." Peter Danton repeated my name aloud, over and over. Each time he said it, he lifted a bale of hay from one of the taller piles and threw it onto a smaller one.

With three or four more tosses, I would be completely exposed.

"I'm going to find you in a moment or two, Alex, and then you and I are going to join the party."

He lifted another block and bounced it off a nearby pile.

"You could scream, of course, but then the only people who might hear you are the men who work for me. The vault is completely soundproofed. Nobody wanted to hear those bombs exploding around them in the good old days," he said. "And the men who work for me don't have a reputation for being the friendliest sort."

I heard another bale land on the floor.

"That's what I get for hiring ex-cons to do my security. They're a little rough around the edges—all the edges—but then again, they don't scare easily out here in the boondocks, which so many people do. Well, there you are!"

I was crouched in a corner of the shed, and now my cover was completely gone.

"You can come to me, Alex, or I'll just get over to you and drag you out. It might take a minute or two longer, but I'll get there."

I stood up. I stepped on the pile of hay between me and Peter Danton. He reached out to grab my arm and pull me down beside him.

"Sorry. I was up most of the night. I just fell asleep back here." I figured I looked dazed enough to make believe I hadn't heard any of the conversation.

"I would have thought you'd be the type to enjoy some fresh air," he said, "which would have been much healthier for you. But now I think it's time for a rendez-vous with your friends in the vault."

I looked out the door of the small shed and thought about making a run for my car. I'd prefer anything to be-ing entombed in a bomb shelter. Mike had a gun and knew how to use it, though the idea of leaving him and Luc trapped behind the steel door terrified me.

"If you want me to take off, I'll just get in the car and go," I said.

"A little late for that plan, don't you think? And don't look so longingly at all that open land out there. My foreman is a great hunter. Unfortunately, he once mis-took his wife for a deer, I guess. Did twelve years for it and I'd say he's completely rehabilitated."

I was backed against the hay bales when Danton grabbed my right arm, above my elbow, with his good hand. "Just listen to what I say and stay calm," he said. "You're walking with me."

Peter Danton led me toward the steel door, the entrance to the vault. I looked back over my shoulder, hoping against hope that Mercer would be arriving any minute. But there was no sign of anyone approaching the graveled parking lot.

"I've got the lives of your dear friends in my hands, Alex, and Luc tells me you're a very emotional girl. High-strung is what he called you."

There would be time for me to argue with Luc about that one later on.

"You'd be wiser to control yourself once we see the others. Maybe we can sort this out and get you on your way."

"I'm sure we can do that," I said, knowing that my brain was scrambling to think of ways to counter whatever Danton had in mind.

"I don't scare easily, Alex. I lost one finger to my own negligence a long time ago in a kitchen, as I told you," he said. He had clamped his other hand on my neck to keep me close to him. "The other one was hacked off by a drug dealer in Nigeria who thought I'd been poaching from his stash. Both times without the benefit of anesthesia."

He laughed at his own story, or maybe at the look on my face as I checked out his mutilated fingers.

"Don't look so surprised, Alex. You and the detective obviously came up here today because—"

"I asked him to bring me here to find Luc. That's all. I was desperate to spend a few hours with Luc before he goes home."

"Such a sweet thought. But I think the truth is that

your friend Chapman believes I knew something about Luigi and his drug business. He'll be happy to see you come in with me, Alex. Both Mike and Luc will be glad you're there."

I tried to dig my heels into the seams of the wooden floorboard, but Peter Danton pulled me forward. "I've learned to work with what I've got left, in case you're thinking there isn't much strength in my hands."

I wanted them off me—off my neck. I shook my head, but he grasped me even tighter.

"Come along, Alex," he said, as he steered me through the opening of the vault. "Don't keep everyone waiting. It's cold in there. Bone-chilling cold."

Fifty-three

The temperature dropped the minute we crossed the threshold into the subterranean shelter. Outside it had been a warm, sunny April afternoon, but once the steel door closed behind us, the fifty-five-degree temperature—and the sudden injection of fear—had me shivering uncontrollably.

Peter Danton kept a firm grip on my neck as he moved me forward. There was a single corridor—a long, gray cement floor lined with cases and cases of wine, stacked floor to ceiling. Overhead, the long fluorescent lights cast an eerie glow in the windowless space.

I could hear voices in the distance. I thought about screaming, but there was no point in creating chaos without an understanding of what had gone on. I knew that Mike had a gun, and it didn't appear that Peter Danton did.

Every ten cases or so, an alley had been created between the cartons, each ending against a solid concrete wall. I looked from side to side but saw no one.

I paused to catch my breath and rub my hands together. The boxes stacked on my right side were different from the wine cases. They were brown cardboard, labeled ENERGY LIFE PACK, which seemed ironic at the moment. The date stamp said 1960, and they had obviously been sealed for more than fifty years. In small print below that was a list of uses: ATOMIC WARFARE/BACTERIA WARFARE/HURRICANES/EARTHQUAKES. I wondered if their contents would be of any help today to interlopers buried alive in an out-of-date bomb shelter.

"Is that you, Peter?" Josh Hanson called out. "You back?"

"Yeah. Is there a problem?"

"Nah. Mike here is asking questions I just can't answer."

I bit my lip as Danton dragged me along beside him.

"What is it you don't understand, Detective?" Danton asked.

We were coming to the end of the corridor, and I could tell from the direction of Josh's voice that the others were around the corner to the left.

The bunker seemed almost like a labyrinth—a small maze with a low ceiling and no natural light, and no exit at the end of any of the rows. The tight, cold space was a claustrophobe's nightmare. It seemed airless, too, because the chilly temperature made it harder to breathe. I closed my eyes to try to concentrate on a way to safely talk us all out of this disaster.

"I'm just trying to learn about all these vintages— what makes them valuable and that kind of thing."

Mike was the first person I saw when we turned the last corner. He was ten feet away from me, holding a bottle of wine from the long rows of shelves on which the bottles had been stacked after being removed from their cases.

Although Peter Danton had let go of my neck, Mike clearly got a look at the panicked expression on my face.

"Coop—what—?"

There was a long table tucked into the far corner behind Mike, where Luc and Josh had been seated with Jim Mulroy. Luc got to his feet immediately and called out my name.

"I'm fine," I said, holding out both hands in front of me and urging both Mike and Luc to stay calm.

"Alex was afraid she was missing out on something tasty," Danton said. "Aren't you guys still drinking?"

There were several open bottles of red wine— and four half-filled wineglasses—on the table at which they'd been sitting before Danton came back out and found me.

Mike started toward me as Luc tried to catch up with him.

"I'm fine!" I shouted, far too loud to be convincing as my voice echoed off the ceiling and wall.

At the same moment, Danton yoked me with his right arm, dragging me back and reaching out with his left toward a crack between the metal racks of the last row of wine bottles.

Before Mike could reach me, Peter Danton dropped his hand from my neck and lifted a double-barreled shotgun, pointing it directly at the three startled men who were facing us.

Fifty-four

"I'm happy to pay for the wine I drank," Mike said, lowering his hand to his side. His off-duty gun was probably in a shoulder-holster under his arm. "No need to shoot."

"On the house, Detective. Keep your hands away from your pockets. More wine and fewer questions, you'd be on your way home."

"Alex," Luc said. "Are you all right?"

I nodded at him while Danton answered. "Sit yourself down, Luc. Back at the table where Jim is."

Luc stood his ground for several seconds, until Danton fired directions at Josh Hanson.

"There are several lengths of rope in that cabinet behind you, Josh," Danton said. "Sit them down and tie their hands to the chair, behind their backs."

"Let me recommend something to you," Mike said. "You and Josh take a flying head start on us, Peter. Get yourselves out of here right now, before anybody else gets hurt. Go right to the airport, if you're smart. You can live like a king in the South of France. Like a deposed dictator or any other kind of thug. I bet Gil-Darsin's villa's already on the market."

"Shut up, Chapman."

"Leave us here for a few hours. Overnight even. You know we can't call out on these phones. Go wherever the hell you want to go and just let us be. You're not wanted for murder in France."

"I didn't kill the girl there," Danton said.

"They're ready to tag that one to Luigi," Mike said. "Not to worry."

I could hardly stop trembling from the combination of cold and terror.

"Give me your gun, Detective," Danton said, as I watched Josh wrap the rope around Luc's hands.

"My day off, Peter. Left my Glock home in bed. I just came for a ride in the country," Mike said, lifting his arms in the air. "All in the name of love. Now, if you let Alex sit down, maybe she'll stop shaking so badly."

"She'll get used to it."

"Come here, Coop," Mike said. "Go sit back there with Luc."

I knew Mike wanted me out of the way in case he and Peter reached the point of exchanging gunshots, but I couldn't bring myself to move farther into the corner of this death trap of a vault.

"She'll stay right here until I see your heat," Danton said, slamming the shotgun against my back.

"I'm telling you, man. Sometimes I just don't pack. Like you, the night you slit Luigi's throat." Mike gestured by running his finger across his neck. "I mean it's more quiet than shooting him, but it left so much fucking blood all over the houseboat. It would have been much neater if you'd just pumped one or two shots in his gut."

"Hurry up, Josh. Time to pat down the detective."

"Stop squirming," Josh Hanson said to Luc, who seemed to be trying to help Mike in his own way.

Mike leaned one hand on the metal shelf below a row a bottles. "You were smart to wear gloves, though. I gotta give you that. Crime Scene tried everything to get DNA outta that place. Not a whit."

"I'd take credit for surprising you with my intelligence, Mike, but then you'd be able to say 'gotcha.'"

Mike was rolling his head to the side. I thought he was signaling me to break away from Danton and take shelter in the next row over.

"Oh, I can still say 'gotcha,' my man. You know they found a pair of latex gloves in the canal, caught up under Luigi's arm, in the material of his jacket. I guess too much Gowanus sludge had gotten inside to get DNA out of them to see who'd been wearing them, and most of his blood had washed off in the canal. Tested positive for blood, but in amounts too minuscule to test."

"Convenient," Danton said. "Search him, Josh."

"Almost there, Peter."

"But there weren't even any traces of blood on the two fingers of the right-hand glove," Mike said. "So I'm thinking you were the killer, and your chopped-off, mutilated digits didn't reach to the tip of the gloves when you were wearing them. So no blood got on them when you sliced the Squid. Not even a drop. How's that for a deduction?"

"You should keep your thoughts to yourself, Detective. In fact, if you hadn't been so curious about narcotics trafficking in Africa fifteen minutes ago, and about what's behind the wine labels in the bottles here, you and these lovebirds might have been on your way back home."

It was Mike who had triggered Danton's suspicions, not Luc. But that hardly mattered, now that we were captured in his lair.

Josh Hanson tugged at the rope behind Luc's back to secure it, did the same to Jim, then started to walk toward Mike. I don't think I had ever seen my friend react so quickly. He swiveled in Hanson's direction, bringing with him a bottle from the shelf he'd been leaning on and cracking it against the side of Hanson's head.

The bottle splintered and the wine spurted out. Hanson fell to his knees and toppled onto his side, screaming in pain. Shards of glass were lodged in the skin on his face like arrows shot out of a bow.

"Run, Coop!" Mike shouted at me.

I pushed at Danton while he used both hands to raise the shotgun. I knocked him off-balance and he cursed at me as he tried to regain his footing.

Luc yelled for me to get out of the way, too, and the last thing I saw before I turned the corner—looking for an escape route—was that Mike had unholstered his revolver and was pointing it at Peter Danton.

Fifty-five

I ran to the massive steel door as fast as I could. I pushed against it, just like I did at the door of Luc's home the night this all began one week ago. Nothing gave, and I didn't know which lever to touch or pull to get the lock to respond to me.

I turned my head and saw Danton eyeing me, having rounded the corner to get away from Mike.

He was coming in my direction, still almost thirty feet away down the long corridor, holding the shotgun with both hands. Behind him, Mike stuck his head out and pointed his revolver at Danton.

Before he could take aim, Danton darted into one of the side aisles. Mike moved cautiously into the center corridor, inching his way forward.

"Look for a panic button, Coop," he called out to me. "There has to be one somewhere."

I didn't want to take my eyes off Mike, for fear that Danton would shoot or charge toward him. I stepped backward toward the door, then glanced from side to side to see if there was anything as obvious as a panic device.

Before I heard the noise, I could see the enormous rack behind Mike's back—almost to the ceiling of the vault, at least fourteen feet high—begin to tilt. Danton must have been pushing at it. I screamed to warn Mike, but the wine cartons began to fall off the uppermost shelves, crashing to the ground all around him as he covered his head with his hands.

The wine was as red as blood, spilling out and gushing from the broken glass as it cascaded over other cases and onto Mike's head and body.

"Are you okay?" I yelled out to him.

"Keep it up, kid. You know I've got a thick head."

There was no way Mike could free himself from the cartons and bottles fast enough to follow Danton. I couldn't see Danton, of course, but I could hear movement as he seemed to be struggling with something— maybe another heavy table or piece of furniture—deep in the row into which he had receded.

I turned around to examine the sides of the great door more closely. Off to my left was a small yellow box, the size of a light switch pad. I tugged at the cover and pulled it open. Inside was a black button with the word ALARM written below it.

I pressed the button, half expecting something to ring inside this airtight space, but there was no sound. I pressed it again, with no idea who might be summoned, if the device was even connected to anyone in the outside world—on or off the grounds of Stallion Ridge.

Now I returned my attention to Mike, who was on his feet, digging his way out of the debris around him. I started to move toward him, but he held out his left arm, motioning me to stay in place. The revolver was in his right hand.

There were two distinct sounds I could hear. The farther one came from Josh Hanson, moaning as though he was still immobilized by pain. The other must have been Peter Danton, dug in behind the overturned shelves of wine, but making noise as though he was scraping something with the end of the shotgun.

I needed to take cover, but there were so few places that afforded it, and I didn't know whether there were openings within any of the other rows in this bizarre maze. I feared that Danton would emerge from some part of this hideaway which he knew so well, ready to shoot his way out.

Each time Mike took a step to position himself closer to the row into which Danton had disappeared, the glass and cardboard beneath his feet gave his movement away.

"Come on out, Danton," he called. "I got you trapped in there. I can wait you out all night."

Mike was trying to peer between the metal racks to look for Danton, so he was no longer paying attention to me. I crouched down and quickly ducked over into the first aisle to my right—Danton was off somewhere to the left—and got down on one knee. If I could eventually move closer to Mike, maybe I could help him draw a bead on his human target.

The scraping noise stopped. Suddenly, there was a blast from the shotgun, aimed in Mike's direction, that sounded like cannon fire because of the confines of the shelter.

My hands reflexively flew up over my ears, and it looked as though the pellets had shattered another dozen bottles of some ridiculously expensive vintage.

Mike swiveled quickly again—obviously safe—and

flattened himself against the wooden wine crates that bordered the adjacent row of shelves.

As I readied myself to go forward to help him, I could see a flash of steel out of the corner of my left eye, as though something on the door was in motion.

I froze in place, watching the enormous handle—the size of a car's steering wheel—turn in a circle, around and around again.

"Mike!" I called out, torn between diverting his attention from Danton and needing to let him know that someone was about to open the vault door.

"Stay back," he said. "Get way back in that aisle, will you?"

Danton fired again, this time spraying the ceiling with shotgun pellets. He was laughing as he spoke. "Find the alarm, did you, Alex? Who do you think is going to get here first? The town police or my foreman?"

Terrified that someone who worked for Peter Danton would be the next man through the door, I kept my eyes riveted on the steel handle. The soundproofing of the shelter made it impossible to hear anyone or anything from outside.

I was so focused on its gyration that I nearly jumped out of my skin when Mike fired his gun. When I turned my head, I could see another bottle smashed by his bullet. This time, a fine white powder—cocaine, no doubt—poured over the side of the divided vessel, like grains of sand running through an hourglass.

Why was Mike wasting a bullet that we might desperately need in the coming seconds?

"Here goes your fortune, Danton. There'll be blow all over the floor of this goddamn place," he said. "What vintage is it? Château Calamari 2012?"

Danton fired again, this time lowering his aim to try to get a piece of Mike.

I directed my attention back to the steel entry. The handle was still, but someone was pushing against the door. As it opened into the room, the man who'd been pressing on the door fell forward onto the ground, grabbing his left leg as he rolled on his right side.

He was dressed entirely in denim—blue work shirt and jeans—and I guessed him to be one of the Stallion Ridge staff. He was bleeding profusely from his leg, and although the soundproofing kept his voice from penetrating the space before the door opened, he was howling now.

Behind him, standing in the doorway with a rifle pointed directly at Mike, was Gina Varona.

Fifty-six

"Put it down, Gina," Mike said before he was able to lift his revolver.

I hadn't liked the woman from the moment her name had come into the mix, and now we were all at her mercy.

"Tell me what's going on," she said, never flinching as she held her position. "Where's Peter?"

Gina was Brigitte's best friend. Of course they were all in this together.

"Getting high," Mike said, since there was no answer from Danton. "What else did you think he'd be doing?"

She had ignored me at first, but still holding the gun on Mike, Gina spoke to me directly. "Get off your knees, Alex. Out of that row, over to Chapman."

I looked at Mike for direction and he shook his head at me. I didn't move.

"Tell me where Peter is," she asked again.

Another blast from Danton's shotgun, this one missing Gina Varona's head by only inches. I was almost as stunned as she seemed to be, and suddenly there was more commotion as Danton—having moved shelves and worked his way out of one dead-ended row—emerged from the next one into the narrow main corridor between Mike and Gina, trying to make his way to the door.

"Stop!" Mike shouted at him.

But Danton ignored the command, and with his weapon steadied on Gina, he continued his mad charge.

It was Mike who fired first, missing Peter Danton altogether, his bullet ricocheting off the end of a wooden crate.

But Gina Varona got off a shot before Danton could pull the trigger, and the killer crashed to his knees—his chest ripped apart by the impact—falling to the cement floor a foot away from where I kneeled.

Fifty-seven

"I'm so sorry, Gina. I didn't trust you from the minute we were introduced," I said.

"I didn't like you much either. What did you walk into here today?"

We were standing together next to the large barn, in the sunlight—Gina, Luc, Mike, Jim, and I. The township police—who had responded to the panic alarm within ten minutes—were swarming around the shed. Two ambulances had left for the local hospital, one with Josh Hanson and the injured foreman on board, and the other with the body of Peter Danton.

"Mike and I drove up here looking for Luc, but we interrupted a business meeting between your partners."

"I found out a little late that I didn't get the invite," Gina said. "Don't you hate when that happens?"

She had an arm around my shoulder, trying to lighten me up.

"Totally." I was taking deep breaths, trying to keep an

eye on Luc, Jim, and Mike as they walked away from me to talk with the cops.

"Luc and Jim Mulroy drove up together," I said. "We came because Luc was supposed to spend the day in town, but left the city without letting us know. We certainly weren't expecting Armageddon at Stallion Ridge, or we'd have brought reinforcements."

"Josh Hanson's the new kid on the block." Gina said. "Peter's been trying to push me out. I think Josh is more his type, in terms of a business partner."

"What made you come up here today?"

"I called the gallery to speak to Peter this morning," she said. "We haven't been getting along too well lately. That's when Eva told me he'd had a call from Jim, and that he disappeared quite suddenly. Said he had to check something here in Connecticut. I decided to drive up and protect my own interests. Nothing's been right since that girl was killed in Mougins."

"But you thought to bring a gun," I said, still wary of Gina.

She smiled. "That's the Tiro a Segno in me. The Rifle Club. I've always got one in the trunk of my car. You never know when you'll get a chance for some target practice."

"So you shot the foreman?" I asked.

"When I drove into the parking lot, I recognized him. He's always been perfectly friendly before. This time he was running into the shed, but came back out when he saw me get out of the car. He threatened me, actually. He was carrying a shotgun and told me to stay away."

"Why?" I said. "Did he say?"

"Just that Peter had set off the panic alarm, and he was going to open the door. I asked him if that was unusual—I mean, had it happened before—and he said it never had. When I asked him who was inside, the guy said there was a detective and—well—you must have been the young woman he mentioned. I didn't have a clue what was going on, but I didn't like the sound of it," Gina said. "But I obeyed him."

"You did?"

She smiled. "Well, I returned to the car, anyway. I came back with my rifle, but he didn't notice me coming because he was unlocking the vault. I got up real close behind him, and when he realized I was there—and armed—he really didn't like the sight of that."

"So he refused to open the door?" I said.

"I nudged him a few times, but he wouldn't change his mind. Most men don't take me seriously until they see me shoot," Gina said. "I just grazed him, Alex. It got the job done."

Mike was making his way back over to us.

"Before I came into the shelter, did Peter Danton tell you anything at all about the skulls?" I asked him. The ancient bones had haunted me since I first saw them in the moonlight in Mougins.

"I never got to that, Coop. They must have been a diversion, cooked up by Lisette and Luigi to keep everyone's attention on the restaurant wars. Luc would be so busy looking for enemies around town that the drug trafficking wouldn't get any attention. It was a good ruse. The bones were old enough so the police didn't have to worry about dead bodies, but spooky enough to be a distraction."

"The one you brought to my apartment, Mike," I said, "was that the only one on the houseboat?"

"Yeah. I guess Luigi just wanted a souvenir."

"How did he get it on a plane?" I asked.

"It was sitting on a Mylar blanket—you know, the kind runners use after a marathon? It probably didn't even scan going through X-ray. And in customs, it was tagged with an 'antiquities' stamp, so nobody even looked inside the wrapping."

I glanced over at Luc, being questioned by one of the police officers. "Poor Luc, the skulls alone made it look like he was connected to both murders. Those skeletons worked for the bad guys on every level."

Mike turned his attention to Gina. "I haven't thanked you properly for what you did in that vault. I'll find a way to do that."

"It'll be easy, Detective. I've got lots of time on my hands."

"In the meantime, I know these guys have questions for you," he said. "And I told them how cool you were under pressure, Gina. I had that gun pointed right at you and you didn't blink."

Gina Varona started down the rise toward the parking lot. "I wasn't worried for a second, Mike. Sergio called me after you'd been questioning him about me at Tiro the other night. He told me, after he'd seen you shoot in the basement there, that you couldn't hit the broad side of a barn."

Fifty-eight

By six o'clock, we had been taken over to Kenner Stables by the local police, joined by Mercer, who had arrived soon after the town cops.

Patti Kenner, one of the kindest, smartest women I'd ever met, was doing her best to calm and comfort us. She had called her personal physician to come tend to the soles of Mike's feet, cleaning out the teeny glass fragments from the broken bottles he'd stepped on and bandaging them with an antibiotic ointment.

Mercer, Mike, Luc, and Gina were at Patti's kitchen table. She had canceled her dinner party and was feeding all of them the delicious meal she'd prepared earlier in the day—individual chicken pot pies in small cast iron skillets. I was on a sofa at the far end of the room.

After the police had interviewed Jim Mulroy, he'd brought a case of 1982 Mouton Rothschild Pauillac for Patti before heading home. He told us it was from Peter

Danton's personal stash. We were on our third bottle by the time the doctor arrived to check me out.

Gina Varona was explaining her long friendship with Brigitte Rouget. "Luc and I were the two steady influences in Brigitte's life," she said. "I've spent a lot of years trying to keep her drug-free, keep her on track for her family."

"You were serious about backing me, too," Luc said. He was leaning back in his chair, his long, thin legs stretched out in front of him. I'd never seen him look so sad.

"We should never have let Peter get involved," Gina said. "I think he was feeding coke to Brigitte all along. Bringing it to her from Africa even a decade ago. You trust everyone, Luc. That's your problem."

"And Coop doesn't trust anyone," Mike said.

"When did you get worried about Peter Danton?" Mercer asked Gina.

She frowned as she answered. "I was really fond of Luigi. I mean, I only knew him from the club, but I thought he was a bright kid, a hustler with a great future. I really liked that Luc was willing to give him such a big break. So first I heard that Luigi was going over to Mougins—to meet Luc—I thought it was really a good thing for us."

"Well, that was the least of it," Luc said.

"Next thing Peter tells me, after Luigi comes home, is he thinks Luigi killed the girl."

"Lisette?" I asked.

"Yes, Lisette. And she used to be Brigitte's supplier. So suddenly, it seemed so obvious to me that there was a drug connection at the base of all this," Gina said. "And then Luigi was found dead in the water."

"Josh Hanson rolled over on Peter while we were waiting for his ambulance to come," Mike said. "Snitched on him. That's how he won himself a free ride back to Brooklyn, with the detectives, as soon as he's treated and released."

"Peter Danton slit Luigi's throat?" Gina asked.

"Yes, for the same reason Luigi killed Lisette. Too much cocaine went missing. Luigi slipped Luc's matchbox into her pocket, just to make it look bad for Luc. Josh said Peter bragged about doing the same thing to Luigi, who'd told him he'd done it. It's a dangerous game, trafficking in drugs," Mike said. "Maybe the most dangerous game."

"But you must have known about Gineva Imports?" I asked Gina.

"We set up a corporation because we had a lot of legitimate goods to bring into the country," she said. "Cocaine wasn't one of them."

"Nor were women," Luc said. "Escorts or prostitutes, or however you want to call them."

"Wine, cheese, truffles, escargot," Gina said. "We had quite a list of good things to import. The corporation was set up in my name and Eva Danton's. Peter was the vice president. I'm sure you'll see he's signed off—or forged our names—on everything else."

"The building next to Luc's restaurant?" I asked.

"What building would that be?" She answered my question with a question.

"I didn't know about it either," Luc said, drawing in his legs and burying his head in his hands. "Apparently my design to restore the dignity and civility of the great Lutèce was the least important part of Peter's plan."

"Has his link to the prostitution ring based in Lille been confirmed?" I asked.

"Interpol will have an answer by Monday," Mercer said.

"It hardly matters at this point," Luc said. "The dream is ruined. There's no point going on."

I stood up to walk over to him. "They'll get this all separated out from you."

He waved me off. "I was stupid, Alex. I was so driven to create this fantasy for myself—for my father—that I let myself lose sight of everything that mattered. I need to go home, darling. I need to go home and figure out what's left of this."

The chief of police opened the back door of Patti's kitchen. "My men are ready, Mr. Rouget. If you're going to get to JFK for your flight, you'll have to leave now. We need to stop at your hotel for your passport and bags."

"Why don't you stay one more day, Luc?" Gina asked.

He stood up to shake hands with Mercer and Mike, and to thank Patti Kenner.

"I think it's better for everyone if I leave now," Luc said. "Whenever the police need me, I'll come back."

"Let me walk you to the car," I said.

Luc laughed, trying to defuse the tension. "Just come out on the steps to say good-bye."

"Who wants a refill?" Mike asked, trying to distract everyone from watching me, I was sure.

The Washington Township patrol car was backed into the drive, the two officers seated in front with the motor running.

I held on to the railing as I went down the stairs after Luc. I was on the bottom step and he was on the ground when he turned to embrace me.

"I'm so sorry I brought such a sordid mess into your life, dear Alex. It was the last thing I ever intended to do."

"No apologies, Luc. There's nothing to be sorry about."

"I had such very different plans for this evening, darling. Someday soon I'll tell you what they were, and maybe by then we can even laugh about it."

"Maybe so," I said, wiping the tears from my eyes.

Luc pulled my head toward him and kissed me—first on each damp eyelid, then on the tip of my nose, and then my mouth.

I hated good-byes. I hated emotional good-byes of every kind. I willed myself to think that this wouldn't be the last time Luc held my face between his hands and told me that he loved me. But I knew better than to believe that.

Fifty-nine

Mercer was driving us back to the city in his beat-up old station wagon. He'd moved Logan's toys off the backseat, and I stretched out to nap for the ride, with one of Patti Kenner's quilts covering me.

I fell asleep somewhere in the rolling foothills of Connecticut—maybe a little too much red wine after all the excitement of the day and the personal drain of Luc's departure. Mike and Mercer were dissecting the details of the crimes and the investigation, but I would have to hear it all again the next time we were together.

"Are we there yet?" I asked.

"You sound like my kid," Mercer said. "Getting closer."

I dozed again, waking up at the tollbooth and then drifting back to sleep. The cool night air and the darkness as I looked out the window were soothing to me.

The next time I opened my eyes, I could see that we were whipping past overhead lights, obviously on a highway.

"The FDR Drive?" I asked. It was the last stretch before we'd reach the exit for my apartment.

"Yes, ma'am."

I started to push back the quilt. "I'd better wake up,
guys. Almost home."

Mike looked over his shoulder at me. "Keep your
head down, kid. We got a slight detour to make."

"What time is it?"

"Eleven fifteen."

"Can't the detour wait till tomorrow?"

"Just not possible, Coop."

"Keith Scully?" I asked. "The commissioner?"

I couldn't think of any other command appearance
we'd have to make at this hour.

"Like that."

I closed my eyes and rested. "You think Luc's airborne?"

"Yeah," Mike said. "He texted to say they made the
flight."

"That's good." It relaxed me to know that he was on
his way back to France and his sons.

I rolled onto my back. Now I could see many more
lights strung out above me, close together. They were
hanging from huge cables, arcing up from the roadway
to tall columns far above, so I knew we were on a bridge.

"Please don't tell me, guys," I said. "Brooklyn?"

"Brooklyn it is," Mike said.

"Scully insists on talking to us in Brooklyn because of
the Gowanus murder?"

"Just go with your imagination, Coop. Let it run
wild."

It wasn't long until we were off the bridge, driving
down the exit ramp. Mercer knew where he was going,

so I just rested and tried to conjure up images more pleasant than those of the day.

Three or four minutes later, the car came to a stop. It seemed to be dark all around us. I pushed the quilt off and sat up, trying to get a sense of our surroundings.

I could see that we were between the Brooklyn and Manhattan Bridges, facing the spectacular outline of Manhattan Island, magically lighted against the dark night sky.

Mike got out and opened my door. I slipped my moccasins back on and stood up.

He took my arm and walked me around the station wagon, and all of a sudden hundreds of lights came on just fifty feet in front of us. I gasped at the sight—a gigantic glass box the size of a small building sitting on the water's edge, with an old-fashioned carousel inside.

I watched in amazement as the carousel began to turn and the antique painted ponies started to trot. The traditional music of the calliope played, as if the entire scene had come alive just for us. Against the cold facades of the restored warehouses of DUMBO—the Brooklyn neighborhood Down Under the Manhattan Bridge Overpass—this stunning confection stood out like a fairy tale brought to life.

"It's your ride, Coop," Mike said. "Let's get moving."

"But it was all dark a moment ago."

A workman was at the door, holding it open for us. The writing in front said JANE'S CAROUSEL. I'd read about it when it opened a few months back. It was a 1922 theme park attraction that had been lovingly restored and installed by the Walentas family, for more than ten million dollars.

"Well, it's open for business now. You work Night

Watch in Brooklyn and pretty soon you find out the world's your oyster."

"I've got nothing to complain about, Mike," I said, leaning on his arm. "But let's forget about oysters and French food for the time being."

"Pick your pony, Coop."

The horses were each more magnificent than the others. They were side by side as the carousel spun around, some painted in soft pastels of lemon and coral, one dressed in the armor of a knight's steed, another outfitted for a cowboy. There must have been close to fifty of them, spinning around inside their dazzling jewel box of a showcase.

Mercer had crossed the street and come back with a large shopping bag. When he returned, they both helped me get up on the moving carousel and held me steady while I climbed onto a palomino every bit as handsome as the horses I'd seen today at Stallion Ridge.

I was riding in the outer lane, beaming as though I'd won the lottery.

Each time we circled, I made out another landmark in the distance. I could see the towers of the criminal courthouse, where yesterday's slaughter had occurred, and the glittering gilded statue of Fame, high above the municipal offices facing City Hall. The Empire State Building was bathed in its own bright lights, and I could even see the high-rise apartments of the Upper East Side forming a backdrop against the horizon.

Mercer rested the brown bag on the floor next to me. He took three cupcakes out of it, along with a candle and a matchbook.

"Is it still my birthday?" I asked, as I watched him light the single candle.

"You got another twelve minutes to enjoy it, Alex," Mercer said.

Mike started to sing while Mercer held the cupcake in front of me. I grabbed the pole with one hand and Mercer's shoulder with the other, gliding up and down with my chosen pony.

"Close your eyes and make a wish," Mercer said.

"Eyes wide open, guys. I have everything I want right here with me tonight."

"You've got us for life, kid. The three musketeers."

"They're too French, Mike. Give me another image."

"Well, did you hear the man?" Mike said, getting down on his knees, fumbling with something I couldn't see. "Close your eyes. Wish or don't wish, that's up to you."

I closed my eyes. And as long as they were closed, I made a wish. Then I opened them and blew out the candle that Mercer was holding.

I looked down and saw that Mike had uncorked another bottle of wine, and he handed us each a paper cup full.

"Cheers, Coop. Happy birthday," Mike said.

"Happy birthday, Alexandra," Mercer said, as the city spun around before me.

"What did you wish for?"

"If I tell you, I'd have to kill you."

"That serious?" Mike said, with a laugh, climbing up on the horse next to mine. "Then let me be the last to know."

"You usually are," Mercer said, leaning his back against my pony to take in the view.

"You're forgetting one thing," Mike said. "The ring."

I sat bolt upright, like I'd been punched in the gut.

"Look, I don't know what you know about that, but this isn't the night—"

"Keep your cool, Coop. Lean over next time around. The brass ring is yours if you can pick it off."

The brass ring of the carousel, I thought to myself. Not Luc's birthday surprise for me, that Joan Stafford had alerted me to.

Mike was talking about the classic carnival prize— happiness, long life, great friends, good luck.

"You just keep this carousel going till I reach it," I said.

"Dizzy yet?" Mike asked.

"Not a chance of it. I'm just beginning to feel good again."

I handed my cup to Mercer, basking in the lights of the city I loved so much. I could see the brass ring hanging from a leather strip on the carousel's frame, and I grabbed for it every time we circled around.

ACKNOWLEDGMENTS

Jane Stanton Hitchcock is one of my favorite writers. Since I first created Alex Cooper, Jane has helped me plot my way out of difficult corners at all hours of the day and night, allowed me to put words in her mouth as Coop's friend, Joan Stafford, and feted me with every completed book. Her brilliant husband, Jim Hoagland, has generously tolerated endless conversations about our fictional alter egos. This time, Jane and Jim introduced me to Mohammed Gil-Darsin and set my backstory in motion.

Sometimes my readers ask which characters in my stories are real and which are not. This is a work of fiction, of course, so none of the people portrayed in these pages are "real." Occasionally, I pay homage to friends for whom I have enormous respect, and they are named as such. One example is the incomparable Andre Soltner—and his wife, Simone—who truly built Lutèce into America's greatest restaurant, as described in a book by one of my sources, Irene Daria (*Lutèce: A Day in the Life of America's Greatest Restaurant*).

But Lutèce was actually created by my dear friend, Andre Surmain, who hired Soltner and later sold the restaurant to him. All the "firsts" Luc Rouget lists to describe his father's accomplishments were the brainstorms of Surmain—who has four wonderful children, none of whom resembles Luc, nor Luc's estranged wife, Brigitte. Many, many years ago, I did spend countless delightful hours in the village of Mougins, dining at Le Relais and marveling at the difficulties of keeping a three-star restaurant at the top of its game. So a special thanks to Andre Surmain—a genius at that business, both artist and showman—for such a delicious introduction to the sometimes treacherous world of fine food and wine. And *merci* again to Andre, Jean-Paul Battaglia, and Mitch and Sarah Rosenthal for those death-defying trips on the Ducati from Mougins all along the Côte d'Azur.

Ken Aretsky's Patroon is one of my favorite places in town. Though I take fictional liberties with a lot of my characters, it's an understatement to say that Diana Lyne and Ken run one of the classiest eateries in New York and answered all my restaurant questions over divine food and first-class wine. Reserve now—you'll love the wine cellar.

After thirty years as a prosecutor, it's impossible for me to turn off my imagination when I read about cases in the morning news. And when sex crimes become high-profile matters, I'm often called on by national media to discuss the facts and issues. To this day, wherever I

go, people ask me about the man known to the world as
DSK—the prominent Frenchman who was charged with
a crime in a Manhattan hotel room. I had no inside track
on the investigation—no leaks at all—but I had the same
intense curiosity as much of the world, and so I decided
to create a fictional case with similar issues, working it with
my own experience and my own "dream team" of colleagues. Cyrus Vance, the District Attorney of New York
County, is my great friend. He is *not* the DA in this series
of books. Paul Battaglia was created fifteen years before
Vance was elected to the job, and it is Battaglia's oversight
of the DA's office that shapes Alex Cooper's investigation,
as it has in every previous book in the series. The actions
Battaglia takes are entirely fictional. None of them are
based on real events, which were no more than a spark
of inspiration for something that would have been within
my characters' legal jurisdiction. There are no similarities
between the scenes in this novel and reality.

There were so many articles and books—most of them
mouthwatering—that I relied on for detail in creating
this story. As always, *The New York Times* was an invaluable source of information. In particular, articles by Liesl
Schillinger, Al Baker, Eric Asimov, Sean Wilsey, Douglas
Martin, Ben Schott, David Segal, Joyce Wadler, Lizette
Alvarez, and J. David Goodman all enlightened and
amused me. Benjamin Wallace's *Town & Country* piece
about "Buried Treasure" was invaluable, too. The books
I most enjoyed were William Grimes's *Appetite City*,
H. Peter Kriendler's *21: Every Day Was New Year's Eve*,
and Marilyn Kaytor's *21: The Life and Times of New York's
Favorite Club*. Though the books by Anthony Bourdain
didn't make it into my novel, they make superb reading
on the subject of food.

I'm so happy with my Dutton family—their expertise and their kindness—Brian Tart, Ben Sevier, Christine Ball, Jamie McDonald, Jessica Horvath, Carrie Swetonic, Susan Schwartz, and Dick Heffernan. And the same to my Little, Brown group in the UK, to David Shelley, Catherine Burke, and all.

Esther Newberg of ICM, great friend and fearless agent, negotiated me through a year of very rough waters, aided by the extremely efficient and ever-cheerful Kari Stuart. Mark Gordon and Josie Freedman—thanks, too . . . and keep trying, will you?

It is impossible for me to express, in the cold type of the written page, what friendship has meant to me in the months that I was trying to create this book. There are too many meaningful names to note them all, but how fortunate Justin and I were to have been embraced by such loving friends.

To Matt and Alex Zavislan, Lisa and Marc Fairstein— who gave us sunshine and hope with every call and visit.

To the women who are my proudest legacy in the law, for their stories and evenings out, dining and wining me with TLC—Martha Bashford, Ann Donnelly, Karen Friedman-Agnifilo, Audrey Moore, Melissa Mourges, and Kerry O'Connell. And to the eight great ladies who have lunched with me once every month for twenty years, "dressing the window" at table #1 at Michael's Restaurant, cheers!

To my favorite doctor, Stanley Schrem, whose skill and compassion allowed Justin to thrive against all odds for so very long; and to doctors Jeff Zack and Sean Kelly— our island medical miracle workers—who partnered with the fantastic nurses at VNA to give us one more spectacular Vineyard summer.

To Louise Grunwald, who has a gift for friendship that is unparalleled. Not only did her "angel flight" to the Vineyard with Ann and Donovan Moore provide days of laughter and happy memories, but she was beside me in the darkest hours, without fail. To Karen Friedman-Agnifilo, who gave new meaning to the expression "night watch" at a most vulnerable moment in my life. Martin and Pinks London, Karen Cooper, Alex Cooper, Susan and Allison Davis, Ann and Vernon Jordan, Alex Denman and Ben Stein, Joan and Bernie Carl, Nancy Clair and Ric Patterson, Cyrus and Peggy Vance, Patty and David Schulte, Colleen McMahon and Frank Sica, Ann and Mike Toth, Alan Levine, Tessa Sookran, Bill Solon, Peter O'Hayer, Allan Howe, and my family—Fairsteins, Feldmans, Zavislans, and David Braunstein—I smile again because of you.

Rabin Sooklall is simply the best person on this planet—and I think of his exquisite care, his loyalty, and his grace every single day.

For my beloved Justin—your dignity, courage, wisdom, brilliance, humor, joy, and boundless capacity for love will live in my heart forever.

Read on for an excerpt from
Linda Fairstein's next novel,

DEATH ANGEL

Coming in July from Dutton

One

"Can you hold up those guys with the body bag, Loo?" I was jogging down the steps from the top of Bethesda Terrace, trying to catch up with Mercer Wallace, when the four cops and two techs from the ME's office passed me on their climb toward the waiting morgue van.

The lieutenant had his back to me, standing on the edge of the lake and pointing at something across the water. Ray Peterson, the man in charge of Manhattan North Homicide, either couldn't hear me shouting because of the distance or wasn't interested in what I had to say.

I swiveled and backtracked up the broad staircase, hoping to overtake the crew carrying the corpse to the roadway on the 72nd Street traverse. But they had already reached the open doors of the transport vehicle by the time I hit the pavement and was stopped by uniformed cops who were stringing yellow crime scene tape across the gaping space between the elegant balustrades.

"Hey, Jack." After more than twelve years as a prosecutor in the Manhattan District Attorney's Office, I knew the morgue attendants almost as well as I knew my doormen. "It's me, Alex Cooper. Give me three minutes with her, please."

Jack picked his head up and turned toward me, just as one of the officers brushed my hand off the tape. "In or out, ma'am?" the cop growled. "You want to ride with the body, that's fine. But you don't get back in here once you walk past this point."

I needed to talk to the lieutenant and to be briefed on the findings along with Mercer, but I also wanted to see the girl whose remains had been found splayed beneath the northern abutment of Bow Bridge early this morning. I wanted to know what she looked like now, before her flesh met the cold instruments of the autopsy room.

Jack called out over the back of the young cop who was restraining me, "No can do, Alex. It's already a madhouse here, between the regulars and the press scavengers. Feel free to drop by my office later on. She won't be on the table until tomorrow."

It was only seven forty-five, but it was obvious that police officers from all over the city were being bused in from their commands to form a perimeter around the roadways that led to the terrace and the lake, which was the very centerpiece of the park. There was nothing more difficult to secure than a crime scene that had no obvious boundaries, in the middle of the most trafficked public space on the planet.

Mercer Wallace, a first grade detective with the Special Victims Unit and one of my best friends, had picked me up at my home just a few blocks from the park entrance. We had passed trucks from every major media outlet, and watched as reporters and camera crews sneaked through the dense spring growth of bushes and plantings to get closer to the vista where death had intruded on a glorious spring morning.

"Alexandra, we're waiting on you." Mercer was shouting at me from beside the fountain at the foot of the steps.

I waved at him to let him know I'd heard him, then watched the van drive off before retracing my way down toward the lake. I'd left the stern cop manning the tape barrier with more pushy onlookers to contend with than just me. It was too early for the thousands of tourists who would flood the park later on this June day, but the daily complement of joggers, power walkers, bikers, dog owners, Rollerbladers, and wildlife aficionados all seemed to have stopped in their tracks, trying to figure out the cause of the commotion below.

This time I took the two-tiered staircase—the eastern one—more slowly than my first descent minutes ago. I looked around at the stunning landscape and the water of the calm lake sparkling with morning sunlight, but my eyes darted from tree to tree as figures—some in blue uniforms but mostly civilians in exercise gear—appeared on every path and between each leafy opening, like characters in a fast-moving video game. I wondered if the killer or killers were among them.

"Don't be looking for your perp, Alexandra," Mercer said. "He's long gone."

"How do you know?"

I joined up with him and we continued on to the huddle of detectives clustered around the lieutenant. I recognized most of them from cases we had worked together—they greeted me by name—while those I hadn't met before acknowledged my presence with a "Good morning, Counselor," the arm's-length term for a prosecutor . . . especially when she or he was treading on NYPD turf.

Mercer finished his thought. " 'Cause she's been dead for months. Just washed up today."

"According to . . .?"

"Johnny Mayes was here before we arrived."

Mayes was a brilliant young forensic pathologist. I nodded, understanding how well he knew his business.

"Thanks for coming over, Alex," the lieutenant said as he put out his cigarette against the side of the fountain before placing the stub in the pocket of his tattered brown jacket. No need to leave his DNA on a butt that would be picked up by crime scene investigators who were already scouring both sides of the shoreline for clues. "I wanted you to eyeball the kid before we moved her, but the paparazzi with the long-distance lenses were scrambling through the brush here. Had to whisk her the hell out before they grabbed one of the rowboats for a close-up."

"Got it, Loo. I'm here for whatever you need."

I'd been the prosecutor in charge of the Special Victims Unit for almost ten years. Our office had long had a practice of assistant DAs "riding" homicides and major felonies—going out on calls with detectives 24/7—to try to make the legal piece of every valid case hold up in court. We went to crime scenes and station houses, hospitals and morgues—taking statements from suspects or witnesses, overseeing lineups, drafting search warrants, and generally lending our expertise on all matters likely to result in arrests.

My specialties were late entries in the field of criminal law. Sexual assault, domestic violence, child abuse, sex trafficking, and homicides related to these acts had been ignored by our justice system since American courts were created. But our office had lobbied for legislative reform and pioneered techniques to allow these victims—too long without voices—to begin to triumph in the courtroom in the late seventies and early eighties, a period when violent crime threatened to devour the island of Manhattan.

Lieutenant Peterson had already lit his next cigarette. "Don't know what we need yet. Don't know much."

"What else did Dr. Mayes say?"

Peterson started to walk along the path that led from the fountain toward Bow Bridge, which arched over the lake to the area of the Ramble. He repeated to me what he had probably just told Mercer.

"Doc says he doubted she was even twenty years old."

"No ID on her?"

"Pretty hard to carry your driver's license when you're naked, Alex."

I could see five men on the far side of the bridge—detectives, no doubt—all of them wearing booties and vinyl gloves. Four were standing at the water's edge, while one was crouching directly beneath the stone archway, his toes about to disappear into the water.

"Is that Mike?" I asked the lieutenant. His thick head of black hair was a giveaway, even at this distance, confirmed by his trademark navy blazer.

"Yeah. A rookie from the Central Park precinct caught the squeal. Mike was working a day tour, so I assigned the case to him."

Mike Chapman had come on the job shortly before I graduated from law school and joined the DA's office. He and Mercer had partnered on many of the worst cases imaginable; they remained close friends after Mercer transferred to SVU, preferring to work with victims who survived their attacks.

The three of us started across the span, a familiar image in scores of park photographs featuring boaters and ice skaters. I couldn't help but look down at the water, as though some clue was about to float by just in time for me to spot it.

Mike ducked out and stepped back to talk to the other guys from the squad. I could see him shaking his head. He hadn't noticed our approach.

"Anything, Mike?" Peterson called out.

"Nothing, Loo," Mike shouted over his shoulder.

"Here's your minder, Chapman," Freddie Figueroa said, laughing as he pointed at me. My relationship with Mike was a source of great amusement to many of our colleagues, who couldn't figure how I tolerated his constant needling yet knew he'd covered my back in more situations than I could count. "You'd better come up with something fast."

"Hey, Coop," Mike said, flashing all hundred megawatts of his best grin. "Hope you brought a crystal ball. This one will take more than your brains."

I started to walk to the end of the bridge but he called me off.

"Stay there. Last thing we need is another pair of footprints in the mud. D'you see my girl?"

I shook my head. "Jack was ready to roll. The locals were about to surround him, so he took off."

"Hal's got plenty of close-ups if you want to take a look."

Hal Sherman, one of the masters of crime scene investigations, came up behind me. He'd been photographing each of the approaches to the lake, on the theory that no one would know what angles were important until we had a sense of what had happened to this victim and where.

"Hey, Alex. Too quiet too long, huh?" Hal said, patting me on the back before he reached for his notepad. "That statue on top of the fountain—any idea what she's called?"

I looked across at the colossal bronze figure of a woman, raised high above the plaza and held aloft by four cherubs, with her wings outstretched as she delivered her blessing over the lake below.

"Sure, Hal," I said, as he scratched the answer on a notepad. "She's the most iconic statue in the park. She's called the Angel of the Waters."

Mike Chapman joined us on the bridge, pulling off his gloves and stuffing them in his rear pants pocket. "That name worked for her once upon a time, Coop. Now she stands up there with the best vantage point of all, sees everything that goes on here but gives us nothing. I'd like to know everything that *she* knows."

"It's not even eight o'clock and you're loaded for bear. Why take it out on an angel?"

"It's not the first body I've had in this lake, Coop. We've got two cold cases—young women who have never been identified, whose files are collecting dust in the squad room."

"How old are those runs, that I don't even know about them?" I asked. "Are you figuring this one falls into some kind of pattern with the others?" I asked.

"I'm just thinking the beautiful statue may be an attractive nuisance. Maybe she blessed the waters a century ago, but now she's a magnet for murder. She's an angel all right," Mike said, staring at the beautiful sunlit figure that towered over us. "A death angel."

Two

Mike led Hal, Mercer, the lieutenant, and me along the path to the first pavilion on the north shore of the lake. The large boathouse itself, where rowboats could be rented by the hour, was to our east. Four of these covered wooden sheds were scattered about the edges of the water as landing docks for rowers, a throwback to their Victorian origins.

We set ourselves up out of the direct sun, and Mike asked Hal to show me the digital photos he had taken when he first arrived.

"So, the initial call to 911 came in at five forty-nine this morning," Mike said. "Two guys out for a run on the pathway approaching Bethesda Terrace from below, to the west. One of them saw what he thought was a head and upper torso of a woman under the bridge, against the foundation, and stopped his friend."

"What time was sunrise?" Mercer asked.

"Five twenty-four. Plenty of light to see across."

"They touch anything?" I asked.

"Too spooked to get closer."

"What if she'd been alive and needed help?"

"Decomposition was evident, Coop, even from a distance," Mike said. "Hal, you got those shots?" He cupped his hand over the viewer as Mercer and I leaned in.

The girl's face was mostly intact, but her skin was a ghastly shade of gray. Her head was cocked to the side, one cheek hugging the concrete structure. The one eye we could see was closed and her mouth was agape, with stringy dark brown hair plastered across her face. The area below her shoulder blade was discolored and it looked like her bones were protruding through what once had been skin.

"Late teens is Johnny Mayes's estimate," Mike said. "No tats, no track marks. No surgical scars. Badly malnourished, lousy dentition, filthy nails all bitten down and cracked. I'm going with homeless."

"How long has she been dead?" I asked.

"Mayes figures it's been a few months, but she was only left in the water for a day or two."

Mercer studied the photographs of the full body taken after the victim had been pulled from the water. "So, a dump job?" Killed somewhere else and deposited in the lake. Dumped here by the murderer.

"Likely. But who knows where she's been all this time? That's a big problem."

"How'd she die?" I asked.

"Blunt-force trauma. Check the photos of the back of her head."

Hal advanced the shots. Some object had crushed the skull with a couple of blows. Two different angles of injury suggested repeated applications of the weapon.

"Does Johnny know what might have caused this?"

"Lead pipe, maybe. Or a baseball bat. I'm hoping Derek Jeter has an alibi, 'cause we're only two months into the season and he's hitting four hundred. Whoever did this has a pretty perfect swing."

"A tree branch, maybe," I said.

"They got redwoods here I don't know about, Coop? I mean, why do you ask me a question and then take your own guess at an answer?"

"I'd like to stop by the morgue later," I said. I was fidgety and knew that I was annoying Mike before we'd even gotten out of the blocks. "I had a good chance to see what immersion in water did to a body when I helped with that girl who was murdered in France this spring."

"Save me, Jesus." Mike closed his eyes and shook his head. "Give me a break for a change, will you? Whose idea was it to call Coop in on this so early?"

The lieutenant looked at Mike, puzzled by his outburst at me. "What—?"

"I wanted her here," Mercer said. "It's going to be her case."

"We don't know that this is a sexual assault yet. Coop spent ten minutes with a lady in a lake on one of her holiday jaunts and—"

"It was a pond, not a lake, but go ahead, Mike. I made some observations that the French police found useful so I thought maybe you would, too."

"Well, tell them to the medical examiner, because he knows how long my vic's been dead and what killed her. You got any wild guesses on figuring out the 'who,' then stick around."

"Drain the lake," I said.

"What?"

"Drain the lake. That might give you her clothing,

some form of ID, possibly the weapon. Maybe even other victims. If this fits together with your cold cases, maybe you get a bit closer to solving the whole thing."

Ray Peterson angled his head and looked at me.

"It's been done before. Draining the lake, I mean."

"Who's going to sign off on that one?" Peterson asked.

"Don't confuse the lake with the reservoir. I'm telling you it can be done."

"You think I don't know that, Coop?" Mike said. "One of my vics was found when the Central Park Conservancy restored this hole ten years back, when all the DA would let you handle were petty thefts."

The reservoir, above 86th Street in the park, had originally been built to hold the city's entire supply of drinking water, piped in by a complicated system from upstate New York and distributed throughout the boroughs via massive underground tunnels. The Jacqueline Kennedy Onassis Reservoir was now more than one hundred acres of exquisite scenery—no longer used to relieve New Yorkers' thirst—forty feet deep and holding a billion gallons of water.

The picturesque lake, on the other hand, was only eighteen acres in area, and just a few feet deep—also man-made by the park's designers, to replace the great untamed swamp that sat on the current site in the nineteenth century.

"Alex is right," Mercer said. "If the commissioner asks the mayor to do it, it'll happen."

Keith Scully had been commissioner for most of the mayor's tenure in office, and they enjoyed a strong respect for each other.

"I've got scuba on its way here," Mike said. "Let's see what they come up with. You're over-the-top, Coop."

"Not if you think this case is linked to your two old ones. About time you solved them, don't you think?"

"That wasn't my point. I was just saying the angel is falling down on her job."

"Missing persons?" Mercer asked.

"Figueroa's going down to look through files. We can't put up a photo or sketch of the girl until the ME cleans her up," Mike said. "And we're going to need a detail, Loo, to canvass the area around the terrace and the perimeter of the lake."

"Yeah. Every morning for at least a week," the lieutenant agreed with Mike. "I'll start them at four a.m. and run it till ten at night. Creatures of habit, these park people."

"Say it, Coop. Stop biting your lip and speak up," Mike said. "You look like you have that burning need to throw another rope out to rescue us."

"I'm not correcting the lieutenant. But today's Friday. A business day. You'll get an entirely different rhythm with any canvass you do over the weekend. Mercer and I had the same experience with our rapist who was targeting bikers up near the reservoir."

Mercer nodded in agreement.

"Tomorrow and Sunday you'll have all the gawkers who hear this story on the news. But most of the working people who jog before going to the office have a different weekend schedule. People sleep in, dogs get walked later, businessmen who ran today at six are pushing a stroller at ten on Saturday. Your heavy days, the ones likely to yield value, will start on Monday."

"I guess I was right about your crystal ball."

"Who's going to be on top of the homeless parkies?" Mercer asked.

"I left that mess to Sergeant Chirico," Peterson said.

"Problem with springtime is that they're all back out on the street. This place is so damn big you can find them anywhere, from the Sheep Meadow to the Blockhouse. Harmless and homeless or toothless and ruthless. Takes all kinds to survive on the streets of this city."

"Detective Sherman!" One of the cops at the top of the steps yelled out to Hal. "You want me to send these guys down?"

Hal gave him a thumbs-up. "That's my Panoscan team, Mike. We'll do a couple of setups on each side of the Bow Bridge from this bank and then a few from the foot of the fountain."

Just a few years in operation, the Panoscan was a vast improvement in crime scene technology. It would take only minutes to assemble a kit with a fish-eye lens to create high-resolution 360-degree images. Things that may not have seemed obvious to first responders—clues possibly overlooked at a scene—would be available to Mike and Mercer by pointing and clicking on the panoramic image from their desktops.

"Great. Let's get out of the way, guys," Mike said, herding the rest of us back across the bridge to the footpath.

I waited until Peterson was a few steps ahead of us. "How come I don't know anything about your two cold cases, Mike?"

"There's a lot you don't know, kid."

"But you usually come to me with—"

"Bags of bones, Coop. Partial remains. That's what I've got. From back in the day, before you hitched yourself to my star. No way to know who they are or how they died. No way to prove they were sexually assaulted."

"Throw in that woman from Brazil who was killed in

the ravine in 'ninety-five," Mercer said, referring to a remote area in the northern end of the park, "and the body
in the Harlem Meer. Both cases colder than the iceberg
that sunk the *Titanic*."

"So what are you two telling me?" I asked, although
the picture was coming together for me without any
more narrative. "Is this like those unsolved murders of
young women out on Long Island, near Gilgo Beach?
Some deranged killer set up shop in the heart of the city's
most populated public space?"

Mike and Mercer exchanged glances over my head.

"We don't know what it is yet. But we do know that
it's been real stable here for the past couple of years,"
Mike said. "So nobody's going public with the bigger
story—do you understand that? Not the district attorney
or any of his flaks, or Scully has me walking a foot post in
Bed-Stuy."

Mike stared at me and I nodded.

"Maybe there's nothing to connect any of these victims with each other. Maybe this poor broken body is a
one-off. That's the approach we're taking for now."

"And so it's your idea just to make believe the park is
a safe place to be?" I asked.

"Safest precinct per square foot of any property in the
city," Mike said. "I think the mayor's got the last word
on what's a threat to his voters, Coop, and when he de-
cides to tell them about that. There's a primary in three
months and he's hoping it's a mandate for another term.
You figure out who this dead girl is and I'll stay on top of
the cold cases."